P9-DLZ-108

THE BOY FROM THE WOODS

Also by Harlan Coben

Play Dead

Miracle Cure

Deal Breaker

Drop Shot

Fade Away

Back Spin

One False Move

The Final Detail

Darkest Fear

Tell No One

Gone for Good

No Second Chance

Just One Look

The Innocent

Promise Me

The Woods

Hold Tight

Long Lost

Caught

Live Wire

Shelter

Stay Close

Seconds Away

Six Years

Missing You

Found

The Stranger

Fool Me Once

Home

Don't Let Go

Run Away

THE BOY FROM THE WOODS

HARLAN COBEN

GRAND CENTRAL PUBLISHING

NEW YORK BOSTON

This book is a work of fiction. Names, characters, places, and incidents are the product of the author's imagination or are used fictitiously. Any resemblance to actual events, locales, or persons, living or dead, is coincidental.

Cover design by Jaya Miceli

Grand Central Publishing
Hachette Book Group
1290 Avenue of the Americas, New York, NY 10104
grandcentralpublishing.com
twitter.com/grandcentralpub

First Edition: March 2020

Grand Central Publishing is a division of Hachette Book Group, Inc. The Grand Central Publishing name and logo is a trademark of Hachette Book Group, Inc.

Library of Congress Cataloging-in-Publication Data

Names: Coben, Harlan, author.
Title: The boy from the woods / Harlan Coben.
Description: First edition. | New York : Grand Central Publishing, 2020.
Identifiers: LCCN 2019041849 | ISBN 9781538748145 (hardcover) | ISBN 9781538702734 | ISBN 9781538748169 (ebook)
Subjects: GSAFD: Suspense fiction. | Mystery fiction.
Classification: LCC PS3553.O225 B69 2020 | DDC 813/.54—dc23
LC record available at https://lccn.loc.gov/2019041849

ISBN: 978-1-5387-4814-5 (hardcover), 978-1-5387-0227-7 (signed edition), 978-1-5387-0273-4 (large print), 978-1-5387-0299-4 (special signed edition), 978-1-5387-4816-9 (ebook), 978-1-5387-5135-0 (international trade)

Printed in the United States of America

LSC-H

10 9 8 7 6 5 4 3 2 1

To Ben Sevier
Editor and friend
Twelve books and counting

THE BOY FROM THE WOODS

From the North Jersey Gazette
April 18, 1986

ABANDONED "WILD BOY" FOUND IN THE WOODS

Huge Mystery Surrounding Discovery of "Real-Life Mowgli"

WESTVILLE, N.J.—In one of the most bizarre cases in recent history, a wild-haired young boy, estimated to be between six and eight years old, was discovered living on his own in the Ramapo Mountain State Forest near the suburb of Westville. Even more bizarre, authorities have no idea who the boy is or how long he had been there.

"It's like Mowgli in the 'Jungle Book' movie," Westville Police Deputy Oren Carmichael said.

The boy—who speaks and understands English but has no knowledge of his name—was first spotted by Don and Leslie Katz, hikers from Clifton, N.J. "We were cleaning up from our picnic when we heard a rustling in the woods," Mr. Katz said. "At first I worried it was a bear, but then we caught sight of him running, clear as day."

Park rangers, along with local police, found the boy, thin and clad in tattered clothes, in a makeshift campsite three hours later. "At this time, we don't know how long he's been in the state forest or how he got here," said New Jersey State Park Police Chief Tony Aurigemma. "He doesn't recall any parents or adult figures. We're currently checking with other law enforcement authorities, but so far, there are no missing children who match his age and description."

For the past year, hikers in the Ramapo Mountain area have reported seeing a "feral boy" or "Little Tarzan" matching the boy's description, but most people chalked up the sightings to urban legend.

Said James Mignone, a hiker from Morristown, N.J., "It's like someone just birthed him and left him in the wild."

"It's the strangest survival case any of us have ever seen," Chief Aurigemma said. "We don't know if the boy has been out here days, weeks, months or heck, even years."

If anyone has any information on the young boy, they are asked to contact the Westville Police Department.

"Someone out there has to know something," Deputy Carmichael said. "The boy didn't just appear in the forest by magic."

PART ONE

CHAPTER ONE

April 23, 2020

How does she survive?

How does she manage to get through this torment every single day?

Day after day. Week after week. Year after year.

She sits in the school assembly hall, her eyes fixed, unseeing, unblinking. Her face is stone, a mask. She doesn't look left or right. She doesn't move at all.

She just stares straight ahead.

She is surrounded by classmates, including Matthew, but she doesn't look at any of them. She doesn't talk to any of them either, though that doesn't stop them from talking to her. The boys—Ryan, Crash (yes, that's his real name), Trevor, Carter—keep calling her names, harshly whispering awful things, jeering at her, laughing with scorn. They throw things at her. Paper clips. Rubber bands. Flick snot from their noses. They put small pieces of paper in their mouths, wad the paper into wet balls, propel them in various ways at her.

When the paper sticks to her hair, they laugh some more.

The girl—her name is Naomi—doesn't move. She doesn't try to pull the wads of paper out of her hair. She just stares straight ahead. Her eyes are dry. Matthew could remember a time, two or three years ago, when her eyes would moisten during these ceaseless, unrelenting, daily taunts.

But not anymore.

Matthew watches. He does nothing.

The teachers, numb to this by now, barely notice. One wearily calls out, "Okay, Crash, that's enough," but neither Crash nor any of the others give the warning the slightest heed.

Meanwhile Naomi just takes it.

Matthew should do something to stop the bullying. But he doesn't. Not anymore. He tried once.

It did not end well.

Matthew tries to remember when it all started to go wrong for Naomi. She had been a happy kid in elementary school. Always smiling, that's what he remembered. Yeah, her clothes were hand-me-downs and she didn't wash her hair enough. Some of the girls made mild fun of her for that. But it had been okay until that day she got violently ill and threw up in Mrs. Walsh's class, fourth grade, just projectile vomit ricocheting off the classroom linoleum, the wet brown chips splashing on Kim Rogers and Taylor Russell, the smell so bad, so rancid, that Mrs. Walsh had to clear the classroom, all the kids, Matthew one of them, and send them all out to the kickball field holding their noses and making *pee-uw* sounds.

And after that, nothing had been the same for Naomi.

Matthew always wondered about that. Had she not felt well that morning? Did her father—her mom was already out of the picture by then—make her go to school? If Naomi had just stayed home that day, would it all have gone differently for her? Was her throwing-up her sliding door moment, or was it inevitable that she would end up traveling down this rough, dark, torturous path?

Another spitball sticks in her hair. More name-calling. More cruel jeers.

Naomi sits there and waits for it to end.

End for now, at least. For today maybe. She has to know that it won't end for good. Not today. Not tomorrow. The torment never stops for very long. It is her constant companion.

How does she survive?

Some days, like today, Matthew really pays attention and wants to do something.

Most days, he doesn't. The bullying still happens on those days, of course, but it is so frequent, so customary, it becomes background noise. Matthew had learned an awful truth: You grow immune to cruelty. It becomes the norm. You accept it. You move on.

Has Naomi just accepted it too? Has she grown immune to it?

Matthew doesn't know. But she's there, every day, sitting in the last row in class, the first row at assembly, at a corner table all alone in the cafeteria.

Until one day—a week after this assembly—she's not there.

One day, Naomi vanishes.

And Matthew needs to know why.

CHAPTER TWO

The hipster pundit said, "This guy should be in prison, no questions asked."

On live television, Hester Crimstein was about to counterpunch when she spotted what looked like her grandson in her peripheral vision. It was hard to see through the studio lights, but it sure as hell looked like Matthew.

"Whoa, strong words," said the show's host, a once-cute prepster whose main debate technique was to freeze a baffled expression on his face, as though his guests were idiots no matter how much sense they made. "Any response, Hester?"

Matthew's appearance—it had to be him—had thrown her.

"Hester?"

Not a good time to let the mind wander, she reminded herself. *Focus.*

"You're gross," Hester said.

"Pardon?"

"You heard me." She aimed her notorious withering gaze at Hipster Pundit. "Gross."

Why is Matthew here?

Her grandson had never come to her work unannounced before—not to her office, not to a courtroom, and not to the studio.

"Care to elaborate?" Prepster Host asked.

"Sure," Hester said. The fiery glare stayed on Hipster Pundit. "You hate America."

"What?"

"Seriously," Hester continued, throwing her hands up in the air, "why should we have a court system at all? Who needs it? We have public opinion, don't we? No trial, no jury, no judge—let the Twitter mob decide."

Hipster Pundit sat up a little straighter. "That's not what I said."

"It's exactly what you said."

"There's evidence, Hester. A very clear video."

"Ooo, a video." She wiggled her fingers as though she were talking about a ghost. "So again: No need for a judge or jury. Let's just have you, as benevolent leader of the Twitter mob—"

"I'm not—"

"Hush, I'm talking. Oh, I'm sorry, I forget your name. I keep calling you Hipster Pundit in my head, so can I just call you Chad?" He opened his mouth, but Hester pushed on. "Great. Tell me, Chad, what's a fitting punishment for my client, do you think? I mean, since you're going to pronounce guilt or innocence, why not also do the sentencing for us?"

"My name"—he pushed his hipster glasses up his nose—"is Rick. And we all saw the video. Your client punched a man in the face."

"Thanks for that analysis. You know what would be helpful, Chad?"

"It's Rick."

"Rick, Chad, whatever. What would be helpful, super helpful really, would be if you and your mob just made all the decisions for us. Think of the time we'd save. We just post a video on social media and declare guilt or innocence from the replies. Thumbs-up or thumbs-down. There'd be no need for witnesses or testimony or evidence. Just Judge Rick Chad here."

Hipster Pundit's face was turning red. "We all saw what your rich client did to that poor man."

Prepster Host stepped in: "Before we continue, let's show the video again for those just tuning in."

Hester was about to protest, but they'd already shown the video countless times, would show it countless more times, and her voicing any opposition would be both ineffective and only make her client, a well-to-do financial consultant named Simon Greene, appear even more guilty.

More important, Hester could use the few seconds with the camera off her to check on Matthew.

The viral video—four million views and counting—had been recorded on a tourist's iPhone in Central Park. On the screen, Hester's client Simon Greene, wearing a perfectly tailored suit with a perfectly Windsored Hermès tie, cocked his fist and smashed it into the face of a threadbare, disheveled young man who, Hester knew, was a drug addict named Aaron Corval.

Blood gushed from Corval's nose.

The image was irresistibly Dickensian—Mr. Rich Privileged Guy, completely unprovoked, sucker-punches Poor Street Urchin.

Hester quickly craned her neck toward Matthew and tried, through the haze of the studio spotlights, to meet his eye. She was a frequent legal expert on cable news, and two nights a week, "famed defense attorney" Hester Crimstein had her own segment on this very network called *Crimstein on Crime*, though her name was not pronounced Crime-Rhymes-with-Prime-Stine, but rather Krim-Rhymes-with-Prim-Steen, but the alliteration was still considered "television friendly" and the title looked good on the bottom scroll, so the network ran with it.

Her grandson stood in the shadows. Hester could see that Matthew was wringing his hands, just like his father used to do, and she felt a pang so deep in her chest that for a moment she couldn't breathe. She considered quickly crossing the room and asking Matthew why he was here, but the punch video was already over and Hipster Rick Chad was foaming at the mouth.

"See?" Spittle flew out of his mouth and found a home in his beard. "It's clear as day. Your rich client attacked a homeless man for no reason."

"You don't know what went on before that tape rolled."

"It makes no difference."

"Sure it does. That's why we have a system of justice, so that vigilantes like you don't irresponsibly call for mob violence against an innocent man."

"Whoa, no one said anything about mob violence."

"Sure you did. Own it already. You want my client, a father of three with no record, in prison right now. No trial, nothing. Come on, Rick Chad, let your inner fascist out." Hester banged the desk, startling Prepster Host, and began to chant: "Lock him up, lock him up."

"Cut that out!"

"Lock him up!"

The chant was getting to him, his face turning scarlet. "That's not what I meant at all. You're intentionally exaggerating."

"Lock him up!"

"Stop that. No one is saying that."

Hester had something of a gift for mimicry. She often used it in the courtroom to subtly if not immaturely undermine a prosecutor. Doing her best impression of Rick Chad, she repeated his earlier words verbatim: "*This guy should be in prison, no questions asked.*"

"That will be up to a court of law," Hipster Rick Chad said, "but maybe if a man acts like this, if he punches people in the face in broad daylight, he deserves to be canceled and lose his job."

"Why? Because you and Deplorable-Dental-Hygienist and Nail-Da-Ladies-69 on Twitter say so? You don't know the situation. You don't even know if the tape is real."

Prepster Host arched an eyebrow over that one. "Are you saying the video is fake?"

"Could be, sure. Look, I had another client. Someone photo-shopped her smiling face next to a dead giraffe and said she was the hunter who killed it. An ex-husband did that for revenge. Can you imagine the hate and bullying she received?"

The story wasn't true—Hester had made it up—but it *could* be true, and sometimes that was enough.

"Where is your client Simon Greene right now?" Hipster Rick Chad asked.

"What does that have to do with anything?"

"He's home, right? Out on bail?"

"He's an innocent man, a fine man, a caring man—"

"And a rich man."

"Now you want to get rid of our bail system?"

"A rich *white* man."

"Listen, Rick Chad, I know you're all 'woke' and stuff, what with the cool beard and the hipster beanie—is that a Kangol?—but your use of race and your easy answers are as bad as the other side's use of race and easy answers."

"Wow, deflecting using 'both sides.'"

"No, sonny, that's not both sides, so listen up. What you don't see is, you and those you hate? You are quickly becoming one and the same."

"Reverse this around," Rick Chad said. "If Simon Greene was poor and black and Aaron Corval was rich and white—"

"They're both white. Don't make this about race."

"It's always about race, but fine. If the guy in rags hit the rich white man in a suit, he wouldn't have Hester Crimstein defending him. He'd be in jail right now."

Hmm, Hester thought. She had to admit Rick Chad had a pretty good point there.

Prepster Host said, "Hester?"

Time was running out in the segment, so Hester threw up her

hands and said, "If Rick Chad is arguing I'm a great attorney, who am I to disagree?"

That drew laughs.

"And that's all the time we have for now. Coming up next, the latest controversy surrounding upstart presidential candidate Rusty Eggers. Is Rusty pragmatic or cruel? Is he really the most dangerous man in America? Stay with us."

Hester pulled out the earpiece and unclipped the microphone. They were already headed to commercial break when she rose and crossed the room toward Matthew. He was so tall now, again like his father, and another pang struck hard.

Hester said, "Your mother...?"

"She's fine," Matthew said. "Everyone is okay."

Hester couldn't help it. She threw her arms around the probably embarrassed teen, wrapping him in a bear hug, though she was barely five two and he had almost a foot on her. More and more she saw the echoes of the father in the son. Matthew hadn't looked much like David when he was little, when his father was still alive, but now he did—the posture, the walk, the hand wringing, the crinkle of the forehead—and it all broke her heart anew. It shouldn't, of course. It should, in fact, offer some measure of comfort for Hester, seeing her dead son's echo in his boy, like some small part of David survived the crash and still lives on. But instead, these ghostly glimmers rip at her, tear the wounds wide open, even after all these years, and Hester wondered whether the pain was worth it, whether it was better to feel this pain than feel nothing. The question was a rhetorical one, of course. She had no choice and would want it no other way—feeling nothing or someday being "over it" would be the worst betrayal of all.

So she held her grandson and squeezed her eyes shut. The teen patted her back, almost as though he were humoring her.

"Nana?"

That was what he called her. Nana. "You're really okay?"

"I'm fine."

Matthew's skin was browner than his father's. His mother, Laila, was black, which made Matthew black too or a person of color or biracial or whatever. Age was no excuse, but Hester, who was in her seventies but told everyone she stopped counting at sixty-nine—go ahead, make a joke, she'd heard them all—found it hard to keep track of the evolving terminology.

"Where's your mother?" Hester asked.

"At work, I guess."

"What's the matter?" Hester asked.

"There's this girl in school," Matthew said.

"What about her?"

"She's missing, Nana. I want you to help."

CHAPTER THREE

Her name is Naomi Pine," Matthew said.

They were in the backseat of Hester's Cadillac Escalade. Matthew had taken the hour-long train ride in from Westville, changing at the Frank Lautenberg Station in Secaucus, but Hester figured that it would be easier and smarter to drive him back to Westville. She hadn't been out to visit in a month, much too long, and so she could both help her distraught grandson with his problem and spend some time with him and his mom, killing the allegorical two birds with one stone, which was a really violent and weird image when you stopped and thought about it. You throw a stone and kill two birds—and this is a *good* thing?

Look at me, throwing a stone at a beautiful bird. Why? Why would a person do such a thing? I don't know. I guess I'm a psychopath, and whoa—I hit two birds somehow! Yay! Two dead birds!

"Nana?"

"This Naomi," Hester said, pushing the silly inner rant away. "She's your friend?"

Matthew shrugged as only a teenager can. "I've known her since we were, like, six."

Not a direct answer, but she'd allow it.

"How long has she been missing?"

"For, like, a week."

Like, six. Like, a week. It drove Hester crazy—the "likes," the "you-knows"—but now was hardly the time.

"Did you try to call her?"

"I don't know her phone number."

"Are the police looking for her?"

Teenage shrug.

"Did you talk to her parents?"

"She lives with her dad."

"Did you speak to her dad?"

He made a face as though that was the most ridiculous thing imaginable.

"So how do you know she's not sick? Or away on vacation or something?"

No reply.

"What makes you think she's missing?"

Matthew just stared out the window. Tim, Hester's longtime driver, veered the Escalade off Route 17 and into the heart of Westville, New Jersey, less than thirty miles from Manhattan. The Ramapo Mountains, which are actually part of the Appalachians in every way, rose into view. The memories, as they have a habit of doing, swarmed in and stung.

Someone once told Hester that memories hurt, the good ones most of all. As she got older, Hester realized just how true that was.

Hester and her late husband, Ira—gone now seven years—had raised three boys in the "mountain suburb" (that's what they called it) of Westville, New Jersey. Their oldest son, Jeffrey, was now a DDS in Los Angeles and on his fourth wife, a real estate agent named Sandy. Sandy was the first of Jeffrey's wives who hadn't been an inappropriately younger dental hygienist in his office. Progress, Hester hoped. Their middle son, Eric, like his father before him, worked in the nebulous world of finance—Hester could never understand what either man, her husband or son, actually did, something with moving piles of money from A to B to facilitate C. Eric and his wife, Stacey, had three boys, aged two years apart, just as Hester and Ira had done. The family had recently moved down to Raleigh, North Carolina, which seemed all the rage nowadays.

Their youngest son—and truth be told, Hester's favorite—had been Matthew's father, David.

Hester asked Matthew, "What time will your mom be home?"

His mother, Laila, like grandmother Hester, worked at a major law firm, though she specialized in family law. She'd started her career as Hester's associate during summers while attending Columbia Law School. That was how Laila had first met Hester's son.

Laila and David had fallen in love pretty much right away. They'd gotten married. They had a son named Matthew.

"I don't know," Matthew said. "Want me to text her?"

"Sure."

"Nana?"

"What, hon?"

"Don't tell Mom about this."

"About . . . ?"

"About Naomi."

"Why not?"

"Just don't, okay?"

"Okay."

"Promise?"

"Stop it," Hester said with a little snap that he needed her to say this. Then, more gently: "I promise. Of course, I promise."

Matthew fiddled with his phone as Tim made the familiar right turn, then left, then two more rights. They were on a storybook cul-de-sac called Downing Lane now. Up ahead was the grand log-cabin-style home Hester and Ira had built forty-two years ago. It was the home where she and Ira raised Jeffrey, Eric, and David, and then, fifteen years ago, with their sons grown, Hester and Ira decided that it was time to leave Westville. They'd loved their home in the foothills of the Ramapo Mountains, Ira more than Hester because, God help her, Ira was an outdoorsman who loved hiking and fishing and all those things that men named Ira Crimstein were not supposed to like. But it had been their time to move on. Towns like Westville are meant for raising children. You get married, you move out from the city, you have a few babies, you go to their soccer games and dance recitals, you get overly emotional at their graduations and commencements, they go to college, they visit and sleep in late, and then they stop doing even that and you're alone and really, like any life cycle, it's time to put this behind you, sell the house to another young couple who move out from the city to have a few babies, and start anew.

There was nothing for you in towns like Westville when you got older—and there was nothing wrong with that.

So Hester and Ira did indeed move on. They found an apartment on Riverside Drive on the Upper West Side of Manhattan facing the Hudson River. They loved it. For almost thirty years they had commuted on that same train Matthew had taken today, changing in Hoboken back in those days, and now, in their advancing years, to be able to wake up and walk or quickly subway to work was heaven.

Hester and Ira relished living in New York City.

As for the old mountain home on Downing Lane, they ended up selling it to their son David and his wonderful wife, Laila, who'd just had their first child—Matthew. Hester thought that it might be odd for David, living in the same house he'd grown up in, but he claimed that it would be the perfect place to start and raise a family of his own. He and Laila did an entire renovation, putting their own stamp on the house, making the interior almost unrecognizable to Hester and Ira during their visits out here.

Matthew was still staring down at his phone. She touched his knee. He looked up.

"Did you do something?" she asked.

"What?"

"With Naomi."

He shook his head. "I didn't do anything. That's the problem."

Tim pulled to a stop in her old driveway at her old house. The memories didn't bother swarming anymore—they just full-on assaulted. Tim put the car in park and turned to look at her. Tim had been with her for nearly two decades, since he'd first immigrated from the Balkans. So he knew. He met her eye. She gave him the slightest of nods to let him know that she'd be okay.

Matthew had already thanked Tim and gotten out. Hester reached for the door handle, but Tim stopped her with a throat clear. Hester rolled her eyes and waited while Tim, a big slab of a man, rolled his way out of his seat into a standing position and opened the door for her. It was a completely unnecessary gesture, but Tim felt insulted when Hester opened the door on her own, and really, she fought enough battles every day, thank you very much.

"Not sure how long we'll be," she said to Tim.

His accent remained thick. "I'll be here."

Matthew had opened the front door of the house and left it ajar. Hester shared one more look with Tim before walking up the cobblestone path—the same one she and Ira installed themselves over a weekend thirty-three years ago—and heading inside the home. She closed the door behind her.

"Matthew?"

"In the kitchen."

She moved to the back of the house. The door of the huge Sub-Zero refrigerator—that hadn't been there in her day—was open, and again she flashed back to Matthew's father at that age, to all her boys during their high school years: Jeffrey, Eric, and

David, always with their heads in the refrigerator. There were never enough groceries in the house. They ate like trash compactors with feet. If she bought food, it was gone the next day.

"You hungry, Nana?"

"No, I'm good."

"You sure?"

"I'm sure. Tell me what's going on, Matthew."

His head came into view. "Do you mind if I just make a little snack first?"

"I'll take you out to dinner, if you want."

"I got too much homework."

"Suit yourself."

Hester wandered into the den with the TV. She smelled burnt wood. Someone had recently used the fireplace. That was strange. Or maybe it wasn't. She checked out the coffee table.

It was neat. *Too neat*, she thought.

Magazines stacked. Coasters stacked. Everything in its proper place.

Hester frowned.

With Matthew busy eating his sandwich, she tiptoed up to the second level. This was none of her business, of course. David had been dead for ten years. Laila deserved to be happy. Hester meant no harm, but she also couldn't help herself.

She entered the master bedroom.

David, she knew, had slept on the far side of the bed, Laila by the door. The king-sized bed was made. Immaculately.

Too neat, she thought again.

A lump formed in her throat. She crossed the room and checked the bathroom. Immaculate too. Still not able to stop herself, she checked the pillow on David's side.

David's side? Your son has been gone for ten years, Hester. Leave it be.

It took a few seconds, but eventually she located a light-brown hair on the pillow.

A long light-brown hair.

Leave it be, Hester.

The bedroom window looked onto the backyard and the mountain beyond. The lawn blurred into the slope and then faded away into a few trees, then more trees, then a full-blown thick forest. Her boys had played there, of course. Ira had helped them build a tree house and forts and Lord knew what. They made sticks into guns and knives. They played hide-and-seek.

One day, when David was six years old and supposedly alone, Hester had overheard him talking to someone in those woods. When she asked him about it, little David tensed up and said, "I was just playing with me."

"But I heard you talking to someone."

"Oh," her young son had said, "that was my invisible friend."

It had been, as far as Hester knew, the only lie David had ever told her.

From downstairs, Hester heard the front door open.

Matthew's voice: "Hey, Mom."

"Where's your grandmother?"

"Right here," he said. "Uh, Nana?"

"Coming!"

Feeling both panicked and like a total idiot, Hester quickly slipped out of the bedroom and into the hallway bathroom. She closed the door, flushed the toilet, and even ran the water to make it look good. Then she headed toward the stairs. Laila was at the bottom, staring up at her.

"Hey," Hester said.

"Hey."

Laila was gorgeous. There was no way around it. She dazzled in the fitted gray business suit that hugged where it should, which in her case was everywhere. Her blouse was a vibrant white, especially against the darkness of her skin.

"You okay?" Laila asked.

"Oh, sure."

Hester made it the rest of the way down the stairs. The two women hugged briefly.

"So what brings you out, Hester?"

Matthew came into the room. "Nana was helping me with a school report."

"Really? On what?"

"The law," he said.

Laila made a face. "And you couldn't ask me?"

"And, uh, also being on TV," Matthew added clumsily. Not a good liar, Hester thought. Again, like his dad. "Uh, like, no offense, Mom, being a famous lawyer."

"That a fact?"

Laila turned to Hester. Hester shrugged.

"Okay then," Laila said.

Hester flashed back to David's funeral. Laila had stood there, holding little Matthew's hand. Her eyes were dry. She didn't cry. Not once that day. Not once in front of Hester or anyone else. Later that night, Hester and Ira took Matthew out for a hamburger at ABG's in Allendale. Hester had left early and come back. She walked into the backyard, into the opening in the woods where she'd seen David disappear countless times to go see Wilde, and even from there, even at that distance with the night wind howling, she could hear the guttural cries of Laila alone in her bedroom. The cries were so raw, so ripping, so pained that Hester thought that maybe Laila would break in a way no one could ever fix.

Laila had not remarried. If there were other men in the past ten years—and there had to have been many, many offers—she had not told Hester about them.

But now, there was this too-neat house and this long brown hair.

Leave it be, Hester.

Without warning, Hester reached out with both arms and pulled Laila in close.

Surprised, Laila said, "Hester?"

Leave it be.

"I love you," Hester whispered.

"I love you too."

Hester squeezed her eyes shut. She couldn't keep tears back.

"Are you okay?" Laila asked.

Hester gathered herself, took a step back, smoothed her clothes. "I'm fine." She reached into her purse and grabbed out a tissue. "I just get..."

Laila nodded. Her voice was soft. "I know."

From over his mother's shoulder, Hester spotted Matthew shaking his head, reminding her of what she'd promised.

Hester said, "I better go."

She kissed them both and hurried out the door.

Tim was waiting for her with the door open. He wore a black suit and chauffeur cap to work every day, whatever the weather or season, even though Hester told him he didn't have to and neither the suit nor the cap ever seemed to fit him right. It could be his bulky frame. It could be that he carried a gun.

As she slid into the backseat, Hester turned for one last look at the house. Matthew stood in the doorway. He looked at her. It hit her yet again:

Her grandson was asking for her help.

He had never done that before. He wasn't telling her the whole story. Not yet. But as she wallowed in her own pity, in her own misery, in this awful hole in her own life, she reminded herself that it was a much bigger and more awful hole for Matthew, growing up without a father, growing up, especially, without *that* father, without that good and kind man, who had been the best of Hester and even more Ira—Ira, who died of a heart attack, she was convinced, because he could never get over the heartbreak of losing his son in that crash.

Tim slid back into the driver's seat.

"You heard what Matthew said?" she asked.

"Yes."

"What do you think?"

Tim shrugged. "He's hiding something."

Hester did not reply.

"So back to the city?" Tim asked.

"Not yet," Hester said. "Let's stop at the Westville police station first."

CHAPTER FOUR

"Well, well, well, as I live and breathe. Hester Crimstein in my little station."

She sat in the office of Westville police chief Oren Carmichael, who, nearing retirement at age seventy, remained what he'd always been—a grade-A prime slice of top-shelf beefcake.

"Nice to see you too, Oren."

"You look good."

"So do you." Gray hair worked so well on men, Hester thought. Damn unfair. "How's Cheryl?"

"Left me," he said.

"Seriously?"

"Yep."

"Cheryl always hit me as dumb."

"Right?"

"No offense."

"None taken."

"She was beautiful," Hester added.

"Yes."

"But dumb. Is that insensitive?"

"Cheryl might think so."

"I don't care what she thinks."

"Me neither." Oren Carmichael's smile stunned. "This back-and-forth is fun."

"Isn't it?"

"But I somehow don't think you're here for my middling repartee."

"I could be." Hester sat back. "What do the kids call it when you do more than one thing at a time?"

"Multitasking."

"Right." She crossed her legs. "So maybe that's what I'm doing."

Hester would say she's a sucker for a man in a uniform, but that was such a cliché. Still, Oren Carmichael looked mighty fit in that uniform.

"Do you remember the last time you were here?" Oren asked.

Hester smiled. "Jeffrey."

"He was dropping eggs on cars from the overpass."

"Good times," Hester said. "Why did you call Ira to pick Jeffrey up instead of me?"

"Ira didn't scare me."

"And I did?"

"If you want to use the past tense, sure." Oren Carmichael tilted his chair back. "Do you want to tell me why you're here, or should we keep with the banter?"

"Think we'll get better at it?"

"The banter? Can't get worse."

Thirty-four years ago, Oren had been on the posse that found the young boy in the woods. Everyone, including Hester, thought that mystery would be solved quickly, but no one ever claimed Wilde. No one ever found out who left him in the woods or how he'd gotten there in the first place. No one ever figured out how long the little boy had lived on his own or how Wilde had survived.

No one—still, after all these years—knows who the hell Wilde really is.

She debated asking Oren about Wilde, just to get an update on him, maybe use that as a way to ease into the rest.

But Wilde wasn't her business anymore.

She had to leave that alone, so she dove into the real reason she was here.

"Naomi Pine. You know who she is?"

Oren Carmichael folded his hands and rested them on that flat stomach. "Do you think I know every high school girl in this town?"

"How did you know she's a high school girl?" Hester asked.

"Can't get anything past you. Let's say I know her."

Hester wasn't sure how to put it, but again the direct route seemed the best. "A source tells me she's missing."

"A source?"

Okay, so not so direct. By God, Oren was handsome. "Yes."

"Hmm, isn't your grandson about Naomi's age?"

"Let's pretend that's a coincidence."

"He's a good kid, by the way. Matthew, I mean."

She said nothing.

"I still coach the basketball team," he continued. "Matthew is hardworking and scrappy like..."

He stopped before he could say David's name. Neither of them moved. For a few moments, the silence sucked something out of the room.

"Sorry," Oren said.

"Don't be."

"Should I pretend again?" he asked.

"No," Hester said in a soft voice. "Never. Not when it comes to David."

Oren, in his capacity as police chief, had gone to the scene the night of the crash.

"To answer your question," Oren said, "no, I don't know anything about Naomi being missing."

"No one called it in or anything?"

"No, why?"

"She's been out of school for a week."

"So?"

"So could you just make a call?"

"You're worried?"

"That's putting it too strongly. Let's just say a call would put my mind at ease."

Oren scratched his chin. "Is there anything I should know?"

"Other than my phone number?"

"Hester."

"No, nothing. I'm doing this as a favor."

Oren frowned. Then: "I'll make some calls."

"Great."

He looked at her. She looked at him.

Oren said, "I guess you don't want me to do this later and call you with the results."

"Why, are you busy right now?"

He sighed. Oren called Naomi's house first. No answer. Then he called the school's truant officer. The truant officer put him on hold. When the officer came back on the line, she said, "So far, the student's absences have been verified."

"You spoke to a parent?"

"Not me, but someone in the office."

"What did the parent say?"

"It's just marked as excused."

"Nothing else?"

"Why? Are you requesting that I take a ride out there?"

Oren looked over the phone at Hester. Hester shook her head.

"No, I'm just checking all the boxes. Anything else?"

"Just that this girl will probably need to either repeat the grade or do extensive summer school. She's been absent a lot this semester."

"Thank you."

Oren hung up.

"Thanks," Hester said.

"Sure."

She thought about it. "I get how you know Matthew," she said slowly. "From me. From David. From the basketball team."

He said nothing.

"And I know you're very active in the community, which is commendable."

"But you're wondering how I know Naomi."

"Yes."

"I probably should have said why from the start."

"I'm listening."

"Remember the movie *Breakfast Club*?" he asked.

"No."

Oren looked surprised. "You never saw it?"

"No."

"Really? Man, my kids had it on all the time, even though it was before their time."

"Is there a point?"

"Do you remember the actress Ally Sheedy?"

She bit back a sigh. "No."

"Not important. In the movie, Ally Sheedy plays a high school outcast who reminds me of Naomi. In one confessional scene, the character lets down her guard and says, 'My home life is unsatisfying.'"

"And that's Naomi?"

Oren nodded. "This wouldn't be the first time she's run away. Her father—and this is confidential—has three DUIs."

"Any signs of abuse?"

"No, I don't think that's it. More like neglect. Naomi's mother walked out, I don't know, five, ten years ago. Hard to say. The dad works long hours in the city. I think he's just in over his head raising the girl alone."

"Okay," Hester said. "Thanks for telling me."

"Let me walk you out."

When they reached the door, they turned to each other full-on.

Hester felt a blush come to her cheeks. A blush. Are you ever too old?

"So do you want to tell me what Matthew said to you about Naomi?" Oren asked.

"Nothing."

"Please, Hester, let's pretend that I'm a trained law enforcement officer who has been on the job for forty years. You casually stop by my office and ask about a troubled girl who happens to be a classmate of your grandson's. The detective in me wonders why and concludes that Matthew must have said something to you."

Hester was going to deny it, but that wouldn't do any good. "Off the record, yes, Matthew asked me to look into it."

"Why?"

"I don't know."

He waited.

"I really don't."

"Okay then."

"He seems worried about her."

"Worried how?"

"Again: I don't know. But if you don't mind, I'm going to look into it a little."

Oren frowned. "Look into it how?"

"I think I'll stop by her house. Talk to the father. That okay?"

"Would it matter if I said it wasn't?"

"No. And no, I don't think there is anything to it."

"But?"

"But Matthew has never asked me for anything before. Do you understand?"

"I think I do, yes," he said. "And if you learn anything while looking into it..."

"I'll call you immediately, promise." Hester took out her business card and handed it to him. "That's my cell number."

"You want mine?"

"That won't be necessary."

He kept his eyes on the card. "But didn't you just say you'd call me?"

She could feel her heart beating in her chest. Age was a funny thing. When your heart starts beating like this, you're in high school all over again.

"Oren?"

"Yes?"

"I know we are supposed to be all modern and woke and all that."

"Right."

"But I still think the guy should call the girl."

He held up her business card. "And by coincidence, I now have your phone number."

"Small world."

"Take care, Hester."

"Just the basics," Tim said, handing sheets back to Hester. "More coming soon."

They stored a printer in the trunk that hooked up to a laptop Tim kept in the glove compartment. Sometimes Hester's paralegals downloaded information to her phone, but Hester still preferred the tactile reading experience of paper. She liked to make notes with a pen or underline important phrases.

Old school. Or just old.

"You have the address for Naomi Pine?" she asked him.

"I do."

"How far away?"

Tim looked at the GPS. "Two-point-six miles, six minutes."

"Let's go."

She skimmed the notes as Tim drove. Naomi Pine, sixteen years old. Parents divorced. Father, Bernard. Mother, Pia. Father had sole custody, which was interesting in and of itself. In fact, Mother had given up all parental claims. Unusual, to put it mildly.

The house was old and worn. The paint had at one time been white, but it was more a cream-to-brown now. Every window was blocked by either a thick shade or cracked shutter.

"What do you think?" Hester asked Tim.

Tim made a face. "Looks like a safe house from the old country. Or maybe someplace to torture dissidents."

"Wait here."

A red Audi A6 in mint condition, probably worth more than the house, sat in the driveway. As she got closer to the door, Hester could see that the house had at one point been a grand Victorian. There was a wraparound porch and detailed albeit worn crown molding. The house had been, she bet, what they used to call a Painted Lady, though the paint was scant and whatever feminine charms she had once possessed had long gone to seed.

Hester knocked on the door. Nothing. She knocked some more.

A man's voice said, "Just leave whatever at the door."

"Mr. Pine?"

"I'm busy right now. If I have to sign for it—"

"Mr. Pine, I'm not here for a delivery."

"Who are you?"

His voice had a little slur in it. He had still not opened the door.

"My name is Hester Crimstein."

"Who?"

"Hester—"

The door finally opened.

"Mr. Pine?"

"How do I know you?" he asked.

"You don't."

"Yeah, I do. You're on TV or something."

"Right. My name is Hester Crimstein."

"Whoa." Bernard Pine snapped his fingers and pointed at her. "You're that criminal lawyer that's always on the news, right?"

"Right."

"I knew it." He startled back half a step, now wary. "Wait, what do you want with me?"

"I'm here about your daughter."

His eyes widened a bit.

"Naomi," Hester added.

"I know my daughter's name," he half snapped. "What do you want?"

"She's been absent from school."

"So? Are you a truant officer?"

"No."

"So what does my daughter have to do with you? What do you want from me?"

He looked the part of the man who'd just come home from a hard day's work. His five-o'clock shadow was closer to seven or eight p.m. His eyes were rimmed with red. His suit jacket was off, the cuffs of his sleeves rolled up, the tie loosened. Hester would bet there was a glass of something in the spirit family already poured.

"May I speak to Naomi?"

"Why?"

"I'm..." Hester tried on her legendary disarming smile. "Look, I don't mean any harm. I'm not here in any sort of legal capacity."

"Then why are you here?"

"I know this is out of the ordinary, but is Naomi okay?"

"I don't understand—why is my daughter any of your business?"

"She's not. I don't mean to pry." Hester tried to consider all the angles on this and decided to go with the most personal and truthful reply. "Naomi goes to school with my grandson Matthew. Maybe she's mentioned him?"

Pine's lips tightened. "Why are you here?"

"I... Matthew and I just wanted to make sure that she was okay."

"She's fine."

He started to close the door.

"Can I see her?"

"Are you serious?"

"I know she's been out of school."

"So?"

Enough with the disarming. She put a touch of steel in her voice. "So where is Naomi, Mr. Pine?"

"What right do you—?"

"None," Hester said. "No right. Zero, zilch. But a friend of Naomi's is worried about her."

"A friend?" He made a scoffing noise. "So your grandson is her friend, is he?"

Hester wasn't sure what to make of his tone. "I'm just asking to see her."

"She's not here."

"Where is she then?"

"That's really not your business."

A little more steel in the tone now: "You said you've seen me on TV."

"So?"

"So you probably know that you don't want to get on my bad side."

She glared at him. He stepped back.

"Naomi is visiting her mother." His grip on the knob of the door tightened. "And Ms. Crimstein? My daughter doesn't concern you or your grandson. Get off my property now."

He closed the door. Then, as though to add emphasis, he bolted the lock with an audible click.

Tim was outside and waiting. He opened the car door as she approached.

"Douche-nozzle," Hester muttered.

It was getting late. Night had fallen. The lighting out here, especially near the mountains, was near nonexistent. There was nothing more to be done about Naomi Pine tonight.

Tim slid into the driver's seat and started up the car. "We should probably start heading back," he said. "Your segment starts in two hours."

Tim met her eye in the rearview mirror and waited.

"How long has it been since we've been to Wilde's?" Hester asked.

"It'll be six years in September."

She should have been surprised at how much time had passed. She should have been surprised that Tim recalled the year and month so quickly.

Should have been. But wasn't.

"Do you think you could still find his road?"

"This time of night?" Tim considered it. "Probably."

"Let's try."

"You can't call?"

"I don't think he has a phone."

"He may have moved."

"No," Hester said.

"Or he may not be home."

"Tim."

He shifted the car into drive. "On our way."

CHAPTER FIVE

Tim found the turn on his third pass along Halifax Road. The thin lane of a road was almost entirely camouflaged so that it felt as though they were driving through a giant shrub. The vegetation scraped across the top of the car like those sponge noodles at a car wash. A few hundred yards south was the Split Rock Sweetwater Prayer Camp of the...what did they call themselves now? Ramapough Lenape Nation or Ramapough Mountain People or Ramapough Mountain Indians or simply Ramapoughs, with their murky genealogy some claim came directly from the indigenous people native to this area or maybe native tribes mixing with the Hessians who fought in the Revolutionary War or maybe runaway slaves that hid amongst the old Lenape tribes before the Civil War. Whatever, the Ramapoughs—she'd keep it simple in her own head—were now a reclusive albeit dwindling tribe.

Thirty-four years ago, when the little boy now called Wilde was found half a mile from here, many had suspected—many *still* did—that he had to somehow be connected to the Ramapoughs. No one had any specifics, of course, but when you are different and poor and reclusive, legends spring up. So maybe a tribeswoman had abandoned a child she'd had out of wedlock or maybe in some whacky tribal ceremony the child had been sent into the woods or maybe he'd wandered off and gotten lost and now the tribe was afraid to claim him. It was all nonsense, of course.

The sun had set. Trees didn't so much line the sliver of road as crowd onto it, the top limbs bending up and over and reaching across like children's arms playing London Bridge Is Falling Down. It was dark. Hester figured that they'd hit one sensor when they made the turn, probably two or three more as they coasted down the road. When they reached the dead end, Tim made a K-turn so they were now facing the way out.

The woods remained silent, still. The car headlights provided the only illumination.

"Now what?" Tim asked.

"Stay in the car."

"You can't go out there alone."

"But can't I?" They both reached for their door handles, but Hester stopped him with a firm "Stay put."

She stepped into the silent night and closed the door behind her.

The pediatricians who'd examined Wilde after his discovery estimated his age between six and eight years old. He could speak. He had learned how, he claimed, via his "secret" friendship with Hester's son David and, more directly, by breaking into homes and watching countless hours of television. Along with living off the land in the warmer seasons, that was how Wilde had fed himself—foraging in human beings' garbage cans, checking wastebaskets near parks, but mostly sneaking (aka breaking) into summer homes and raiding the fridge and cupboards.

The child didn't remember any other life.

No parents. No family. No contact with any human other than David.

One memory, however, did come back. The memory haunted the boy and now the man, kept him up at night, startling him awake in cold sweats at all hours of the night. The memory came to him in snap-flashes with no discernible narrative arc: a dark house, mahogany floorboards, a red banister, a portrait of a man with a mustache, and screams.

"What kind of screams?" Hester had asked the little boy.

"Terrible screams."

"No, I understand that. I mean, are they the screams of a man? A woman? In your memory, who is screaming?"

Wilde had considered that. "I am," he told her. "I'm the one screaming."

Hester folded her arms, leaned against the car, and waited. The wait didn't last long.

"Hester."

When Wilde stepped into view, Hester's heart filled and exploded. She couldn't say why. It had just been that kind of day maybe, and seeing her son's best friend—the last person to see David alive—just overwhelmed her yet again.

"Hi, Wilde."

Wilde was a genius. She knew that. Who knew why? A child comes out hardwired. That was what you learned as a parent—that your kid is who he is and what he is and that you, as a parent, greatly overstate your importance in his development. A dear friend once told her that being a parent is like being a car mechanic—you can repair the car and take care of the car and keep the car on the road, but you can't fundamentally change the car. If a sports car drives into your garage for repairs, it isn't driving out an SUV.

Same with kids.

So part of it was, well, that was what Wilde was genetically hardwired to be—a genius.

But experts also claim that early development is hugely important, that something like ninety percent of a child's brain develops by the age of five. But think about Wilde by that age. Imagine the stimulation, the experiences, the exposure, if as a small child he really did have to take care of himself, feed himself, shelter himself, comfort himself, defend himself.

What would that do to intensify a brain's development?

Wilde stepped into the headlights so she could see him. He smiled at her. He was a beautiful man with his dark sun-kissed complexion, his build of coiled muscles, his forearms looking like high-tension wires straining against the rolled-up flannel shirt, the faded jeans, the scuffed hiking boots, the long hair.

The very long hair of light brown.

Like the strand she'd found on the pillow.

Hester dove right in: "What's up with you and Laila?"

He said nothing.

"Don't deny it."

"I didn't."

"So?"

"She has needs," Wilde said.

"Seriously?" Hester said. "'She has needs'? So you're being—what, Wilde?—a Good Samaritan?"

He took a step toward her. "Hester?"

"What?"

"She can't love again."

Just when she thought that she couldn't hurt any more, his words detonated another explosive device in her heart.

"Maybe one day she can," Wilde said. "But right now, she still misses David too much."

Hester looked at him, feeling whatever had been building inside her—anger, hurt, stupidity, longing—deflate.

"I'm safe for her," Wilde said.

"Nothing's changed for you?"

"Nothing," he said.

She wasn't sure how she felt about that. At first, everyone thought that they'd find the boy's real identify fast. So Wilde—an obvious nickname that stuck—had stayed with the Crimsteins. Eventually, Child Services placed him with the Brewers, a beloved foster family who also lived in Westville. He started school. He excelled in pretty much everything he tried. But Wilde was always an outcast. He loved his foster family the best he could—the Brewers even officially adopted him—but in the end, he could only live alone. Other than his friendship with David, Wilde couldn't really connect to anyone, especially adults. Take whatever abandonment issues any normal person might have and raise them to the tenth power.

There had been women in his life, lots of them, but they couldn't last.

"Is that why you're here?" Wilde asked. "To ask about Laila?"

"In part."

"And the other part?"

"Your godson."

That got his attention. "What about him?"

"Matthew asked me to help find a friend of his."

"Who?"

"A girl named Naomi Pine."

"Why did he ask you?"

"I don't know. But I think Matthew might be in trouble."

Wilde started toward the car. "Tim still driving you?"

"Yes."

"I was about to hike over to the house. Give me a lift and tell me about it on the way."

In the backseat, Hester said to Wilde, "So this is a fling?"

"Laila could never be a fling. You know that."

Hester did know. "So you spend the whole night?"

"No. Never."

So, she thought, he really was the same. "And Laila is okay with that?"

Wilde replied by asking a question of his own: "How did you figure it out?"

"About you and Laila?"

"Yes."

"The house was too tidy."

Wilde didn't respond.

"You're a neat freak," she said. That was a polite understatement. Hester didn't understand official diagnoses or any of that, but Wilde had what a layman might consider obsessive-compulsive disorder. "And Laila is anything but."

"Ah."

"And then I found a long brown hair on David's pillow."

"It isn't David's pillow."

"I know."

"You snooped in her bedroom?"

"I shouldn't have."

"Yes."

"I'm sorry. It's just weird. You get that, right?"

Wilde nodded. "I get it."

"I want Laila happy. I want you happy."

She wanted to add that David would want that too, but she couldn't. Probably sensing her discomfort, Wilde changed topics.

"So tell me what's up with Matthew," Wilde said.

She filled him in on the Naomi Pine issue. He watched her with those piercing blue eyes with the gold flakes. He barely moved as she spoke. Some had nicknamed him—probably *still* nicknamed him—Tarzan, and the moniker fit almost too well, as though Wilde were playing into that role, what with the build and the dark skin and the long hair.

When she finished, Wilde said, "Did you tell Laila about this?"

She shook her head. "Matthew asked me not to."

"Yet you told me."

"He didn't say anything about you."

Wilde almost smiled. "Nice loophole you found there."

"A corollary of my occupation. Love me for all my faults."

Wilde looked off.

"What?"

"They're pretty tight," Wilde said. "Laila and Matthew. Why wouldn't he want her to know?"

"That's what I'm wondering."

They sat back in silence.

When he was eighteen years old, Wilde had gone to West Point, where he finished with all kinds of honors. The whole Crimstein clan—Hester, Ira, all three boys—had taken the forty-five-minute drive to the United States Military Academy for Wilde's graduation. Wilde then served overseas, mostly in some kind of special force—Hester could never remember what it was called. It was secret stuff, and even now, all these years later, Wilde couldn't or wouldn't talk about it. Classified. But in a song with a too familiar refrain, whatever Wilde saw over there, whatever he did or experienced or lost, war had pushed him over the edge or maybe, in his case, it had awoken the ghosts of his past. Who's to say?

When he finished serving and returned to Westville, Wilde gave up the pretense of trying to assimilate into "normal" society. He started working as a private investigator of sorts at a security firm called CRAW with his foster sister Rola, but that didn't really pan out. He bought a small trailer-like dwelling that brought minimalism to a new level and lived off the grid in the foothills of the mountains. He moved the dwelling around a bit, though he was always within shouting distance of that road. Hester didn't understand the technological minutiae of how Wilde knew when he had visitors. She just knew it had something to do with motion detectors and sensors and night cameras.

"So why tell me about this?" Wilde asked.

"I can't be out here all the time," she said. "I have court in the city. I have the TV appearances, obligations, stuff like that."

"Okay."

"And who would be better at tracking down a missing person than you?"

"Right."

"And then there was that hair on the pillow."

"Got it."

"I haven't been there for Matthew enough," Hester said.

"He's doing fine."

"Except he thinks a girl who's been missing from school is in serious danger."

"Except that," Wilde agreed.

When Tim made the turn, they both spotted Matthew walking away from the house. It was a teenage walk—head down, shoulders hunched protectively, feet scraping the ground, hands jammed aggressively deep into his jeans' pockets. He had white AirPods in his ears and didn't hear or see them until Tim nearly cut him off with the car. Matthew pulled out one of the earpieces.

Hester stepped out of the car first.

Matthew said, "Did you find Naomi?"

When he spotted Wilde getting out of the passenger door, Matthew frowned. "What the . . . ?"

"I told him," Hester said. "He won't say anything."

Matthew turned his attention back toward his grandmother. "Did you find Naomi?"

"I spoke to her father. He said she's fine, that she's visiting her mother."

"But did you talk to her?"

"The mother?"

"Naomi."

"Not yet, no."

"Then maybe her dad is lying," Matthew said.

Hester looked over at Wilde.

Wilde stepped toward him. "Why would you think that, Matthew?"

Matthew's gaze darted everywhere but on theirs. "Could you just, uh, make sure she's okay?"

It was Wilde who moved closer to the boy, not Hester. "Matthew, look at me."

"I am."

He wasn't.

"Are you in trouble?" Wilde asked.

"What? No."

"Talk to me then."

Hester stayed back. Here was the main reason she worried so about this new relationship between Laila and Wilde. It wasn't about David's memory and the pain of him being forever gone—or at least, not only about that. Wilde was Matthew's godfather. When David died, Wilde had been there. He answered the call, stepped up his role in Matthew's life. He wasn't a father or stepfather or anything like that. But Wilde was there, more as an involved uncle, and Hester and Laila had been grateful, believing, sexist as this might sound, that Matthew still needed a man in his life.

How would the romantic relationship between Laila and Wilde affect Matthew?

The boy wasn't stupid. If Hester saw the signs in a few minutes, Matthew had to know about the romance too. So how was the boy handling his godfather shacking up some nights with his mother? What would happen to Matthew if the relationship went south? Were Laila and Wilde mature enough to make sure Matthew didn't get hurt in the fallout—or were they being naïve in their thinking?

Matthew was taller than Wilde now. When the hell had that happened? Wilde put a hand on the boy's shoulder and said, "Talk to me, Matthew."

"I'm going to a party."

"Okay."

"At Crash's house. Ryan, Trevor, Darla, Trish—they'll all be there."

Wilde waited.

"They've been picking on her more lately. On Naomi." Matthew closed his eyes. "Supercruel stuff."

Hester joined them. "Who has been picking on her?"

"The popular kids."

"You?" Hester asked.

He kept his eyes on the ground.

Wilde said, "Matthew?"

Matthew's voice, when he finally spoke, was soft. "No..." He hesitated. They waited. "But I let it happen. I didn't do anything. I should have. Crash and Trevor and Darla played a prank on her. A mean one. And now...now she's gone. That's why I'm going to Crash's party. To see if I can learn anything."

"What kind of prank?" Hester asked.

"That's all I know."

A car driven by one teen with another riding shotgun pulled up to them. The driver honked the horn.

"I have to go," Matthew said. "Please...just keep looking too, okay?"

"I'm having someone from my office trace down Naomi's mother," Hester said. "I'll talk to her."

Matthew nodded. "Thanks."

"Is there anyone else we should talk to, Matthew? A friend of Naomi's maybe?"

"She has no friends."

"A teacher, a family member—"

He snapped his finger and his eyes lit up. "Miss O'Brien."

Wilde said, "Ava O'Brien?"

Matthew nodded. "She's, like, an assistant art teacher or something."

"And you think—?" Hester asked.

The driver honked the horn again. Hester silenced it with a glare.

"I gotta go. I'm hoping to learn something at the party."

"Learn what?" Hester asked.

But Matthew didn't reply. He hopped into the backseat of the car. Wilde and Hester watched them drive away.

"You know this Miss O'Brien?" Hester asked Wilde.

"Yes."

"Should I ask how?"

Wilde said nothing.

"That's what I thought. Will she talk to you?"

"Yes."

"Good." When the car disappeared around the bend, Hester asked, "What do you think?"

"I think Matthew isn't telling us everything."

"Maybe Naomi's mother calls me back. Maybe she lets me talk to Naomi."

"Maybe," Wilde said.

"But you don't think so."

"No, I don't think so."

They both turned and looked down the cul-de-sac toward the Crimstein homestead.

"I have to get back to the city to do my show," Hester said.

"Uh-huh."

"I don't have time to get into this with Laila now."

"Probably best," Wilde said. "Do your show. I'll talk to Laila, then I'll talk to Ava O'Brien."

Hester handed him a business card with her mobile number on it. "Stay in touch, Wilde."

"You too, Hester."

CHAPTER SIX

When Laila answered the front door, she asked, "What's wrong?"

"Nothing."

"Then why are you using the front door?"

Wilde always came in through the back door. Always. He hiked through the woods that came up behind the Crimstein house. He'd been doing that since the days David sneaked him inside when they were little boys.

"Well?"

Laila had this passion and energy that turned her beauty into a living, breathing, pulsating entity. You couldn't help but be drawn in, to watch, to want to be a part of it.

"I can't stay for dinner," he said.

"Oh."

"Sorry. Something just came up."

"You don't owe me an explanation."

"I can come back later, if you want."

Laila studied his face. He wanted to tell her about Matthew and this Naomi situation, but after weighing the pros and cons, he'd decided that keeping his godson's confidence trumped informing on him to his mother. For today anyway. For now. It was a close call, but Laila would understand.

Maybe.

"I have an early morning anyway," Laila said.

"Got it."

"And Matthew is out tonight. I don't know what time he'll get back."

Wilde mimicked her in the gentlest way as he quoted her: "'You don't owe me an explanation.'"

Laila gave him a smile. "Ah, what the hell. Come back if you can."

"Might be late."

"I don't care," she said. Then: "You didn't tell me why you're using the front door."

"I spotted Matthew on the street."

Not a lie.

"What did he say to you?"

"That he was going to a party at someone named Crash's house."

"Crash Maynard," she said.

"As in?"

"Yeah, the Maynard Manor. Son of Dash."

"Dash has a son named Crash?"

"His father loved the movie *Bull Durham* or something. Can you believe that?"

He shrugged. "When your name is Wilde..."

"Touché."

Darkness had fallen. The lullaby of crickets played, his constant comforting companion. "I better go."

"Wait." Laila dug into her jeans pocket. "No need to play mountain man." She pulled out her key fob and tossed it to him. "Take my car."

"Thank you."

"You're welcome."

"I may not be gone long."

"I'll be here, Wilde."

Laila closed the door.

Eight months ago, when Wilde first encountered Ava O'Brien, she was living off Route 17 in a sprawling condo development of dull grays and beiges. That night, as they stumbled under popping fluorescent streetlights back to her place, Ava had made a joke about how the condos looked so much alike that she often stuck her key in the wrong door.

Wilde had no such issue. He still remembered the exact address and location.

No one answered on the first knock. Wilde knew the condo layout. He checked the window on the upper right. The light was on. That didn't mean much. He looked for a passing shadow. Nothing.

He knocked again.

Shuffling feet. A pause. It was nearly nine p.m. now. Ava O'Brien was probably looking through the peephole. He stood and waited. A moment later he heard a sliding chain. The knob turned.

"Wilde?"

Ava wore a big terry cloth robe. He knew the robe. He had even worn it.

"Can I come in for a second?" he asked.

He tried to read her face to see whether she was happy or sad to see him. Not that it would change anything. Her expression, however, seemed mixed. There was maybe surprise. There was maybe some joy. There was also something else—something in her expression that he couldn't quite put his finger on.

"Now?"

He didn't bother replying.

Ava leaned forward, met his eye, and whispered, "I'm not alone, Wilde."

Ah, so now he could quite put his finger on it.

Her face softened. "Ah, Wilde," she said in a voice too tender. "Why tonight?"

Maybe he shouldn't have come. Maybe he should have left this to Hester.

"It's about Naomi Pine," he said.

That got her attention. She glanced behind her, stepped out onto the stoop, and closed the door.

"What about Naomi?" she asked. "Is she okay?"

"She's missing."

"What do you mean, missing?"

"She's one of your students, right?"

"Sort of."

"What do you mean, sort of?"

"What do you mean, she's missing?"

"Did you notice she's been absent?"

"I assumed she was sick." Ava tightened the terry cloth robe. "I don't understand. What's your interest in this?"

"I'm trying to find her."

"Why?" When he didn't reply right away, Ava asked, "Did you ask her father?"

"My colleague"—easier than trying to explain about Hester—"did."

"And?"

"He claims that Naomi is with her mother."

"He said that?"

"Yes."

Now Ava looked genuinely concerned. "Naomi's mother hasn't been a part of her life for a long time."

"So we've been told."

"How did you end up coming to me?"

"A source"—again easier—"claimed that you're close to her."

"I still don't understand. Why are you looking for Naomi? Did someone hire you?"

"No. I'm doing it as a favor."

"A favor for whom?"

"I can't tell you. Do you have any idea where she is?"

The door behind her opened. A big man with one of those superlong beards filled the doorway. He looked at Ava, then at Wilde. "Hi," he said.

"Hi," Wilde said.

He looked back at Ava. "I better be going."

"No need," Wilde said. "This won't take long."

The bearded man looked at Ava some more. Then, as if he'd seen an answer there, he nodded to himself. "Rain check?" he asked her.

"Sure."

He kissed her on the cheek, slapped Wilde on the back, and jogged down the steps. He slid into his GMC Terrain, headed out in reverse, and waved goodbye. Wilde turned back toward Ava and considered making an apology. She waved that away.

"Come on in."

Wilde sat on the same red couch where he and Ava had first kissed. He quickly scanned the room. Nothing much had changed since he'd spent those three days here with her. On one wall, there were two new paintings hung the slightest bit crookedly—one watercolor of what looked like a tormented face, one oil painting of the Houvenkopf Mountain, which wasn't far from here.

"The paintings," he asked. "You do them?"

She shook her head. "Students."

He had figured that. She didn't like displaying her own work. *Too personal*, she'd told him when he asked. *Too self-involved. Too easy to see all your flaws.*

"Either of them by Naomi?"

"No," Ava said. "But go ahead if you want."

"Go ahead and what?"

She gestured to the walls. "Straighten them. I know how antsy it's making you."

At night, while Ava had slept, Wilde would go around, sometimes with a level, and make sure the paintings were indeed completely straight. It was one of the reasons why he was glad he had nothing hung up in his own abode.

As Wilde started to adjust the paintings, Ava took a seat in the chair farthest away from him. "You need to tell me why you're looking for her."

"No, I don't."

"Excuse me?"

He finished finagling with the mountain watercolor. "We don't have time for explanations. Do you trust me, Ava?"

She pushed the hair back from her face. "Should I?"

There may have been an edge in the tone, he couldn't be sure.

Then: "Yes, Wilde, I trust you."

"Tell me about Naomi."

"I don't know where she is, if that's what you're asking."

"But she's one of your students?"

"She will be."

"What does that mean?"

"I encouraged her to sign up for Intro to Watercolors next semester. She'll be my student then."

"But you already know her?"

"Yes."

"How?"

"I do cafeteria duty three days a week. With the cutbacks, they were woefully understaffed." She leaned forward. "You went to that high school, didn't you?"

"Yes."

"You're not going to believe this, but when the two of us were, uh"—she looked up as though searching for the right word before shrugging and settling for—"together, I had no idea who you were. I mean, about your past."

"I know."

"How?"

"I can always tell."

"People treat you differently, right? Never mind. It doesn't matter. I imagine you were an outcast at that place, right?"

"To some degree."

"To some degree," she repeated, "because you're strong and attractive and probably athletic. Naomi is none of those things. She is *that* girl, Wilde. The full-on, grade-A, bullied outcast. Somehow—and this will sound awful—but there is something about her that makes it easier for people. Human nature that no one wants to discuss. There is a bit of us that enjoys the spectacle. Like she deserves it. And it's not just students. The other teachers smirk. I'm not saying they like it, but they do nothing to defend her."

"But you do."

"I try. It often makes it worse. I know that's a cop-out, but when I stood up for her, well, let's just say it didn't help. So what I do instead, I pretend she gets in trouble—I hope that maybe gives her cred or something—and part of her punishment is, she can't sit in the cafeteria during lunch. I take her to the art studio. Sometimes, if I get out of cafeteria duty, I'll sit with her. I don't think it helped much with the students, but at least..."

"At least what?"

"At least Naomi gets a break. At least she gets a few minutes of peace during the school day." Ava blinked away a tear. "If Naomi is missing, she probably ran away."

"Why do you say that?"

"Because her life is hell."

"Even at home?"

"I don't know if hell is the right word, but it isn't great there either. Do you know Naomi was adopted?"

Wilde shook his head.

"She talks about it more than an adopted kid should."

"In what way?"

"Fantasizing about being rescued by her real parents, for example. Her adoptive parents had to go through all kinds of interviews and screenings, and when they passed, they were awarded an infant—Naomi—but then pretty much right away, the mom couldn't handle it. They even tried to return her to the orphanage. Do you believe that? Like she was a package delivered by UPS. Anyway, her mother had a breakdown. Or claimed to. She abandoned Naomi and her father."

"Do you know where the mother is now?"

"Oh, she's"—Ava frowned and made air quotes with her fingers—"'recovered.' Remarried a rich guy. Naomi says she lives in a fancy town house on Park Avenue."

"Has Naomi said anything to you lately? Anything that might help?"

"No." Then: "Now that you mention it."

"What?"

"She seemed a little . . . better. More relaxed. Calm."

Wilde didn't say anything, but he didn't like that.

"Now it's your turn, Wilde. Why are you asking?"

"Someone is worried about her."

"Who?"

"I can't say."

"Matthew Crimstein."

He said nothing.

"Like I said, Wilde, I didn't know who you were when we met."

"But you know now."

"Yes." Her eyes were suddenly bright with tears. He reached out and took her hands in his. She pulled away. He let her. "Wilde?"

"Yes."

"You need to find her."

Wilde walked back to the condo parking lot. He drove Laila's BMW twenty yards to a dumpster. Hester had been correct. Laila was a slob. A beautiful slob. She kept her own self meticulously neat and clean and freshly showered. But her surroundings did not follow suit. The backseat of her BMW had coffee cups and protein bar wrappers.

Wilde put the car in park and emptied it out. He wasn't a germophobe, but he was glad that she had antibacterial lotion in the glove compartment. He looked back at Ava's house. Would she call back the big guy with the bigger beard? Doubt it.

He didn't regret his time with Ava. Not in the slightest. In fact, there had been a strange pang when he first saw her, something akin to... longing? Maybe it was justification or rationalization, but the fact that he couldn't connect long term didn't mean he didn't appreciate new experiences with new people. He never wanted to hurt them, but maybe it was even worse to patronize them or hand them some bullshit line. He settled on being completely truthful, not sugarcoating it, not being too faux protective.

Wilde slept outside. Even on those nights.

It was hard to explain why, so sometimes he would leave a note, sneak back to the woods for a few hours, and then be back by the morning. Wilde couldn't fall asleep when someone else was with him.

It was that simple.

Outside he dreamt a lot about his mother.

Or maybe it wasn't his mother. Maybe it was another woman in that house with the red banister. He didn't know. But in the dream, his mother—call her that for now—was beautiful, with long auburn hair and emerald eyes and the voice of an angel. Was this what his mother really looked like? The image was a bit too perfect, perhaps more delusion than reality. It could be something he just conjured up or had even seen on TV.

Memory makes demands that you often can't keep. Memory is faulty because it insists on filling in the blanks.

His phone rang. It was Hester.

"Did you talk to Ava O'Brien?" Hester asked.

"Yes."

"Are you proud of me for not prying about how you know her?"

"You're the model of discretion."

"So what did she say?"

Wilde filled her in. When he finished, she said, "That part about Naomi seeming calm. That's not good."

"I know," Wilde said.

When people decide to end their lives, they often exhibit a sense of calm. The decision has been made. A weight, oddly enough, has been lifted.

"Well, I have news," Hester said. "And it's not good."

Wilde waited.

"The mother called me back. She has no idea where Naomi is."

"So the father lied," Wilde said.

"Maybe."

Either way, it wouldn't hurt for Wilde to pay the dad a visit.

Someone called out to Hester. There was some commotion in the background.

"All okay?" he asked.

"I'm about to go live on air," Hester said. "Wilde?"

"Yes."

"We need to do something fast, agreed?"

"It could still be nothing."

"Is that what your gut is telling you?"

"I don't listen to my gut," Wilde said. "I listen to the facts."

"Bullshit." Then: "Are the facts worried about this girl?"

"This girl," he agreed. "And Matthew."

There was more commotion.

"Gotta go, Wilde. We'll talk soon."

She hung up.

Hester sat at the news desk on a leather-backed stool, set a tad too high for her. Her toes barely touched the floor. The teleprompter was lined up and ready to roll. Lori, the on-duty hairstylist, was working some final touches, which involved two-finger plucking, while Bryan, the makeup artist, added some last-second concealer. The red countdown clock, which resembled the timer on a TV-drama bomb, indicated that they had under two minutes until air.

Her cohost for tonight played on his phone. Hester closed her eyes for a second, felt the makeup brush stroke her cheek, felt the fingers gently pull her hair into place. It was all oddly soothing.

When her phone vibrated, she opened her eyes with a sigh and shooed Lori and Bryan away. She normally wouldn't take a call this close to going on air, but the caller ID told her it was her grandson.

"Matthew?"

"Did you find her yet?"

His voice was a desperate hush.

"Why are you whispering? Where are you?"

"At Crash's house. Did you speak to Naomi's mother?"

"Yes."

"What did she say?"

"She doesn't know where Naomi is."

Her grandson made a sound that might have been a groan.

"Matthew, what aren't you telling us?"

"It doesn't matter."

"It does."

His tone turned sullen. "Forget I asked, okay?"

"Not okay."

One of the producers yelled, "Ten seconds to air."

Her cohost pocketed his phone and sat up straight. He turned to Hester, saw she had the phone pressed against her ear, and said, "Uh, Hester? You're doing the intro."

The producer held up his hand to indicate five seconds. He tucked his thumb to show it was now four.

"I'll call you back," Hester said.

She put the phone on the table in front of her as the producer dropped his index finger.

Three seconds may seem like a very short time. In television terms, it's not. Hester had time to glance at Allison Grant, her segment producer, and nod. Allison had time to make a face and nod back so as to indicate that she would comply with Hester's request but she would do so reluctantly.

Still, Hester had prepared for this. There were times you investigated—and there were times you instigated.

It was time for the latter.

The producer finished his countdown and pointed at Hester.

"Good evening," Hester said, "and welcome to this edition of *Crimstein on Crime*. Our lead story tonight is—what else?—upstart presidential candidate Rusty Eggers and the controversy surrounding his campaign."

That part was on the teleprompter. The rest was not.

Hester took a deep breath. *In for a penny, in for a . . .*

"But first, breaking news just coming in," Hester said.

Her cohost frowned and turned toward her.

The thing was, Matthew was scared. That was what Hester couldn't shake. Matthew was scared, and he had asked for her help. How could she not do all she could?

A photograph of Naomi Pine filled television screens across the country. It was the only photograph her producer Allison Grant had been able to find, and that had taken some doing. There was nothing on social media, which was really strange in today's society, but Allison, who was as good as they came, dug up the website for the school photographer who took the official Sweet Water High portraits. Once Allison promised that they would keep the watermark with his logo on it, the photographer had agreed to let them use it on air.

Hester continued: "Tonight, a local girl from Westville, New Jersey, is missing and needs your help."

From the parking lot outside Ava's condo, Wilde weighed his options. There really wasn't much more to do when he thought about it. The hour was getting late. So Option One: He could just drive back to Laila's house and gently pad upstairs to the bedroom where she'd be waiting and...

Yeah, did he really have to review other options?

To cover his bases, he texted Matthew: Where are you?

Matthew: At Crash Maynard's.

Laila had told him that earlier, but he wasn't sure he was supposed to know.

Wilde: Is Naomi there?
Matthew: No.

Wilde debated what to type next, but then he saw the dots dancing, indicating that Matthew was typing.

Matthew: Shit.
Wilde: What?
Matthew: Something bad is going down.

Wilde's thumbs didn't move as fast as he wanted them to, but he finally managed to type: Like what?

No reply.

Wilde: Hello?

The utopian image from Option One—Laila upstairs in that bedroom, warm under the covers, reading legal briefs—rose up in front of him so real he could smell her skin.

Wilde: Matthew?

No reply. The Laila-related image turned to smoke and drifted into the ether.

Damn.

Wilde started up the road toward Maynard Manor.

CHAPTER SEVEN

Matthew was in Crash Maynard's enormous mansion on the hill.

The mansion's exterior looked old and kind of Gothic with marble columns. It reminded Matthew of that snooty golf club his grandmother took him to because one of her clients was getting some kind of award. Hester hadn't liked being there, he remembered. As she sucked down the wine—too much wine as it turned out—her eyes began to narrow. She glanced around the room, frowning and muttering under her breath about silver spoons and privilege and inbreeding. When he asked her what was wrong, Hester had looked her grandson up and down and said, loud enough for those nearby to hear: "You're half Jew, half black—you'd doubly not be allowed in this club." Then she paused, raised a finger in the air, and added, "Or maybe you'd be two tokens in one." When an elderly lady with frozen dollops of snow-white hair made a tut-tut, shh-shh noise in her direction, Hester had told her to blow it out her ass.

That was Matthew's grandmother. Nana never avoided a controversy if she could create one.

It was both mortifying and comforting. Mortifying, well, that was pretty obvious. Comforting because he knew that his grandmother always had his back. He never questioned it. Didn't matter that she was small or seventy or whatever. His grandmother seemed superhuman to him.

There were about a dozen kids at what parents insisted on calling a "party" but was really just a gathering in Crash's "lower level"—Crash's parents didn't like calling it a basement—which may have been the coolest place Matthew had ever been. If the exterior was old school, the interior couldn't have been more state of the art. The home theater was closer to a full-fledged cinema with mod digital sound design and forty-plus seats. There was a cherrywood bar and real-theater popcorn machine out front. The corridors were lined with a mix of vintage movie posters and posters for Crash's dad's television shows. The arcade room was a mini replica of the Silverball, the famed pinball palace on the Asbury Park boardwalk. Down one corridor was a wine cellar with oak barrels. The other became an underground tunnel leading to a regulation-sized basketball court, a replica—lots of replicas—of the Knicks' floor at Madison Square Garden.

No one ever hung out on the basketball court. No one ever used the pinball arcade. No one was ever really in the mood to watch anything in the movie theater. Not that Matthew had been here a lot. For most of his life, he'd been on the outs with the popular crowd, but recently, Matthew had wormed his way back in. Truth be told, he loved it here. The popular kids did the coolest things, like when Crash had that birthday bash in Manhattan. His dad had rented black limos to transport them, and the party had been in some huge place that used to be a bank. All the boys got to be "escorted" in by past contestants on Dash Maynard's reality show *Hot Models in Lingerie*. A famous TV star had DJed the party, and when he introduced "my best friend and our birthday boy," Crash had ridden in on a white horse, a real horse, and then his father drove in behind him in a red Tesla he'd given his son as a present.

Tonight most of the kids had ended up in the "regular" TV room—a ninety-eight-inch Samsung 4K Ultra HD hanging on the wall. Crash and Kyle played Madden video football, the rest of the gang—Luke, Mason, Kaitlin, Darla, Ryan, and of course Sutton, always Sutton—lay sprawled across upscale beanbag chairs as though some giant being had tossed them from the sky. Most of his friends were high. Caleb and Brianna had gone off to a room down the corridor to take their hookup to the next level.

The room was dark, the blue light from both the television and individual smartphones illuminating his classmates' faces, turning them a ghostly pale. Sutton was on the right, uncharacteristically on her own. Matthew wanted to take advantage of that opening, and so he looked for a way to move closer to her. He'd had an unrequited crush on Sutton since seventh grade—Sutton with the almost supernatural poise and blond hair and perfect skin and melt-your-bones smile—and she was always nice and friendly and a sixth-degree black belt in how to keep guys like Matthew in the friend zone.

On the big screen, Crash's video quarterback threw a deep pass that went for a touchdown. Crash jumped up, did a little celebration dance, and shouted at Kyle, "In your face!" This led to some halfhearted laughs from the spectators, all of whom were on their phones. Crash looked around as though he'd expected more in the way of a reaction. But it wasn't happening.

Not tonight anyway.

There was something in the room, a whiff of fear or desperation.

"We need more munchies?" Crash asked.

No one responded.

"Come on, who's with me?"

The halfhearted murmurs were enough. Crash hit a button on the intercom. A woman's Mexican-accented voice said, "Yes, Mr. Crash?"

"Can we get some nachos and quesadillas, Rosa?"

"Of course, Mr. Crash."

"And can you crush up some of that homemade guac?"

"Of course, Mr. Crash."

On the screen, Crash kicked off. Luke and Mason drank beers. Kaitlin and Ryan shared a joint while Darla vaped with the latest flavors from Juul. The room had been Crash's dad's cigar room and they had done something to it so you couldn't really smell the new smoke. Kaitlin passed an e-cigarette to Sutton. Sutton took it, but she didn't put it in her mouth.

Kyle said, "Man, I love Rosa's guac."

"Right?"

Crash and Kyle high-fived and then someone, maybe Mason, forced up a laugh. Luke joined in, then Kaitlin, then pretty much everyone except Matthew and Sutton. Matthew didn't know what they were all laughing about—Rosa's guacamole?—but the sound had zero authenticity, like they were all trying too hard to be normal.

Mason said, "She check in on the app?"

Silence.

"I was just saying—"

"There's nothing," Crash said, interrupting him. "I got an app that gives updates."

More silence.

Matthew slipped out of the room. He headed toward the relative privacy of the nearby wine cellar. When he closed the door behind him, he sat on a barrel that read Maynard Vineyards—yes, they owned a vineyard too—and called his grandmother.

"Matthew?"

"Did you find her yet?"

"Why are you whispering? Where are you?"

"At Crash's house. Did you speak to Naomi's mother?"

"Yes."

Matthew felt his heart beating in his chest. "What did she say?"

"She doesn't know where Naomi is."

He closed his eyes and groaned.

"Matthew, what aren't you telling us?"

"It doesn't matter."

"It does."

But he couldn't say anything. Not yet. "Forget I asked, okay?"

"Not okay."

Through the phone, he heard a male voice say, "Ten seconds to air." Then someone else mumbled something he couldn't make out.

"I'll call you back," Hester said before disconnecting the call.

As he took the phone away from his ear, a familiar voice said, "Hey."

He turned to the wine cellar entrance. It was Sutton. She was still blinking away the dark of the TV room.

"Hey," he said.

Sutton had a bottle of beer in her hand. "You want some?"

He shook his head, afraid that Sutton would think it was gross to share his germs or something. Then again, hadn't she asked him?

Sutton looked around the wine cellar as if she'd never seen it before, though she had always been with the popular crowd. Always.

"What are you doing in here?" she asked.

Matthew shrugged. "I don't know."

"You don't seem yourself tonight."

It surprised him that Sutton would notice something like that.

He shrugged again. Man, did he know how to woo girls or what?

Then Sutton said: "She's fine, you know."

Just like that.

"Matthew?"

"Do you know where she is?"

"No, but . . ." Now it was her turn to shrug.

His phone buzzed. He sneaked a peek.

Where are you?

It was from Wilde. Matthew quickly texted back: At Crash Maynard's.

Is Naomi there?

No.

Sutton stepped toward him. "They're a little worried about you."

"Who?"

"Crash and Kyle, the others." She looked at him with those blue eyes. "Me too."

"I'm fine."

Now her phone buzzed. When she read it, her eyes widened. "Oh my God."

"What?"

She looked up at him with those gorgeous eyes. "Did you . . . ?"

He heard a commotion from down the corridor.

Matthew typed: Shit.

Wilde: What?

Crash burst into the wine cellar as Matthew hit send on: Something bad is going down.

Kyle came in right behind him. They both had their smartphones in their hands. Crash stormed toward Matthew so fast that Matthew actually put his fists up as though preparing to ward off a blow. Crash stopped, raised his hands in a surrender motion, and smiled.

The smile was oily. Matthew felt something roil in the pit of his stomach.

"Whoa, whoa," Crash said in a voice that aimed for comforting but slithered down Matthew's back like a snake. "Let's slow down here."

Crash Maynard was surface handsome—wavy dark hair, brooding boy-band expression, thin frame adorned in the latest fashion. When you took a closer look at him, you could see that Crash was nothing special, not in any way really, but as Hester once joked about a rich girl she wanted Matthew to date, "She's beautiful when she's standing on her money."

Crash always wore a big silver smile-skull ring. It looked ridiculous on his thin, smooth finger.

With that oily smile still on his face, Crash lifted his phone and turned it toward Matthew. "Do you want to explain this?"

He pushed down on the screen using the finger with the smile-skull ring. The ring seemed to wink at Matthew. A video sprang to life, starting off with the familiar network news logo. Then his grandmother came on the screen.

"But first, breaking news just coming in . . ."

A photo of Naomi appeared on the screen.

"Tonight, a local girl from Westville, New Jersey, is missing and needs your help. Naomi Pine has been missing for at least a week now. There have been no reported sightings or ransom demands, but friends are concerned that the teen may be in danger. . . ."

Oh no. . . .

Matthew felt his stomach tumble. He hadn't thought about that, that Nana might go live on the air with the story. Or was that what he'd secretly been hoping? He wasn't surprised by how fast the news—according to the timer on the app, less than two minutes—had disseminated amongst his friends. That was how it worked now. Someone maybe had a news alert on Naomi Pine or maybe a parent had seen the story and right away texted their kid and said, *"Doesn't this girl go to your school?!?!"* or maybe someone followed CNN on Twitter. Whatever, that was how it was now, how quickly word got out.

Crash's smile didn't flicker. "That's your grandmother, right?"

"Yeah, but..."

Crash beckoned for more with his smile-skull-ring hand. "But?"

Matthew said nothing.

Crash's tone was mocking. "Did you say something to Grandma?"

"What?" Matthew tried to look offended by the suggestion. "No, of course not."

Still smiling—a smile that now eerily echoed the one on his ring—Crash stepped forward and put his hands on Matthew's shoulders. Then, without the slightest warning, he drove his knee upward, straight into Matthew's groin. Crash pulled down on Matthew's shoulders for extra leverage.

The blow lifted Matthew onto his toes.

The pain was immediate, white hot, all-consuming. Tears filled Matthew's eyes. Every part of his body shut down. His knees caved, and he collapsed to the floor. The pain rose from his stomach, paralyzing his lungs. Matthew pulled his knees to his chest and curled himself into a fetal ball on the floor.

Crash bent down so his mouth was right near Matthew's ear. "Do you think I'm stupid?"

Matthew's cheek was pressed against the floorboard. He still couldn't breathe. It felt as if some part of him was irretrievably broken, as if he would never be right again.

"You drove here with Luke and Mason. They told me you were standing with your grandmother when they picked you up."

Breathe, Matthew told himself. *Try to breathe.*

"What did you tell her, Matthew?"

He gritted his teeth and managed to open his eyes. Kyle was by the door on lookout. Sutton was nowhere to be seen. Had she set him up? Would she really do that to...? No. Sutton couldn't know the story was about to come out or any of that. And she wouldn't...

"Matthew?"

He looked up, the pain still ripping through him.

"We could kill you and get away with it. You know that, right?"

Matthew stayed frozen. Crash made a fist and showed him the silver skull.

"What did you tell your grandmother?"

CHAPTER EIGHT

Two floors above the wine cellar, in a circular turret on the western wing of the massive estate, Dash Maynard and his wife, Delia, sat in burgundy leather wingback armchairs in front of an oversized fireplace with ceramic "white birch" logs and gas-fed flames. This room, an addition they'd put on three years ago, was the "Beauty and the Beast" library and featured floor-to-ceiling built-in oak bookshelves with a rolling ladder on copper rails.

Dash Maynard read a biography on Teddy Roosevelt. He loved history, always had, though he had no interest, thank you very much, in being a part of it. Before he hit it huge with the both famous and infamous self-help talk show *The Rusty Show* and then in a new genre that the networks dubbed "upscale game-ality"—an awkward blend of "game show" and "reality"—Dash Maynard had been an award-winning documentary filmmaker. He'd won an Emmy for his searing PBS short on the Nanking massacre of 1937. Dash loved research and interviews and on-location filming, but he'd excelled in the editing room, able to take countless hours of video and turn it into a compelling narrative.

Delia Reese Maynard, the chair of the political science department at nearby Reston College, read through student essays. Dash liked to watch her when his wife read student papers—the furrow of the brow, the thinning of her lips, the slow nod when she got excited about a section. Over the summer, Dash and Delia—Double Ds, some jokingly called them—had celebrated their twenty-fifth wedding anniversary by taking their sixteen-year-old son Crash and their fourteen-year-old twin daughters Kiera and Kara on their yacht through the Baltics. During the day, they'd set down the anchor in a secluded island cove to swim and jet-ski and wakeboard. In the afternoons and evenings, they toured ports of call like Saint Petersburg and Stockholm and Riga. It had been a marvelous trip.

Dash thought of that time now, that family vacation away from this damn country, as the calm before the storm.

They were lucky people. He knew that. People liked to classify them as "Hollywood elites," but Dash had been born and raised in a modest three-family town house in the Bedford-Stuyvesant neighborhood of Brooklyn. Both his parents had taught at Hunter College's main campus in Manhattan. Dash's name came from his father's favorite author, Dashiell Hammett. He and Delia first bonded—really bonded—over old mystery novels when they browsed first editions of Raymond Chandler, Agatha Christie, Ngaio Marsh, and of course, Dashiell Hammett at a used-book store in Washington, DC. At the time, the two barely paid political interns working on Capitol Hill couldn't afford any first editions. Now this very room housed one of the greatest collections in the world.

As they say, life comes at you fast.

Dash and Delia had spent the last ten years, since Dash's production company had really hit it big with a prime-time show where big-name celebrities disguise themselves as "ordinary" Americans and live amongst them for six months, trying to balance the fame and money thing with the core values of family and study that they both revered. It was a constantly evolving calibration.

The balance had worked for the most part. Sure, Crash was a

little spoiled and acted out, while Kiera had some mild issues with depression, but that seemed to be the norm today. As a couple, Dash and Delia could not have been closer. That was why nights like this—his son throwing a small party downstairs while his parents enjoyed the quiet of each other—meant so much to them.

Dash loved this. He reveled in it. He wanted to live the rest of his life this way.

But he couldn't.

There was a knock on the library door. Gavin Chambers, a former Marine colonel who now worked in the ever-expanding private security industry, stepped into the room before Dash had a chance to say, "Come in." Chambers still looked the longtime Marine—the buzz cut, the ramrod posture, the steady gaze.

"What's the matter?" Dash asked.

Chambers looked over at Delia, as though maybe it would be best if the little lady left. Dash frowned. Delia didn't move.

"Go on," Dash said.

"A television report just aired," Chambers said. "There's a young girl missing. Her name is Naomi Pine."

Dash looked at Delia. Delia shrugged.

"And?"

"Naomi goes to school with Crash. They are in several classes together."

"I'm still not sure—"

"She's been communicating with your son. Texts mostly. Also the journalist who reported her missing just now? Her name is Hester Crimstein. Her grandson Matthew is downstairs with Crash."

Delia put the student papers down on the side table. "I still don't see how this connects to us, Colonel."

Chambers said, "Neither do I..."

"So?"

"...*yet*." Then for emphasis, Chambers repeated the sentence: "Neither do I *yet*." He stood at attention and stared straight ahead.

"But with all due respect, I don't believe in coincidences, especially right now."

"What do you think we should do about it?"

"I think we need to talk to your son and figure out his relationship to Naomi—" His phone buzzed. He put it to his ear with a snap, almost as though he were saluting a superior officer. "Yes?"

After three seconds, Gavin Chambers pocketed the phone.

"Don't leave this room," he told them. "There's been an incident."

Racing along Skyline Drive toward Maynard Manor—man, what a pompous name—Wilde hoped to feel his phone buzz with another text from Matthew.

It didn't.

The last text just kept coming back to Wilde, taunting him: Something bad is going down.

Wilde might not go with his gut—that was what he'd told Hester—but as he turned into the manor's driveway, every instinct told him that he should pay heed to that message.

Something bad is going down.

Maynard Manor sat atop thirty acres of disputed mountain the Ramapough people claimed as their own. There were barns for a dozen horses and a track for steeple jumping and a pool and a tennis court and who knew what else. The centerpiece was an enormous Classical Revival Georgian home, built by an oil tycoon in the Roaring Twenties. The upkeep on the thirty-five-room estate had been so steep that the manor had fallen into disrepair for nearly a quarter century, until Dash Maynard, mega television producer and cable-network owner, and his wife, Delia, swept in and brought the place back to its former splendor and then some.

From the ornate gate where Wilde had to stop, the manor house was still a solid quarter-mile drive up the mountain. Wilde could see some distant lights, but that was about it. He pressed the intercom button while checking his phone, hoping maybe he just didn't feel the buzz.

Nothing from Matthew.

He sent another text: I'm at the guard gate.

"May I help you?" the intercom said.

Wilde had his driver's license out. He held it up to the camera. "I'm here for Matthew Crimstein."

Silence.

"Matthew is a friend of Crash's."

"What's your relationship to him?"

"To Matthew?"

"Yes."

Odd question. "I'm his godfather."

"And what is the purpose of your visit?"

"I'm here to pick him up."

"He arrived in Mason Perdue's vehicle. We were told that he was leaving with him."

"Well, the plans have changed."

Silence.

Wilde said, "Hello?"

"One moment, please."

Time passed.

Wilde hit the intercom button again.

No reply.

He pressed down on the button and held it down.

Nothing.

He checked for wires near the gate. None. The fence had no electrocution setup. That was good. It was high with spiked tops, but none of that would be an issue. There were security cameras, of course, lots of them. That didn't matter to him either. If anything, he wanted to be seen.

Wilde threw the car into park and stepped out. He eyed the gate. Twelve feet high, he guessed. Bars spaced six inches apart.

The seam where both halves of the metal gate met would be the way to go. Thicker bar. Get a running start. Just up and over. Wilde had spent his life climbing—mountains, trees, rocks, walls, as a child, as a civilian, as a soldier. This gate, even with the spikes on top of every bar, would offer him little resistance.

He took two large steps toward the gate when he heard the voice from the speaker say, "Halt. Do not—"

He didn't hear the rest.

Wilde leapt, his foot hitting the bar in midstride. He hoisted himself up, as though running vertically, grabbed the bars with both hands, and tucked his legs. He spun, let go with his left hand, and put his feet out. The soles of his shoes hit the bars on the other side, slowing him. He let go and dropped to the ground as two cars sped toward him.

Not one car. Two.

That seemed like overkill.

Or maybe not. Dash Maynard had been in the news lately. Rumor had it—a rumor Dash Maynard adamantly denied—that he videoed everything when people were on his shows, including conversations in the dressing rooms. Rumor further had it that these videos could take down a lot of top celebrities and politicians, most notably former self-help guru and current United States senator Rusty Eggers, the budding tyrant running for president and gaining ground.

Both cars pointed their headlights at him and screeched to a stop. Four men, two from each car, got out. Wilde kept his hands out where they could see them. The last thing he wanted was for someone to do something stupid.

The two from his left, big men, began to approach him. They both had their chests puffed out, their arms swinging with a little too much alpha preening. One wore a hoodie. The other, the one sporting dyed-Thor locks, had a suit jacket that didn't fit well.

Didn't fit well, Wilde noted, because he had a gun holster under the left armpit.

Wilde had known too many guys like these two. They wouldn't be an issue, except for the weapon. He braced himself, sifting through his options, but the man who got out of the car on the right—close-cropped gray hair, military bearing—held up a hand and stopped them. Clearly the leader.

"Hey there," Gray Hair shouted to Wilde. "Nice fence hop."

"Thanks."

"Please keep your hands visible at all times."

"I'm not armed."

"We can't let you go any farther."

"I don't have any interest in going any farther," Wilde said. "I'm here for my godson, Matthew Crimstein."

"I understand. But we have a policy."

"Policy?"

"All the minors who entered tonight had to inform us of how they were leaving," he began, the very voice of reason. "We clearly explained to them that no one is allowed in unless they are specifically invited or properly vetted. Matthew Crimstein came in with Mason Perdue. That was who Matthew told us he would be leaving with. Now you show up unannounced..."

He spread his hands, not only the voice of reason but the very essence of reason. "Do you see our dilemma?"

"So contact Matthew."

"We have a policy about not disturbing social gatherings."

"Lots of policies," Wilde said.

"Helps keep the order."

"I want to see my godson."

"I'm afraid that won't be possible at this time." The gate behind him opened. "I'm going to have to ask you to leave now."

"Yeah, that's not happening."

Gray Hair might have smiled.

"I'm going to ask you one more time."

"Matthew texted me to pick him up now. So that's what I'm doing."

"If you'll just go back to the other side of the gate—"

"Yeah, again, that's not happening."

The big guys didn't like Wilde's attitude. They furrowed their rather enormous brows. Dyed-Thor turned to Gray Hair, hoping for permission to take this to the next level.

"You have no legal standing, Mr. Wilde." The use of his name threw him, but only for a millisecond. He'd shown his driver's license at the gate. "You're not the boy's father, are you?"

Gray Hair smiled. He knew the answer, more specifically than just the part about Wilde being Matthew's godfather, which meant somehow he knew the history.

"More to the point, you're a trespasser who illegally scaled our security fence."

They all took a step closer. Wilde stared straight ahead, at the leader, but using his peripheral vision, he could see Thor sidle a little closer, hunching down like he was some sort of invisible ninja. Wilde didn't shift his eyes.

Gray Hair said, "We would be within our rights to meet your threat with physical force."

So they were there now, all of them, standing on the same narrow precipice off which so many men over the entire course of human history had slipped and then plunged into bloody violence. Wilde still didn't believe that they would go there, that they would risk a big incident which might make the news or social media and awaken whatever controversy had finally quieted down. But you never know. That was the thing with the precipice. It was slippery. The best-laid plans do indeed go awry.

Man may be evil or good, that wasn't the issue. The issue was that man rarely considered the consequences of his actions.

In short, man was often just plain stupid.

That was when it all changed.

At first, the change was noticed only by Wilde. For scant seconds, the knowledge was his and his alone. Two seconds, maybe three, no more. Then, he knew, this advantage—and the change would be, he hoped, an advantage—would be null and void.

Wilde felt what he had come to know as The Disturbance.

There were those who called it an omen or a harbinger or a premonition, something that gave his already heightened capabilities a supernatural undertone. But that wasn't it. Not really. Over the millenniums, man has adapted both for better and worse. A recent example: Navigation GPS. Studies show that parts of our brain—the hippocampus (the region used for navigation) and the prefrontal cortex (associated with planning) are already changing, perhaps even atrophying, because we now rely on GPS navigation. That's happened in a few years. But take the whole spectrum of mankind's history, how we sat in caves and forests, sleeping figuratively with one eye open, no protection, our primitive survival instinct in overdrive, and then think of how that has softened and eroded over the years with the advent of homes and locked doors and civilization's give and take. But Wilde didn't have that. From the time he could remember, Wilde grew up with those primitive impulses awakened. He understood before he could articulate it that a predator could attack at any time. He learned to sense it, to be attuned to any sort of Disturbance.

You still see this in nature, of course, in animals with supersensitive hearing or smell or sight, who flee before the danger gets too close. Wilde had this ability too.

So he'd heard the sound. No one else had. Yet.

It was just a rustling. That was all. But someone was running toward them. More than one probably. Someone was in danger and sprinting fast. Someone else was giving chase.

Without so much as glancing away from Gray Hair, Wilde glided a little closer to Thor. He wanted to be as close to the armed man as possible.

A second later, no more, Wilde heard the scream: "Help!"

Matthew.

This was where Wilde had to fight off his instincts and let his training take over. Instinct told him to run toward his godson's cry. That would be the natural reaction. But Wilde had braced for this moment. The scream, coming from behind Gray Hair and up the hill toward the house, made all heads turn. That, too, was natural and expected. If you hadn't known that the scream was a possibility, you couldn't help but react.

Thor looked in the direction of Matthew's scream too.

And away from Wilde.

That was all the opening Wilde needed. The rest took a second, no more. Spinning with his left elbow at the ready, Wilde struck Thor in the side of his head. At the same time, before Thor could stumble back, Wilde's right hand dove into the opening of the jacket. His fingers found the butt of the gun in the holster under Thor's arm.

By the time Matthew yelled "Help!" for a second time, Thor was on the ground, and Wilde had the gun up and aimed, moving the muzzle between Gray Hair and the other two men.

Wilde said, "Breathe wrong and I'll shoot you dead."

From the ground, Thor groaned and lunged toward him. Wilde kicked him in the head. The slapping of feet on driveway drew closer. For a second, they all waited. Matthew turned the corner, sprinting seemingly for his life, two other boys not far behind him.

Matthew pulled up, a look of confusion crossing his face. The two other boys did the same.

"Go through the gate," Wilde told Matthew. "Get in the car."

"But—"

"Do it."

One of the boys said, "We were just playing, is all. Tell him, Matthew. Tell him we were just playing."

Keeping his hands in the air, Gray Hair slid in front of the boy speaking. "Stay behind me, Crash."

"It's just a game," Crash said.

"A game," Wilde repeated.

"Yeah, it's called Midnight Skull." He pointed to the smile-skull ring on his hand. "It's like night tag. Tell him, Matthew."

Matthew didn't move. His eyes were glassy with near tears. In the distance, Wilde heard a car engine start. Reinforcements.

"Matthew, car now!"

Matthew snapped out of it and hurried toward the gate. Walking backward so as to keep the gun aimed at them, Wilde did the same. He kept his eyes on Gray Hair. He was the leader. The others wouldn't make a move without him. Gray Hair nodded as if to say, *It's okay, get out of here, we won't stop you.*

Ten seconds later, Wilde sped away with Matthew in the seat next to him.

CHAPTER NINE

Hester was back in her limo when she saw the calls coming in.

She'd expected that. You can't just drop a bomb like this one about a missing girl and not expect something to explode. It was, in fact, her hope—that someone would come forward or act or make a mistake or do something so that they'd know what really happened. Right now, when you added all the pros and cons, the options and possibilities, Hester figured that the girl had run off and was perhaps contemplating suicide. Not to be too cold and analytical, but if the awful task were already completed, well, there was nothing anyone could do. But if Naomi had taken pills, for example, or slit her wrists, or maybe she was just off someplace, standing on the edge of a high-rise or bridge, then this was the best chance to save her.

Then again—because you have to see every side—maybe Hester's pushing would do the opposite. Maybe it would make the girl panic and act or, if she were being held, maybe it would make the kidnappers react with violence. Hester understood the risks. But she was not a woman who took stock in inaction.

The first call she took had a caller ID that read CHIEF WESTVILLE POLICE. That would be Oren, she thought.

"That was fast," Hester said.

"Huh?"

"I mean, I'm flattered, Oren, but next time, wait a few days. It makes you look a little desperate."

"Uh, I am a little desperate. What the hell was that report, Hester?"

"You saw it? Thanks for being a fan."

"Do I sound like I'm in the mood?"

"Something isn't right with Naomi's disappearance," Hester said.

"Then you should come to me."

"I did, remember?"

"I do. So what changed?"

"Her father said Naomi was with the mother. The mother said she's not with her. Her teacher—"

"Wait, you talked to her teacher."

"Art teacher or guidance counselor or something, I don't remember. Ava something."

"When did you have time to talk to her?"

This part would not go so smoothly. "I didn't. Wilde did."

Silence.

"Oren?"

"Wilde? You got Wilde involved in this?"

"Look, Oren, I probably should have given you a heads-up before I went on the air—"

"Probably?"

"—but I have a really bad feeling. You need to put some resources into this."

Silence.

"Oren?"

"Matthew put you onto this," Oren said. "Why?"

Now it was her turn to be silent.

"Whatever your grandson is hiding, he has to come clean now. You know this."

As they sped off from Maynard Manor, Wilde asked, "What happened?"

"It's like Crash said," Matthew said through a wince. He was still trying to catch his breath. "We were playing a game."

"You're going to lie to me now?"

Matthew blinked back the tears. "You can't tell Mom."

"I'm not going to."

"Good."

"Because you are."

"No way. I'll tell you, but we can't tell her."

"Sorry, it isn't going to work that way."

"Then I'm not telling you a thing."

"Yeah, Matthew, you are. You're going to tell me what happened. And then you're going to tell your mother."

He hung his head.

"Matthew?"

"Okay."

"So what happened?"

"Did you know what Nana was going to do?"

"Do?"

"She went on the air about Naomi. She told everyone she's missing."

Wilde had wondered whether that was going to be her next move. Hester had been worried about leads drying up. What better way to beat the brush?

"What did she say?"

"I didn't really hear it," Matthew said. "But Crash and Kyle and the others did."

"And they got upset?"

Matthew started blinking.

"Matthew?"

"Crash kneed me in the balls." More tears came to Matthew's eyes. A few spilled out.

Wilde felt his hands tighten on the steering wheel.

"They wanted to know what I told her. I rolled away. When I saw an opening, I ran."

"You're okay now?"

"Yeah."

"You want me to take you to a doctor?"

"No, I'll be a little sore, I guess."

"Most likely. Does Crash have something to do with Naomi?"

"I don't know. It's..."

"It's what?"

"You can't tell anyone, okay? About Naomi. About tonight."

"We've already been through this, Matthew."

"I'll figure out how to tell Mom. But tomorrow, okay? Tonight I don't want to say anything."

As he turned onto Matthew's street, he heard the whoop of a siren and the blue squad-car lights came on. A voice over the loudspeaker said, "Pull over immediately." They were right down the street from the house, no more than two hundred yards, so Wilde signaled out the window that he was going to cruise up to it. The car hit the siren again and spun right alongside them.

The familiar voice over the loudspeaker—they both knew Oren Carmichael—said in a tone that left no room for argument: "Immediately!"

To Wilde's surprise, Oren cut them off with his squad car, forcing them to the curb. Oren opened his car door and made his way toward them. By the time he arrived, Wilde had the window down.

"What the hell, Oren. You know we live right down the block."

Oren arched an eyebrow. "We?"

Mistake, Wilde thought. "I meant Matthew, this car. You know what I mean."

Oren looked inside the car. He nodded at Matthew. Matthew said, "Hey, Chief."

"Where are you coming from, son?"

Wilde said, "Maynard Manor."

"Why were you there?"

"Why would you care?" Wilde countered.

Oren ignored him. "Son?"

"I was at a party," Matthew said.

Oren took a longer look at Matthew now. "You don't look so good, Matthew."

"I'm fine."

"You sure?"

Wilde wasn't sure whether they should tell Oren about the incident in the house or not. Before he had a chance to say anything, Matthew said, "I'm fine, Coach. We were playing Midnight Skull."

"What?"

"It's like tag or something. Running around outside. That's why I look like this."

Oren Carmichael frowned. He glanced at Wilde. Wilde gave him nothing. Then Oren said, "Why did you ask your grandmother to look for Naomi Pine?"

Ah, Wilde thought, so that explained the sudden stop. Oren wanted to corner Matthew alone—away from both his mother and grandmother, two renowned attorneys—so he could get less evasive responses.

Wilde said, "Don't answer."

Oren didn't like that. "What?"

"I'm telling him not to answer."

"You don't have any legal standing here, Wilde."

"Yeah, I've been hearing that a lot tonight. But I'm not letting you question him without his mother present."

"I don't know where Naomi is," Matthew blurted out. "That's the truth."

"So why did you ask your grandmother to find her?"

"I'm just worried about her, okay? She hasn't been in school and..."

"And?"

Wilde said, "Matthew, not another word."

"And kids pick on her, is all."

"Are you one of those kids, Matthew?"

Wilde put his hand up. "Okay, that's it. This conversation is over."

"Like hell—"

Wilde restarted the car.

"Turn that engine off right now," Oren snapped.

"You charging us with something?"

"No."

"Then we are on our way. You can follow us to Matthew's house if you'd like."

But Oren didn't follow them.

As Wilde pulled the car into Laila's driveway, the front door opened. It was dark now, but with the light behind her, Wilde could make out Laila's silhouette standing in the doorway. She held her hand up high and awkwardly waved. When Wilde and Matthew got closer, he could see that she was holding her mobile phone.

"There's a call for you," she said to Wilde. Then she added: "On my phone."

He nodded, and she handed it to him. He put the phone to his ear.

"We good?"

It was Gray Hair. Wilde wasn't surprised. They would have

seen the license plate. Guys with his kind of juice would have no trouble getting a registration, a name, an address, phone numbers both home and mobile. Laila was the car's owner. That would be the number they'd try.

"I guess," Wilde said.

"Crash may have acted inappropriately."

"Uh-huh."

"But the boy is under a lot of pressure. We hope you'll understand."

"There's a missing girl," Wilde said.

"He doesn't know anything about her."

"So why's he under a lot of pressure?"

"Other things."

"Can I ask your name?" Wilde said.

"Why?"

"Because you know mine."

There was a pause. "Gavin Chambers."

"As in Chambers Security? As in Colonel Chambers?"

"Retired colonel, yes."

Whoa, Wilde thought. The Maynards were not messing around when it came to security. He was tempted to move away so Laila wouldn't hear, but from the look on her face, that would only get him in hot water.

"Do you know what Crash did to Matthew, Colonel?"

Laila's eyes widened when she heard that.

"We have CCTV in the basement area," Gavin replied.

"So you saw it?"

"I did. Sadly, that particular footage no longer exists. Accidental deletion. You know how it is."

"I do."

"Will you accept our apologies?"

"I wasn't the one assaulted."

"Will you please pass them to young Matthew then?"

Wilde said nothing.

"It's my job to keep the Maynards safe, Mr. Wilde. There is much more at stake here than a teenage brawl."

"Like what?"

But Chambers didn't answer. "I know you're good at what you do. But I'm good too. And I have vast resources. If there is conflict between us, it probably won't end well. There will be collateral damage. Do I make myself clear?"

Wilde looked at Laila and Matthew. The collateral damage.

"I'm not a big fan of threats, Colonel."

"Neither one of us wants to spend our lives looking over our shoulders, correct?"

"Correct."

"That's why I'm extending a hand of friendship."

"Friendship seems a bit strong."

"I agree. More like, to quote the French, détente. You can keep the gun, by the way. We have plenty of others. Good night, Mr. Wilde."

He hung up. Laila said, "What the hell was that?"

Wilde handed her phone back. His mind was working overtime. The immediate threat—the one he'd worried most about—was that Maynard's guys would come after them. That threat seemed to be neutralized for now. Matthew was home. He was safe. So now Wilde turned his attention back to Naomi Pine.

The father had told Hester that Naomi was with the mother. That was a lie. It seemed obvious that Naomi's father was thus the place to start.

Laila asked, "Did that call have something to do with Naomi Pine?"

Matthew let out a small groan. "You know about that?"

"Everyone knows about that. After your grandmother's report, the school sent out an emergency text. All the parent boards on social media are lighting up. Do you want to tell me what's going on, please?"

"Matthew will," Wilde said, tossing her the car keys. "I have to go."

"Wait, go where?"

It would take too long to explain. "I'll try to come back, if that's okay."

"Wilde?"

"Matthew will explain."

He turned and ran toward the woods.

CHAPTER TEN

There is a theory, introduced by psychologist Anders Ericsson and made popular by Malcolm Gladwell, that ten thousand hours of practice makes you an expert in a given field. Wilde didn't buy it, though he understood the appeal in the simplicity of such encouraging pop slogans.

He sped now through the woods, his eyes already accustomed to the dark. Theories like Ericsson's didn't take into account intensity and immersion. Wilde had run through woods like these since before he could remember. Alone. Adapting. Surviving. It wasn't practice. It was life. It was ingrained. It was survival. Yes, the hours mattered. But intensity matters more. Imagine if you have no choice. If you hike through the forest for fun or because your dad likes it, it isn't the same as being forcibly immersed, of knowing the woods well or dying. You can't fake that. A man does an experiment, tries to see what it's like to be blind, so he covers his eyes—no, sorry, that isn't the same thing as being blind. You can always take the blindfold off. It's voluntary and controlled and safe. Some coaches tell kids to play like their life depends on it. That's probably sound motivational advice, but if your life doesn't depend on it—and it doesn't—the intensity will pale compared to the real thing.

The best athletes? It is life and death, in their minds. Now imagine how much better they'd be if the stakes were really that high.

That was Wilde in the woods.

As he got closer to the Pine residence, he spotted a squad car and three news vans from local stations. The scene wasn't frantic—this wasn't the biggest story of the year or anything like that—but the news van had obviously heard Hester's report and the cops had in turn asked them to move down the block away from the house. Wilde spotted Oren Carmichael by the Pines' front door, talking to a guy who had to be the father, Bernard Pine. The father seemed upset, not about a missing daughter but about the police and media intrusion. He gestured wildly while Carmichael kept showing him his palms to calm him down.

Wilde's phone double-buzzed, indicating an incoming text. He checked and saw it was from Ava O'Brien:

Did you find Naomi?

He was tempted not to reply. But that didn't feel right. Not yet.

There was the moving-dots pause. Then Ava wrote: Come over tonight. I'll leave the door unlocked.

More moving dots: I miss you, Wilde.

He pocketed the phone without a reply. Ava would get the message, much as he hated to send it this way.

Wilde crept out of the woods. He kept low and headed toward the neighboring backyard. No one spotted him. He stayed down. Naomi's father finished whatever he had to say to Oren and slammed the door. For several seconds, Oren Carmichael didn't move, almost as if he expected the door to reopen. When it didn't, he turned away and headed for his car. Another cop—this one far younger—met him there.

"Keep the press back," Carmichael said.

"Yes, Chief. Are we going in?"

Oren frowned. "Going in?"

"You know, like doing a search of the house."

"The father says she's safe."

"But that reporter on TV—"

"A TV report is not evidence," Oren snapped. "Get the press out of here."

"Yes, Chief."

When the kid left, Wilde saw no harm. He stood upright and approached the car. Because he'd had enough with itchy fingers, he called out as soon as he could possibly be seen. "Oren?"

Carmichael turned. When he saw who it was, he frowned. "Wilde? What are you doing here?"

"What did the father say about Naomi?"

"Not your business, is it?"

"You know he lied to Hester, right?"

Oren Carmichael sighed. "Why on earth did Hester involve you in this?"

"The father told Hester that Naomi is with her mother."

"And maybe she is."

"Is that what he told you just now?"

"He said she's safe. He asked me to respect her privacy."

"And you're going to do that?"

"Neither parent has filed a missing person report."

"So?"

"So it's almost midnight. You want me to kick his door down?"

"Naomi could be in danger."

"And what, you think the father killed her or something?"

Wilde didn't answer.

"Exactly," Oren said, clearly exhausted by it all. "This is a girl who has run away before. My guess? That's what this is."

"Maybe it's something worse."

Oren slid into the driver's seat. "If that's true, we'll find that out, too, eventually." He stared up from the squad car. "Go home, Wilde."

He drove off as Wilde headed back to the woods. He stopped behind the first tree and slipped on a thin black mask that covered everything except his eyes. He kept it with him always. The world now had more CCTV cameras than people. Or so it seemed. You never know. So Wilde, who had a thing about privacy in this privacyless world, always came prepared.

When Oren's squad car was out of sight, Wilde circled back so that he was now behind the Pine house. There were lights on in the kitchen, one upstairs bedroom, and in the basement. As a child, he had broken into countless lake homes and summer cabins. He'd learned to silently case them, circle them, check the driveways and lights, see who if anyone was home. To break in, he'd search for unlocked doors or windows (you'd be surprised how often it was that simple), then move on to other means. If the locks were too strong or the alarm system too complicated, young Wilde would search for another house. Most of the time, even as a child, he had known to leave no trace of his being there. If he slept in a bed, for example, he made sure that it was made the next morning. If he ate their food or needed supplies, he was careful not to consume or steal too much, so that the owners wouldn't notice.

Had someone taught him all this when he was too young to remember? Or was it instinctive? He didn't know. In the end, man is an animal. An animal does what it has to do to survive.

It was probably that simple.

The phone in his pocket buzzed. The phone was a personally designed burner. That was all he used and never for more than a week or two. At night, he turned it off. He didn't keep it with him—he knew that, even when the phone was off, it was possible to trace—and usually left it buried in a steel box by the road.

It was Hester: "Are you with Laila?"

"No."

"Where are you then?"

"Casing Naomi's house."

"You have a plan?"

"I do."

"Tell me."

"You don't want to know," he said.

Wilde hung up and moved closer to the house. Loads of homes now had motion detector lights that snap on when you approach. If that were to be the case, Wilde would simply sprint back into the woods. No harm, no foul. But no lights came on. Good. He kept close to the house. The closer to the wall, the less chance of being seen.

He checked the kitchen window. Bernard Pine, Naomi's father, sat at the table and played with his phone. He looked nervous. Wilde circled the perimeter and peered in through the first-floor windows. No one else present, no other movement.

Wilde bent down and checked the basement windows. The shades were drawn all the way—blackout shades—but Wilde still spotted the small sliver of light.

Someone down there maybe?

He had little trouble climbing onto the second-floor overhang. He worried about the structure, if it could hold his weight, but he decided to risk it. There was a light in a corridor that shone through what appeared to be the father's bedroom. He climbed toward the corner back window, cupped his hands against the glass, and looked into the room.

A computer monitor displaying a dancing-lines screen saver provided the only illumination. The walls were blank. There were no posters of teen heartthrobs or favorite rock groups or any of the expected teenage girl clichés, except, perhaps, the bed, which was low to the floor and blanketed with stuffed animals—dozens of them, maybe hundreds, in various sizes and colors, mostly bears but there were giraffes and monkeys and penguins and elephants. It was hard to see how Naomi could fit in the bed with all of them. She must have just jumped in, like she was living inside one of those claw-crane arcade games.

Naomi was an only child, so Wilde was pretty sure that this was her bedroom.

The window was locked with a vinyl lever sash lock with keeper. Routine security for a second-floor room. Most burglars don't scale walls to reach second floors. Wilde was, of course, different. He reached into his wallet and plucked out a loid—short for "celluloid"—card. Better than a credit card. More flexible. He slid the loid between the two sash frames and moved the lever into the unlocked position. It was that simple. Five seconds later, he was inside the room.

So now what?

Quick check of the closet revealed the following: a pink Fjällräven Kånken backpack on the top shelf, clothes neatly hung, no bare hangers. Meaning? He wasn't sure. The backpack was empty. If she'd run away, wouldn't she have packed it? Wouldn't there be some signs of missing clothes?

Nothing conclusive, but interesting.

There was a time, Wilde imagined, where it would pay to check the desk drawers or perhaps look under the pillow or mattress for a diary, but nowadays most teens keep their secrets in their tech devices. The phone would be better to search, of course, the place we store our lives, and no, that wasn't a comment on today's youth. Adults too. Mankind has surrendered any pretense of privacy to those devices for the sake of... hard to say what. Convenience, he guessed. Artificial connections maybe, which might be better than no connection at all.

But it was not for him. Then again, real connections didn't seem to be his bag either.

Had the police tried to ping Naomi's location via her phone?

Maybe. Probably. Either way, he texted Hester to give it a try.

Naomi's desktop computer had been left running. He moved the mouse, afraid that there might be a password blocking access. There wasn't. He brought up her web browser. Naomi's email information—name and password—had been saved for easy access. She was NaomiFlavuh, which seemed sweet and a little sad. He clicked and got in right away. He almost rubbed his hands together, hoping that he had hit the mother lode. He hadn't. The emails couldn't have been more innocuous—class assignments, college recruitment spams, coupons and offers from the Gap and Target and retailers unknown to Wilde with names like Forever 21 and PacSun. Kids today, he knew from his interactions with Matthew, text or use some sort of parent-proof app. They don't email.

He stopped for a moment and listened. Nothing. No one coming up the stairs. He moved the mouse's cursor up to the top and hit the history button. He hoped that Naomi hadn't cleared her cache recently.

She hadn't.

There were searches on eBay for stuffed animals. There were links to forums and Reddits that talked about collecting stuffed animals. Wilde glanced behind him at the bed. The stuffed animals had been laid out with some care. Several animals stared back at him. He thought about that for a second, about this girl who had been bullied all her life, how she must have rushed home after school, fleeing the taunts and abuse, maybe leaping high onto her bed, escaping into this lonely, self-created menagerie.

The thought flooded him with a surprising rage.

People had bullied this girl her whole life. If someone did more to her, if someone went the extra mile or forced her to do something desperate...

He bottled it and turned back to the task at hand. He still had the mask on his face. If by some chance Bernard Pine were to come upstairs or spot him—unlikely, really—Wilde would blow past him and run away. There would be nothing to identify him. His height and build—six feet, one eighty-five—would give them nothing.

Whoa. Pay dirt.

Naomi had been researching her classmates. There were six,

maybe seven of them, but two names stuck out right away. One was Matthew's. The other was Crash Maynard's. The searches on Matthew—as well as his other classmates—were surface and quick. Did this mean anything? Or did teens Google each other all the time? You meet someone, you search online about them. Of course, Naomi had known these kids forever. She had grown up with them, gone to school with them, been a victim of their taunts and blows.

So why now?

He skimmed down through the rest of her Google searches. Nothing much stood out, except for an odd two-word search followed by an odd three-word search:

> challenge game
> challenge game missing

He focused on the added word: Missing.

He clicked through the links. As he started reading, his heart sank. He was midway through the pages when he heard a noise that startled him.

Footsteps.

Not close. Not coming up toward him. That was what was odd. There was only one person in the house. The father. Bernard Pine. He was in the kitchen. But these steps weren't coming from the kitchen. In fact, now that he thought about it, he had not heard a sound coming from downstairs the entire time he had been up here.

The footsteps were faint. They were coming from inside the house, but...

Wilde closed down the browser and slipped across the room and into the corridor. He looked down the stairs. The footsteps were louder. Wilde could hear a voice now. Sounded like Bernard Pine. Who was he talking to? Wilde couldn't make out the words. He crept closer to the top of the stairs so he could hear better.

The door beneath the stairs flew open.

The basement door.

Wilde jumped back. The voice was clear now, easy to understand.

"It was on the goddamn news! That woman was here too. What do you mean, who? That lawyer from TV, the one who did the report."

Bernard Pine closed the basement door behind him.

"The cops just came. Yes, the chief, Carmichael, he knocked on the door. They're probably still..." Wilde had his back pressed against the wall, but he risked a look. Bernard Pine had his mobile phone in one hand. With the other, he pushed aside a curtain and looked out into his front yard.

"I don't see them right now, no. But I can't...I mean, Carmichael might be right down the block, watching. There were news vans here too.... We are probably being watched."

We? Wilde thought.

Unless Pine considered himself royalty, "we" meant more than one person. Except that Wilde had cased the house. He had only spotted one person. Bernard Pine. If someone else was here, there was only one place that person could be.

The basement.

"Yeah, Larry, I know you told me not to do this, but I didn't think I had a choice. I don't want to get caught. That's the big thing now."

Pine hurried up toward the stairwell where Wilde stood on the landing. He was hustling now, jumping the steps two at a time. Relying on reflexes, Wilde dove back into Naomi's bedroom and rolled toward a corner. Pine passed him on the landing without glancing into his daughter's room.

The basement, Wilde thought.

He didn't wait long. The moment Pine was past the door and in his own bedroom, Wilde came out. Moving on the balls of his feet—not the toes, the toes made noise—he padded down the steps. He spun to his right and came to the basement door. He tried the knob. It turned.

He opened the basement door silently, stepped inside, closed it behind him.

There was a faint light below him. Wilde had two choices here. Choice One: Tiptoe down the steps and sneak slowly toward whatever was to be found. Choice Two: Go for it.

Wilde went for Choice Two.

He took off his mask and strolled down the cellar stairs. He didn't disguise it. He didn't hurry nor did he dawdle. When Wilde arrived at the bottom, he turned toward the light.

Naomi opened her mouth.

"Don't scream," Wilde said to her. "I'm here to help you."

CHAPTER ELEVEN

The basement had been finished on the cheap. The walls were faux wood made of some kind of vinyl, stuck up on the concrete with adhesive. The sofa was a hand-me-down convertible that was right now open into a queen-sized bed.

It was blanketed with stuffed animals.

Naomi Pine sat on the sofa's armrest, her shoulders slumped, her eyes down, so that her hair hung in front of her face like a beaded curtain. She wasn't skinny, which in today's world was to say she was probably overweight, but Wilde didn't really know. She was neither pretty nor ugly, and while her looks should be irrelevant, they weren't, not in the real world and especially not in the teen world. So he looked at her, at her whole being, and it stirred his heart. In truth, if he could be totally objective and maybe it was the history of the situation talking, Naomi Pine looked, above all else, like an easy target. That was indeed the vibe. Some people look smart or dumb or strong or cruel or weak or brave or whatever. Naomi looked like she was always in mid-cringe, as though she were asking the world not to hit her, and that just made the world sneer in her face.

"I know you," Naomi said. "You're the boy from the woods."

Not exactly accurate. Or maybe it was.

"Your name is Wilde, right?"

"Yes."

"You're our boogie man, you know."

Wilde said nothing.

"Like, parents tell little kids not to go in the woods because the Wild Man will grab them and eat them or something. And like, when kids tell ghost stories or try to scare each other, you're kinda the star of the show."

"Terrific," Wilde said. "Are you scared of me?"

"No."

"Why not?"

"I'm drawn to outcasts," she said.

He tried to smile. "Me too."

"You ever read *To Kill a Mockingbird*?" she asked him.

"Yes."

"You're like our Boo Radley."

"I guess that would make you Scout."

"Yeah, right," Naomi said with a roll of her eyes, and his heart felt it again.

"Who is Larry? I heard your dad on the phone."

"He's my uncle. He lives in Chicago." Naomi lowered her head. "Are you going to tell?"

"No."

"So you'll just leave?"

"If you want." Wilde moved closer to her and made his tone as gentle as he could. "The Challenge," he said.

Naomi looked up at him. "How do you know about that?"

He'd seen it on her computer, but he'd also remembered reading about it a few years back. The article had called it the 48-Hour-Challenge, though it was later dismissed as an urban legend. It was an online game of sorts, albeit a fairly awful one. Teens would vanish on purpose so that their parents would panic and think that their child had been kidnapped or worse. The longer you "disappeared," the more points you'd accumulate.

"It doesn't matter," Wilde said. "You were playing it, right?"

"I still don't understand. Why are you here?"

"I was looking for you."

"Why?"

"Someone was worried."

"Who?"

He hesitated. Then he figured, why not. "Matthew Crimstein."

She may have smiled. "Figures."

"Figures why?"

"He probably blames himself. Tell him he shouldn't."

"Okay."

"He just wants to fit in too."

Wilde could hear movement from upstairs. Her dad no doubt. "What happened, Naomi?"

"You ever read self-help books?"

"No."

"I do. All the time. My life..." She stopped, blinked back tears, shook her head. "Anyway, they always talk about making small changes. The self-help books. I tried that. It doesn't work. Everyone still hates me. You know what that's like? Every day to feel your whole insides twist up because you're scared to go to school?"

"No," Wilde said. "But it must suck."

She liked that answer. "It does. Big time. But I don't want you to feel sorry for me, okay?"

"Okay."

"Promise?"

He crossed his heart with his right hand.

"Anyway," Naomi said, "I decided to go for it."

"Go for what?"

"Change." Her face lit up. "Total change. One big move, one big thing, so I could erase my past as a loser and start again. Do you get that?"

He said nothing.

"So yeah, I took the challenge. I disappeared. At first, I hid in the woods." She managed a smile. "I wasn't scared of you at all."

He smiled back.

"I lasted two days."

"Was it rough?"

"No, I liked it actually. Out there. On my own. You get that, right?"

"I do."

"Heck, you probably get it better than anyone," she said. "It was like an escape, a reprieve. But my dad, look, he's not the most on the ball. What I am, okay, I mean, me being a loser—"

"You're not a loser."

Naomi shot him a look that told him he was patronizing her and she was disappointed by it. He held up his hands as though to say, *My bad*.

"Anyway, it's not his fault. All this. But he doesn't make it better either, you know what I mean?"

"I think so."

"So I was gone two days, and he started texting. He was going to go to the police, which is part of the game, right. Also . . . I was worried he'd start drinking too much. Whatever, anyway, I didn't want that. So I came home, even though I knew forty-eight hours wouldn't be enough. Then I told my dad what I was doing."

Wilde heard the footsteps now. He didn't turn, didn't worry. "And your dad decided to help?"

"He got it right away. He thinks I'm a loser too." Naomi held up her hand. "Don't say it."

"Okay."

"I just wanted to, you know, fit in. Impress them."

"By them, you mean Crash Maynard?"

"Crash, Kyle, Sutton, all of them."

Wilde wanted to launch into a little speech about how you shouldn't want to impress bullies or how trying to fit in was always the wrong move, that you should stay true to yourself and stick to your principles and stand up to the abuse—but he was sure that Naomi had heard it all before and he would again sound patronizing. Naomi knew all the angles here better than he ever could. She'd lived them every day. He hadn't. She hoped that this move—the Challenge—would make her "cooler," and who knows, maybe she was right. Maybe Crash and his cohorts would be impressed when she came back. Maybe it would change everything for her.

Who the hell was he to tell her it wouldn't work?

"My dad had the idea. I could just hide down here. He'd just pretend to be worried."

"But then the cops showed up for real."

"Right. We didn't count on that. And he can't tell the truth. Imagine if that gets out—what he'd done, what I'd done. I mean, I'd get demolished in school. So he's freaking out right about now."

The basement door opened. From the top of the stairs, Bernard Pine called down. "Naomi?"

"It's okay, Dad."

"Who are you talking to, honey?"

Naomi's smile was bright now. "A friend."

Wilde nodded. He wanted to ask whether there was anything he could do, but he already knew the answer. He headed toward the basement stairs. Bernard Pine's eyes widened when he came into view.

"Who the—?"

"I was just leaving," Wilde said.

"How did you . . . ?"

Naomi said, "It's okay, Dad."

Wilde walked up the stairs. As he passed Bernard Pine, he stuck out his hand. Pine took it. Wilde handed him a card. No name, just a phone number.

"If I can help," Wilde said.

Pine glanced toward the windows. "The police might see you. . . ."

But Wilde shook his head and started toward the back door. He had his mask in his hand now. "They won't."

One minute later, Wilde was back in the woods.

As Wilde headed back toward Laila's, he called Hester.

"Naomi is fine."

He explained.

When he finished, Hester shouted, "Are you shitting me?"

"This is good news," he said. "She's safe."

"Oh, great, fine, she's safe, la-di-dah. But in case you missed it, I just went live on air saying a teenage girl went missing. Now you tell me she's hiding in her own basement. I'm going to look like a fool."

"Ah," Wilde said.

"Ah?"

"That's all I got. Ah."

"And all I got is my reputation. Well, that and my good looks."

"It'll be okay, Hester."

She sighed. "Yeah, I know. You going back to the house?"

"Yes."

"So you'll tell Matthew?"

"I'll tell him enough of it."

"And then you'll go to bed with Laila?"

He didn't reply.

"Sorry," she said.

"Get some sleep, Hester."

"You too, Wilde."

The next day, Naomi was back in school. She hoped no one would ask too many questions. But they did. Soon her story collapsed, and the truth—that she had "cheated" in the game of Challenge—came to light.

If school life had been hell for Naomi before, this latest revelation raised that hell to the tenth power.

A week later, Naomi Pine disappeared again.

Everyone assumed that she'd run away.

Four days after that, a severed finger was found.

PART TWO

CHAPTER TWELVE

One Week Later

A car pulled into his hidden road.

Wilde knew that because he'd laid down a rubber hose alarm, the kind you see every day at gas stations across this country, at the entranceway. Old school but more effective in this setting—animals set off motion detectors. They'd trip every hour with false alarms. Only something heavier, like cars, triggered the hose alarm.

He had just been staring at the small screen at the time, more specifically at an email from one of those ancestry sites with a subject that trumpeted, "WE HAVE YOUR DNA RESULTS RIGHT HERE!" when the notification about the intruder popped up. Wilde had been debating whether to click the link or let sleeping dogs lie, just as he'd debated whether to take the test at all, whether to begin this journey down a probably dark path in the first place. Submitting his DNA under a pseudonym, he'd concluded, was safe enough. He didn't have to look at the results. He could just let them sit there behind that link.

There were those who would wonder why Wilde had waited so long, why he hadn't already taken this obvious step. With companies like 23andMe and Ancestry.com advertising nonstop about how they'd helped reunite hundreds if not thousands of long-lost relatives, wouldn't it be natural for Wilde to send in his own swab and perhaps learn his own origin story? The extemporaneous, unthought-out answer was yes, of course—but when he took more time with it, when he contemplated the full ramifications, Wilde wasn't so sure.

Should Wilde, a man who enjoyed living off the grid, a man who really couldn't connect to most people, open the door to meeting strangers who could claim him as blood and thrust themselves into his life?

Did he want that?

What possible good could come from learning about his past?

The rubber hose alarm triggered the rest of Wilde's more state-of-the-art system. Most times, especially a few years back, if a car pulled onto the road, it was by mistake. A wrong turn. Wilde had, in fact, set up a clearing right past the road's entrance so as to make it easy for a car to realize its error, K-turn, and head back out. Now though, with the overgrowth of vegetation in full effect, the turnoff wasn't really visible from the main road, so those accidental visitors were far rarer.

Still, they happened. And that could be the case here.

When the second and third motion detectors kicked in, it became clear that the car had no intention of turning around. That meant that someone was looking for him.

Wilde lived in a customized spheroid-shape pod called an Ecocapsule. The Ecocapsule was a micro smart house or off-the-grid eco-abode or compact mobile home, whatever you wanted to call it, created by a Slovakian friend he met while serving in the Gulf. The structure resembled a giant dinosaur egg, though Wilde, using five different matte colors, had painted it camouflage to keep it hidden from view. The total living space was small, under seventy square feet, one room, but it had all he needed—a kitchenette with a cooking plate and mini fridge, a full bathroom with water-saving faucet and showerhead and an incinerator toilet, which turned waste into ash. The furniture was build-ins—table, cabinets, storage, a folding bed that could be either a twin or double—all made from lightweight honeycomb panels with an ash-wood veneer finish. The egg exterior was made from insulated fiberglass shells overlaid on a steel framework.

The Ecocapsule was—no reason to pretend otherwise—supercool.

There were those who would assume from the dwelling that Wilde must be an "eco-nut" or extremist. He wasn't. The capsule gave him privacy and protection. It was self-sustainable and thus totally off the grid. There were photovoltaic power cells on the roof and a pole with a wind turbine that could be mounted when he needed more battery charge. The spheroid shape made collecting rainwater easy, but if there was a dry spell, Wilde could add water by any source—lake, stream, a hose, whatever. The water would then be cleaned via reverse-osmosis water filters and UV LED lamp, making it instantly potable. The storage tank and water heater were adequate for one man, though Wilde would confess to enjoying luxuriating under Laila's jet-propulsion showerhead and seemingly limitless supply of hot water.

There was no washer and dryer, no microwave, no television. He didn't really care. His electronic needs consisted of a laptop and phone, which were easy enough to power up in the capsule. There were no thermostats or light switches—all of those sorts of functions were performed via the smart-home app.

The pod was also easy to put on a trailer and move, something Wilde did every few weeks or months, even if the move was only fifty or a hundred yards. At this stage of the game, it was probably overkill to move that often, but when his home stayed in one place too long, it felt to him as though the pod (and thus he himself?) were taking root.

He didn't like that.

Right now, Wilde was standing outside the gull wing door, taunted by that DNA site link. The sensors and cameras, all set up to solar power cells, streamed digital videos to his smart device. He took a look as the car on the screen—a red Audi A6—came to a stop. The driver's door opened. A man half fell out and took some time to right himself. Wilde recognized him. They had met only once.

Bernard Pine, Naomi's dad.

"Wilde?"

Wilde heard him through the microphones in place. He was still too far away to hear him without that. He hurried down the familiar path toward the road. The hike was a little more than a quarter mile. He had a weapon in his pod—a standard military-issue Beretta M9—but he saw no reason to pack it. He didn't like guns and wasn't a good shot. The night at Maynard Manor, when he'd taken the gun off Thor, he'd been glad that he hadn't been required to fire it, not so much because he didn't want to hurt anyone, but because from that distance, Wilde's marksmanship with a handgun could kindly be described as suspect.

Wilde silently came up behind Bernard Pine.

"What's up?"

Pine startled and spun toward him. Wilde wondered how he had learned about this spot, but it wasn't really that much of a secret. This was how you contacted Wilde. People knew that.

"I need your help," Pine said.

Wilde waited.

"She's missing again," Pine said. "Naomi, I mean. She didn't run away this time."

"Did you contact the police?"

"Yes."

"And?"

He rolled his eyes. "What do you think?"

They thought, of course, that she ran away again. Her Challenge game, Pine explained, had been exposed as a hoax, which just fueled the school bullies. The taunts intensified. Naomi had grown even more despondent. For the police, there was also the

Boy (or in this case, Girl) Who Cried Wolf aspect of the whole thing too.

"I'll pay you," Pine said. "I've heard..." He stopped.

"Heard what?"

"That you do stuff like this. That you were a hotshot investigator or something."

That, too, was an overstatement. He'd been the W in the security firm CRAW, his specialty being overseas protection and defense. Because of his unusual status—and because no one could even find a birth certificate for him—he handled the most sensitive cases that required the greatest amount of secrecy. When he'd made enough money, he quit the daily routine but stayed on as a silent partner at CRAW, officially "retiring" into that murky part of any business called "consulting."

"She didn't run away," Pine repeated.

There was a slur in his speech. Pine had the whole after-work-drinks thing going on—the bloodshot eyes, the wrinkled shirt, the loosened tie.

"Why do you say that?"

Pine mulled that over. Then he said, "Would it sway you at all if I said a father just knows?"

"Not in the least."

"She was taken."

"By?"

"I have no idea."

"Any signs of foul play?"

"Foul play?" He frowned. "Are you for real?"

"Any evidence at all she was taken?"

"I have the absence of evidence."

"Meaning?"

Bernard Pine spread his hand and smiled in a creepy way. "Well, she's not here, is she?"

"I don't think I can help you."

"Because I can't prove she was taken?"

Pine staggered toward Wilde a little too quickly, as though he was going to attack. Wilde took a step back. Pine stopped and held up his hand in surrender.

"Look, Wilde or whatever the hell they call you, have it your way. Let's say Naomi ran away. If that's the case, well, she's out there all alone." He lifted both arms and spun, as though to indicate his daughter might be in these specific woods. "She's been traumatized by those Neanderthals in her school and now she's scared and sad and . . . and she needs to be found."

Tough for Wilde to admit, but that made sense.

"Will you help me? No, not me. Forget me. You met Naomi. I can tell you connected with her. Will you help Naomi?"

Wilde stuck his hand out. "Give me your car keys."

"What?"

"I'll drive you home. You can tell me everything you know on the way."

CHAPTER THIRTEEN

Hester tried to focus, but she also felt giddy as a schoolgirl.

Her guest right now on *Crimstein on Crime* was famed activist/attorney Saul Strauss. The topic, like the topic of nearly every broadcast on every show right now, was the disruptive presidential campaign of Rusty Eggers, a talk-show guru with a sketchy background.

But her mind heading into commercial break was on the text she'd just received from Oren Carmichael:

> I know you're going on air. Can I come up and talk when you're done?

She'd giddily—man, she was too old for all this giddy—replied yes and that she'd leave Oren's name at reception and he could come up at any time. She almost typed one of those emoji hearts or smiley things at the end, but a fly-through of common sense restrained her.

But still.

Coming out of commercial, Hester read the quick bio on Saul

Strauss off the teleprompter—son of an old-school Republican governor from Vermont, served in the military, graduated from Brown University, taught at Columbia Law School, worked tirelessly now as a staunch defender of the underserved, of the downtrodden, of green causes, for animal rights... in short, he never met a bleeding-heart cause he didn't betroth with total ferocity.

"Just to be clear," Hester said, diving straight in, "you are suing the producers of *The Rusty Show*, but not Rusty Eggers himself, is that correct?"

Hester guessed that Saul Strauss was in his early sixties. He had the trappings of a stereotypical liberal arts professor—long gray hair in a ponytail down his back, flannel dress shirt under corduroy burnt-orange sports coat, complete with the patches on the sleeves, facial hair that sat somewhere between fashionable and Amish, reading spectacles dangling from a chain around his neck—but no matter how he dressed, Hester could still spot the steeliness of the old Marine.

"Exactly. I represent one of the advertisers for *The Rusty Show*, who is justifiably concerned that he was sold a false bill of goods."

"Which advertiser?"

Strauss's hands, folded on the desk, were thick, enormous, his fingers like sausages. Last time he'd been on, Hester had rested her hand on his forearm during the conversation, just for a second. The forearm felt like a marble block.

"We've asked the judge to keep my client's name confidential for now."

"But you're suing for fraud?"

"Yes."

"Explain."

"In short, we feel that *The Rusty Show* defrauded my client and other advertisers by deliberately hiding information that could be damaging to their brands."

"What information?"

"We aren't sure yet."

"Then how can you sue?"

"My client in good conscience connected their company to Rusty Eggers and his television program. We believe that when they did so, both the network and Dash Maynard—"

"Dash Maynard being the producer of *The Rusty Show*?"

Saul Strauss grinned. "Oh, Dash Maynard was much more than that. The two men are longtime friends. Maynard created the show—and really, he created the fake entity we now know as Rusty Eggers."

She debated following up on the fake entity thing, but it would keep. "Okay, fine, but I still don't understand your claim."

"Dash Maynard is sitting on information damaging to Rusty Eggers—"

"You know that how?"

"—and by not revealing what that damaging information is, even with all the NDAs in place, Dash Maynard knew that he was selling advertising for a program that could blow up at any moment and harm my client's brand."

"But it didn't blow up."

"Not yet it hasn't."

"In fact, *The Rusty Show* is off the air. Rusty Eggers is now a leading candidate to be the next president of the United States."

"Exactly, that's the point. Now that he's running for office, there will be much more scrutiny. When Dash Maynard's damaging tapes are released—"

"Wait, do you have any evidence that these tapes even exist?"

"—my client's business will be seriously and maybe irrevocably harmed."

"Because they advertised on the show?"

"Yes, of course."

"So in short, you're suing for a fraud that hasn't happened and that you have no proof was committed based on something you don't know exists or even if it does, how or if it would damage you. That about sum it up?"

Strauss didn't like that. "No, that's not—"

"Saul?"

"Yes?"

Hester leaned forward. "This lawsuit is complete nonsense."

Strauss cleared his throat. The big hands tensed. "The judge said we had standing."

"You won't for long. We both know that. Can we be honest here? Just between us? This is a frivolous suit designed to raise awareness and pressure Dash Maynard into releasing tapes that might be embarrassing to Rusty Eggers and derail his campaign."

"No, that's not the case at all."

"Are you a backer of Rusty Eggers?"

"What? No."

"In fact"—Hester had the pull quote on a graphic that they put on the screen now—"you said, 'Rusty Eggers needs to be stopped at all costs. He is a deranged nihilist who could lead us into unimaginable horrors. He wants to tear down the world order, even if it kills millions.'" Hester turned to him. "You said that, right?"

"I did."

"And you believe it?"

"Don't you?"

Hester wasn't about to be drawn into that one. "And so if Dash Maynard has something in his possession damaging to Rusty Eggers, you believe that this information should be released to the public."

"Of course it should," Strauss said. "We are voting for the most powerful position in the world. There should be total transparency when it comes to a candidate."

"And that's really the point of this lawsuit."

"Transparency is important, Hester. Don't you agree?"

"I do. But you know what I think is much more important? The Constitution. The rule of law."

"So you're defending Rusty Eggers and Dash Maynard?"

"I'm defending the law."

"I don't want to sound hyperbolic—"

"Too late."

"—but if you saw Hitler coming to power—"

"Oh, Saul, don't start with that. Please."

"Why not?"

"Just don't. Not on my show."

Saul Strauss leaned toward the camera and addressed it directly. "Dash Maynard may have tapes that could change the course of human history."

"Well, as long as you don't want to sound hyperbolic," Hester said with an eye roll. "By the way, how do you even know these tapes exist?"

Strauss cleared his throat. "We, uh, have our sources."

"For example?"

"Arnie Poplin, for one."

"Arnie Poplin?" Hester couldn't keep the skepticism from her voice. "Arnie Poplin is your source?"

"One of them, yes." Strauss cleared his throat. "He has direct knowledge—"

"Just to clarify for our viewers, Arnie Poplin is the celebrity has-been-turned-conspiracy-nut who appeared as a contestant on *The Rusty Show*."

"That characterization is misleading."

"Arnie Poplin claimed, did he not, that 9/11 was an inside job?"

"That's not relevant."

"This same Arnie Poplin calls my producer weekly demanding to be a guest so he can air some new whacked-out theory involving UFOs or chemtrails or some similar malarkey. Seriously? Arnie Poplin?"

"With all due respect—"

"That's never a good way to begin a sentence, Saul."

"—I don't think you see the danger in this Rusty Eggers campaign. We have an obligation to air these tapes and save our democracy."

"Then find a legal way to air them—or there isn't much of a democracy to save."

"That's what I'm doing."

"With this dinky fraud case?"

"I can start by going after someone for a parking violation," Strauss said, "and if I stumble across a murder, well, so be it."

"Wow, that's a stretch, but it seems to be a philosophy you and Rusty Eggers have in common then."

"Pardon me?"

"Ends justifying the means—a tale as old as time. Maybe you two should find your own country?" Strauss's face turned scarlet, but before he could counter, Hester spun to the camera. "We'll be right back."

A producer shouted, "Clear."

Saul Strauss was not a happy man. "Jesus, Hester, what the hell was that?"

"Arnie Poplin? Are you for real?" She shook her head and checked her texts. There was one from Oren sent two minutes ago:

On the way up.

"I have to go, Saul."

"My God, did you hear yourself? You just compared me to Rusty Eggers."

"Your lawsuit is nonsense."

Saul Strauss put his hand on her arm. "Eggers is not going to stop, Hester. The destruction, the mayhem, the nihilism—you get that, right? He basically wants anarchy. He wants to tear down everything you and I cherish."

"I have to go, Saul."

Hester unclipped the microphone from her lapel. Her producer Allison Grant waited in the wings. Hester tried to be nonchalant.

"Do I have a visitor?" she asked.

"You mean that Giant Yum in the police-chief uniform?"

Hester couldn't help herself. "He's cute, right?"

"Welcome to Beefcake City. Population: Him."

"Where is he?"

"I put him in the greenroom."

Every studio has a greenroom, a place for guests to sit before they come on air. They are, for some odd reason, never actually green.

"How do I look?" Hester asked.

Allison inspected her to the point where Hester feared that she'd do a horse-purchase check on her teeth. "Smart."

"What?"

"Having him come by right after you go on air. Makeup and hair already done."

"Right?" Hester smoothed her business skirt and headed down the corridor. The greenroom was loaded up with posters of the network anchors and talking heads, including one taken three years ago of Hester, turned to the side, arms crossed, looking tough. When she entered the room now, Oren was standing with his back toward the door, looking at her poster.

"What do you think?" Hester asked.

Without turning toward her, Oren said, "You're hotter now."

"Hotter?"

He shrugged. "'Prettier' or 'more beautiful' don't seem to fit you, Hester."

"I'll take hotter," she said. "I'll take hotter and run."

Oren turned and smiled. It was an awfully good smile. She felt it in her toes.

"Nice to see you," he said.

"Nice to see you too," Hester said. "And I'm sorry about that whole Naomi thing."

"Water under the bridge," Oren said. "I imagine it ended up being more embarrassing for you than me."

It had been. When it was discovered that Naomi was just playing a prank, there had been plenty of online ridicule. Hester's enemies—everyone on social media had enemies—reveled in her error. When two days later she commented on a controversial election court decision in California, a dozen Twitter Nuts (that's what Hester called them) pounced with a fury: "Wait, isn't she the one who thought a kid's prank was a national emergency?" This was the way now for both sides—and yes, she even hated the phrase "both sides"—now: Discredit any legitimate argument with something, no matter how long ago or obscure, the person got wrong in the past. As if only perfection deserved your consideration.

"She ran off again," Oren said.

"Naomi?"

"Yes. Her father came to see me. He insists it's more than that."

"What will you do?"

"What can I do? I put it on the radio so if my guys see her, they'll call it. But the signs seem pretty clear that she's a runaway."

"I imagine she's been under a lot of stress."

"Yes. That's my concern too."

Hester still had questions about the whole Naomi mess—notably, why did Matthew insist she get involved?—but once the ending came, Matthew shut down and shrugged it off as a vague worry about a classmate.

"So what brings you here?" she asked.

"Seems enough time has passed."

"Pardon?"

"You said not to call too soon. It would make me look desperate."

"So I did."

"And being a little old school, I thought I would ask you out the old-fashioned way."

"Oh."

"In person."

"Oh."

"Because no one has a rotary phone anymore."

"Oh."

He smiled again. "This is going well."

"Should I say 'Oh' again?"

"No, I think I got the gist. Would you like to have dinner with me sometime?"

"I should probably fake indifference. Say something about checking my busy schedule."

Oren said, "Oh."

"Yes, Oren. I would like to have dinner with you very much."

"How's tomorrow?"

"Tomorrow is good."

"Seven?"

"I'll make a reservation," she said.

"Will I need to wear a tie?"

"No."

"Good."

"Good."

Silence.

He stepped forward as though he might hug her, then thought better of it. He gave an awkward half wave and said, "Bye then."

She watched him walk past her and out the door.

Yep, Hester thought, holding back the urge to leap up and click her heels. *Giant Yum.*

CHAPTER FOURTEEN

Rusty Eggers turned the television off with a little too much drama and tossed the remote onto the white couch.

"It's just a silly nuisance suit."

Gavin Chambers nodded. They'd been watching Hester Crimstein's interview with Saul Strauss from Rusty's sleek, chrome-n-white penthouse. The penthouse of this particular high-rise was made up of floor-to-ceiling windows offering the most breathtaking views of the Manhattan skyline imaginable—mostly because the penthouse was in Hoboken, New Jersey, not Manhattan, and so it faced the city rather than stood amongst it. New Yorkers on the Hudson River have the okay view of New Jersey—New Jerseyans on that same Hudson River have the jaw-dropping view of New York City. Right now, at night, with the lights of the buildings twinkling off the Hudson, the river looked like diamonds strewn out on black velvet.

"A judge will toss it out before it gets anywhere," Rusty continued. He spoke with great confidence. Rusty always spoke with great confidence.

"I'm sure you're right," Gavin Chambers said.

"I thought Hester Crimstein was good in that interview," Rusty said.

"She was."

"Fair. Called Strauss out on his bullshit."

"Yes."

"But he won't go away easily, will he?"

"Saul Strauss?" Gavin Chambers shook his head. "He will not."

"You know him, right?"

"Yes."

"You served together."

They had. In the Marines. A lifetime ago. Gavin had always admired Saul Strauss. Saul was tough and scrappy and brave—and yet wrong about pretty much everything.

"How long has it been since you saw him?"

"A long time."

"Still," Rusty said. "There must be a bond. From your time overseas."

Gavin didn't reply.

"Do you think you can talk to him?"

"Talk to him?"

"Get him to back off."

Saul Strauss used to be what Gavin would consider committed and passionate in a namby-pamby, Kumbaya-like, eco-green, granola-y, unrealistic sort of way, but more and more, the Sauls of the world had raised their rhetoric to the dangerously hysterical, especially when it came to Rusty Eggers.

"Not a chance," Gavin said.

"So Strauss is a true hater?"

Gavin Chambers and Saul Strauss both came from politically mixed marriages—conservative fathers, liberal mothers. Gavin had taken after his old man while Saul became a proper mama's boy. There had been a time when they could talk and debate in a spirited way. Gavin would say that Saul was naïve and a bleeding heart. Saul would say that Gavin was overly analytical and Darwinian. Those relative niceties now seemed a long time ago.

"He's become a zealot," Gavin said.

"I figured that," Rusty said.

"Uh-huh."

"In some ways, we are the same, your friend Saul and I. We both believe that the current system is rigged. We both believe that the system has failed the American people. We both believe the only way to fix it is to first upend it."

Rusty Eggers stared out at the view. He was a New Jersey boy through and through—born poor in the Ironbound district of Newark to a Ukrainian father and a Jamaican mother, attended all-male St. Benedict's Prep on Martin Luther King Boulevard in the heart of the city, earned an academic full ride to Princeton University—all of which was why he stayed in his home state rather than moving across that river. He loved the view, of course. Trains and ferries could get him into midtown or Wall Street in less than half an hour. New Jersey was also a big part of Rusty's rep—The Three S's, he liked to say—a sliver of Springsteen, a sliver of Sinatra, a sliver of the Sopranos. Rusty came across as gruff yet lovable, urban yet safe, a big teddy bear of a man with a shock of rust-colored (ergo the nickname) hair. He was light skinned enough to pass as white, yet black enough so that the racists could get behind him to prove that they weren't really racists.

Rusty Eggers was also, Gavin Chambers knew, brilliant. The only child in a close-knit family, Rusty had double-majored in philosophy and political science at Princeton. He'd made his first fortune by creating a board game that mixed personal opinions and trivia called PolitiGuess. Life seemed to be going swimmingly for Rusty until a tractor trailer, driven by a man who'd popped too many amphetamines to keep on a ridiculous delivery schedule, crashed through the divider on the New Jersey Turnpike and slammed head-on into a car carrying the Eggers family. Rusty's mother and father both died instantly. Rusty was seriously injured and spent two months in a hospital bed. As the family driver on that particular night, even though it was not in any way his fault, Rusty suffered survivor's guilt. He became unmoored. He sunk into a painkiller addiction and then diagnosable depression. It was bad for a while.

Fast-forward through three terrible years.

Though some claim that he never fully recovered from this dark period, Rusty Eggers, sporting a limp he carried to this day, eventually rose from the ashes like a phoenix with the help of his old friends Dash and Delia Maynard. Rusty would claim, as so many had before him, that he'd pulled himself up by the bootstraps, but in truth, it had been the Maynards who gave him the boots and tugged on those straps with all their might. With Dash's help, Rusty Eggers became television's most trusted self-help guru. Two years ago, he'd ridden that fame and goodwill to a landslide victory to become a United States senator as, in his own words, the "Complete Independent."

Rusty's motto: *Parties Are for Weekends, Not Politics.*

Now, like every political upstart from Obama to Trump, Rusty Eggers had foregone waiting his turn and was aiming for the highest office in the land with early success.

With his back to Gavin, still staring out the window, Rusty asked, "How are they faring?"

He was talking about the Maynards. "They're fine. A little stressed perhaps."

"I'm sure your presence helps with that."

Rusty's apartment's décor was fittingly spare, nothing gold or marble, just whites and minimalism. The view was the thing, those floor-to-ceiling windows.

"I appreciate you doing this for me, Gavin."

"I'm billing for it."

"Yes, but I know you don't go into the field anymore."

"I do," Gavin said. "But rarely. Senator?"

Rusty frowned. "We've known each other too long for you to start calling me that."

"I'd prefer it."

"As you please, Colonel," Rusty replied with a small smile.

"You know besides running my securities firm, I'm an attorney."

"I do."

"I don't do much practicing," Gavin continued, "but I passed the bar so that anything you or any client tells me is covered under attorney-client privilege."

"I trust you anyway. You know that."

"Still, you have that protection too—that *legal* protection. I wanted you to know that. I'm your trusted friend, yes, but legally I can't reveal anything you tell me."

Rusty Eggers turned with a smile on his face. "You know I want you in my cabinet."

"This isn't about that."

"National security advisor. Maybe secretary of defense."

Didn't matter how much he tried not to get excited by this notion—retired colonel Gavin Chambers, ex-Marine, was still human. The idea of serving in a cabinet made him heady. "I appreciate your confidence in me."

"It's deserved."

"Senator? Let me help you."

"You are."

"The thing is, I've heard the rumors—"

"They are just that," Rusty said. "Rumors."

"Then why am I guarding the Maynards?"

Rusty turned to him. "Are you familiar with the horseshoe theory of politics?"

"What about it?"

"Most people think, politically speaking, that the right and the left are on a linear continuum—meaning that the right is on one side of the line, and the left is obviously on the other. That they are polar opposites. Far apart from one another. But the horseshoe theory says that the line is, well, shaped more like a horseshoe—that once you start going to the far right and the far left, that the line curves inward so that the two extremes are far closer to one another than they are to the center. Some go as far as to say it's more like a circle—that the line bends so much that far left and far right are virtually indistinguishable—tyranny in one form or another."

"Senator?"

"Yes?"

"I studied political science too."

"Then you'll understand what I'm trying to do." Rusty came closer, wincing as he limped. The shattered leg from that terrible night too often tightened up. "Most Americans are in the middle relatively speaking. Most are somewhat left or right of that center. Those people don't interest me. They are pragmatic. They change their minds. Voters always think the president has to appeal to those folks—the center. Half the country more or less is right, half is left, so you need to grab the middle. That's not what I'm doing."

"I don't see what that has to do with the Maynards," Gavin said.

"I am the next evolution of our outrage-fueled, social-media-obsessed political culture. The final evolution, if you will. The end of the status quo."

Rusty had the fire in his eyes, the smile rocking. There was no one else in the room and yet Gavin could hear the cheers of millions.

"My point is, if my enemies think my close friends Dash and Delia have something, *anything*, on me, they'll stop at nothing, including hurting them, to get it."

"So you're doing this just to protect close friends?"

"You find that hard to believe?"

Gavin made a face and put the tip of his index finger near the tip of his thumb to indicate a wee bit. Rusty laughed. It was an explosive laugh. Such charm in that laugh. So disarming. "I've known Delia since our days at Princeton. Did you know that?"

Gavin did, of course. He knew the entire legend. Rusty had

dated Delia during their junior year. They broke up while working a summer internship on Capitol Hill for the Democrats, where Delia then fell for and married another summer intern from that Capitol Hill class, a budding documentary filmmaker named Dash Maynard. That, oddly enough, was how Rusty and Dash met—in DC, doing summer internships for the Dems.

That was where it all started.

"The Maynards know more about me than anyone," Rusty said.

"Like what?"

"Oh, nothing dire. It's not like they have any serious dirt on me. But Dash taped everything back in the day. Everything. Backstage. Private gatherings. There are no smoking guns, but, I mean, in all that material, there must be moments my enemies could use, don't you think? A moment when I was rude to a guest or snappy with an employee or maybe I put my hand on a woman's elbow, whatever."

"And specifically?"

"Nothing comes to mind."

Gavin didn't believe him.

"Just keep an eye on them for a few more weeks. Then this will all be over."

CHAPTER FIFTEEN

When Bernard Pine unlocked his front door, Wilde didn't wait for permission. He headed straight for the staircase.

"Hold up, where do you think you're going?"

Wilde didn't reply. He started up the steps. Bernard Pine fell in behind him. That was fine. Wilde entered Naomi's bedroom and flicked on the lights.

"What are you looking for?" Pine asked.

"You want my help, right?"

"Yes."

Wilde stared at Naomi's bed, at all the stuffed animals on it. "Does Naomi have a favorite?"

"A favorite what?"

"Stuffed animal."

"How would I know?"

Wilde opened the closet and checked the shelf.

"Her backpack," he said to Pine.

"What?"

"When I was here last time—"

"Wait, when the hell were you in my daughter's bedroom?"

Did Wilde want to go into it? Judging by the look of bafflement and perhaps even hostility sneaking onto Pine's face, he probably had to. "The day you and I met."

"But I saw you in the basement."

"And before that, I was in the bedroom."

"With my daughter?"

"What? No. Alone. You know that. She was in the basement."

Pine shook his head, as though trying to clear it. "I don't understand. How did you get in her bedroom?"

"That's not really important right now. What is important is that Naomi's backpack is missing."

Wilde pointed to the shelf. Pine followed the gesture, saw the empty shelf, and shrugged. "It's probably at her school. In her locker. I saw her take it lots of times. Every day, in fact."

"What color backpack?"

"Black, I think. Maybe dark blue."

"I'm talking about the pink one she kept on this shelf."

Again Pine looked baffled. "How would you know...you looked in her closet?"

"Yes."

"Why?"

Wilde tried to keep the impatience out of his tone. "Because I was looking for her. Like now."

"I don't know anything about a pink backpack."

Wilde gave the closet a more thorough look. The pink Fjällräven Kånken backpack he'd seen on that shelf was definitely gone. He also checked the hangers. Last time he'd been in this room, all the hangers had been taken. He counted four empty ones now. Three more hangers lay scattered on the floor, as though she'd ripped the clothes off those hangers quickly.

Obvious conclusion: She packed clothes into that pink backpack.

Wilde shifted his gaze back to the bed and the stuffed animals.

He closed his eyes for a second, tried to recall what the bed looked like last time he was here, hoping that he'd be able to tell if any were missing. But it was pointless. If one or more of them were missing, it might confirm the fact that Naomi intentionally ran. But did he need that extra proof?

"She ran away," Wilde said to him.

"You can't know that."

"Mr. Pine?"

"I'd prefer it if you called me Bernie."

"What aren't you telling me, Bernie?"

"I'm not sure what you mean."

"You know more than you're saying."

He started rubbing his chin. Wilde tried to read him. Nothing was coming through clearly. Was he a loving albeit distracted father? Or was there something more? There was definitely a quality in the man he didn't trust. Was Bernard Pine a danger or was Wilde just being his usual cynical self?

Then: "Naomi sent me this text yesterday."

Pine handed Wilde his phone. The message was two short sentences:

> Don't worry. I'm safe.

"I know what you're thinking," Pine said.

Not much question about it now. Backpack and clothes gone. No signs or hints of any abduction. No ransom or demands or anything like that. Now throw in the other factors—the heightened bullying, her past history of running off, the failed Challenge game.

The conclusion was obvious.

"There's something else you should know," Pine said.

Wilde looked at him.

"Someone hurt her." His eyes were wet now. "And I'm not talking about the usual bullying."

"What are you talking about then?"

"Physically."

The room went still.

"You better explain," Wilde said.

It took him a little time to gather himself. Pine stared down at his hand. He had a school ring with a garnet stone. He started twisting it around his finger. "When I came home from work the day before she disappeared, Naomi had a frozen bag of peas on her right eye. It was black the next morning."

"Did you ask her about it?"

"Of course."

Wilde waited. Bernard Pine started biting hard on his thumbnail.

"She said she walked into a door."

"Did you believe her?"

"Of course I didn't believe her," he snapped. "But that's all she would say. You ever try to get a teenager to tell you something? You can't force it out of them. She said she was fine and went up to her room."

"Did you check up on her?"

"You don't have kids, do you, Wilde?"

Wilde took that as a no.

"It's all connected," Pine said.

"What is?"

"That game of Challenge, those kids who were picking on her, the fact that she's gone again. Something isn't right." He tilted his head and looked at Wilde as though seeing him for the first time. "Why were you so invested in my daughter?"

Wilde didn't reply.

"Did you even know Naomi before that night?"

"No."

"Yet you broke into my house to find her. A girl you didn't even know. Why would you do that?"

That was when Bernard Pine pulled out a handgun.

Wilde didn't hesitate. The moment he realized what was happening he was already on the move. No one with a gun expects that. Not at first. One of the two men in this room—Wilde—was highly trained in combat. The other wasn't. Pine had made the mistake of standing too close. Wilde took a quick step toward him. With one hand, he snatched the gun. With the other, he formed a classic chop and delivered it without much force to Pine's throat. If you throw that blow too hard, you do permanent damage. Wilde was just aiming for a choke, a gag reflex, a muscle release.

It did the trick.

Pine staggered back, one hand on his neck, the other waving in some sort of surrender. The weapon now in Wilde's hand felt light. He popped the revolver's chamber open and checked.

No bullets.

Pine had his voice back. "I was just trying to scare you."

Idiot, Wilde thought. But he said nothing.

"You get it, right? You break into my house, you start some kind of relationship with my daughter—you, the weirdo who lives alone in the woods. I mean, if you were in my shoes, wouldn't you wonder?"

"I don't know where your daughter is."

"So explain it to me then: Who got you involved in finding her during the Challenge game?"

Wilde wasn't about to tell him. But when he stepped back and looked at it objectively, Pine did raise an interesting point. Matthew had never really explained it all, had he?

"Give me your phone," Wilde said.

"What, why?"

Wilde just held out his hand. Pine handed it over. Wilde clicked the message button and found the text from Naomi saying Don't worry, I'm safe. He skimmed up to see the rest of the conversation. He stopped.

"What?" Pine asked.

There were no other texts between the two of them—between father and daughter.

"What happened to the rest of the messages?"

"What?"

"I assume this wasn't the first time you and Naomi texted."

"No, of course not. Wait, what are you doing?"

Wilde checked the call history. Yes, there were phone calls to Naomi. But not many. The last had been more than a month ago.

"Where are the rest of the texts between you two?"

"What, I don't know. They should be there."

"They're not."

Pine shrugged. "Can someone delete them?"

Someone can. The user of the phone.

"Why would you get rid of your messages with your own daughter?"

"I didn't. Maybe Naomi cleared them out."

Not likely.

Wilde started typing.

"What are you doing?" Pine asked.

Wilde ignored him. He typed into the message field:

> Hey, Naomi, it's Wilde.

She may not think it's really him. She may think it's her father tricking her.

> Aka Boo Radley.

Only she would get that reference.

> I'm using your dad's phone. He's worried about you.
> So am I. Let me know you're okay.

Wilde gave his current burner number and told her she could text or call. Then he tossed the phone back to Pine, but he pocketed the weapon.

It was time to talk to Matthew. He headed for the door.

"Will you help me?" Pine asked.

Wilde didn't break stride. "I'll help Naomi."

CHAPTER SIXTEEN

As soon as he was out of the Pine house, Wilde checked the burner number he'd texted to Naomi, hoping for a quick response.

Nothing.

If Naomi had just run off, wouldn't she reply to him right away? He might be deluding himself, but he thought so. There had been some sort of connection between them in that basement, two outcasts who kind of understood one another, but again maybe that was more him projecting than anything substantive.

He texted Matthew:

> You home?

The dots danced before the word "Ya" popped up.

> Mind if I come by?

Matthew's reply was a thumbs-up emoji.

As Wilde took to the woods, he called Hester.

"Articulate," she said as she picked up.

"What?"

"A friend of mine says that when he answers. I thought it was cute. What's up?"

"Naomi Pine is missing again."

"I heard."

"How?"

She cleared her throat. "Oren told me." Her voice sounded a little funny.

"What did he say?"

"That her dad came to him. That he made a big fuss but she probably ran away again."

"The dad came to me too."

"What does it look like?" Hester asked.

"Like she ran away on her own."

He filled her in on the missing clothes and backpack and text to her dad not to worry.

"The text I dismiss," Hester said. "If someone grabbed her, they could have taken her phone and sent anything."

"Right."

"But the clothes plus her past suggest she ran away."

"Agree."

"Either way—and I don't know how to put this subtly—"

"Not your strong suit anyway, Hester."

"—but this isn't our business anymore. Unless you need the money."

"I don't."

"So?"

"So two things," he said.

"Let me guess," Hester said. "Thing One: You met Naomi. You liked her. You want to help her, even if she ran away. You're worried about her."

"Yes."

"And Thing Two?"

"You know Thing Two, Hester."

There was a sigh. "Matthew."

"He didn't tell us everything that first time. We let it go when we found Naomi. The dad said she had bruises. Like someone hit her."

"Oh come on, you don't think Matthew—"

"Of course not. But I don't think he's told us everything either."

"And you like the girl."

Wilde thought about it. "Yes. And she's alone. She has no one."

"How about that teacher you were bedding?"

Wilde frowned. "Did you really say 'bedding'?"

"You'd prefer '*shtupping*'?"

"Better than 'bedding,'" Wilde said. "We can try Ava, but in the end she's just a schoolteacher, not a relative or friend."

"So what's your plan?"

"I'm going to talk to Matthew."

"Now? I wouldn't push him."

"I won't. Do you have contacts with the phone company?"

"I may," she said.

"Can you ping Naomi's phone? Find out where it is?"

"I can try."

"Or you can ask Oren to do it," Wilde said, "after you bed him."

"Funny."

Wilde pocketed the phone. The woods were never silent. Some days he got all intuitive and insightful about that, about the effects of quiet without silence, but for him it was different. It wasn't necessarily enjoyable—it was what he needed. He didn't lose his mind when he went to the "big city" or anything like that. He liked the change sometimes. But this was home. If he stayed away too long—if he didn't escape to this quiet for long periods of time—it was something akin to a diver and the bends.

Sounded like Zen-level bullshit. Maybe it was.

Matthew was waiting for Wilde in the kitchen.

"Mom's not home," Matthew said.

Wilde knew. Laila had told him she'd be out late. "Naomi is missing again."

Matthew didn't reply.

"Did you notice? At school or anything?"

"Yeah."

"And?"

Shrug. "And I figured she'd run away or something. The last week has been brutal. I figured she needed a break."

"You were very concerned last time."

"And that ended up being nothing."

"Why were you so concerned?"

Matthew shifted his feet. "I told you."

"You got wind of this Challenge game?"

"Right."

"Yeah, I'm not buying that, Matthew."

His eyes went wide. "You think I'm lying?"

"Probably by omission. But yes."

Matthew shook his head, feigning offense. Then he said, "It's nothing."

"Tell me anyway."

"I don't feel comfortable—"

"Then feel uncomfortable," Wilde said.

"Hey, you're not my father, you know?"

"Really?" Wilde gave him a hard gaze. "You want to play that card?"

Matthew looked down. His voice was soft. "Sorry."

Wilde waited.

"I hurt her."

Wilde felt his pulse pick up, but he stayed silent.

"There was this dance thing. Like a party."

"When?"

"Two months ago."

Matthew stopped.

After some time passed, Wilde said, "Where was the party?"

"Crash Maynard's place. It was *like* a party, but it wasn't really a party. It was more like a school function. A few years ago, a bunch of kids got wasted at a school dance, so we aren't allowed to hold them in the gym anymore. So the Maynards volunteered to host. The whole class was there."

"Naomi too?"

"The whole class, yeah." Matthew kept his eyes on the floor.

Wilde folded his arms. "Go on."

"Naomi brought a stuffed animal. A penguin. I think for her it was like a therapy pet or something, I don't know. It wasn't like she was being freaky about it. It was small. She kept it in her handbag. But she showed it to some of the girls. They started giggling about it. Anyway, Crash goes over and starts talking to her. He's being all nice, showing her his stupid skull ring. Which means something is up. Anyway, it's just to distract her. She's smiling and so happy... and then two of the other guys run over and it's like they purse-snatch her. She cries out and runs after them toward the woods behind the estate. Everyone's laughing."

Matthew paused.

"Including you?"

"Yeah, but I don't think it's funny."

"But you see this happen?"

"I was talking to Sutton Holmes."

Sutton Holmes. Wilde and Matthew don't have too many of those man-to-mans, but Wilde knew about Matthew's crush. The only person who had ever been in Wilde's Ecocapsule was Matthew. When the boy needed to get away, Wilde brought him there. Something about the outdoors, the camping, the being one with nature, whatever label you wanted to use, it seemed to always lead to opening up.

"It's dark by now," Matthew continued. "The Maynards rented these portable lights like you see at an outdoor baseball game. Half the kids are carrying flasks, so they're mixing in vodka and grain alcohol with whatever sweet concoction the Maynards are serving. But I'm watching the woods. I'm waiting for Naomi to come back. Five minutes passed, maybe ten. Then Kyle emerges from the woods. He's holding up his hand. At first, I can't see what's in it, but when he gets closer"—Matthew shut his eyes—"it was the head of the stuffed penguin. Just the head. Like the stuffing is leaking out."

Wilde felt his heart sink.

"Everyone is cheering."

Wilde tried to keep the judgment out of his voice. "You?"

"You want to hear this or not?"

He was right. There would be time enough later. Matthew looked so small right now. Wilde reminded himself that Matthew was the little boy who lost his father in a car crash. He'd just been trying to fit in, something Wilde never quite got because he'd wanted the opposite for himself.

"I was pretty wasted by now."

"Wasted meaning...?"

"Drunk."

"High too?"

"No, I didn't take any drugs. But I had a lot to drink. I know that's never an excuse for anything, but I think it matters. I was stumbling around and somewhere along the way, as it got later and later, I realized that no one was leaving. See, a parent had caught on to the fact that a lot of us were wasted and figured it'd be safest if we stayed on the estate until we sobered up."

Made sense, Wilde thought.

"So I'm watching Crash take out a lighter. He flicks it and there's a flame. And then he sets Naomi's penguin on fire. Just like that. He had this big smile on his face. He looked around, I think, because he wanted to see Naomi's reaction, and I realized that she hadn't come back since she chased those guys who took her penguin."

Matthew grabbed an apple and moved into the living room. Wilde followed him.

"What happened next, Matthew?"

Matthew stared down at the apple, cradling it in his palm, and Wilde wondered whether he was seeing that penguin. "I wish I could explain how I felt."

"Try."

"Crushed. Depressed. Sutton was with Crash now. Couples were starting to hook up and disappear. I just felt, I don't know, out of place and angry and stupid and I'm drunk so all that is just... so I go looking for her. For Naomi. It's dark. But thanks to you, I know my way around the woods. I stumble at one point, and my face smacks a tree. I'm even dizzier. My lip is bleeding. And then I found her. She's just sitting on a rock. I can see her profile, and in the moonlight, Naomi looks really pretty. I move closer. She doesn't turn, even though she has to hear me. There are no tears on her face. Her eyes are dry. I ask her if she's okay. She says, 'It's just a stupid stuffed toy.' And she seems to mean it. Like she really doesn't care. I move a little closer, and my legs kinda give way, and I collapse next to her. We're by that brook behind the Maynards'. I guess the noise is supposed to be nice and all, but you know what I remember thinking at the time?"

"No."

"The noise makes me need to take a leak. So I excuse myself. I duck behind the nearest tree. That's how drunk I am. Right there. I drop trou and... anyway, I zip up and come back and sit with her. We start talking. It was nice. I've known Naomi my whole life. I don't think we ever talked before. Not like that anyway. And again, I'm drunk and the brook babble is now kinda soothing and there's the moonlight and I got a million things rushing through me. I don't know how late it is. In the distance I see the stadium lights go off. So at some point, I kiss her. Or maybe she kisses me. Whatever, it's consensual on both our parts. I don't want you to think it wasn't. It was definitely okay by her. We make out. And in my mind, I don't know how to describe it. Part of me is so into it, right? I mean, most of me. I don't know if I like her or not. I don't even think that matters. I can't explain it better."

Teenagers, Wilde thought. A boy and a girl at a party. We may not like it, but it's a tale as old as time.

"You want to hear something awful?"

Wilde gave him a small nod.

"We start going at it a little harder. Her hand is on my leg, all that. And part of me is like, Yeah, awesome. And part of me is like, Wow, look at you—you're with the biggest loser in the school." Matthew stopped, raised his hand, shook his head. "I'm not explaining this right. And it doesn't matter. Because right then, with her hand on my leg and my hand under her shirt, a big spotlight hits us in the face. We both jump back. I can hear laughter. Hard to make out, but for sure I can hear Crash and Ryan and...Naomi runs. Like a rabbit. She jumps up and takes off. I can't even see. The light is still in my eyes. I raise my hand to block it. Everyone is laughing and mocking me for being with *her*. I'm all blinking and I can feel tears start coming. I just want to die, you know? I'm thinking I'm never going to live this down. And for the next two months, I don't. Wherever I was on the social ladder, I'm tossed down to the bottom. Not as low as Naomi. But down there."

"What did you say?" Wilde asked. "To the guys laughing at you."

"That it was nothing. That I was just having fun." He swallowed. "I...I said that she's easy."

"Classy."

Matthew closed his eyes. Wilde backed off.

"Did you talk to Naomi about it?"

"No."

"Seriously?"

Matthew didn't reply.

"When did you next see her?"

"At school, but we avoided each other." Matthew thought about it. "It was more me avoiding her, to be honest. It was really bad for a few weeks."

Wilde wanted so very much to play a small air violin. "This is all awful," Wilde said, "but I'm still not sure why you were so concerned when she went missing."

"Because I'm not done with the story."

Tears flooded the boy's eyes. Wilde felt his heart drop.

"I'm going to skip the excuses, okay? Because there is no excuse. I got a small taste of what Naomi went through for years. Just a small taste. And I couldn't take it. So when Crash came to me with a way to get back into their good graces, I took it. That's all that matters. Not why. Just that I did it."

"What did you do?"

"It was a prank."

"What was?"

He didn't reply.

"Matthew?"

"I asked Naomi to meet me. Like, on a date. I texted that I wanted to see her again, not to tell anyone, at that same spot behind the Maynards'."

"How did she reply?"

"She said yes." He shrugged. "She seemed excited."

Matthew closed his eyes.

Wilde worked hard to keep his expression neutral. "And?"

"And I pranked her."

"How?"

"I sort of didn't show."

"Hey, Matthew?"

Matthew looked up.

"This isn't a time to be cute with your wording. What do you mean, sort of didn't show?"

"I didn't show. And I was supposed to ghost her so when she texted me 'where are you' I wasn't supposed to reply."

"But you did?"

"Yeah."

"What did you say?"

"I said, 'I'm sorry.'"

"What did she say?"

"Nothing. She never spoke to me again."

He flashed back to that basement. Naomi's words about Matthew: *"He probably blames himself. Tell him he shouldn't. He just wants to fit in too."*

Maybe Naomi forgave him, and maybe Matthew was looking for absolution, but Wilde wasn't about to be the one to give it to him.

"So what happened when Naomi went to the brook by herself?"

"Crash showed up. Others in the group."

"And?"

"And I don't know. Or at least I didn't. That's why I contacted Nana. The next day, Naomi vanished. I thought...well, I don't know what I thought. I thought they'd done something to her."

"Like what?"

"Like, I don't know," he said, throwing up his hands. "But it ends up, Naomi was okay. You found her. Crash just told her about that stupid Challenge game. Got her to go along with it. That's all."

Wilde heard what he thought might be a car pulling into the driveway. He moved down the hall and looked out the window. A tall man in obvious designer threads got out on the driver's side of a shiny black Mercedes-Benz SL 550. He hurried to the passenger side, hoping to be ever the gallant gentleman, but Laila had already opened the door and gotten out too.

So that was why Laila had told Wilde she'd be out late.

Without another word, Wilde padded down the stairs and out the back door. Matthew would get it. They'd all been here before. Laila wouldn't bring Designer Threads into the house. Not yet. Not with Matthew home. But she'd ask Wilde to stay away from her for a while and Wilde would and Laila would try and in the end it wouldn't happen. Wilde shouldn't wish for that. He told himself he didn't, that he just wanted Laila happy. But for now, Laila would give this guy a go—and Wilde would take up with other women. He'd still see Laila platonically—she'd never want him out of her or especially Matthew's life—and then one day Designer Threads would be gone and Wilde would stay the night. Maybe that cycle was okay. Maybe that was how it was supposed to be. Or maybe Wilde should make himself less available and not be such a convenient out for her. Maybe he made it too easy for her to give up on a new relationship. Maybe not. Maybe she's better off with Wilde and she should forget Designer Threads. Maybe Wilde was self-rationalizing. And maybe, just maybe, he shouldn't be deciding what Laila really wants or needs or what's best for her.

Meanwhile it was late. He'd find Ava O'Brien in the morning. Maybe there'd be something there. Maybe, he thought as he paused and listened to the Mercedes pulling out of the driveway, he meant that in two ways.

CHAPTER SEVENTEEN

The first thing Wilde did when he rose at five a.m. was to check his text messages. There were none. Naomi had still not replied to his text. What did that mean? He had no idea.

Wilde threw on shorts and stretched in front of the Ecocapsule. The morning air was crisp. He sucked in a deep breath, felt the tingle. Wilde started most days with a walk-run through the woods. When he reached a peak, he took out the phone and texted Ava O'Brien and asked to see her at school. It was only five fifteen so he didn't expect an answer, but Ava was an early riser too, he remembered, as he watched the dancing dots indicating a response was coming soon. She suggested the teacher parking entrance behind the high school at one p.m. Wilde typed back:

> We are both up. How about I come over now?

Again the dancing dots. Then: Not a good time.

Wilde remembered the big bearded man and nodded to himself: One PM. Teacher parking entrance.

He finished up his hike, set up a lawn chair, started reading.

He had been a voracious reader for as long as he could remember. When the park rangers found him all those years ago, Wilde could already read, something that had perplexed the experts. Surely, they claimed, the only explanation was that the young boy was lying or confused—someone had fed him and clothed him and educated him. He couldn't have taught himself to read. But as far as Wilde knew, he had. He'd broken into homes and watched television, including so-called educational television shows like *Sesame Street* and *Reading Rainbow*. More to the point, in one house he'd found educational videotapes on how to teach your child to read.

That, he was sure, was how he'd learned to read.

Which brought him back to the DNA genealogy test.

He hadn't yet looked at the results. Did he want to? Did he need that confusion in his life? He was content as he was. He liked being a minimalist in every way, including the people in his life. So why open that door?

Was he curious?

He put down his book. It was a hardcover novel. He mostly read actual physical books rather than something on an e-reader, not because he disliked the technology or enjoyed the tactile experience of turning pages, but simply because he used enough electronic equipment up here and so printed material, read and then donated, served him best.

He found the email from the DNA site. Two months ago, he'd signed up under an alias and spit into the test tube. Wilde had several fake aliases. They were in metal storage boxes, advertised as both fire- and waterproof, buried in the woods within a hundred yards of here. There was also cash in the boxes, plus bank accounts in all those names, plenty of easy ways for Wilde to vanish if need be.

He clicked the link and then he typed in the username and password he'd set up when he sent in his DNA sample. It led to a page announcing his Ancestry Composition, which in his case was all over the place, the largest percentage being vaguely "Eastern

European." So what did that tell him? Nothing. Did it change the way he felt or get him closer to any truth? Nope, not really.

The smaller banner under his Ancestry Composition read:

> You have over a hundred relatives! Click the link to learn more!

Should he?

His mother or father could be behind that click. Wow, when you first thought about that. But then again, so what if they were? Most people sought these answers because they felt as though something was missing, that the answers could somehow fill some vague void. Most people wanted more people in their lives—more family, more relatives. Wilde did not. So why open this particular Pandora's box?

Then again, ignorance was never bliss. Wilde firmly believed that. So why not click the link? He didn't need to do more than take a quick peek for now. Just click and see whether the information is out there.

He tapped down on the link.

Wilde felt as though he were a contestant on a game show and the hostess was drawing a curtain and maybe there'd be a brand-new car or maybe there'd be nothing.

It turned out to be a lot closer to nothing.

There was no mother match, no father match, no full-sibling match, no half-sibling match. In fact, the closest relative listed was a second-to-third cousin with the initials PB who shared 2.44 percent of Wilde's DNA and eight segments. There was a small graph with the following explanation:

> You and PB may share a set of great-grandparents. You could also be from different generations (removed cousins) or share only one ancestor (half cousins).

It was something more than nothing, but not a lot more. He could, he guessed, contact PB and start working up some kind of family tree, but right now, today, with Naomi running away and Matthew deservedly haunted by what he'd done to her and Laila dating Designer Threads (not that he cared about that last one, he reminded himself), the idea exhausted him.

It could wait.

Wilde hadn't been back to Sweet Water High School since his own graduation. As he got closer, the ghosts joined him. Or at least, one ghost. He could almost feel David, Matthew's father, sidle up next to him. They'd walked like this together pretty much every day until David got his license during their junior year and drove them. The memories moved in for the kill, but Wilde battled back.

Not now. No distractions.

There had been no security guards when Wilde had attended. That wasn't the case anymore. The crisply uniformed rent-a-cops were both serious and armed. They had their eyes on him the moment he hit the main road. Wilde took the most visible approach, smiling and keeping his hands in plain view.

Hands in plain view approaching a high school. What a world.

"What can we do for you?" the taller cop asked.

"I'm supposed to meet Ava O'Brien in the teacher lot."

The other rent-a-cop sported a pencil-drawn mustache and looked young enough to be, if not still a student here, that guy who graduated a year or two earlier and spends all his time cruising around town in a beat-up sedan. He checked his clipboard for Wilde's name while the taller cop tried to stare him down. Wilde didn't mind that or the pat-down or the pocket emptying or the stroll through the metal detector. Sad how the world was now—really, did you want to arm two guys like this and stick them near a school? Do we really want to protect our children by giving guns to two underpaid cop wannabes and then mixing them in with a bunch of wiseass teens? Seemed a recipe for disaster. Wilde had worked in the security industry, so he knew that a lot of his competitors stoked these parental fears so they could cash in with big school contracts.

Create the problem—then monetize the solution.

The young armed guard made a phone call, and two minutes later, Ava O'Brien was leading him down a corridor. He liked the way Ava walked, which might seem like an odd thing to be thinking about, but there it was. She looked beautiful and strong.

It must have been between classes because the only sound was their feet on the linoleum. Wilde flashed back to his own years in these hallways. He still knew his way, of course. Do you ever forget? When they passed the gymnasium, Ava gestured to the portraits on the wall.

"I get to see your face every day."

There were probably fifty faces under the listing "Sweet Water Sports Hall of Fame." Wilde had been inducted under Track and Field. He didn't attend the ceremony. Not his scene. During his senior year, Wilde had set almost every running record in the school—hurdles, sprints, miles. The school's football coach tried to convince him to go for tailback, but Wilde didn't like team sports with their comradery and rah-rah high fives. He didn't like the football team in particular. Too tribal and clan-like.

"You look angry in the picture," Ava said.

"I was aiming for macho."

She studied it a second. "I'd say you didn't hit that mark."

"I rarely do."

His eyes scanned down the plaques searching for Rola Naser. It didn't take long. Rola's beaming smile—no attempt at macho here—hit him like a sunburst. That was how Rola Naser was—beaming, loquacious, earnest, enthusiastic—even at home. Pretty much the opposite of Wilde. Maybe that was a forced facade, her way of compensating for her upbringing, but if so, Wilde rarely saw her break character.

"Soccer captain," Ava said, following his eyes and reading Rola's plaque. "Wow, she was an all-American?"

"Rola was the best soccer player the school ever had."

"Was she a close friend?"

"Sister," Wilde said. Then: "Foster sister."

Ava led him into a classroom-cum-art-studio. There were splashes of color everywhere. Wilde took it all in. The room was comforting, what with the creations of the über-amateurish blended in with the super-gifted, the half-baked sculptures with works that could find a place in a museum. There was just life here. Lots of life.

"So I checked already," Ava began.

Her tone was matter-of-fact. Wilde waited.

"Naomi has been out for a few days," Ava said. "The absences are unexcused. The school has sent out warnings by email."

"I heard it was bad when she got back from the last disappearance."

"Heard from whom?"

"Her father," he said. No reason to bring Matthew in. Wilde quickly updated her on the rest—Bernard Pine reaching out to him, Naomi's bedroom, the missing clothes and backpack.

"Yeah, it was bad," she said when he finished. "As expected."

"How did Naomi react?"

"To the bullying?"

"Yeah."

"Naomi, I don't know, maybe she became withdrawn. I tried to get her to open up, but she didn't share much."

"Was there anyone else she might have talked to?"

"Not that I know of." Ava tilted her head. "She told me you were the one who found her. She said you two talked in her basement."

"Yes."

"She liked you, Wilde."

"I liked her too."

"Did she tell you why she went along with that awful game?"

"She hoped that it would be a reset," Wilde said.

"A reset?"

"A way to start again with her classmates. A do-over. She thought that maybe if she did it, really made a splash, everyone would look at her differently."

Ava shook her head. "I get it, but..."

Wilde said nothing.

"I wish these kids could understand how short high school is," she said.

"They can't."

"I know. My grandfather up in Maine turned ninety-two recently. I asked him what that was like—reaching that age. He said it's a finger snap. He said, 'One day I turned eighteen. I joined the army. I headed south to basic training. And now I'm here.' That fast. That's what he said. Like he got onto a bus with his duffle bag in 1948 and he got off now."

"He sounds like a cool guy," Wilde said.

"He is. I'm not sure why I told you that, except that if it's hard for us, two adults, to believe that—that our lives are going to whiz by that fast—it's impossible to convince a bullied sixteen-year-old girl that the world isn't this stupid high school."

Wilde nodded. "So do you have any thoughts on where Naomi is?"

"I think we both agree she probably ran away."

"Probably."

Ava asked, "Did you try her mother?"

"I thought you said—"

"Yeah, I know. But that was before. What Naomi said to you about starting over? She said something like that to me too. But after what happened with that Challenge game, she knew that it couldn't happen here, in this town. The fresh start meant a fresh place."

"So you think she could be with her mom?"

"Naomi told me her mother was going on a trip. I didn't really think about it at the time, but maybe there was longing in her voice."

"Do you know where the mother was going?"

"Just overseas."

"Okay, I'll reach out."

Ava looked at her watch. Wilde caught the hint.

"You probably have a class," he said.

"Yeah." Then: "About those texts I sent you the other night."

Wilde knew the ones she meant, of course: Come over tonight. I'll leave the door unlocked. And then: I miss you, Wilde.

"Don't worry about it."

"I wouldn't want anything more than we had. I just, I mean, I had a lonely moment."

"I get them too."

"You do?"

He saw no reason to repeat himself.

"It was odd," she said, "what we had. Now isn't the time. But..."

"It was nice," Wilde said. "Really nice."

"But it couldn't last, could it?" She didn't ask it with regret or anything like that.

Wilde didn't respond.

"It was like one of those vibrant creatures that only survive a short time. A whole life cycle packed into a few days."

He thought that was well put. "Yeah, pretty much."

They both stood. Neither was sure what to do. Ava stepped toward him and kissed his cheek. He looked in her eyes and almost told her that he was available. Almost. But he didn't.

Change the subject: "Do you know the Maynard kid?"

She blinked, took a step back. "Crash? By reputation."

"Which is?"

"Crappy. He used to torment Naomi, though maybe there was something more."

"More?"

"He doth protest too much methinks," Ava said in her best Shakespearean accent.

"Like he had a crush on her?"

"I wouldn't say that. He's dating Sutton Holmes. But I think Naomi fascinates Crash in ways that he probably couldn't quite articulate himself."

"Is Crash Maynard in school today?"

"Probably, why?"

"What time does school let out?"

CHAPTER EIGHTEEN

Hester donned her swim cap and did laps for forty-five minutes in the indoor pool on the lower level of her office high-rise. Swimming laps—freestyle down the lane, breaststroke back—had been her major exercise activity for two decades now. Before that, she hadn't really liked the pool. Changing out of a wet suit is a pain. You smell like chlorine. It does awful things to your hair. It is numbingly boring. But it was that last point—numbing boredom—that eventually sold Hester on it. Moments of pure alone, of pure silence, of yes, pure boredom—rote strokes you'll repeat hundreds if not thousands of times this very week—ended up being what others considered Zen. With her body encased in water and chemicals, Hester rehearsed summations, testimony, and cross-examinations.

Today though, alone in that pool, her body gently slicing through the water, she didn't think about work. She thought about Oren. She thought about tonight.

It's just a dinner, she reminded herself.

He'd asked her out.

It isn't a date. Just a meal with an old friend.

Wrong. A man doesn't drive to your place of work and ask you to share a meal as two old friends. This was not a drill. This *was* a date. The real McCoy.

Hester showered, blew out her hair, got dressed in her best power suit. When she got off the elevator, Sarah McLynn, her assistant, handed her a bunch of messages that needed her attention. Hester grabbed them, headed into her corner office, and closed the door. She sat at her desk, took a deep breath, and brought up the web browser.

"Don't, Hester," she said out loud.

But since when did Hester Crimstein take advice from anyone, especially from Hester Crimstein?

In the search field, Hester typed in "Cheryl Carmichael."

Yep. Oren's ex.

Half of Hester floated up and out of her body and tsk-tsked disapprovingly. The other half—the half still in the chair—frowned at the floating half and countered, "Yeah, right, like you're too good for this."

Hester hit the return button and let the screen load. The top searches were for a Cheryl Carmichael who worked as a professor at CUNY. Uh-uh, no—that was definitely the wrong Cheryl Carmichael. Hester scanned down the page. She wasn't sure what she'd find online about a divorced woman in her mid-to-late sixties. But when she found the right one—Cheryl Carmichael living in Vero Beach, Florida—what Hester uncovered was far worse than she'd imagined.

"My God..."

Cheryl Carmichael was all over social media. Her Instagram account had more than 800,000 followers. Her vertical Instagram bio or whatever you called it read:

Public Figure
Fitness Model
Influencer and Free Spirit
"I love life!"
#Over60andFabulous

Gag me, Hester thought.

Under the bio was an email address to write "For Inquiries." Inquiries? What kind of inquiries? Hester's mind spiraled down a prurient hole until she realized that by "inquiries" she meant paid endorsements. Yes, for real.

Companies paid Cheryl to pose with their products.

Looking at the photos on display made Hester's stomach knot. Cheryl, who used to have flowing locks down to the middle of her back—Hester remembered her at the Little League field in tight shorts and a tighter top, the dads pretending not to stare—now sported that mod, short, spiky hair. Her physique, which was on display in many risqué pictures with hashtags reading #bikinibabe #fitgoals #squats #loveyourself #beachbum, was all that and more.

Ugh. Cheryl Carmichael was still a knockout.

Hester's mobile rang. She checked the number and saw it was from Wilde.

"Articulate," she said.

"What are you doing?"

"Making myself feel immensely inadequate."

"Pardon?"

"Never mind. What's up?"

"Did the phone company get back to you?" Wilde asked.

He was talking about Naomi's phone. "They're monitoring it. So far, no activity."

"Meaning the phone is off?"

"Yes."

"Can they tell when and where it was powered off?"

"I'll check. Did you talk to Matthew last night?"

"Yeah."

"And?"

"And it might be better if you talk to him directly."

Wilde didn't want to betray Matthew's trust. Hester understood.

"There is one other thing you can do for me," Wilde said.

"I'm not much in the mood to put a lot of resources on this. I mean, unless you have some real evidence Naomi didn't just run away."

"Fair enough," Wilde said. "Can you make one more call to Naomi's mother?"

He briefly filled her in on his conversation with Ava O'Brien the art teacher.

"So if the mother took the kid, wouldn't she tell the father?" Hester asked.

"Who knows. A quick call to the mom might put it to rest. If you're too busy—"

"What, you're going to call? What would you say? 'Hi, I'm a single male in my late thirties looking for your daughter'?"

"Good point."

"I'll do it."

"You okay, Hester?"

She was staring at a photograph of Cheryl Carmichael in a one-piece that could be a cover shot for the *Sports Illustrated* swimsuit issue. "I'm average at best."

"You sound grouchier than usual."

"Maybe," she said. "Where are you?"

"Still at the high school. I want to try to question the Maynard kid."

Wilde hung up the call with Hester and turned to Ava.

"You sure about this?"

"Yes."

"It might blow back on you."

Ava shrugged. "I'm out at the end of the year anyway. All the part-timers are. Budget cuts."

"Sorry."

She waved it away. "It's time I moved back to Maine anyway."

They'd stayed in the same art room. Wilde had slowly circled, checking out the various student works throughout the room. It was, in some ways, the greatest museum he'd ever seen. There were drawings and watercolors and sculptures and mobiles and pottery and jewelry, and while the talent level was naturally all over the place, the heart and creativity were never less than mesmerizing.

They stood by the door and waited for the final bell.

"This wasn't an art room when I was here," he said.

"What was it?"

"Shop with Mr. Cece."

She smiled. "Did you make a lamp or footstool?"

"Lamp."

"Where is it now?"

He had given it to the Brewers, his foster-cum-adoptive parents who retired to a gated community in Jupiter, Florida. Wilde and his foster sister Rola had helped the Brewers move in eight years ago, renting a U-Haul for the long drive down Interstate 95. Rola kept wanting to stop at roadside oddities along the way, like the UFO Welcome Center in South Carolina and America's smallest church in Georgia.

Wilde hadn't been back to Florida since.

When the bell trilled, Wilde slipped into a supply closet. Ava stood near the door to the corridor.

Two minutes later, Crash Maynard came in. "You wanted to see me, Miss O'Brien?"

Wilde left the closet door open a crack so he could watch.

Ava said, "Yes, thank you."

Crash touched a clay sculpture standing by the stool.

"That's still drying," Ava warned him.

"I don't get why you paged me. I haven't taken an art class since freshman year."

"This isn't about art. Why don't you have a seat?"

"My mom's waiting for me, so—"

"Do you know where Naomi Pine is?"

Wilde liked that. No reason to play around.

"Me?" Crash said it as though the very notion that he might know was the most shocking and incomprehensible concept ever uttered. "Why would I know?"

"You and Naomi are classmates."

"Yeah, but..."

"But?"

Crash gave a chuckle that seemed both nervous and cocky at the same time. "We aren't exactly friends or anything."

"But you talk."

"No, we don't."

Ava folded her arms. "Why should she tell me that you did?"

"Naomi said that?"

"Yes."

Crash gave it a second. You could see the wheels turning as an aw-shucks smile spread across his face. "I shouldn't say this."

"But?"

"I think Naomi might have a thing for me."

"And if she did?"

"Well, I mean, if she said we talked"—shrug—"I don't know, maybe she was trying to show off or something."

"Show off?"

"Yeah. Or, I don't know, I'm nice to her and all. So, like, if she says hi to me, I say hi back."

"Wow," Ava said. "That *is* nice."

The sarcasm went right over his head. "But really we don't have any serious interaction. You know what I mean?"

"I think I do," Ava said. "Now tell me about the night Matthew ghosted her or whatever you call it at your house."

Silence.

"Crash?"

He lifted his phone into view and touched a button. Wilde didn't like that. "My mom is texting me, Ms. O'Brien."

"Okay."

"I have to go."

"Answer my question first."

"Yeah, I don't know what you're talking about."

"Yes, you do. Naomi told me—"

"She told you?"

"Yes—"

"Then there's no reason to ask me about it," Crash said, which, Wilde had to admit, was a pretty decent rejoinder. "I'd better leave now, Ms. O'Brien."

"I want to know—"

Crash spun toward her, getting a little too close. "I don't know anything about Naomi Pine!" The aw-shucks tone was gone. "Nothing!"

Ava didn't back away. "You saw her that night."

"So what if I did? She was on my property."

"Why did you tell Matthew Crimstein to prank her?"

"Did Matthew tell you that?" He shook his head. "Look, I'm allowed to leave, right? You can't force me to stay, can you?"

"No, of course not—"

"Then I'm out of here."

Wilde figured, *Why not?* He opened the closet door and said, "I can stop you." He crossed the room and positioned himself so that his back was against the door, literally blocking the teen's exit. Ava shot him a look and shook her head. The look and headshake both said that this wasn't the way to handle it.

Crash scowled. "What is this?"

"Tell us where Naomi is," Wilde said.

His eyes narrowed. "You came to my house the other night. You're the one who grabbed the gun from my guard."

Ava shot Wilde another look. He ignored it.

"You're not in trouble," Wilde said, which may or may not have been true. "We just need to find Naomi."

The door behind Wilde suddenly burst open, hitting him in the back and throwing him off balance. Thor surged through the door, lowering his shoulder like a blitzing linebacker. Wilde cursed himself. Of course, the kid would have security. Of course, he'd use his phone to signal he needed help. Stupid of Wilde to be caught off guard.

Now he was in serious trouble.

Thor leapt toward Wilde. No hesitancy. Wilde was still trying to get his bearings.

But it was too late.

Thor wrapped his muscled arms around Wilde, his shoulder in the midsection, and drove Wilde back. Squeezing and lifting Wilde right off the ground, Thor kept his legs going, ready to slam Wilde into the floor.

This was definitely not good.

Thor was mad. Probably upset about being embarrassed when Wilde disarmed him in front of his boss. This was payback.

Wilde debated his next move. There really wasn't one. He was off his feet, in a bear hug, with milliseconds before he hit the floor. If they were standing or slowed down, he might try to headbutt the big man's nose. But Thor had lowered his face into Wilde's chest.

That wouldn't work.

Nothing would.

He would have to brace for the blow and recover. Plan the next move.

At the last possible moment, Wilde twisted his body hard. It didn't stop him from getting slammed to the ground. Not at all. He got slammed on the Formica, slammed hard. The air whooshed out of him. But by twisting his body, Wilde had wrenched Thor's grip enough so that instead of Thor's arm landing on the meaty flesh beneath the forearm, his elbow took the brunt of the fall.

That hurt too.

One man had a hurt elbow. But the other man—Wilde—couldn't breathe.

Distance, Wilde thought.

That was his only thought. Distance. Get away from his attacker. Put as much space as possible between himself and Thor.

Regroup, recover.

Still on the floor, Wilde tried to ignore the desire, nay, the absolute *need* to breathe. That was the thing. He'd had the wind knocked out of him before. It was paralyzing and awful, but what he'd learned with experience was that the paralysis was mostly caused by fear—you *feel* as though you'll suffocate, that you'll never breathe again. That shut down everything. Orders from the brain to the feet or legs were cut off. But Wilde now knew, despite all his primitive instincts telling him otherwise, that his breath would eventually return, faster if he didn't panic, and so he fought through the temptation to just stay where he was and curl up into a ball until he could recover his breath.

With his lungs bursting, Wilde log-rolled away.

"Get off him!" Ava shouted.

But Thor was relentless. He dove on top of him, driving his knees into the small of Wilde's back. The jolt sent what felt like shards of glass up his spine. Ava tried to pull Thor away, but he shrugged her off like so little dandruff. Wilde tried to spin, to help, but Thor was having none of it. He snaked his arm under Wilde's, and the grappling began in earnest. When you look at old movies or training films, it was all about the strikes. Men stood and threw punches, sometimes kicks. The majority of fights, however, ended up on the ground. Grappling matches. Thor would have the size and weight advantage. He'd have the element of surprise. He'd have the fact that Wilde was still trying to catch his breath.

The key to victory often involved sacrifice. Wilde watched enough football to know that the quarterbacks who stood in the pocket, who didn't wince even when a three-hundred-pound lineman was about to demolish them like a freight train, those were the ones who succeeded. The greats took the hit while never losing focus on their target.

That was what Wilde did right now.

He let the bigger man land a few blows. Because he had one target.

A finger.

He shifted, knowing that Thor would have to grab him near his shoulder to keep him in place. He waited for that. He concentrated on that—Thor's hand heading for his shoulder—and only that. And when Thor reached for him, Wilde let go with both hands, grabbed one of Thor's fingers, and bent it back with everything he had.

The finger broke with an audible snap.

Thor howled.

Distance, Wilde thought.

He rolled away again. He could see the toxic mix of rage and pain in Thor's face. The big man prepared to launch himself again, but a voice cut through the air like a reaper's scythe. "That's enough."

It was Gavin Chambers.

CHAPTER NINETEEN

Once in the school parking lot, Gavin Chambers packed Thor, who was cradling his broken finger as though it were a wounded pet, into a black Cadillac Escalade and sent him on his way. He put a sheepish Crash into a white Mercedes-Benz S-Class coupe, driven by Crash's mother. The mother—Wilde knew that her name was Delia—was having none of it. She got out of the car and demanded an explanation from Gavin. Wilde stood too far away to hear what was being said—but he was still close enough to get pierced by the occasional maternal eye-dagger.

Kids from the school had gathered. Wilde recognized Kyle and Ryan and Sutton and a few of the other kids Matthew had told him about over the years. Matthew was there too, looking properly mortified. He met Wilde's eye as if to say, *What gives?* Wilde gave him nothing in return.

Eventually, Delia Maynard got back into her car, slammed the door, and drove away with Crash in the passenger seat. The onlookers, including Matthew, dispersed. Gavin Chambers made his way back over to Wilde and said, "Let's take a walk."

They strolled between a fence and the building's brick back.

Wilde could see the football field, and more relevant to his past, the quarter-mile track that encircled it. That was the spot of his purported "glory days," though no waves of nostalgia washed over him. He didn't suddenly see himself as a sprinting teen or anything like that. You move forward in life. You may give the old you a nod every once in a while, but the old you is gone and not coming back. That was often a good thing.

"I thought the girl was found," Gavin said.

"She's gone again."

"You mind telling me about it?"

"Yeah, I do."

Gavin shook his head. "What you did here—confronting the kid like that, injuring my man—it makes me look bad." He stopped. "I thought we had an understanding."

"That was before Naomi vanished again."

"And you have evidence that Crash is involved?"

Wilde didn't say anything.

Gavin put his hand to his ear. "I can't hear you."

"It was why I was asking him questions."

"I think you went a little too far, don't you? His mother is furious. She wants to report the art teacher."

"It's on me, not her."

"Noble of you, but I'm not sure the school board will agree."

"Threatening the schoolteacher's job," Wilde said with a small shake of the head. "That's kind of beneath you, isn't it?"

Gavin smiled. "It is, yes. I read up on you, Wilde. Most of your military record is classified, but, well, I'm not without means. Very impressive. Your whole life story is. But as I said before, I have the manpower and resources. So here is our new deal. I'll question the kid for you. If Crash Maynard knows anything about this girl, I'll tell you."

They kept walking.

"I have a question," Wilde said.

"I'm listening."

"Last time we talked you said there was much more at stake here than a teenage brawl."

"Is that a question?"

"What's at stake?"

"You don't want to know."

"Seriously?"

Gavin Chambers smiled. "It has nothing to do with Naomi Pine."

"Does it have something to do with Rusty Eggers?"

Another black Cadillac Escalade pulled in front of them. Gavin slapped him on the back and moved toward it.

"Stay in touch," he said to Wilde, "but stay away."

When Wilde entered the woods on his way back to the Ecocapsule, Matthew was waiting for him, pacing, his hands in tight fists. "What the hell was that all about?"

"You seem upset," Wilde said.

Wilde headed up the path. Matthew fell in behind him.

"Well?"

"Well what?"

"What were you doing at my school?"

"I asked Crash Maynard about Naomi."

"At my school? Are you kidding me?"

"That a problem, Matthew?"

"I have to go to school here. You get that, right?"

Wilde stopped.

"What?" Matthew asked.

"Did you already forget what you did to her?"

That shut the boy up. Wilde watched the blood drain from Matthew's face. The woods stood silent, solemn. Matthew's voice, when he found it, was soft. "No."

His chin was down—and ah damn, just like David. The echo

of the father was so strong on the son's face right now that Wilde almost took a step back. A few seconds later, Matthew's chin rose. He saw the expression on Wilde's face and snapped, "Cut that out."

"I'm not doing anything."

"Yeah, you are," Matthew said. "You know I hate when you give me that 'oh my God, he looks like his dad' face."

Wilde couldn't help but smile. "Fair enough."

"Just stop it."

"Okay, I'm sorry." Wilde mimed wiping away the expression on his face with his hand. "See?"

Matthew sighed. "You can be so lame."

Wilde smiled.

"What?"

"That's the kind of thing your father would have said."

Matthew rolled his eyes. "Will you stop?"

He often warned Matthew that he would bring up his father, like it or not. He didn't do it to appease David's ghost or any of that—dead was dead in Wilde's worldview—but for Matthew. He had been robbed of his father. It doesn't mean he should be robbed of the memory or influence.

"So what would Saint Dad say about this?" Matthew asked in the most grudging tone he could muster.

"About what?"

"About what I did to Naomi?"

"He'd be pissed."

"Would he ground me?"

"Oh yeah. He'd also make you apologize."

"I tried to." Then: "I will."

"Cool. And your dad wasn't a saint. He messed up plenty. But he also made amends."

They were heading across the ravine, not far from the Ecocapsule, when Matthew said, "Always?"

"Always what?"

"Did he always make amends?"

Wilde felt something flutter inside his chest. "He tried."

"Mom thinks you're hiding something about the night of the accident."

Wilde didn't break stride, but the words stung. "She told you that?"

"Are you?"

"No."

Matthew eyed him. Forget David—the kid was more like Laila when he gave him the skeptical eye. Then Matthew blinked and said, "Doesn't matter, does it? He's dead either way."

Wilde thought about it and decided that his comment didn't require a response.

Matthew asked, "So what did Crash tell you?"

The subject change plus the alternate definition of the word—"Crash" the name as opposed to "crash" as in the accident—threw him for a moment. "Not much. But he seemed nervous."

"So you think, what, that Crash did something to Naomi?"

"All signs still indicate she ran off on her own."

"But?"

"But something isn't adding up for me."

Matthew smiled at that. "Didn't you teach me that there is always chaos?"

"Anomalies are to be expected, but there is still a certain pattern to the chaos."

"A pattern to the chaos," Matthew repeated. "That doesn't make much sense."

True enough, Wilde thought.

"I think..." Matthew stammered. "I think what I did to Naomi that night. Not showing up. I feel guilty, I guess. This is all my fault in some ways, right?"

Matthew waited. Wilde waited.

Then Wilde said, "You want me to say something comforting here?"

"Only if you feel it."

"I don't."

They arrived at the Ecocapsule. Matthew, the only guest he ever had out here, liked to do homework in the tighter confines. "Fewer distractions," he told Wilde. Matthew wanted to study for a physics test. The kid was good in the sciences. Wilde stayed outside and read his book.

Two hours later, Matthew emerged.

"Good study sesh?" Wilde asked.

"Yes, thank you. And never say 'sesh' again."

They made the trek back toward Matthew's house. When they arrived, Wilde said he wanted some water. Normally he'd leave once he made sure Matthew was inside, but what with the strangeness around Naomi and even Crash, it might pay to hang around until his mother got home.

He also wanted to see Laila for two reasons. The first was what Matthew had just told him—that Laila still questioned the official account of what happened on that treacherous mountain road all those years ago.

"Matthew?"

"Yeah?"

Wilde thought back to Ava's conversation with Crash. "Anything you're keeping from me?"

"Huh?"

"About Naomi."

"No."

Matthew handed him the glass of water. Then he headed up to his bedroom and closed the door. He didn't tell Wilde what he was up to and Wilde didn't ask. Wilde sat in the den and waited. At seven p.m., Laila's car glided into the driveway. He stood when she opened the door.

"Hey," Laila said when she saw him.

"Hey."

"I've been meaning to talk to you," Laila said.

This was the second—and more important—reason Wilde had stayed.

"Yeah, I know," Wilde said.

Laila stopped. "You know?"

"I was here the other night with Matthew when you pulled up. I ducked out the back."

"Oh," Laila said.

"Yeah."

"Early days," Laila said. "I don't know if it'll go anywhere—"

"You don't need to explain—"

"—but it might."

Laila just looked at him. He got the message. She was ready to take the relationship with Designer Threads to the next level. The physical level, for those slow on the take.

"No worries," Wilde said.

"Plenty of worries," Laila countered.

"I mean—"

"I know what you mean, Wilde."

He nodded and stood. "I better go."

"It won't be weird, right?"

"It never is, is it?"

"Sometimes it is, yeah," Laila said. "And sometimes you stay away too much."

"I don't want to intrude."

"You won't intrude. But Matthew still needs you. I still need you."

He crossed the room and kissed her cheek with almost too much tenderness. "I'll be here when you need me."

"I love you, Wilde."

"I love you too, Laila."

He smiled. She smiled. Wilde felt something in his chest crack a little. Laila . . . well, he didn't know what she felt.

"Good night," he said, and left by the back door.

CHAPTER TWENTY

Hester chose the restaurant—RedFarm, a modern dim sum joint that mixes delicious with casual and a touch of food humor. Her favorite dumplings, for example, were called "Pac Man" and looked like the ghostly creatures from the old video game. RedFarm didn't take reservations, but Hester came often and so she knew a guy who could get her a corner table when she needed it. The vibe here was creative and cool rather than romantic and quiet, but hey, first date.

No pressure, right?

Oren had trusted Hester to order. Now the table was loaded up with dumplings—three-color vegetable, shrimp and mango, pork and crab soup (another favorite), crispy oxtail, black truffle chicken.

"Heaven," Oren muttered between bites.

"You like?"

"It's so delicious I'm almost forgetting how wonderful the company is."

"Smooth line," Hester said. "Can I ask you about your ex-wife?"

His chopsticks had just clamped down on a dumpling. "Seriously?"

"I'm not good with subtlety."

"Nice demonstration of that."

"And it's on my mind."

"My ex-wife is on your mind?"

"I just have a few questions. I can sit here and let them distract me or I can just ask them."

Oren picked up the dim sum. "I don't want you distracted."

"I found Cheryl's Instagram page."

"Ah," he said.

"You've seen it?"

"I haven't, no. I don't do social media."

"But you know about it?"

"I do, yes."

"Do you still think about her?"

"I'm supposed to answer no, right?"

"I saw the pics."

"Uh-huh."

"So I don't blame you."

"Of course I still think about her—but not like that. We were married for twenty-eight years. Do you still think of Ira?"

Hester didn't answer right away. She had tried on a dozen outfits before settling on this dress. It was only as she caught her reflection in a window on the street that she realized it was a dress Ira always said made her look sexy.

"We both have pasts, Hester."

"I just..." She wasn't sure how to put it. "We're so different. Cheryl and I."

"Yes."

"I know this is only a first date, but she's just so... sexy."

"So are you."

"Don't patronize me, Oren."

"I'm not. I get it. But this isn't a competition."

"Thank God for that. You said Cheryl left you."

"She did and she didn't."

"Meaning?"

"I think I left her first. At least emotionally. She left me because in part I left her." He put down his chopsticks and wiped his napkin with his chin. His movements were deliberate now. "When the kids were gone, I think Cheryl felt adrift. You know our town. It's about raising families. When that's gone, well, you, Hester, have a career. But Cheryl just looked around her and the kids are gone and I'm still going to work every day and she's either at home or playing tennis or going to Zumba or whatever."

"So she just ended it?"

"One of us doesn't have to be at fault. Divorce doesn't mean your marriage was a failure."

"Uh, sorry to disagree, but divorce seems to be pretty much the definition of a failed marriage."

Oren clenched his jaw and turned away for a moment. "Cheryl and I had twenty-eight years together. We raised three good kids. We have a grandchild and another on the way. Put it this way: If you owned a car for twenty-eight years and then it breaks down, does that make the car a failure?"

Hester frowned. "That analogy is a stretch."

"Then how about this one? If life is a book, we are both starting new chapters. She'll always be important to me. I'll always wish her happiness."

"She's just—to continue with this analogy—not in your chapters anymore?"

"Exactly."

Hester shook her head. "God, that's so mature I want to barf."

Oren smiled. "Not until I try that crispy oxtail dim sum please."

"Okay, one final question," Hester said.

"Fine, go ahead."

Hester cupped her hands in front of her chest. "Cheryl had a boob job, right? I mean, those puppies are high enough to double as earrings."

Oren laughed as Hester felt her phone vibrate. She counted the pulses in her head.

"Three pulses," she said. "I have to take it."

"What?"

"One pulse is just a regular call. Two pulses means it's work. Three, it's something important and I should pick it up."

Oren gestured with both hands. "Pick it up already."

She put the phone to her ear. It was Sarah McLynn from her office.

"What's up?" Hester asked.

"Are you on your date?"

"You're interrupting it."

"Sneak a photo of him. I want to see."

"Was there another reason for this call?"

"Does there have to be?"

"Sarah."

"Fine. I reached out to Naomi's mother like you asked."

"And?"

"And she refuses to talk to you. She said to mind your own business and hung up."

Gavin Chambers was at the window of his office high-rise in midtown, looking down at the "protestors"—a ragtag group of aging grunge-ola that probably numbered no more than twenty—mulling inside the building's courtyard. The chant—"Release the tapes!"—was hardly catching fire. The quasi-vagrants held up signs for every left-wing cause. Two of the women donned faded pink knit caps. According to the various signs, they wanted to Free Palestine, Resist, Abolish ICE—but their hearts didn't seem to be in it today. The march looked to Gavin more like a languid sway.

Delia joined him at the window. "Isn't that—?"

"Saul Strauss," Gavin said with a nod. His old war buddy wasn't hard to spot, Saul being close to six six and sporting the long gray ponytail that was so on point it could only be there to *be* on point.

Dash finished up a phone call and moved next to his wife. There was an ease between Dash and Delia, always, a flow, and while Gavin had had plenty of great relationships in his life, he envied these two. People can fool you—they fool you every day—but Gavin had been hanging around the Maynards long enough to recognize that Dash and Delia were the real deal, the kind of love that makes yours, no matter how good, seem somewhat inadequate. It wasn't just what they said. It wasn't just how they looked at each other or casually touched. There was an intangible here, that mix of great friendship and physical attraction, and maybe that was something Gavin was projecting on them, but when they talk about a soulmate, one person in this world that is perfect for you and almost impossible to find, Dash and Delia seemed to have done just that.

"What do the protestors want?" Delia asked.

"You can hear them," Gavin said. "They want the tapes."

"There are no tapes," Delia replied.

"They don't believe that."

"Do you, Gavin?" she asked.

"Doesn't matter."

"That's not an answer."

"I'll protect you either way."

Dash finally spoke. "That's not what she asked."

Gavin looked at Dash, then back at Delia. "Of course there are tapes," Gavin said. "Are they as damaging to Rusty as our hemp-adorned friends below would like to believe? Not for me to say."

Dash moved back toward his office desk. "You understand the situation then."

Gavin didn't bother with a response.

"We aren't safe," Delia said, moving with her husband. "If Crash could be approached like that in his very school—"

"That won't happen again."

Dash put his arm around his wife's shoulder. Again Gavin

couldn't help but notice the ease, the naturalness, the tenderness, in this everyday move. "Not good enough."

"Who was that man?" Delia asked.

"Crash didn't tell you?"

Delia shook her head. "He said he kept asking about Naomi Pine."

"They call him Wilde."

"Wait, he's that weird mountain guy they found in the woods?"

"Yes."

"I don't get it. What does he have to do with Naomi Pine?"

"He is something of a surrogate parent for Matthew Crimstein. For some reason, Matthew and his family are interested in Naomi's whereabouts."

"Crimstein," Dash repeated. "As in Hester?"

"Yes."

No one liked that.

"Crash swears he doesn't know anything about Naomi," Delia said. When Gavin didn't respond, she asked, "Do you think he does?"

"Crash has been in touch with her. Naomi Pine, I mean. As you probably know, she disappeared a week or so ago playing a game called Challenge."

"Some of the mothers were talking about that."

"Crash . . . encouraged her to do it."

"Are you saying he forced her?"

"No, but peer pressure was a major factor."

"You don't think Crash did something bad to this girl, do you?"

"Very doubtful," Gavin said. "He's too monitored."

They both were visibly relieved.

"But that doesn't mean he knows nothing about it."

"So what do we do? I don't like this." Delia looked down at the courtyard again. Saul Strauss was staring straight up, almost as though he could see them through the one-way windows. "I don't like any of this."

"I would suggest the family take a bit of a break from this town. Maybe travel overseas."

"Why?"

"People perceive Rusty Eggers as an existential threat."

Gavin Chambers waited for one of them to argue this point. Neither did.

Delia said, "Gavin?"

"Yes."

"We are safe, right? You won't let anything happen to our son."

"You're safe," Gavin said. "He's safe."

CHAPTER TWENTY-ONE

Matthew made himself a peanut butter and jelly sandwich, sat alone at the kitchen table, ate it, still felt hungry, made a second, and was eating when there was a knock on his back door.

He looked out the window and was surprised—closer to shocked—to see Crash Maynard. Prepared for anything, Matthew carefully opened the door halfway.

"Hey," Crash said.

"Hey."

"Can I come in a second?"

Matthew didn't move or open the door any wider. "What's up?"

"I just..." Crash used his sleeve to wipe his eyes. He looked out at the yard. "Remember when we used to play kickball out here?"

"In fifth grade."

"We sat next to each other in Mr. Richardson's class," Crash said. "He was out there, wasn't he?"

"Yeah."

"But he was also kinda awesome."

"He was," Matthew agreed.

"We were tight then, remember?"

"Yeah," Matthew said. "I guess."

"It was easier."

"What was?"

"Everything. No one really cared about who had the big house or what other people thought. We just...we cared about kickball."

Matthew knew this wasn't exactly true. It may have been a more innocent time, but it wasn't that innocent.

"What do you want, Crash?"

"To say I'm sorry."

Tears streamed down his cheeks. His voice was more a sob now.

"I'm so damn sorry."

Matthew stepped back. "Why don't you come in?"

But Crash didn't move. "There is so much shit going down around my house right now. I know that's no excuse, but it's like I'm living on top of a volcano and I'm waiting for it to erupt."

Gone was the high-school-hallway confidence, the swagger, the sneer. Matthew wasn't sure what to make of this, but something felt very wrong. "Come on in," he tried again. "We used to drink Yoo-hoo, right? I think my mom still has some in the fridge."

Crash shook his head. "I can't. They'll be looking for me."

"Who?"

"I just wanted you to know, okay? I'm really sorry I hurt you. And Naomi. What I did..."

"Crash, just come in—"

But Crash was already running away.

Wilde didn't feel like going back to his Ecocapsule yet.

His regular hangout—as much as one could say he had such a thing—was a bar located in the atrium lobby of the glass-towered Sheraton hotel on Route 17 in Mahwah, New Jersey. The hotel advertised itself as "unfussy yet upscale," which seemed pretty close to the truth. This was a hotel for businesspeople, here for one night, maybe two, and that worked for both the guests and Wilde.

The Sheraton's bar had a nice open feel, being in a glass atrium. The bartenders, like Nicole McCrystal who gave him a welcoming smile as he entered, stayed the same, while the clientele, mostly young executives blowing off a little steam, constantly changed. Wilde liked hotel bars for that latter reason—the transient nature, the openness, the rooms and beds being conveniently located only an elevator ride away should they be needed.

Was it too soon?

Probably, but how long should Wilde give it? A week? Two weeks? The wait seemed arbitrary and unnecessary. He wasn't heartbroken. Neither was Laila.

It was what it was.

"Wilde!" Nicole called out, clearly happy to see him.

She brought him a beer. When it came to beer, he was, like the hotel, "unfussy," but he enjoyed whatever local ale was on tap. Today, that was a "blonde lager" from the Asbury Park Brewery. Nicole leaned over the bar to buss his cheek. Tom down at the other end gave him a wave.

"Been a while," she said to him.

Nicole smiled. She had a kind smile.

"Yeah."

"Back on the prowl?"

He didn't reply to that one because he didn't yet know the answer.

She leaned toward him. "A few past conquests were asking about you."

"Don't call them that."

"What name would you prefer?" A guy bellied up to the other end of the bar and raised his hand. Nicole said, "Think it over and I'll be back later."

Wilde took a deep sip from his mug and listened to the hum of the hotel. His phone buzzed. It was Hester.

"Wilde?"

He could barely hear her over the background noise on her end. "Where are you?" he asked.

"At a restaurant."

"I see."

"I'm on a date."

"I see."

"With Oren Carmichael."

"I see."

"You're a great conversationalist, Wilde. Such enthusiasm."

"Do you want me to yell, 'Yippee'?"

"Naomi's mother won't talk to me."

"What do you mean by that?"

"What do you think I mean? I mean she won't talk to me. She refuses to return my calls. She says her daughter is none of my business."

"So Naomi is with her?"

"I don't know. I was going to send my investigator over to her house, but get this: She's vacationing in the south of Spain."

"So maybe Naomi is traveling with her. Maybe Naomi needed to escape all the bullying so her mother took her to Spain."

"Where are you, Wilde?"

"I'm at the Sheraton bar."

"Careful," Hester said. "You hold your liquor like an eighteen-year-old co-ed at her first mixer."

"What's a mixer?"

"You're too young to know."

"For that matter, what's a co-ed?"

"Funny. Let's talk in the morning. I have to get back to Oren."

"You're on a date," Wilde said. Then: "Yippee."

"Wiseass."

At some point, Wilde found himself talking to Sondra, a redhead in her early thirties with tight slacks and an easy laugh. They sat at the quiet end of the bar. She'd been born in Morocco, where her father had been working for the embassy. "He was CIA," she told him. "Pretty much all embassy employees are spies. Not just the USA ones. All over. I mean, think about it. You get to bring in whoever you want to a protected location in the heart of a foreign country—of course you're going to send your best counterintelligence people, right?" Sondra had moved around a lot as a kid, embassy to embassy, mostly in Africa and the Middle East. "My hair fascinated them. There are so many superstitions surrounding redheads." She'd gone to UCLA and loved it and got a degree in hotel management. She was divorced and had one son, age six, at home. "I don't travel much, but I do this trip every year." Her son was staying with his dad. She and her ex got along. She liked staying at this Sheraton. They always upgraded her room to the presidential suite. "You have to see it," she said in a tone that could knock a movie rating from PG to R. "Top floor. You can see the skyline of New York from it. It's three rooms, so like, if we just wanted to have a drink in the living room space, I mean, I don't want you to think..."

Eventually Sondra gave him a key card.

"They gave me two when I came in," Sondra quickly explained. "One for the living room, one for the bedroom, you know what I mean?"

Wilde, still nursing his second blonde lager, assured her that he did.

"Anyway, I can't sleep yet with the time change. I'm going to do some work in the living room, if you want to come up later and have a nightcap."

Nightcap. Mixer. Co-ed. It was like he was living in 1963.

He thanked Sondra but promised nothing. She headed to the elevator. He stared at the key card so as not to stare at her. A drink, she'd said. In the living room—not the bedroom. Maybe that was all it was. Maybe it was nothing more than that.

Then a tall man with a ponytail asked, "Are you going to go up?"

The tall man grabbed the stool right next to him, despite the fact that there had to be twenty open ones.

"She's very attractive," the tall man said. "I like redheads, don't you?"

Wilde said nothing.

The tall man stuck out his hand. "My name is Saul," he said.

"Strauss," Wilde added.

"You know who I am?"

Wilde didn't reply.

"Well, I'm flattered."

Wilde had seen Strauss on Hester's show every once in a while. He was a good talking head—an endearing mix of that super-progressive college professor with the cred of being a bona fide war hero. Wilde was not a fan of pundits. They came on television to either confirm your narrative or piss you off, and either way, that wasn't healthy for anyone.

"I didn't catch your name," Strauss said.

"But you know it."

"Does anyone?" He gave Wilde an inquisitive look that must wow the college—to use Hester's vernacular—co-eds. "They call you Wilde, right? You're the infamous boy from the woods."

Wilde pulled out the necessary bills from his wallet and dropped them on the bar. "It was nice meeting you," he said, rising.

Strauss was unruffled. "So you're going up to her room?"

"Seriously?"

"I don't mean to pry."

"Hey, Saul—can I call you Saul?"

"Sure."

"Why don't we skip the rest of the foreplay and get to it?"

"Is that your plan when you go upstairs?" Strauss quickly raised a palm. "Sorry, that was going too far."

Wilde started to walk away.

Strauss said, "I hear you had a run-in with the Maynard kid today."

Wilde turned back to him.

"You asked me to skip the foreplay, right?" Strauss said.

"Heard from whom?"

"I have my sources."

"And they are?"

"Anonymous."

"Bye then."

Strauss put his hand on Wilde's forearm. His grip was surprisingly strong. "It could be important."

Wilde hesitated, but then he sat back down. He was curious. Strauss was a partisan—who wasn't nowadays?—but he'd also hit Wilde as something of a straight shooter. Instinctively, Wilde had thought that the best move was to simply blow the man off, but with a little more time to reason, he started to wonder what he had to lose by listening here.

Not a thing.

Wilde said, "I'm looking for a teenage girl who probably ran away."

"Naomi Pine."

Wilde shouldn't have been surprised. "Your sources are good."

"You're not the only one here who is ex-military. What does Crash Maynard have to do with Naomi Pine?"

Strauss was all business now.

"Maybe nothing."

"But?"

"She's an outcast. He's Mr. Popular. Yet there's been some interaction."

"Could you be more specific?" Strauss asked.

"Why don't you ask your 'source'?"

"Do you know anything about the Maynards' relationship with Rusty Eggers?"

"I know that Maynard was his producer."

"Dash Maynard created Eggers."

"Okay."

Strauss leaned in closer. "Do you realize how dangerous Eggers is?"

Wilde saw no reason to answer that one.

"Do you?" Strauss insisted.

"Let's say I do."

"And you've heard about the Maynard tapes?"

"I don't see the connection," Wilde said.

"There may not be one. Wilde, can I ask you a favor? Not a favor really. You're a patriot. You want those tapes released, I'm sure."

"You don't know what I want."

"I know you want the truth. I know you want justice."

"And I don't know that you bring either of those things."

"Truth is an absolute. Or it used to be. The Maynard tapes should be released because the people should know the truth about Rusty Eggers. Who can argue with that? If the people see the truth—the full truth—and still want to hand the keys to the country to this nihilist, okay, that's one thing."

"Saul?"

"Yes."

"Get to the point."

"Just keep me informed—and I'll keep you informed. It's your best bet for finding that girl. You served admirably because you love this country. But Eggers is a threat like none this country has faced before. He's hoodwinking this nation with his charisma, but his supposed 'manifesto' is really a call for anarchy. It'll lead to food shortages, worldwide panic, constitutional crises, and even war." Saul slid a little closer and lowered his voice. "Suppose the Maynard tapes show the real Rusty Eggers. Suppose they open people's eyes to the grave dangers right in front of them. This is bigger than any mission we undertook overseas, Wilde. You have to believe me on that."

He handed Wilde a card with his mobile phone and email. Then he slapped him on the back and walked past the reception desk toward the door.

Wilde pocketed Saul Strauss's business card and stood.

He meandered toward the lobby bathroom, urinated for a fairly long time, then—to quote-paraphrase Springsteen—he checked his look in the mirror and wanted to change his clothes, his hair, his face. He splashed water on his cheeks and tidied himself up as best he could. He walked to the glass elevator and pressed the up button. Nicole the bartender caught his eye and gave a small nod. He didn't know how to read it or if it meant anything at all, so he gave her a small nod back.

To get to the top floor you needed to slide a key card into the slot. He did that with the card Sondra had given him. He rode up, leaning against the glass, looking down as the lobby grew smaller and smaller. Faces swirled through his mind's eye—Matthew, Naomi, Crash, Gavin, Saul, Hester, Ava, Laila. Laila.

Shit.

He got out and headed down the corridor. He stopped in front of the door with the brass sign reading PRESIDENTIAL SUITE in fancy script. He looked at his key card. He looked at the door. Sondra was beautiful. You could criticize this type of relationship or label it or consider it empty or whatever other judgment card you feel like pulling out, but it was all a matter of perspective. He and Sondra could link up and have something special. Just because it didn't last did not make it less so. Cliché, sure, but everything dies. A beautiful rose lives but a short time. Certain termites can survive for sixty years.

A Bon Jovi song came to mind. Man, first Bruce now Jon. How New Jersey could he be?

"Want to make a memory?"

Wilde took one more look at the door, thought of Sondra and that long red hair fanned across his chest. Then he shook his head. Not tonight. He would head back down to the lobby and call her from the house phone. He didn't want her waiting up for him.

That was when the door opened.

"How long have you been standing here?" Sondra asked.

"Minute or two."

"Want to talk about it?"

"Probably shouldn't."

"Talk?"

"I'm not much of a talker."

"But I'm a supergood listener," Sondra said.

He nodded. "Yeah, that's true."

She took a step back. "Come on in, Wilde."

And he obeyed.

CHAPTER TWENTY-TWO

When Wilde woke up, the first thing he thought about—even before he realized that he was in a strange yet familiar hotel room rather than his Ecocapsule—was Laila.

Damn.

Sondra sat in a chair with her feet tucked under. She looked out the window, her face lit by the morning sun. For a few long moments, neither one of them moved. She stared out the window. He stared at the profile of her face. He tried to read her expression—serenity? regret? contemplation?—and he realized that whatever he deduced would probably be wrong. Human beings were never that simple to read.

"Good morning, Sondra."

She turned to him and smiled. "Good morning, Wilde." Then: "Do you have to leave right away?"

Again, despite the warning he had just given himself on human beings, he tried to read her. Did she want him to leave—or was she giving him an out if he wanted to take it?

"I have no plans," he said. "But if you do—"

"How about we order some breakfast?"

"That sounds great."

Sondra smiled at him. "I bet you know the breakfast menu by heart."

He didn't reply.

"I'm sorry. I didn't mean..."

Wilde shook it off. She asked him what he wanted to eat. He told her. She stepped into the suite's living room and picked up the phone. Wilde got out of bed naked. He was padding toward the bathroom when his phone erupted.

Not buzzed or rang or vibrated. Erupted.

He quickly snatched it up and stopped the alarm.

"Everything okay?"

He looked at the screen. The answer was no.

He swiped left, which some might find ironic under the circumstances. It wasn't Tinder—it was his security system. A car had pulled into his hidden road. No big deal. The alarm doesn't sound for that. It just triggers the other motion detectors. Two of them had gone off. As he watched the screen, a third lit up. That meant people, at least three, were walking in the woods in search of his home. He swiped left again. A map came up. A fourth alarm triggered. They were traveling from the south, east, and west toward the Ecocapsule.

"You have to go," Sondra said.

Wilde wanted to explain. "Someone is trying to find where I live."

"Okay."

"I mean, this isn't some bullshit excuse."

"I know," she said.

"How long are you staying in town?"

"I'm leaving today."

"Oh."

"'Oh' or 'whew'?" She held up her hand. "Sorry, that was uncalled for. I know you won't believe this, but this is new to me."

"I believe it," he said.

"It's not new to you though."

"No, it's not."

"You didn't sleep well," she said. "You called out a lot. You rolled around like the blankets were binding you."

"I'm sorry if I kept you awake."

There was really nothing more to say. Wilde got dressed quickly. There was no kiss goodbye. There was no true goodbye. He preferred it that way. Sondra stayed in the suite's other room while he got ready, so maybe she did too.

There was no time to travel on foot, so Wilde grabbed a taxi parked outside the Sheraton. He didn't give the driver an address because he didn't really have one. He had him drive up Mountain Road. Wilde rarely traveled on this stretch of highway. Too many bad memories. When the driver took the curve, the same curve David's car had taken so many years ago, Wilde felt his hand grip the seat. He eased his breathing. The small white cross was still there, something Hester probably would have found unnerving if not ironic. Wilde had no idea who had put it there all those years ago. He'd been tempted to remove it—it had been there too long—but who was he to intervene?

"There are no houses up here," the driver told him.

"I know. Just pull over when I tell you."

"You going for a hike?"

"Something like that, yeah."

Half a mile later, he gave the driver the signal. He handed the man a twenty for an eight-dollar fare and got out near the mountain's peak. His small hidden road—the access point for his visitors—was closer to the mountain's base. He normally climbed up the hill toward his home. Today he'd climb down, checking the security map on his phone as he did. From what he could make out from the motion detectors, his visitors were approaching the capsule slowly and carefully and from all sides with almost military precision.

Disturbing.

Why were they coming for him? And equally if not more important: *Who* was coming for him?

One might think it a stroke of luck that Wilde happened to be out the night of this invasion, but that wasn't the case. If he'd been home, the alarms would have roused him. He would have taken off before they got within five hundred yards of the Ecocapsule. He'd long ago set up escape routes and hiding places, just in case anyone ever tried to get to him.

He could be gone in no time.

No one knew these woods like he did. In here, in this thicket, they would have no chance against him. It didn't matter how many of them there were.

But the questions remained: Who were they, and what did they want?

Wilde eased down the mountainside, letting gravity make the journey easier. He veered to his right by a forked tree, toward the closest triggered motion detector. Being in the woods, amongst animals and wildlife, the motion detector could be accidentally set off quite easily. A deer goes by. A bear. Even squirrels or raccoons sometimes. But Wilde had a system, one alarm dominoing to the next before any warnings were issued, proving the movements had to be somewhat calculated and thus most likely human. Between the car parked on his road—ding one—and the follow-up triggers, he knew that this was no false alarm. It wasn't one man or even two or three. More likely there were five or more.

Coming for him.

It was eight a.m. The woods were cool, that early crisp still in the air. Wilde moved with pantherlike quiet. He didn't really have a plan here. It was mostly reconnaissance. Keep your distance. Learn about your adversary. Check out their positions and numbers.

Try to figure out what the hell they want with him.

He slowed when he reached the rock formation with a trigger motion detector. He checked the device, just to see if there was some kind of malfunction that might explain why so many had gone off. The detector was intact. He picked up the pace now.

And there they were.

Two men together working in tandem. Smart. One he could pick off, take out before he communicated with the others. But two would be much more difficult. They were dressed head-to-toe in black. They had their heads on a swivel, one taking the lead and looking forward, the other pulling up the rear. They stood far enough apart, so again they couldn't be taken down by one assailant.

Professionals.

Wilde moved in for a closer look. They both wore earpieces. Probably communicating with the others. These guys were coming in from the north. There were teams coming in from the south, east, and west too. Assuming two men a team, that meant a minimum of eight opponents.

Wilde was good at tracking, obviously better than any of these guys, but that didn't make him invisible. Overconfidence leads to mistakes. The men were armed. Their eyes constantly swept the landscape, and realistically, if Wilde wasn't careful, there was a decent chance he could be spotted.

Every once in a while, the taller man checked something on his smartphone screen and changed their direction slightly. Whatever app they were using, it was clearly leading them to the Ecocapsule. Wilde had no idea what the technology was, but then again if someone wanted to find his home badly enough, there were tracking devices that would eventually lead them to it. He'd always known that. He'd prepared for it.

Knowing the men's ultimate destination made it easier. Wilde didn't have to follow closely. He veered off toward one of his safe boxes. He had six of them in the woods, all hidden in spots no one would find, all opened by using his palm print rather than a combination lock. This one was up in a tree. He climbed, found it taped under the large branch, opened the box. Wilde took out the gun.

He was about to close it up without taking out the false identity papers, but then he thought better of it. Suppose he had to run?

Better safe than sorry.

He slid back down the tree and made his way toward the Ecocapsule. He moved quickly now, wanting to arrive before the tentatively moving team he'd been following got there.

And then what?

He'd figure that out when the time came. He hurried ahead, moving with ease.

He located the hill approximately two hundred yards from where the Ecocapsule sat. He climbed a tree so that he would be high enough to look down on the clearing. He'd wanted to put the capsule in a denser part of the forest, but that blocked the sun, which made storing solar energy that much more difficult. Still, it would pay off now. Once he reached the top of the tree, he'd be able to see the men approaching from a safe spot.

Wilde grabbed a branch, pulled himself up, and looked down.

Damn. They were already there.

Four men. Surrounding the capsule. Armed. Two more—the two Wilde had been following—came into the clearing. So now it was six men.

The leader approached the capsule cautiously.

Wilde recognized him.

Wilde scrolled through his phone's call history and hit the return-call button. Gavin Chambers was reaching for the Ecocapsule's door when he must have felt the vibration in his pocket. He took out his phone, looked at it, glanced at his surroundings. He hit the answer button and put the phone to his ear.

"Wilde?"

"Don't touch my house."

Gavin took a harder look around now, but there was no way he'd be able to spot Wilde up in the tree. "Are you inside this thing?"

"No."

"I need you to open it."

"Why?"

"Something has happened. Something big."

"Yeah, I figured that."

"How?"

"Are you joking? You have at least four armed teams circling my place in the woods. You don't have to be a trained detective to figure out 'something big' has happened. So what is it?"

"The Maynards."

"What about them?"

"I need to look inside your home. Then I need to take you to them. Are you nearby or are you watching me on some kind of camera I missed?" He looked up again, shading his eyes. "Either way, I'm not going to find you, am I?"

"No."

"I'm trespassing on your turf."

"Yet here you are."

"Had to do it, Wilde. Had to flush you out one way or the other."

"So now what?"

"I could take an axe to your house and see what's inside."

"Not your style," Wilde said.

"No, it's not. Tell you what. I'll send my men away."

"Sounds like a good start."

"But then I'll need to see you."

Wilde didn't reply. Gavin Chambers barked out some orders. The men complied without complaint. When they were gone, Gavin Chambers put the phone back to his ear. "Come out now. We need to talk."

"Why? What's wrong?"

"Another kid is missing."

CHAPTER TWENTY-THREE

Hester still had the stomach flutters when she woke up.

The flutters had started last night at eleven p.m. when Oren had walked her to her door—he wouldn't just leave her at the curb or even in that elevator, too much a gentleman—and kissed her. Or did she kiss him? Didn't matter. It was a kiss. A real kiss. He wrapped one arm around her waist. Okay, yes, that was nice. But with the other hand—his big hand—with the other big, wonderful hand, he cupped the back of her head and tilted her face up and, in one word...

Swoon.

Hester melted. Right there. Hester Crimstein, attorney-at-law, knew that she was too old to melt or swoon or feel the same stomach flutters she felt when she was thirteen years old and Michael Gendler, the handsomest boy in her class, sneaked away with her at Jack Kolker's bar mitzvah and they made out in the small room behind the rabbi's office. Oren's kiss was so many things at once. It surged through her, of course, making her heady and dizzy and totally lost in the moment, yet another part of her was outside the body, eyes wide open, watching in amazement and thinking, *Holy shit, I'm being wrecked with a kiss!*

How long had the kiss lasted? Five seconds? Ten? Thirty? A full minute? Not a full minute. She didn't know. Did her own hands wander? She'd replayed the kiss—The Kiss, it deserved to be capitalized—a hundred times, and she still couldn't be sure. She remembered her hands on his strong, round shoulders, how that felt right and safe and oh how she loved those shoulders—and what the hell was wrong with her anyway?

She remembered how soft The Kiss had started, how Oren started to pull away gently, how they came back together, how The Kiss grew hungrier, more passionate, how it ended so tenderly. He had kept his hand on the back of her head. He looked her in the eye.

"Good night, Hester."

"Good night, Oren."

"Can I ask you out again?"

She bit back several snappy rejoinders and went with, "Yes. I'd really like that."

Oren waited until she was inside the apartment. Hester gave him a smile as she closed the door. Then, alone, she broke into a little happy dance. She couldn't help herself. She felt both flighty and a fool. She got ready for bed in a daze. Sleep, she was sure, would not come, but it had, quickly, the adrenaline rush leaving her spent and exhausted. She slept, in fact, beautifully.

Now, this morning, Hester was left with the flutters. Just that. The flutters. Last night now felt surreal, like a dream, and she wasn't sure whether this feeling was something she longed for or something she feared. Did she need this in her life? She was content already, satisfied in both personal life and career. Why risk it? It wasn't just a question of being too old for such immature emotions. She was set in her ways now. She liked being set in her ways. Did she really want something like this upending everything? Did she want to risk hurt or embarrassment or any of the millions of things that could and probably would go wrong?

Life was good, wasn't it?

She reached for her phone and saw a message from Oren:

> Too soon to text? I don't want to look desperate.

Swoon. Swoon all over again.

She typed back: Stalker.

She saw the three dots signaling he was writing her back. Then the three dots vanished. She waited. No reply. She felt a brief surge of panic.

> I was kidding! No, it's not too soon!

No reply.

> Oren?

This was exactly what she meant—who wanted to feel this way? Who wanted their heart in their throat and to be worried that maybe she did the wrong thing or that maybe this was just a game to him and hey, it was only one date and one kiss (The Kiss) so calm the F down already.

Her phone rang. She hoped that it was Oren, but the caller ID displayed another number she recognized. She pressed answer and put the phone to her ear.

"Wilde?"

"I need your help."

Wilde stepped into view by the Ecocapsule. He held his phone in the air.

Gavin Chambers frowned at him. "What are you doing?"

"I'm on a live video call," Wilde said.

"With who?"

"Whom," a female voice coming from the phone said. "With *whom*. Prepositional phrase, sweet stuff."

Wilde continued to walk toward Gavin. Gavin squinted at the screen.

"Hi, Gavin. My name is Hester Crimstein. We met once at a dinner party at Henry Kissinger's."

Gavin Chambers glanced up at Wilde as if to say, *Really?*

"Don't make that face, *bubbalah*," Hester said. "I'm recording all this. Do you understand?"

Gavin closed his eyes and let loose a long sigh. "For real?"

"No, for fake. I want you to know that if anything happens to Wilde—"

"Nothing is going to happen to him."

"Cool, handsome, then we'll have no issue."

"This isn't necessary."

"Oh, I'm sure it's not, but when you have a dozen armed men sneak up on my client's home—a home which you subsequently threatened to destroy—label me paranoid, but as his attorney—and just to make it clear for the record, I am your attorney, correct, Wilde?"

"Correct," Wilde said.

"So as his attorney, I want this on the record. You, Colonel Chambers, approached my client's home with armed men—"

"This is public land."

"Colonel Chambers, do you really want to spend time arguing detailed legalese with me?"

Gavin sighed. "No, I do not."

"Because I can do that. I'm not in a rush. Are you in a rush, Wilde?"

"I got all day," Wilde said.

"Fine, sorry," Gavin said, "no legalese, let's move on."

"Now what was I saying?" Hester continued. "Right, you approached my client's home with armed men. You threatened to break into said home and even destroy it. Don't roll your eyes.

Me, I would have you arrested, but my client, against my high-priced advice, is still willing to talk to you. He seems to have what I would consider badly placed trust in you. I will honor his wants while also making our position on this clear: If Wilde is harmed in any way—"

"He won't be harmed."

"Shush, you, listen. If he's harmed or held against his will, if I call him back and cannot reach him or you do anything other than what he requests, I will become a permanent part of your life, Colonel Chambers. Like shingles. Or piles. Only worse. Do I make myself clear?"

"Crystal."

"Wilde?"

"Thanks, Hester. Okay to disconnect?"

"That's up to you," she said.

"Yeah, thanks."

He hit a button and slipped the phone into his pocket.

Gavin Chambers frowned. "You called your mommy?"

"Wow, now you've hurt my feelings."

"What I wanted to tell you was supposed to be in complete confidence."

"Then call me on the phone next time instead of sending armed men."

Gavin gestured toward the capsule. "I was a little surprised we found your place so easily. I figured you'd set up decoys. You ever read about the Ghost Army in World War Two?"

Wilde had. "The Twenty-Third Headquarters Special Troops."

"Whoa," Chambers said. "Label me impressed."

The Twenty-Third, aka the Ghost Army, were an elite force of artists and special effects soldiers who worked "tactical deception." They'd use stuff like inflatable tanks and rubber airplanes and even create a soundtrack of war, all to create the twentieth-century version of a Trojan horse.

"How did you find it?" Wilde asked.

"Drone with a sensor," Gavin Chambers said. He gestured toward the Ecocapsule. "Please open the door."

"No one is inside."

"And opening it will prove that."

"Don't trust me?"

Exhaustion emanated from him. "Can we just check this box, please?"

"Who are you looking for?"

"No one."

"You just said—"

"That was before you decided to blab to someone with a TV show."

"She's my attorney. If I tell her not to tell anyone, she won't."

"You can't be that naïve." Gavin Chambers looked off and shook his head. He was weighing a decision, but it was a fait accompli. There was only one way this could go. "It's about Crash Maynard."

"What happened to him?"

"He's missing."

"A runaway or—"

Gavin took out his gun. "Just open the goddamn door, Wilde."

"Are you serious?"

"Do I look in the mood to continue this?" He did not. He looked like a worn garment fraying at the edges. "I told you that Crash is missing. Let me eliminate your hovel, so we can find him."

Wilde wasn't afraid of the gun, nor was he tempted to draw his own, but he also saw no reason to antagonize the man any further. He got what was happening here: Crash Maynard had vanished, and Wilde was as likely a suspect as anybody.

The Ecocapsule door opened by the same kind of remote you use to unlock your car door. Wilde reached into his pocket, pulled out the remote, and pressed the button with his thumb. Gavin tucked the gun back into the holster as the hatch door rose. He leaned his head in, looked around, pulled his head back out.

"Sorry about the gun."

Wilde said nothing.

"Let's go."

"Where?"

"The Maynards want to see you. In fact, they insist on it."

"Going to pull the gun again if I refuse?"

"You really going to hold that over me?" Gavin started down the path. "I said I was sorry."

Neither man spoke during the short ride to Maynard Manor. In the morning sun, the mansion glittered atop a clearing of grass so uniformly green it might have been spray-painted that color. The painstakingly mowed lawn looked to be an almost perfect square, the house being dead center, with what Wilde estimated to be about three hundred yards of grass on each side before you reach the woods. There was an Olympic-sized pool on the right, a tennis court on the left, and a regulation soccer pitch with freshly laid-out lime in the back.

The SUV came to a stop by an ornate carriage house. Gavin got out of the vehicle. Wilde followed.

"Before we go any further, I need you to sign this."

Gavin handed Wilde a piece of paper on a clipboard with a pen attached.

"It's a standard NDA—that's a nondisclosure agreement."

"Yeah," Wilde said, handing it back to him, "I know what an NDA is."

"If you don't sign, I can't tell you any more about what's going on."

"Buh-bye then."

"God, you're a pain in the ass. All right, forget the NDA. Come on."

Gavin started walking toward the woods in the back-left corner of the estate.

"Did you really think I, what, I kidnapped the boy?" Wilde asked.

"No."

"Or hid him in my capsule?"

"Not really, but it was a possibility."

Gavin kept walking. He stopped in the side yard midway between the house and the woods. "There is where we lose him."

"Care to elaborate?"

"This morning, Crash wasn't in his bedroom. We checked the CCTV footage. Security here is fairly extensive as you might imagine. CCTV covers the exterior from the home to right about where we are standing." He took out his mobile phone, swiped across, turned it toward Wilde. "This is Crash walking past where we are now, probably heading in that direction."

He pointed to the woods behind him and hit the play button. The camera must have had a night filter on it. On the screen, Wilde watched as Crash traveled from the house, across where they now stood, seemingly on his way to the woods. The time stamp in the lower left-hand corner of the video read 2:14 a.m.

"Anyone else show up on the CCTV before or after him?" Wilde asked.

"No."

"So you figure Crash ran away."

"Probably. All we know for certain is that he walked toward those trees." He turned toward Wilde. "But someone with a strong knowledge of the woods could have been lying in wait."

"Ah," Wilde said. "That's where I come in."

"To a degree."

"But you really don't think I had anything to do with it."

"Like I said—I was checking the boxes."

"So I'm here because I happened to question Crash yesterday."

"Hell of a coincidence that, don't you think?"

"And Naomi Pine is also missing," Wilde said.

"Hell of a coincidence that, don't you think?"

"So there is a connection?"

"Two kids from the same high school class disappear," Gavin said. "If there's not a connection..."

"...it's a hell of a coincidence, don't you think?" Wilde finished for him. "What else you got?"

"They've been communicating."

"Naomi and Crash?"

"Yes."

"Recently?"

"I don't know. The kid stays ahead of our monitoring—WhatsApp, Signal, whatever apps they use. They're encrypted. My job isn't to spy on the family. It's to protect them."

"Why?"

"Why what?"

"Why are you protecting them, Gavin? And I mean you, specifically. You read up on me, I read up on you. You don't do fieldwork anymore, and Dash Maynard is just a television producer. So you're not here simply to protect him and his family. You're here because of Rusty Eggers."

Gavin smiled. "What a deduction. Should I applaud?"

"Only if you feel it's appropriate."

"I don't. It doesn't matter why I'm here. Two teens have disappeared. You want to find one, I want to find the other."

"Pool our resources?"

"We have the same goal."

"I assume you brought me out here for a reason."

"The Maynards insisted, actually. I figured while you're here, I'd get your take."

Wilde looked toward the woods and spotted a path. "You think that's where Crash was headed?"

"From the angle of the walk on the video, yes. But more than that, that's also the spot where he recently encountered Naomi Pine trespassing."

Crash hadn't "encountered" Naomi—he'd pranked, intimidated, and bullied her. Or at least, that was how Matthew described it. But now was not the time to get into semantics. Wilde started toward the path in the woods to get a better look.

"I assume you don't have any CCTV coverage of where we are now," Wilde said.

"That's correct. We only worry about people near the estate. We aren't interested in people, especially family members, who voluntarily choose to leave."

"So," Wilde said, "your working theory is that Crash met Naomi out here and that they are hiding somewhere together?"

"Seems most likely."

"Yet you still panicked."

"We didn't panic."

"You had armed men swarm my house."

"Stop with the dramatics. These are not ordinary times, Wilde. The family is under enormous stress and pressure. Threats have been made—violent and awful threats. You may have seen something about it on the news."

He nodded. "The Maynards have tapes that could destroy Rusty Eggers."

"It's not true, but people believe any crackpot conspiracy they see online."

They entered the woods via the path. Wilde checked the dirt for footprints. There were a fair number, mostly fresh. "You and your men went through here this morning?"

"Of course."

Wilde frowned, but in a sense it didn't matter. Crash Maynard had come out here on his own. There was no one else on the tape. Was Naomi or someone waiting for him? Hard to say via physical evidence. There was a small clearing to the left with the rock where Matthew and Naomi met up. Wilde headed over to it. He knelt down, felt under and around it, and found a few butts, both tobacco and cannabis.

"If this place isn't covered by CCTV, how did you know about Crash's 'encounter' with Naomi?"

"One of my men was walking the grounds. He heard a bunch of kids laughing."

"And he didn't step in?"

"He's security, not a babysitter."

A noise familiar to Wilde cut through the air. He looked skyward, through the branches reaching up to the sky of deep dark blue. The chopping sound from the whirring rotors grew louder. Wilde didn't suffer from PTSD—at least, not the kind that could be clinically diagnosed, but there wasn't a guy who served over there that didn't cringe at this sound.

He stepped back into the clearing as the helicopter hovered above the side yard. As it descended toward the ground, Wilde sneaked a glance at Gavin Chambers, hoping to get a read on the situation, but if this arrival was known to him, his expression wasn't giving that away. Even from this distance, Wilde could feel the wind from the rotors of the Bell 427 twin-engine copter, maybe the most commonly used for short flights from, say, New York City out to here, as it touched down. The engine turned off. Whoever was inside waited until the rotors stopped spinning completely. Then the pilot came out and opened the door.

Hester Crimstein stepped out of the copter. She spotted Wilde and Gavin, smiled, and spread her arms wide.

"Can I make an entrance, boys, or what?"

CHAPTER TWENTY-FOUR

Five minutes later, they were all ensconced in the Maynards' over-the-top library turret. Hester sat across from Dash and Delia. Gavin Chambers stood behind the Maynards. There was an empty burgundy leather wingback chair next to Hester, purportedly for Wilde, but he chose to stand too.

"Can we get you a beverage?" Dash Maynard asked.

Hester looked at Wilde, arching an eyebrow at the word "beverage," as if understandably annoyed by the use of the word in casual conversation.

"We're good," Hester said.

"We appreciate you agreeing to join us on such short notice," Dash continued.

"You sent a helicopter and offered to pay double my regular rate," Hester said. "How's a girl to refuse?"

Delia Maynard had yet to speak. There was a slight tremor in her pale face. Her eyes stared out, unfocused. For a few long moments, no one spoke.

"Hey, listen, I can wait all day—double my usual superexpensive-though-worth-it rate? Mama's gonna buy herself a new pair of Louboutins, you know what I'm saying?"

Dash glanced at Delia. Wilde glanced out the window behind them. The view was magnificent. The manor was so high up that you could see the skyscrapers of Manhattan above the tree line.

"I'm joking," Hester said.

"Pardon?"

"Yes, you offered to double my fee. But I don't work that way. I'll bill you the same hourly rate as every other client—no more, no less. And I don't like wasting time, even if I'm on the clock. I don't need money that badly. I'm rich already. Not as rich as you, Mr. Maynard—"

"Call me Dash."

"Okay, Dash, cool. Since you seem a little hesitant, let me set a few ground rules to get us off the ground, okay?"

"Yes," he said, clearing his throat, "that might be helpful."

"First thing: You said on the phone that you wish to engage my services."

"Yes."

"So now I'm your attorney. Wonderful, mazel tov." She glanced up over Dash's shoulder to Gavin Chambers. "Please leave. This is a private meeting between my client and myself."

"Oh no," Dash said. "It's okay if Gavin—"

"It's not okay with me," Hester interjected. "I'm now officially your attorney. What you divulge to me gets locked away under attorney-client privilege. In short, no one can compel me to reveal what you're about to say. Mr. Chambers here doesn't get that same legal recourse. He can, like it or not, be compelled to reveal the contents of this conversation. So I want him out." Hester glanced to her right. "You too, Wilde. Skedaddle."

Dash said, "But we trust Gavin—"

"Dash? You told me to call you Dash, right? Dash, this is pretty simple. I'm setting up ground rules, like I told you. Rule One: If you want to hire me, you're going to have to listen to me. If you don't want to listen to me, well, my driver is on his way out here—I'll skip that helicopter with that *farkakte* noise on the way back, thank you—and should be arriving soon. I'll head back into the city and charge you for the visit, and we will go our separate ways. This isn't a democracy. I'm your Dear Leader for Life. We understand Rule One?"

Dash looked as though he might argue, but Delia put a hand on his leg.

"We understand," Delia said.

"Good."

Gavin said, "I don't like it."

"In another lifetime," Hester said, "I'll care, really. I'll shed tears. But for now, shush and depart."

Dash nodded to Gavin. Gavin threw up his hands and started for the door. Wilde followed behind him.

"Wait," Delia said.

Both men stopped.

Delia looked at Hester. "We've gotten a full briefing on Wilde's background."

"You don't say."

"He's still a licensed investigator with CRAW Securities," Delia said. "You used to employ him to do work for you, correct?"

"And if I did?"

"Employ him again," Delia said. "For our situation. Then anything he would hear would fall into attorney-client work product, right?"

"Hey, nice thinking." Hester spun and looked back at Wilde. "Want to work for me?"

"Sure," Wilde said.

"Then sit down. Don't stand over me and lurk, it gives me vertigo."

A few moments later, Gavin Chambers was out of the room. The four of them sat in the leather chairs, Delia and Dash on one side of the teak coffee table, Hester and Wilde on the other.

"I don't understand," Dash said. "If you could hire Wilde as your investigator, why can't you hire Gavin."

"Because," Hester said.

"Because why?"

"Because I said so. You flew me out here on a helicopter because I assume your situation is urgent. Let's get to it, shall we?"

Wilde raised his hand. "Not yet."

Hester turned to him. "What?"

"Colonel Chambers was trying to monitor your son's communications."

"Of course he was," Dash said. "That was part of his job."

But Hester had already put both hands on the arms of the chair, and with a grunt, she lifted herself to a standing position. "Let's go outside."

"What for?" Dash asked.

"For all we know, your new chief of security put listening devices in this room."

That knocked both Dash and Delia back for a moment.

"You don't understand," Dash said. "We trust Gavin implicitly."

"You don't understand," Hester countered. "I don't. And I'm not so sure your wife does either." She started for the door. "Come on, let's get some fresh air. It's nice outside, it'll do us all some good."

Dash once again looked at Delia. She nodded and took his hand. They headed down a spiral staircase, passing a confused Gavin Chambers, and headed outside. Their twins were practicing with a coach on the soccer pitch.

"The girls don't know what's going on," Dash said. "We'd like to keep it that way."

They walked toward the middle of the yard, nearly taking the same path their son had on that CCTV recording last night. The day was gorgeous, almost mockingly so. Wilde saw Hester spot the view of Manhattan, her home now, and she watched the skyscrapers as though they were old friends.

When they were far enough from the house, Hester said, "So why am I here?"

Dash launched straight into it. "This morning, when we woke

up, our son Crash was gone. The early signs pointed to him visiting a friend late at night or, at worst, running off. Mr. Wilde here knows the situation."

Hester said, "Okay."

Delia cupped a hand over her eyes to block the sun. She looked up at Wilde. "Why did you corner our son at the school yesterday?"

"Whoa." It was Hester. "Don't answer that. Let's get me up to speed before we start down any of those roads, okay?"

"The road is a simple one," Delia said. "Because of our current situation—"

"What situation?"

"Last night, Saul Strauss was a guest on your show," Delia said.

"Right, so?"

"He made accusations involving us."

"I assume you're talking about you guys possessing incriminating tapes?"

Delia nodded. "Purportedly on Rusty Eggers, yes."

"I thought he was full of it," Hester said. "They exist?"

"No," Delia said, "they do not."

No hesitation, Wilde noted. Didn't mean she was telling the truth, of course. But there was zero pause, zero wrong body language—just a straight-up denial.

"Go on," Hester said.

"When we discovered Crash was missing," Dash said, "Colonel Chambers and his team immediately started a search. All early signs pointed to the fact that our son ran away on his own. There is CCTV of him leaving the manor alone, seemingly voluntarily." Dash turned his glare onto Wilde. "Still—and I think this is a natural response—Colonel Chambers made sure that the man who yesterday held our son against his will at his school wasn't involved. You know this, of course, Ms. Crimstein—you saw it on FaceTime. We want to know the reason why Mr. Wilde here felt the need to confront our son in his own school. I think our concern is understandable."

Hester nodded. "So that's why you had Chambers bring Wilde here."

"Yes."

"And you figured by hiring me, you'd get him to talk."

Delia spoke up now. "No. We hired you because things have changed."

"What do you mean?"

"We don't think Crash ran away on his own anymore."

"Why not?"

"Because," Delia said, "we just received a ransom note."

The ransom note had come in via anonymous email.

Dash handed his phone to Hester, who hunched over so her body would block the sun glare on the screen. Wilde read it over her shoulder:

> We have your son. If you do not do exactly what we say, he will be executed. We don't want that, but we believe in freedom and freedom always comes at a price. If you contact the FBI or law enforcement, we will know about it and we will immediately execute Crash. If you think you can contact the authorities without us knowing, you are wrong. We were able to kidnap your son despite all your expensive security. We will know, and your son will suffer greatly.
>
> Our request is simple. We believe that the truth will set you free. For that reason, we want you to turn over the tapes you have on Rusty Eggers to us. All of them, especially the oldest. There will be no negotiating on this. The stakes are too high.

> Please follow these Instructions exactly.
>
> On the bottom of this email is a link to an anonymous drop box which works through what is commonly known as the Dark Web via several VPNs. The link is not active yet.
>
> At exactly 4PM, click the link and upload all videos that you have on Rusty Eggers per the prompts.
>
> You will see a special folder set aside for the truly damaging tape. We know the tape exists, so please do not pretend otherwise. The link will be useless again at exactly 5PM.
>
> If we don't get what we want, your son will face the consequences.

That was it. On the bottom was indeed a hyperlink with lots of jumbled numbers, letters, and symbols of all sorts.

Hester read the message several more times. Wilde watched her and waited. Eventually Hester handed the phone back to Dash. Both of their hands were shaking.

"You want my advice?" Hester asked.

"Of course."

"Contact the FBI."

"No," Delia said.

"You read the message," Dash added. "No law enforcement."

"I get that, but in my view, contacting the professionals gives you your best chance. Only the four of us have seen this email, am I correct?"

They both nodded.

"So Wilde leaves now. We know people at the FBI. Good

people who will keep it quiet. Wilde tells one of those people what's what—"

"No," Dash said. "No way."

"Delia?" Hester said.

"I agree with my husband. For now, we do this on our own."

They were not going to change their minds, not yet anyway, so Wilde shifted gears. "According to the time stamp, the email was sent a little more than an hour ago. What time did you first see it?"

Dash made a face. "What does that have to do with anything?"

Delia replied, "Pretty much right away."

"That's when you called me?" Hester asked.

"Yes."

Hester saw where Wilde was going with this. "And may we make an observation?" she asked.

"Of course."

"You didn't tell your chief of security about it."

Dash let loose a sigh. "I wanted to."

"Yes, but your wife didn't." Hester faced Delia. "Because you see what I see."

"And what do both of you ladies see that I can't?" Dash asked with a hint of irritation.

"Gavin Chambers works for Rusty Eggers. His loyalty is to him, not you. I didn't send him out of the room just because he could be legally compelled to talk. I wanted him out because you aren't his first priority. Protecting Rusty Eggers is. Do you understand?"

"I do," Dash said, "but even if I agree with that, our interests here are the same."

Hester tilted her head. "Are you sure about that? I mean, let's say hypothetically that the choice is your son dies or all your tapes are released to the public. Which side do you think Rusty Eggers is going to take?"

Silence.

"And I want you to consider something else," Hester went on. "If this really is a kidnapping, who would be your most likely suspect?"

"Radicals," Dash said.

"Well, that's pretty vague, but let's go with that. Let's say it was radicals. So these radicals figured a way to get your son to go out on his own into the woods and then, what, they nabbed him on your own property and dragged him off at, I don't know, gunpoint or whatever?" Hester rubbed her chin. "Does that seem likely?"

"So what are you saying?" Delia asked.

"Nothing yet. I'm spitballing. Honestly. That's all. It could be, for example, that your son concocted all of this."

Delia looked skeptical. "I don't think so."

"Maybe Crash just ran away. Maybe he's fine and safe and hiding. Maybe he sent this email."

"Why would he do that?"

"I don't know. Spitballing, remember? But that's a possibility, right? Another possibility is that Naomi Pine is involved. We know she ran away already. Did she give him the idea? Are they together? We know that Crash and Naomi were classmates. So maybe the two of them are in this together. I don't know, but that's another possibility. Are you with me so far?"

Dash frowned, but Delia said, "I think so."

"So now let's suppose the kidnapping is on the up-and-up. I don't mean to sound cold and analytical, but for now, let's try to keep emotion out of our thinking, okay? Let's say someone found a way to lure your son out into the woods and grab him. One possibility is that, yes, it's just as it appears. Many, uh, radicals want Rusty Eggers to go down. So a team of experts—CIA or military trained—carried out this operation. Doubtful but okay, maybe. Which leads me to the one last possibility I can't get out of my head."

Delia said, "We're listening."

"Gavin Chambers is behind this," Hester said. "He is the

complete insider. He knows the CCTV setup. He knows everything. He told your son to come meet him out in the woods. And he took him."

Dash made a scoffing noise. "That's ridiculous."

"Motive?" Delia asked, ignoring her husband's reaction.

"Maybe Rusty told him to do it. Maybe Rusty wants to flush out any secrets you might have." Hester thought that maybe she scored on that one—with Delia at least. She took a step closer. "Listen, Delia, you felt something, didn't you? That's why you didn't tell Gavin Chambers. Something about him made you hesitate."

"I wouldn't go that far," Delia said.

"Then—"

"I just... he works for Rusty Eggers. Like you said. I acted out of an abundance of caution, not because I really suspect he'd take our child."

Hester turned to Wilde and caught the look on his face. "You have something to add?"

"A few things odd in the ransom email," Wilde said.

"Go on."

"First, what do they mean by 'especially the oldest' tape?"

"I'm not sure," Dash said, "but I assume they mean outtakes from season one."

Wilde waited a beat. Give them a pool of silence. People often dove in. Dash and Delia did not.

After a few more seconds passed, Hester said, "What else, Wilde?"

"If the kidnappers just want the truth out there, why not demand that you release the tapes to the media or post them on a public forum? Why would the kidnappers ask you to send them to their private drop first?"

"I'm not following," Dash said.

"It could be nothing," Wilde said. "Or it could be that the kidnappers want to control the information for themselves, not release it."

The four of them stood there for a few long moments. A lawn mower shattered the silence. Then another.

"But there's nothing on the tapes," Dash said. "That's the key thing. We don't have any dirt."

Delia nodded. "At worst, what we have is slightly embarrassing to Rusty. That's all."

Wilde listened to them both and reached a simple conclusion.

They were lying.

CHAPTER TWENTY-FIVE

They had almost six hours until the link was active.

Wilde knew a few basic rules about negotiating with kidnappers. Rule One: Don't ever agree to the first offer. A life may be at stake, but every negotiation is about power and control. The kidnapper had most of it, but you, the victim's family, are the only buyer in the market for the particular "product" they are selling. So you have some power too. Open a dialogue. All the other rules—keep emotion out of it, start low, be patient, demand proof of life—flow from this basic premise.

There was only one problem.

Wilde had no way to reach the kidnappers.

There were no emails, no mobile numbers, nothing. Wilde tried hitting reply to the ransom email, but the message bounced back.

The clock was ticking, so they divided up the chores. Dash would prepare the videos in case they decided to upload some or all of them. Delia would contact Crash's closest friends to see whether any of them saw Crash recently or knew where he might be.

"Keep it low-key," Hester suggested to Delia. "You're a nervous mom not sure where your kid spent the night, that's all."

Wilde would continue searching for Naomi because the early theory remained the best one: There was a connection between Naomi's disappearance and Crash's. In short, if you find Naomi Pine, you most likely find Crash Maynard.

There was yet another matter Wilde had to handle. He spotted Gavin Chambers standing by the tennis court smoking a cigarette.

"I'm surprised you smoke," Wilde said.

"The bad guy always smokes." Chambers threw the butt on the ground and stomped it with his heel. "And he litters." He squinted up at the sun. "Your idea to move the meeting outside?"

Wilde saw no reason to reply.

"The library isn't bugged. You can have a guy sweep the place."

"Okay."

"So you officially throwing me out?"

"No," Wilde said.

"Then you want to fill me in on what's going on?"

"As much as I can."

"Hey, Wilde?"

Wilde looked up at him.

"Don't insult me with your bullshit, okay? I know Hester isn't just worried about privilege. I'm viewed as Rusty Eggers's man."

"Hmm. Sure you weren't listening in?"

Gavin liked that one. "Even Captain Obvious could have figured that one out. Rusty was the one who brought me in, so someone feels that's where my loyalty will be."

"Isn't it?"

"Would it do me any good to say no?"

"Probably not."

"Either way, I just want to find the kid. So what's the plan?"

"Most of the guards here were employed before you came on board."

"Right. I brought in three men with me, including Bryce."

"Bryce?"

"The blond guy you keep tangling with."

"Okay. So Bryce and the other two are out."

"Leaving you with Maynard's untrained rent-a-cops?"

"I'll bring in a few of my own people," Wilde said.

"Ah, I see." Gavin Chambers smiled. "From your old agency?"

He had already called Rola, who was more than game. She was, in fact, on her way with a crew in hand. "Yes."

"You guys ever handle a kidnapping?" Gavin asked. "Because—no offense—you'll screw it up."

"Funny."

"What?"

"Before you seemed pretty certain Crash was a runaway, not a kidnapping."

"Yeah, that was before the Maynards called Hester Crimstein and tossed me out. And that was before I walked into that library and saw their faces. They were trying to hold it together—that's what Dash and Delia do—but they were clearly coming undone." Chambers reached into his jacket pocket and pulled out a pair of sunglasses. "By the way, did you tell them?"

Wilde waited. When Chambers didn't say anything more, Wilde said, "Okay, I'll bite. Tell them what?"

"That you met with Saul Strauss at the Sheraton bar."

Wilde shouldn't have been caught off guard, but he was. He was also more than a little upset with himself that he hadn't spotted their tail. Had his heart-to-heart with Laila really thrown him off that much? "Impressive."

"Not really."

"Question: If your men were following me, then you knew I wasn't at my capsule this morning. You also knew I didn't take the boy."

"That's a question?"

"Why the big show of force in the woods, if you knew I wasn't there?"

"We didn't know."

"You just said you were following—"

"Not you, Wilde. We weren't following you."

Strauss. They were following Strauss.

"Saul Strauss is a loon—and a threat," Gavin said. "You can see that."

"I can," Wilde said.

"So what did he want with you?"

Wilde considered how to answer this.

"I'm not going away," Gavin Chambers said. "We can either work together like we said before—I know more about Crash, you know more about Naomi—or I can just bulldoze my way into representing Rusty's interest without your cooperation."

Wilde wasn't certain of the right move here, but the old proverb about keeping your friends close and your enemies closer echoed in his head.

"Strauss knew Naomi was missing," Wilde said.

"How?"

"I don't know. But he knew there was a connection between Naomi and Crash."

"Why the hell would Saul Strauss care about Naomi Pine?" Chambers asked.

Something else surfaced in Wilde's head, one of the first things Saul Strauss had said to him: *"I hear you had a run-in with the Maynard kid today."*

Saul Strauss had known that Wilde had been at the school.

How had he known that?

There were witnesses in the parking lot, of course, but the only other person who might know more than that, the only other person who could really say what had gone on in that art room, was Ava O'Brien.

But no. How would Ava be involved in this?

She couldn't be. She was just a part-time art teacher.

Wilde said, "You have a relationship with him, right?"

"Saul Strauss? We served together. I saw him yesterday when he protested by the Maynards' office."

"So maybe the first step is to find him," Wilde said.

"You don't think I thought of that already?"

"So—"

"Remember how he walked out of the Sheraton hotel?"

Wilde nodded. "He walked toward the back exit."

"Maybe," Gavin said.

"What do you mean?"

"My men saw Strauss go in. They never saw him go out. We lost him."

The Maynards had given Wilde a Lexus GS to use. As he slipped behind the driver's seat, he called Ava O'Brien. The call went into her voicemail. No one he knew ever checked voicemail, so he sent Ava a quick text:

Need to talk ASAP.

No immediate reply, no dancing dots. He wasn't sure what he would ask her anyway. If Ava O'Brien was somehow aligned with Saul Strauss... no, that made no sense.

Speaking of Strauss.

As Wilde pulled into Bernard Pine's driveway, he took out the business card Saul Strauss had given him and dialed the number. It went straight to voicemail.

"It's Wilde. You told me to call if I had any information. I do. You'll want to hear it."

He didn't know whether that was strictly true, but he figured that that message might get Strauss's attention. Wilde thought about Ava. He thought about Strauss. He thought about Gavin and Crash and yes, of course, Naomi.

He was missing something.

Bernard Pine, Naomi's father, opened his front door before Wilde could ring the bell.

"Do you know a man named Saul Strauss?" Wilde asked.

"Who?"

"Saul Strauss. He's on TV sometimes. Maybe Naomi has mentioned him."

Pine shook his head. "Never heard of him. Have you found anything new?"

"Have you?"

"No. I'm going to the police again. But I don't think they'll listen."

"Do you know if Naomi's passport is still here?"

"I can take a look," Pine said. "Come on in." He stepped back and let Wilde inside. The foyer smelled stale. Wilde spotted the half-full glass and half-full bottle of bourbon on the coffee table. Bernard spotted him spotting it.

"Taking a personal day," Bernard said.

Wilde saw no reason to reply.

"Why do you need her passport?"

"Any chance Naomi is with her mother?"

Something skittered across his face. "Why do you ask that?"

"We called her."

"You called Pia?"

No reason to clarify that the call was made by Hester's office. "Last time we called, your ex-wife straight-up told us that Naomi wasn't with her. This time she wouldn't reply. We also have a report your ex is overseas."

"Which is why you asked me about her passport." Pine led Wilde to a home office in the back of the house. Standard stuff—desk, computer, printer, file cabinet. Wilde spotted an electric bill and something from the cable company on the right. The checkbook was out. The screensaver was a generic ocean shot, probably one of the computer default screens. The paperweight was a Lucite-block award with Bernard's name on it, some kind of "salesman of the month" type thing. There was a classic photograph of a golf foursome at a pro-am outing, Bernard beaming on the far right as he held his driver.

There were no photographs of his daughter.

Bernard Pine rummaged through the drawer, ducking his head for a better look. "Here."

He pulled out the passport. Wilde held out his hand. Bernard hesitated and handed Naomi's passport over. There was only one foreign stamp—Heathrow Airport in London three years ago.

"Naomi is not with my ex," Pine said.

There was no doubt in his tone.

"Can I show you something?"

Wilde nodded.

"I don't want you to think I'm weird or anything." Bernard Pine turned around to the file cabinet. He fumbled for a key, unlocked it, opened the bottom drawer. He reached into the back and pulled out a magazine in protective wrap. The magazine was called *SportsGlobe*. The publication date was from two decades ago. On the cover was a swimsuit model.

There was a yellow Post-it marking a page. Pine carefully turned to it.

"Pia," he said, with a longing that made even Wilde pull up. "Gorgeous, right?"

Wilde looked down at the model in the floss bikini.

"This was taken a year after we met. Pia mostly modeled lingerie and bikinis. She tried out for *Sports Illustrated*'s swimsuit issue. You remember how big that used to be?"

Wilde said nothing.

"So Pia goes on an audition or whatever they call it and you know what *Sports Illustrated* tells her?"

He stopped and waited for Wilde to answer. To keep things moving, Wilde said, "No."

"They say she's too curvy. That's the word they used. Curvy. They thought her..."—he cupped his hands in front of his chest—"had to be fake. Can you believe that? They said they were so great, they had to be implants." He gestured toward the photograph. "But those are real. Amazing, right?"

Wilde said nothing.

"I sound like a pig, don't I?"

Wilde chose the lie that would keep him talking. "Not really."

"Pia and I met at a club in the East Village. I couldn't believe my luck. I mean, every guy wanted her. But we just hit it off. She was so beautiful. I couldn't stop staring at her. We fell pretty hard. I was working at Smith Barney back then. Making pretty sweet dollars. Pia was modeling just enough. I'm not saying it was perfect. Beautiful women, women who look like this, they always have a little crazy. It comes with the package, I guess. But back then I found that so exciting, you know, and she was just so superhot. We were in love, we had money, we had the city, we had no responsibilities..."

Bernard closed the magazine with care, as though it were a fragile religious text, and slipped it back into the protective plastic. He turned back to the file cabinet, placed it in the back, locked the drawer.

"We were together about a year when Pia told me that she couldn't have children. This will sound weird, I guess, but we never talked about it before. I don't know, I guess she worried about my reaction. But—and this might surprise you—I was thrilled. We were having a blast. I didn't want a baby messing it up, and, man this will sound awful, I loved her bod so much. I had friends with hot wives. Not hot like Pia. But hot. And after childbirth, well, you know what I'm saying?"

Wilde said, "Uh-huh."

"I'm just being honest."

Wilde said, "Uh-huh" again.

"So we got married. Big mistake. Pia and me, we were good before we made it official. But then you start hanging around other married couples and they're all having babies. Pia, well, what I thought was her being eccentric and maybe a little moody? Now that's more like depression or bipolar or something like that. She started staying in bed all day. She didn't take any more jobs. She even put on a few pounds."

Wilde wanted to feign a gasp and say "how awful," but he stayed silent.

"So now, of course, Pia wants a baby. I don't know if it's the best thing, but I love her. I want her happy. And we wouldn't be the first people to think a baby could save our marriage, right? So we start talking about surrogates and all that, but in the end, I find this adoption agency in Maine. You pay a little more, but they make things smoother. The agency told us we would have a healthy baby in six months. Pia, well, it worked. She heard that news, she started taking care of herself again. We were back, except, you know, she became obsessed with the arrival. Suddenly she didn't want to live in the city anymore. The city was dirty, she said. It's no place to raise a child. So she found this place"—Bernard spread his hands—"in the real estate section of the *Times*. You know. Like unusual homes. So we bought it and moved out here two days before Naomi came home to us. It was all going to be great."

Bernard Pine stopped.

"So what happened?" Wilde asked.

"I read somewhere that even adoptive mothers can suffer from postpartum depression or something similar. I don't know if that's what it was, but Pia kinda lost herself. It was awful. She couldn't connect to her daughter in any way. Not even in like a cellular way. It was like our baby was a new kidney Pia's body was rejecting."

Interesting way to put it, Wilde thought. "So what did you do?"

"I hired nannies. Pia kept firing them. I tried to get her to see a shrink, but she flat-out refused. And I still had a job. The commute from out here to the city, no matter how you slice it, is at least an hour each way." He closed his eyes hard, then opened them. "One day, I came home and there was a bruise on Naomi's arm. She fell, Pia said. Another day, there was a cut over her eye. The girl is clumsy, Pia said."

Bernard made a fist and put it near his mouth. "This is very hard to talk about."

"Do you want a glass of water or something?"

"No, I want to get through this before I chicken out. I've never told this story. Not to anyone. I should have done more, I guess. I should have insisted Pia get help or..."

He stopped again, exhausted, and for a moment, Wilde feared that he wouldn't go on.

"We've come this far," Wilde said. "Tell me the rest."

"I started to get scared for Naomi's health. So one day, I didn't go to work. I just pretended like I was heading to the bus, but I hung in town. I can't say exactly why. Something felt extra-off that morning. Or maybe I had a premonition, I don't know. I came home an hour after I left. Totally unexpected. I could hear the screaming from the driveway. Both of them. Screaming. I ran inside. They were upstairs. Pia was giving her a bath. The water. It was so hot, I could see the steam coming up off the top."

He squeezed his eyes shut now.

"That was it. The straw that broke the camel's back. I forced Pia to get help, though 'help' is a relative term. We got divorced—quietly. No reason to let the world know what happened, right? Pia gave up all parental rights. Buying my silence maybe. Or maybe she just knew that she'd never care. That was fifteen years ago. Naomi hasn't seen her mother since."

Wilde tried to wade past what he'd just heard, tried to get past this horrible tale and keep moving ahead with his investigation. Then: "Are you sure?"

"What do you mean?"

"Could Naomi and your ex have started seeing each other behind your back?"

"I don't think so. Pia still battles with severe mental health issues, but she's managed to lasso in a rich new husband. My guess? She stopped thinking about Naomi long ago."

CHAPTER TWENTY-SIX

Hester called Aaron Gerios, a former FBI Special Agent who'd worked hostage situations and kidnappings. "I have a hypothetical situation for you."

"A hypothetical," Gerios repeated.

"Yes," Hester said. "You know what the word 'hypothetical' means, don't you, Aaron?"

"When you call, it means the situation is real, not hypothetical, but you can't tell me who it is."

"I'll pretend you said that in a hypothetical way."

Hester laid out the kidnapping-ransom situation. The suggestions Aaron made were pretty close to what Wilde had already set up. In short, they were doing everything right, considering the circumstances. Gerios also questioned the likelihood that this was a legitimate kidnapping.

"It sounds more like this kid is pranking his parents."

"Could be."

"Or some hot girl seduced him into doing this."

"A man thinking with his dick first," Hester said. "I didn't know such a thing existed."

"You've always been a naïve waif, Hester."

"Yes. Yes, true. Thanks, Aaron."

"No worries. But may I offer you one last piece of repetitive advice?"

"Sure."

"Convince your hypothetical parents to contact the very real FBI. Even if it's a big nothing, these situations tend to go sideways when we aren't involved."

Aaron hung up.

Hester was still walking the grounds of Maynard Manor. There was little doubt that the estate was grand in the old-school way in which it was intended to be, but some of the modern touches were jarring. Right now, Hester was walking past a "sculpture garden" with somewhat tacky bronze likenesses of the Maynard family from several years ago. The twin girls who were now fourteen—Hester couldn't remember their names, something with K's like Katie or Karen—looked to be about seven or eight in the bronze. One flew a bronze kite while the other kicked a bronze ball. Bronze Crash was probably around twelve or thirteen and carried a lacrosse stick on his shoulder like Huck Finn with a fishing pole. Bronze Delia and Bronze Dash watched their bronze children and laughed. The entire Bronze Maynard family were laughing, their faces frozen in that laugh, forever and ever, and that was kind of creepy.

Hester's phone buzzed. The caller ID read OREN. Despite everything, her cheeks still flushed just seeing his name.

"Articulate," Hester said.

"Why do you answer the phone that way?"

"Long story."

"Can I hear it sometime in the very near future?"

She smiled. "How near?"

"I'm on backup duty tonight, so I have to stay in the area. What's your schedule look like?"

"I'm in town."

"Visiting Matthew and Laila?"

"Something else," Hester said. "Business."

"Oh. Are you free for dinner then? It won't quite be last night, but I'm powerful enough to get us a table at Tony's Pizza and Sub. I'll even pay."

"Thank you for that, by the way."

"For what?"

"For letting me pay last night. For thanking me and not playing the macho card and insisting."

"I was trying to be a modern, sensitive man. How did I do?"

"Very well."

"I never understood that really."

"What?"

"This will sound too politically correct."

"Go on."

"Let's face it. You make a lot more money than I do. I'm not being all evolved here. Just the opposite. But I never get the guys who get all bent out of shape when the woman makes more money. The way I've always looked at it, if I'm lucky enough to be with a highly successful woman, that makes *me* look better. The more successful my girl is, the more I look good. Make sense?"

He said "my girl." Swoon.

"So," Hester said, "your being so evolved is really being self-involved?"

"Exactly."

Hester realized again that she was smiling in a way she normally never smiled. "I like it."

"That said, I got tonight's check. Which will be less than the tip on last night's dinner. Sevenish? Unless you're heading back into the city tonight."

Hester thought about it. She didn't know what the status of this would be, but either way, she would need to stick around—and she would probably need to eat. They made the plans tentative and then they hung up.

Hester wandered back toward the house. The grounds were

immense and held no appeal to Hester. The constant tranquillity grew unnerving.

Hester headed inside and found Delia on the phone in that library that was a little too Disneyesque. Delia spotted Hester and waved her in. She put a finger to her lips to signal silence and hit the button for the speakerphone, so Hester could listen too.

Delia said, "Thanks, Sutton, for getting back to me."

"I would have called back sooner, Mrs. Maynard, but I was in class." The girl sounded very much like a teenager. "Is Crash okay?"

"Why do you ask?"

"Well, he's not in school today."

"When did you last talk to him?"

"Crash? We texted last night."

"What time, Sutton?" Delia asked.

There was a hesitation.

"He's not in any trouble," Delia said. "But he went out last night, and I haven't heard from him today."

"Can you hold on a second?" Sutton asked. "I can look up exactly on my phone."

"Sure."

There was a short delay and then Sutton said, "One forty-eight a.m."

"What did he say?"

"He just said he had to go."

"That's it."

"Yeah. 'Gotta run.' That was it."

"Do you have any idea where he might be?"

"No, sorry. I'm sure it's nothing. I can check with Trevor and Ryan and the guys."

"That would be great, thanks."

"The only thing is," Sutton began.

"Yes?"

"I mean, I don't want you to worry or anything. But he usually texts me. A lot. I mean, we all do. We have group chats and just regular texts and Snapchat and whatever else. I mean, I can't remember the last time he didn't text me in the morning."

Delia put a hand to her neck. "Did you text him?"

"Just once. No reply. You want me to try again?"

"Yes, please."

"I'll let you know if I hear anything."

Delia looked over at Hester. Hester mouthed the word "Naomi" at her. Delia nodded.

"Is Crash friendly with Naomi Pine?"

Silence.

"Sutton?"

"Why would you ask about Naomi?"

Delia looked over at Hester. Hester shrugged.

"Well, Naomi is missing—"

"And you think Crash is with her?"

The disbelief in her voice was palpable.

"I don't know. I'm just asking. Are they friends?"

"No, Mrs. Maynard. I don't want to be mean, but Naomi and Crash travel in very different circles."

"And yet he encouraged her to play that Challenge game, right?"

"I have to go to class. If I hear from Crash, I'll let you know right away."

Sutton hung up.

Hester said, "Is that Crash's girlfriend?"

"On and off. Sutton is probably the most popular girl in the school."

"And Crash is one of the most popular boys," Hester said.

"Yes."

"So maybe the popular boy suddenly has a thing for the ostracized girl."

"Sounds like a bad teen rom-com," Delia said with a shrug. "Then again, it wouldn't be the first time."

"Maybe even his bullying her—"

"My son didn't bully her."

"—or whatever you want to call it. Maybe it was like that little boy in the playground who pulls the girl's pigtails because he likes her."

Delia didn't like that. "That little boy usually grows up to be a sociopath."

"What's on those tapes, Delia?"

The change of subject caught Delia Maynard off guard. That was the purpose, of course. Hester was studying her face, looking for the tell. She thought she saw one. Not one hundred percent sure. Hester had been questioning people for a very long time. More than most, she could see a lie, but those who claimed to be "foolproof" were, to quote half of the word, usually the fools.

"There's nothing important," Delia said.

"Then contact the FBI."

"We can't."

"Which suggests that you have something to hide. Sorry, I'm not great with subtle, so let me get right to it: I think you're lying. Worse, you're lying to me. So let me make this clear. I don't care what you're hiding or what's on those tapes. If I know about it and I'm your attorney? It stays secret."

Delia smiled but there was no humor in it. "Always?"

"Always."

"No matter what?"

"No matter what."

Delia crossed the room and looked out the window. The view was spectacular, but it didn't seem to be bringing Delia Maynard much peace or comfort or joy. "I told you I watched your show the other night. When Saul Strauss was on."

"What about it?"

"Strauss started to raise the 'if you could have stopped Hitler' speculation. You cut him off."

"Of course I did," Hester said. "It's utter nonsense on a thousand levels."

"So let's say hypothetically I knew something that could have stopped Hitler—"

"Oh please—"

"—and I confide it to you under attorney-client privilege."

"Would I tell?" Hester said. "No."

"Even if it means letting Hitler rise to power?"

"Yes, but it's a dumb hypothetical," Hester said. "I don't want to get too deep into this, but have you read much on the Hitler paradox? In short, if you went back in time and killed baby Hitler, the changes may be so massive that everything would change, almost every birth thereafter, and so you and I wouldn't be here. But that's not why this is dumb. It's dumb because I can't read the future or go back in time. The future is all conjecture—none of us have a clue what it will be like. So I can tell you that whatever your grave secret is, I won't tell. No matter what. Because I don't know if it will really stop the next Hitler. I also don't know if stopping the next Hitler is even desirable. Maybe if I stopped Hitler, a more competent psycho would have risen instead—after those German scientists developed a nuclear bomb. Maybe it would have gone even worse. Do you see what I'm saying?"

"I do," Delia said. "There are too many variables. You may think you're stopping a slaughter—and end up creating a bigger one."

"Exactly. I've heard some horrible confessions in this job. Gruesome, terrible..." Hester closed her eyes for a moment. "And maybe the world would have been better if I broke my oath. But only on a micro level. Justice for that family maybe. Preventing another tragedy and even worse. But in the end, I have to believe in the system, flawed though it may be."

Delia nodded slowly. "There's nothing on those tapes."

"You're sure?"

"I am. There are some things Rusty's enemies may try to use against him. But there is no smoking gun."

"Okay then," Hester said. Her phone buzzed. She saw a text from Wilde:

My security people will be there within the half hour.

Delia was about to make another call. Hester watched her for a moment. Delia felt the eyes on her and looked up. "What?" Delia said.

"Let me add one caveat to the above," Hester said, "mother to mother."

"Okay."

"If it meant saving my son, I'd talk."

Delia didn't move.

"I'd scream, I'd shout, I'd reveal everything. That's where all our paradox theories would go out the window. If I could go back in time, if I could reveal a truth and it would bring my son back to me, I'd do it in a heartbeat. Do you understand?"

"I think so."

Hester's eyes stayed dry as she nodded and turned away.

CHAPTER TWENTY-SEVEN

The team from Wilde's old security firm pulled up in two vehicles.

The first car was a forest-green Honda Odyssey minivan. The driver was Rola Naser, the firm's founder. When Rola opened the car door, Wilde could hear her kids screeching from the backseat. The radio was blasting out a Wiggles tune about fruit salad being yummy.

"Mommy will be right back," Rola said.

Neither the screeching nor the music paused for that announcement. Rola got out of the minivan and started toward Wilde. Her blue blazer had a stain on the lapel. She wore Puma sneakers and Mom jeans. A diaper bag of some sort was slung over her shoulder.

She stomped toward him, head high. Rola was barely five feet tall so she had to look up to meet his eye. Wilde braced himself.

"Are you kidding me, Wilde?"

"What?"

"'What?'" Rola said, doing a pretty good, pretty sarcastic impression of him. "Don't even with that, okay?"

"Sorry."

"I deserve better from you, do I not?"

"You do, yes."

"So how long has it been?" Rola asked.

"I don't know," he said.

"Yes, you do. *Two* years. *Two* frigging years, Wilde. Last time I saw you was when Emma was born."

Emma was Rola's fifth child—three boys, two girls, all under the age of twelve. Years ago, Rola had been his foster sister at the Brewers' house. Over the years, the Brewer family had almost forty foster kids go through their lives, and all had been made better by the experience. Some stayed only a few months. Some, like Wilde and Rola, stayed years.

"And this stain you keep staring at"—she pointed to her lapel—"the one I know you are *dying* to clean off me? That's Emma's spit-up, thank you very much. What do you have to say to that?"

"Gross?"

She shook her head. Rola's background, like his, was something of a mystery. Her mother was a Sunni Arab who fled the kingdom of Jordan, arriving in the United States pregnant and unmarried. She'd cut off all ties to family and friends from her native country. She never spoke of them. She never told anyone, not even Rola, who her father was.

"What the hell, Wilde? Two years."

"Sorry," Wilde said again. He looked toward the minivan. "How is everyone?"

Rola arched an eyebrow. "For real?"

"What?"

"'How is everyone?'" Rola repeated, doing the impression again. "That's the best you can do? You don't visit. You don't call."

"I called," he said.

"When?"

"Today. Just now."

Rola's mouth dropped open. "Are you for real right now?"

He said nothing.

"You called because you needed help."

"Still a call," he said.

Rola shook her head and said with deep regret in her voice: "Ah, Wilde. You'll never change, will you?"

He had warned Rola when she'd insisted he be her full-time partner that there was no way he could last. She knew and even understood, but Rola had always been the craziest sort of rah-rah optimist, even when she had no right to be. In the Brewer house, Rola had been outgoing and boisterous and engaged and social and never stopped talking. She'd loved the frenzy of activity, the shuffling of foster kids in and out, in part, Wilde thought, because she hated being alone.

Rola craved a crowd the way Wilde craved solitude.

More than overcoming the obstacles, Rola had excelled—valedictorian of her high school class, vice president of the class, captain of her soccer team on every level. As a college standout athlete, she'd been heavily recruited by the FBI. She joined, rose up the ranks quickly, and then when Wilde came home from the army, she somehow convinced him to open a private investigation firm with her. She had decided to call it CRAW—Chloe, Rola, And Wilde.

Chloe, now deceased, had been the Brewers' dog.

"CRAW," Rola had said at the time. "The name is cute, right?"

"Adorable."

Wilde had tried to hang on and fit in and go to the office, but in the end, he couldn't stick it out. It wasn't his way. He tried to give her back his shares, but Rola wouldn't take them. She still wanted his name on the door, so every once in a while, he did some extracurricular work for her.

He knew that he should be better about communicating—return calls, be more present, reach out every once in a while, say yes to a social engagement. And he did care about Rola and Scott and their kids. He cared a lot. But he couldn't do more. It just wasn't in him.

"I brought everything," Rola said, transitioning quickly into serious work mode.

She shrugged the bag off her shoulder and handed it to him.

He frowned. "Is this a diaper bag?"

"Don't worry. It's brand-new. No germs. If someone opens it, they'll just find clean baby clothes and clean diapers. You can tell them you're a caring uncle, though that will obviously be a big character stretch. Do you need me to show you where the hidden pockets are?"

"I think I'll figure it out."

"I packed four GPS trackers, three throwaway phones. You need a blade?"

"No."

"There's still one in the snap-flap closure. Where I keep the wipes."

"Terrific." Wilde looked at the other car. It was a black Buick. "I need three people to cover the Maynards at all times."

"Three of our best are in the Buick," Rola said. She nodded. The car doors opened, and her security team stepped out.

"All women," Wilde said.

"That a problem?"

"Nope."

"You're so progressive, Wilde. And the flaming redhead on the right isn't a woman. Zelda is gender non-binary."

Zelda gave him a little wave. Wilde waved back.

"The four of us will rotate shifts," Rola said.

"Wait. You?"

"Yes me. I'll be in the first group."

"You can't bring your kids to the Maynards'."

"Really, Wilde? I didn't realize. Thanks for telling me. Can I just jot that down?" Rola mimed a pen in her hand and pad in her palm. "Don't. Bring. Kids. To. A. Kidnapping." She put away the air pen. "There. All set."

"Ah, Rola," he said, now mimicking her. "You'll never change, will you?"

That made her smile.

Wilde looked back over at the Honda Odyssey. "So who's in your car?"

"Emma and the twins."

The twins, he remembered, were six.

"I'm dropping Zoe and Elijah at a friend's birthday in Upper Saddle River at a place called the Gravity Vault. One of the moms said she'd watch Emma until Scott gets there. I'll be at the Maynards' within the half hour."

"Okay."

"Anything I should know?"

"You know the drill."

Rola gave him a mock salute. "Right."

For a second, the two of them stood there, unsure what to do.

"I got to go," Wilde said, awkwardly pointing behind him with his thumb. Then he spun away. He didn't turn around, but he heard the black Buick peel away, and Rola calmly say, "Zoe, let go of your brother's hair," as she climbed back into the minivan.

Ten minutes later, Wilde arrived at the 7-Eleven down the block from the high school. Ava had texted him that she would meet him here because the school itself, after yesterday's physical altercation with Thor-Bryce, was off-limits. Wilde headed inside, watched the hot dogs circle, saw the Slurpee machines. Nothing changes at a 7-Eleven. Time flows forward everywhere except in a 7-Eleven.

As Ava O'Brien pulled into the parking lot, Wilde felt his phone buzz. He checked the screen and saw it was Gavin Chambers.

"Where are you?" Gavin asked.

"Seven-Eleven."

"Are you serious?"

"I could snap a picture of a Slurpee as proof."

"Wait there."

"Why?"

"Something you need to see. Don't move."

Chambers hung up. Ava came in and without preamble asked, "What's so important?"

No hello. No greeting of any sort. Maybe Ava was upset about yesterday. She looked more harried today, though no less beautiful. Her eyes sparkled when they looked up at him.

Following her lead, Wilde got to the point: "Do you know Saul Strauss?"

Ava made a face. "That activist on TV?"

"Yes."

"I know who he is, sure."

"I mean, do you know him personally?"

"No. Why?"

"You've never spoken to him or communicated with him in any way?"

"No. Again: Why?"

"Because he knew about my encounter with Crash at your school."

"So did everyone else," Ava said. "We ended up out in the parking lot, remember?"

"He knew more than that."

"I don't understand. What are you asking me here?"

"I'm trying to figure out Saul Strauss's source."

The sparkling eyes caught fire. "This is why you dragged me out of school during my free period? I'm not his source, Wilde. And why would someone like Saul Strauss care about any of this anyway?"

Wilde said nothing.

Ava looked annoyed. "Hello?"

He didn't know how much to tell her. He believed her about not knowing Strauss—and even if she did, he couldn't follow the line of logic. Suppose Ava worked with Strauss somehow. Suppose Ava told Strauss that Wilde had confronted Crash about a missing teenage girl. So what follows? Strauss kidnaps the boy? Did that make any sense?

Too many missing pieces.

"Crash Maynard is missing," Wilde said.

That surprised her. "Wait, when you say 'missing'—"

"Ran away, hiding, kidnapped, whatever. Last night he was home. Today he's gone."

Ava took that in for a moment. "You mean like Naomi?"

"Yes."

She took two steps toward the back so that they were now standing by the chips and salty snacks. He didn't interrupt with a question. Not yet. He wanted to give her some time.

"That may explain some stuff," Ava said.

"Like?"

"I thought Naomi was... I don't know. 'Lying' is too strong a word. 'Exaggerating' is too mild."

Wilde waited. When she didn't say anything else, he asked, "What about?"

"Crash."

"What about him?"

"Naomi has been hinting lately that she had a secret boyfriend—someone super popular. I didn't take it seriously. Do you remember that old bit about the guy who says, 'Oh, I have a hot girlfriend, but you wouldn't know her'?"

Wilde nodded. "She lives in Canada or something."

"Right."

"You thought Naomi was making it up."

"Or imagining it, whatever. Yeah, at first."

"And then?"

"Then after I pushed a little, she told me that the boy was Crash Maynard. She said the whole Challenge game was a cover and that Crash got jealous because she went into the woods with Matthew."

Matthew.

"What did you say to that?" Wilde asked.

"I started wondering whether Crash was setting her up again."

"Pretending to like her so he could ultimately humiliate her?"

"Yes. Like in *Carrie*. Or, wait, wasn't the boy who asked Carrie out in the movie nice? Didn't he try to defend her but then the bullies poured pig's blood on her?"

Wilde didn't remember. "So you think maybe Crash *does* like her?"

"I don't know," Ava said, chewing on her lower lip. "But maybe the simplest answer is the best one—Naomi and Crash are together. Maybe they just want a few days alone. Maybe it isn't our business."

Something wasn't adding up. Or it was adding up too neatly.

"I have to get back," Ava said.

"Let me walk you to your car."

They headed out to the parking lot. Ava hit the unlock button. He wanted to open the door for her, but that felt too faux chivalrous. When she got into the driver's seat, he signaled for her to lower the window for a moment. She did. Wilde leaned against the opening.

"I also talked to Naomi's dad."

"And?"

"He said Naomi's mother was abusive."

He filled her in on the details of his conversation with Bernard Pine. As Ava listened, her eyes glistened with tears. "Poor Naomi. I knew the relationship hadn't been good obviously. But that?" Ava shook her head. "I better go."

"You'll be okay?"

"Yeah, I'm fine."

"You want me to stop by your place later?" he asked.

The words just came out. Wilde hadn't planned them. That wasn't like him.

Ava looked surprised. She took another swipe at her eyes and turned to him. "When?"

"I don't know. Tonight maybe. Tomorrow. We can just talk."

Ava looked out the front windshield rather than at him.

"No pressure," Wilde added. "I may not be free anyway, what with Crash and Naomi—"

"No, I'd like that."

Ava reached through the open window and put her hand on his face. He waited. She looked as though she was about to say more, but in the end, she just took her hand away. She put the car in reverse, pulled out, and headed back toward the school.

CHAPTER TWENTY-EIGHT

"So you got Arnie Poplin ready?" Hester asked.

Hester stood facing the computer monitor in the Maynards' state-of-the-art studio/office. The room was white and steel and looked more like something you'd find in a refurbished Manhattan loft rather than this old estate, but there it was. There were television screens lining the walls. Her producer Allison Grant was on the line.

Rola Naser, someone Hester had known for many years, was setting up the live feed. Hester had always liked Rola, admired her strength under adversity. When Rola and David were teens at the same high school, she'd even hoped that maybe her David would ask her out. She even pushed him a little, surprise, surprise. David never listened, of course, claiming that it would be "weird" because Rola was "like Wilde's sister."

What if he had? Would everything have changed? Would David still be alive?

"Okay, he's connected in now," Allison said.

Hester shook away the ghosts and leaned toward Rola. "Did you hear that?"

"Got it," Rola said as she typed.

Hester's idea was a simple albeit an unreliable one. Saul Strauss had said that his source on the Maynard tapes was Arnie Poplin. Arnie Poplin was, if nothing else, an attention whore. Hester got Allison to track him down with the promise of a "pre-interview" that could lead to a live segment.

Rola said, "You see that monitor on that wall?"

"You mean that gigantic TV?"

"Yes, Hester, the gigantic TV."

"I see it. I think you could see it from space."

"Stand over there," Rola said. "I'm going to patch Arnie Poplin through."

"Stand where exactly?"

"There's a spike on the floor."

And so there was. A spike was what studios or theaters called the mark, usually made with electrical tape, to tell you where to stand or where to place a piece of the set. Hester stood on it.

Rola said, "Ready?"

"As I'll ever be. Will Arnie be able to see you in the room?"

"No. His camera will be focused on your face only. It's why I chose that monitor."

"Great, thanks." Hester smiled at her. "It's really good to see you, Rola."

"And you, Hester. Ready?"

Hester nodded. Rola clicked a few more keys, and the screen came to life. Arnie Poplin's familiar (though more bloated) face filled the screen, huge and close-up, too close-up—see-his-skin-pores close-up. Hester was tempted to take a step back, but alas, the spike.

"Hi, Arnie."

He scowled a little too theatrically. "What the hell is this, Hester?"

They'd met over the years at one thing or another. Twenty-five years ago, Arnie Poplin had starred in a hit family sitcom as the hilarious neighbor. For three years he was beloved and famous.

Then, poof, it was over. Like many, he ended up fighting the withdrawal pains from two of society's most potent addictions—drugs and fame. People underestimate the power of that bright, warm beacon known as fame—and how dark and cold it gets when that beacon goes out.

So Arnie desperately tried to hang on. Allison Grant half joked that Arnie Poplin would appear at the opening of a garage door. He tried to bow and scrape his way onto game shows, reality shows, home and garden shows, cooking shows—anything to turn on that beacon—less bright, less warm—for even a few seconds.

Hester said, "I wanted to ask you—"

"You think I'm an idiot?"

He was sweaty and red-faced.

"I saw your Saul Strauss segment, Hester. Do you know what you called me?"

"A celebrity has-been-turned-conspiracy-nut," Hester said.

His mouth dropped open in what she assumed was mock surprise. It took him a few seconds to work up the bluster again. Actors. "You expect me to just forgive you for that?"

"You have two choices here, Arnie. You can disconnect this call or Skype or whatever this video-cloudy thingy is, or you can tell me your side of it."

"You won't believe me."

"Probably not. But if you can convince me you're telling the truth, even a little bit, I'll have you on the show."

"Solo segment?" Arnie rubbed his face. "I don't want some point-counterpoint crap."

"One-on-one interview. Just you and me."

He crossed his arms and pretended to think it over for a millisecond. "What do you want to know?"

"Tell me about the Rusty Eggers tapes you claim Dash Maynard has in his possession."

"They exist."

"How do you know?"

"I was on *The Rusty Show*. You know this, right?"

"Right."

"Big ratings when I was on. No one talks about that."

Hester sighed. "Arnie."

"Right, right. So anyway, I overheard them. Rusty and Dash. They were talking about the tapes. Dash swore he'd destroyed them."

"So if Dash destroyed them—"

"Oh come on. No one really destroys tapes, Hester. You know that. And Rusty knew it. That's why he was so upset. He knew that Dash would never get rid of them totally. Why would he?"

"Dash Maynard swears he doesn't have any damaging tapes."

"Yeah, well, Dash is a selfish prick, isn't he? He has this big empire. You ever been to his house? It's like something out of Gatsby."

"Have you seen the tapes?" Hester asked.

"Me? No."

"So how do you know they exist?"

"I heard them."

"Heard the tapes?"

"No. I heard Dash and Rusty arguing about them."

"What did they say exactly?"

"It was late at night, see. I was the only one still around. They thought I was gone. That they were alone. Can I tell you the truth though?"

"Yeah, that'd be nice, Arnie."

"I passed out on the toilet."

"Sorry?"

"Yeah, I was in the studio office. In a toilet stall. Sitting down on—"

"I got the visual, Arnie."

"Anyway, I was snorting some coke, whatever. I don't know. I passed out. When I woke up, the bathroom was totally dark. It was ten at night. I pulled up my pants. They were still down around my ankles."

"Hey, thanks for that detail."

"You want the whole story, don't you?"

"Boxers or briefs?"

"Huh?"

"Never mind," Hester said. "You pulled up your pants."

"Right, I pull up my pants. But like I said, it's totally dark. I mean, pitch black. I feel my way to the latch. You know, the one that opens the stall."

"Yes, Arnie, I know about those latches. We have them in women's bathrooms too."

"Anyway, it's still dark. I feel my way out of the can. I get into the hallway. I'm worried that maybe they lock the doors at night. Like maybe I can't get out. You know what I mean?"

"Right, go on."

"Then I hear voices. Two men."

"Let me guess. Rusty and Dash."

"Right. And they're arguing. I get closer. I heard Rusty say, 'You got to get rid of the tape. You have to promise me.' He's drunk. I can hear it in his voice. Rusty is usually in control, but he's got that sloppy-drunk thing going on. And he keeps saying, 'You don't get what it could do to us, you should destroy it, you don't want anyone to ever know.'"

"And what did Dash say?"

"He just said don't worry, no one would ever know, he'd make sure of it. But Rusty kept insisting. He kept begging Dash to delete it, but then he'd sort of take it back."

"What do you mean, take it back?"

"He knew, Hester. Rusty knew."

"Knew what?"

"That Dash Maynard would never really delete it. Dash sees himself as a serious documentarian or journalist or something. An observer. I wouldn't be surprised if even that conversation was recorded. I'm telling you. There were bugs everywhere. Maybe even in that bathroom."

"Uh-huh," Hester said. This was sounding more and more like a waste of time. "So what else?"

"That's not enough?"

"Not really."

"They knew I was there."

"Did they say something?"

"No, but three days later, I got called in for a surprise urine test. They found drugs in my system. I was fired. Me. Their big ratings draw. Not only that, the test was leaked to the media. You know why, right? It was a plot to discredit me. I was clean."

"You just told me you took cocaine—"

"That was three days earlier!"

He was getting more and more agitated, shifting in his seat, eyes darting, sweat beads popping up on his forehead, and Hester bet that Arnie Poplin was on something right now. "They needed to discredit me. They needed to get rid of me."

"Okay, thanks."

"Rusty killed someone."

Hester stopped. "What do you mean?"

"That's what Dash has on him."

"Are you saying," Hester began slowly, "that Dash Maynard has a tape of Rusty Eggers committing murder?"

"I can only tell you what I heard."

"Which was?"

"Rusty saying, 'I didn't mean to kill him, it was an accident.'"

"Those were his exact words?"

"No. I don't know. That was the meaning. Rusty killed someone. That was their bond. Dash even said that, now that I think of it."

"Said what?"

"That he'd never tell because that was their bond. Something like that. That all the good things that came after were based on that bond. I'm telling you, Hester. They're killers. Or Rusty is. Dash has the proof. He has a legal obligation to release that information, doesn't he?"

Hester thought about her earlier conversation with Delia, about what she knew and wouldn't reveal despite attorney-client privilege. She glanced over at Rola. Rola shrugged as if to say she didn't know whether to believe him or not.

"So can I come on the show?" Arnie Poplin said. "I'm free tonight if you want to do it then."

CHAPTER TWENTY-NINE

Gavin Chambers pulled into the 7-Eleven lot in a blue Chevrolet Cruze. Alone. Gone for now at least were both the driver and the SUV. Discretion? Maybe. He slid out of the Chevy wearing a baseball cap and sunglasses, which, Wilde thought, was always a dumb disguise because the only people who don that look are trying to disguise themselves. Then again it was sunny out. Maybe Gavin was just wearing them because they were comfortable.

Maybe not everything is a freaking clue.

"Why are you at a 7-Eleven?" Gavin asked.

"The Slurpee isn't reason enough?"

Gavin sighed. "So what have you learned?"

"I learned not to move because you had something you needed me to see. At least, that's what you told me on the phone."

He shook his head. "You remind me of my first wife."

"Was she hot too?"

"A hot mess."

Wilde checked his phone. "Do you mind giving me a lift back to the Maynards'? We can talk on the way."

"Suit yourself." He hit the unlock button on the remote. As

they got in, Gavin dropped the bomb: "We know that there's been a ransom demand."

He started up the car and put it in reverse.

Top four possibilities, Wilde thought.

One, Chambers was completely fishing. That didn't seem likely.

Two, what with the panic around the Maynards, Chambers had simply surmised that there must have been a ransom demand. If so, that was a hell of a guess.

Three, he did indeed have certain areas of the house bugged. Very possible. Rola would run a sweep and he'd know about that soon enough.

Four, Gavin had an inside source.

Whatever, Wilde wasn't going to confirm or deny. At the traffic light, Gavin Chambers turned and stared at him. Wilde stared back. For a few moments, neither of them blinked. When the light turned green, someone behind them honked their horn. Gavin shook his head and muttered something under his breath as he pulled out his phone.

"You know I told you that Crash stayed a step ahead of us with the messaging apps—Snapchat, Signal, WhatsApp, whatever?"

"Yes."

"One of my best tech guys found a message received on his ISP last night at 2:07 a.m. via a new app called Communicate Plus. It's encrypted so the message and sender get automatically deleted a minute after the file is opened. I obviously don't know the details, but somehow, don't ask me how, my tech guy was able to get the tail end of the last message before it was erased."

He handed Wilde his phone. The message read:

> Of course I forgive you. I know you did that to fool your friends. I'm waiting at the same place right now. So excited!!!

There were three heart emojis at the end.

Wilde asked the obvious: "Do you know where the message came from or who sent it?"

"No. We know it had to be someone else with this app obviously, but the contact and incoming ISP or whatever gets deleted."

Wilde stared at the message. He read it again.

"Did someone make a ransom demand?" Gavin asked.

"You said you already know."

"What?"

"Your exact words were, 'we know that there's been a ransom demand.' If you know, there's no reason to ask me."

"Can you stop being a pain in the ass for five minutes? Rusty wants to help."

"I'm sure he does."

"And we both know who wrote that message."

He meant, of course, Naomi.

"Assuming you're right," Wilde said, "what do you want to do about it?"

"Did you check Naomi's house?"

"I visited the father."

"Did you check the whole house? Last time that's where she was the whole time, right? In the basement?"

Wilde said nothing. He checked his watch. It was almost three p.m., an hour until the deadline. When they approached the gate in front of the Maynard house, Wilde said, "Thanks for the ride."

"You know I'm right," Gavin said.

"About?"

"About everything. You know Naomi is somehow involved in this."

"Uh-huh. What else are you right about?"

He gave him the dagger glare. "That you and your sister can't handle this alone."

"I'm not calling the shots," Wilde said.

"If you tell the Maynards to bring us back in, they'll listen to you."

Something here, something about this whole encounter, was definitely not adding up.

"Thanks for the ride, Gavin. Stay in touch."

Rola met him by the Maynards' security gate in a golf cart.

"I'll drive you up to Hester."

He sat beside her as they started up the drive. The grounds were overmanicured. Many would find that beautiful. Wilde did not. Nature paints her canvas, then you come along and think you can improve it. No. Nature is supposed to be, pardon the wordage, wild. You tame it, you lose what makes it special.

After he filled her in, Rola asked, "So what do you need from me?"

"The ransom note."

"What about it?"

"It asked specifically for the 'oldest' tapes."

"Meaning?"

"The first time Dash Maynard met Rusty Eggers was in DC when they were Capitol Hill interns. See if you can find out anything about that time period."

"Like what?"

"Like I have no idea. Did they room together? Hang out? It's a long shot, I admit."

"I'll put some researchers on it."

"Also, see if you can locate Saul Strauss. He has to be Suspect Number One here."

"Okay. Anything else?"

Wilde thought about it and then figured better safe than sorry. "I need you to go to Naomi Pine's house when it gets dark."

Rola looked at him. "Weren't you just there?"

"I need the place searched."

"For?"

"Crash and Naomi."

Rola nodded. "On it."

Hester sat alone on a stone bench facing the Manhattan skyline. As Wilde approached, she turned toward him and shaded her eyes. With her other hand she patted the concrete. "Sit with me."

He did. For a moment, neither of them spoke. They just stared at the skyline over the trees. The sun was at the height where everything—buildings, trees, formations—looked like it had angel halos.

"Nice," Hester said.

"Yes."

"And boring." Hester turned to him. "You want to go first?"

"No."

"Didn't think so," Hester said. Then: "I talked to Arnie Poplin." She filled him in.

"Killed someone," Wilde said when she finished.

"That's what he claims he heard."

"I assume you weren't the first person he told this to."

"I would highly doubt it."

"So why hasn't anyone reported it?"

"Because Arnie Poplin is an attention-seeking, unreliable drug addict with an axe to grind."

"Okay."

"Journalists would be wary of him under any conditions, but Rusty Eggers rides the refs better than anyone."

"Rides the refs?"

Hester squinted into the sun. "A good friend of mine was a star basketball player in college. A first-round draft pick out of Duke. You a basketball fan at all?"

"No."

"Then you wouldn't know him. Anyway, he's taken me to a few

games at Madison Square Garden. College mostly. You know what I always notice?"

Wilde shook his head.

"The way the coaches rant and scream at the referees. These little men in their suits and ties spend the entire game running up and down the sidelines, having nonstop tantrums like toddlers wanting candy. It's embarrassing to watch. So I asked my friend, the basketball star, what was that all about, and he said it's an intentional strategy. People by nature want to be liked. Not you, not me. But people in general. So if you scream at the refs every time they blow the whistle on you—legitimate or not—they are more likely to give you a call."

Wilde nodded. "And that's what Rusty does with the media."

"Exactly. He constantly berates them and so they cringe and get scared, to keep within the metaphor, to blow the whistle. All politicians do it, of course. Rusty is just better at it."

"We should still confront Dash with what Arnie Poplin told you."

"Done already."

"And?"

Hester shrugged. "What do you think? Dash denied it. He called it 'rubbish.' He actually used the word too. Rubbish."

"Unfortunate. Your takeaway?"

"Same as yours."

"They're hiding something."

"Right." She patted his leg. "Okay, *bubbalah*, so what did you learn?"

Wilde started by telling her what Bernard Pine said about his ex-wife abusing Naomi. Hester just shook her head. "This world."

"Something isn't sitting right with that."

"What do you mean?"

"I don't know," Wilde said. "I still think we need to talk to Naomi's mother. I told Rola to find her."

"Good. What else?"

Wilde told her about the app communication between Crash and maybe Naomi as well as Ava's conversations with Naomi about a budding relationship between the two teens.

"All signs point to Crash and Naomi being together," Hester said.

Wilde said nothing.

"So let's say that's true for the moment," she continued. "Let's say these two teens secretly fell for each other and decided to run off."

"Okay."

Hester shrugged. "How does that turn into a ransom demand?"

Wilde didn't reply. He checked the time. "Less than an hour to the kidnapper's deadline. Should we head inside?"

"They said to meet at 3:45 p.m. in the library."

"They, meaning Dash and Delia Maynard?"

"Yes."

"Any idea what they plan on doing?"

"They don't want to tell us until then."

Wilde looked back at the view. "That's not normal."

"No, it's not."

They both faced the view now. Hester closed her eyes and let the rays warm her.

"How to put this delicately," Hester said.

Wilde kept his eyes on the distant skyscrapers. "Delicately," he repeated. "Not your forte, Hester."

"True, so here goes: I was thinking about spending the night at Laila's, but I don't want to sleep over if you are."

Wilde couldn't help but smile. "I definitely won't be."

"Oh."

"Doesn't mean it's a good idea to stay though."

"Oh," Hester said. And then again: "*Oh*. Really?"

Wilde said nothing.

"Can I be nosey?"

"I assume that's a rhetorical question."

"It's been six years since we really communicated."

"I'm sorry about that," he said.

"Me too, and I hope it's not because of David."

David. Saying the name out loud stilled even the trees.

"I don't blame you. I never have. You understand that, right?"

Wilde didn't answer. "Is that what you want to be nosey about?"

"No," Hester said. "I won't say you're like a son to me because that's way over the top. I have three sons. They're the only ones like a son to me. But I was there from the beginning—from the first day you came out of the woods. We were all there. Me. Ira. David, of course."

"You were very good to me," Wilde said.

"That's not why I'm raising this either, so let me put it bluntly. Those online DNA genealogy tests have become super popular. I even took one a few years ago."

"Any surprises?"

"Not a one. I'm so boring."

"But you want to know if I took one," he said.

"It's been six years," she said. "So yes, I want to know if you took one."

"I did. Very recently, as a matter of fact."

"Any surprises?"

"Not a one. I'm so boring too."

"Seriously?"

"No parents or siblings. The closest thing was a second cousin."

"That's a start," she said.

Wilde shook his head. "No, Hester, it's not. If you're looking for a missing kid—son, brother, whatever—you'd be on that DNA site. No one is looking for me, ergo no one cares. I don't mean that in a pity-me way. But they left a small child alone in those woods for years—"

"You don't know that," Hester said, interrupting.

Wilde turned to look at her, but she wouldn't look back at him.

"Don't know what?" he asked.

"How long you were out there."

"Not exactly, no."

"It could have been days."

Wilde didn't know what to make of this. "What are you talking about? Your son and I played for years."

"Years." Hester made a scoffing sound. "Come on."

"What?"

"You were two little boys. You think you could have kept a secret like that for years?"

"That's what we did."

"That's what you *think* you did. You know how time slows down when you're little. It could have been days, maybe weeks, but years?"

"I have memories, Hester."

"I don't doubt that. But don't you think maybe it could have been just a few days' worth? You always say you have no memory of any time before you were in the woods. So maybe—just hear me out, okay?—maybe something happened to you, something so traumatic that you blocked everything from before. Maybe, since you've retained nothing about your life from before this traumatic event, those memories are now magnified and so what may have been a few days seem like years."

That wasn't what happened. Wilde knew that.

"Hikers spotted me months and even years earlier."

"They said they spotted a little boy. Might have been you, might have been someone else."

But Wilde wasn't buying it. He remembered breaking into homes—lots of them. He remembered traveling miles. He remembered that red banister and those screams.

"It doesn't matter," Wilde said. "Even if you're right, no one looked for that boy."

"That's why you need to find out the truth—to feel whole."

Wilde made a face. "Did you really say 'to feel whole'?"

"Not my finest moment, I admit. But you know what I mean.

You have issues with intimacy and connection, Wilde. That's not a secret. It doesn't take a genius to see it all began with this abandonment. So maybe if you got some understanding of what caused it, of what really happened—"

"I'd be more normal?"

"You know what I mean."

"It won't change anything."

"That's probably so," Hester said. "Then again, there's another reason."

"That being?"

"I'm curious as hell," Hester said, throwing up her hands. "Aren't you?"

Wilde checked his watch. "Fifteen minutes to the ransom deadline. Let's go find the Maynards."

CHAPTER THIRTY

The Maynards sat in the same two burgundy wingback chairs. Not surprisingly, they both looked stressed to the max. Their skin was drawn, complexions ashen, their eyes bloodshot. Somewhat surprisingly, they were both smartly dressed in expensive couture. Dash, sporting tan slacks with a crease that could slice deli meat, did the talking.

"Please fill us in on anything new," Dash said to Wilde.

Wilde did his best. They both listened without moving, almost as though they were trying to stay perfectly still and not show anything or maybe, more likely, they were just working hard to hold it together and figured that if any part of them cracked, that would be it, they'd totally burst open. When Wilde finished, Dash and Delia turned to one another. Delia nodded once.

"Delia and I have talked this to death. We've reviewed the evidence. We've tried to map out a timeline of what our son did last night. We've talked to both of you extensively, and we've bounced around the various theories we've heard."

He reached out and took his wife's hand.

"The truth is, we don't know whether this is a kidnapping

or a hoax or something else entirely. Neither, it seems, do either of you."

"I don't," Hester said. "Wilde?"

"Impossible to know for certain."

"Exactly," Dash said. "Which is why, after extensive discussion, Delia and I have decided that the best course of action, the safest course, is to send the tapes. We can't send them all. The file would be too large, plus, well, how would anyone know how many hours we have? I don't even know."

"Why do you have so much footage?" Hester asked.

"It's always been my way," Dash said.

"He's a documentarian first," Delia added.

Wilde nodded, looked about the room, then decided to go for it. "Is that why you're taping us now?"

Silence. Then Dash: "What are you talking about?"

Wilde took out his phone. "I have a network scanner app that detects if there are listening devices or cameras in a room. Right now, it's spotting networks and ISPs that can only be explained by the fact that we have cameras on us."

Dash leaned back and crossed his legs. "I'm a documentarian. I record our lives as well. I don't think I'll ever use it—"

"Do we have to do this now?" Delia snapped.

"No," Wilde said. "You're right. Let's concentrate on the task at hand."

It had all been a bluff. There were indeed apps for scanning or mapping out networks and detecting hidden cameras. People were using them to make sure, for example, that Airbnb hosts weren't spying on them. But Wilde didn't have one on his phone.

It was five minutes until the 4:00 p.m. deadline. A laptop was set up on the oak coffee table between them. Dash hit the link that had been sent to them before. A screen came with a countdown clock indicating the link would be live in four minutes and forty-seven, forty-six, forty-five seconds.

"My team will try to trace down the ISP when we go live,"

Wilde said, "but I'm told that even a simple VPN will prevent us from getting anything significant."

They silently watched the clock go under the four-minute mark.

"So what's on the tapes?" Hester asked.

"Outtakes from the show," Dash said. "Behind-the-scenes stuff. The writers' room where we hashed out ideas. Stuff like that."

"Uh-huh," Hester said. "In the ransom email, they asked you to upload the 'truly damaging' tape to a special folder."

Hester waited. No one spoke.

"Are you going to do that?"

Delia said, "Yes."

"What's on it?"

"We don't see how that's relevant to you."

"Excuse me?"

"We don't want to share any of this. We are being forced to for the safety of our son."

"So you're willing to share it with an anonymous kidnapper, but not your attorney?"

"We see no reason to show it to anyone," Dash said. "But as Mr. Wilde here pointed out, these people didn't ask for a public release. So perhaps they'll keep it to themselves, perhaps not. Either way, this is not a confidence we want to betray, even to you. We are betraying it, if you will, for the safety of our son."

Hester looked at Wilde and shook her head. Then she turned back and glared at both of the Maynards. "I hope you two know what you're doing."

When the clock clicked down to zero, Dash Maynard refreshed the page. The page was simple. There were two yellow boxes. One was marked: VIDEOS-UPLOAD, the other: SPECIAL FOLDER-UPLOAD.

Under them, the instructions said:

> Click both links. We will not communicate
> with you until the videos start uploading.

Whoever was behind this, Wilde said, was good. No negotiation, no back-and-forth.

Dash let loose a long breath. Delia placed a comforting, familiar hand on his shoulder.

"Here goes," Dash said.

He clicked first the special folder button, then the videos one. The files began to upload. A minute passed. Then another. Finally, a new icon appeared. An envelope. Dash moved the cursor over it and clicked it.

> We will need to review the files.
> If you did as we requested, your son will be returned to you tomorrow at exactly noon. We will contact you with his location.

Delia's eyes filled with tears. "At noon?"

Dash took his wife's hand.

"Our son has to spend another night with these people?"

"He'll be okay," Dash said. "We've done all we can."

"Have we?" Delia asked.

Silence.

Dash turned toward Wilde and Hester. "What do we do now?"

"If you still don't want to go to the authorities—" Hester began.

"We don't."

Hester shrugged. "Then I guess we wait."

When they were back outside, Hester said to Wilde, "We aren't going to wait, are we?"

"I'm not sure what we can do."

"Are you going to hang here?" Hester asked.

"If I'm not on the grounds, I'll be close by."

"Same," Hester said. "I may go out and grab a bite to eat, if that's okay."

"Of course it's okay."

Hester started to wring her hands together, twisting the rings on her fingers. For the first time, Wilde noticed that she was no longer wearing her wedding band. Had she been six years ago? He couldn't remember.

"With Oren Carmichael," she added.

Hester Crimstein blushed. She actually blushed.

"Second date in two nights," Wilde said.

"Yes."

"Yippee."

"Don't be a wiseass."

"If you don't want to sleep at Laila's, maybe you can sleep at Oren's."

"Stop that." Her blush deepened. "I'm not a hussy, you know."

Wilde smiled. It felt nice to be normal, even if only for a few seconds. "Go to dinner," he said. "Enjoy."

"He's a nice man," she said. "Oren, I mean."

"And he's a hunk with broad shoulders."

"Is he? I barely noticed."

"Go, Hester."

"You'll call if there are any changes?"

"I will."

"Wilde?"

He turned.

"There's been no one since Ira."

"Then it's about time," Wilde said.

Tony's Pizza and Sub looked exactly like its name.

There was a counter with two guys in white aprons flipping pizzas. There was a letter-board menu above their heads for walk-ins who didn't want table service or, if you took a booth, a waitress, always a local high school girl, handed you a menu that was both laminated and sticky. The tablecloth, no surprise, was checkered red. Each table was cluttered with a napkin dispenser, an assortment of shakers for parmesan and oregano and the like, and a half-burned candle jammed into the top of an empty Chianti bottle. A television that hung from the ceiling played either sports or the news. Right now, it was playing Hester's very own network.

Decked out in his cop uniform, Oren sat in a booth toward the back. He stood the moment he spotted her, which seemed very formal in this place.

"Hey," Oren said.

He kissed her cheek and took her hand. Hester gave his hand a squeeze and slid into the booth.

"I bet you've been here a million times," Oren said.

Tony's was a town mainstay and less than a mile from her old house. It also purportedly had the best pizza within a ten-mile radius.

"No," Hester said. "In fact, this is the first time I've been here in more than thirty years."

"Seriously?"

Hester nodded. "On the first night we moved into town, Ira and I brought the boys here for dinner. We were exhausted and starved—it'd been a long day. Anyway, there was only one open table, but they wouldn't let us sit there unless we promised to order full dinners and no pizza. I don't remember the details, but whatever, they were rude to us. So Ira got furious. He was slow to anger, Ira, but when he did...anyway, we left without eating. Ira wrote the owner a letter, if you can believe it. Typed it up. But he never heard back. So Ira forbade us from going or ordering from them. I don't know how many thousands of dollars they lost over the years from that incident. The boys, they were so loyal to Ira that even if they were invited to a birthday party here or their

Little League team came after a game, they'd refuse to eat." Hester looked up. "Why am I telling you this story?"

"Because it's interesting," Oren said. "Do you want to go someplace else? The Heritage Diner maybe?"

"Can I tell you a funny thing?"

"Sure."

"I had my assistant check. Tony's was sold four years ago. If the old ownership was still here, I wouldn't have come."

Oren smiled. "So we're safe to stay?"

"Yes." Hester shook her head. "I'm sorry."

"For?"

"Bringing up Ira like that. First date I bring up Cheryl. Second date I bring up Ira."

"Getting all the elephants out of the room," Oren said. "I like that. Why are you in town anyway? Visiting Matthew and Laila?"

Hester shook her head. "Doing work for clients."

"In our little hamlet?"

"I can't say more."

He got it. The waitress dropped off a slice of margherita pizza for each of them. Hester took a bite and closed her eyes. It tasted like nirvana.

"Good, right?" Oren asked.

"I'm hating Ira right about now."

He chuckled and picked up his slice. "I'm guessing the Maynards."

"What?"

"Your clients. The Maynards. I would have guessed just Dash Maynard, but you said you were visiting clients. With an S."

"I can't confirm or deny—"

"I wouldn't expect you to."

"Why do you think it's the Maynards?"

"The helicopter. When they fly in, they have to clear the airspace with us. So I know it flew out of Manhattan this morning.

Then you pulled up in an Uber, not your black Escalade driven by Tim."

"I'm impressed," Hester said.

Oren shrugged. "I'm a trained detective."

"I can't talk about it though."

"I don't want you to talk about it," he said. "I'm just really glad you're here with me."

Despite everything—the ghosts, the ransom, this place—Hester could feel her face blush to the color of the pizza's tomato sauce.

"I'm glad I'm here too," Hester said.

For a few minutes, the world shrunk down to the size of the gorgeous man across the table from her and the ambrosia-like pizza on the table between them. She relished the escapism. It wasn't something Hester often craved. She liked being in the mix. She found it stressful to be out of the loop.

A few people stopped by the table, mostly to see Oren, but some of the faces were familiar to her too. The Gromans, who used to play tennis with Ira on Saturday mornings. Jennifer Tallow, that super-nice librarian whose son had been friendly with Jeff. Everyone knew Oren, of course. When you're a cop that long in a town this size, it's its own form of celebrity. She couldn't tell whether Oren enjoyed the attention or was polite to a fault out of obligation.

"When exactly do you retire?" she asked him.

"Three months from now."

"And your plans?"

Oren shrugged. "They're fluid."

"Do you think you'll stay in town?"

"For right now."

"You've lived out here a long time," she said.

"Yes."

"Ever think about living in a city instead?"

"Yes," he said. "I think about it."

When his phone sounded, the expression on his face hardened. "That's my work ring. I have to take it."

Hester gestured for him to go ahead. It was interesting, she thought, the echo between him having a "work ring" and her last night with her various phone vibrations. Oren picked up the phone and said, "Yep." A few seconds passed. "Okay, who is closest to Tony's? Good, okay, have him swing around and pick me up." He hung up the phone.

"Sorry, I have to go. I might not be long if you want to wait or..."

"No, that's okay. I told Laila I'd come by."

He stood. "Are you sure?"

"Yes, no problem. I'll get an Uber."

"Okay, thanks." He threw two twenties down on the table. "I'll call you later."

"An emergency?" Hester asked.

"It's just a car accident on Mountain Road. I'll call you when I'm done."

Oren hurried for the door as a squad car pulled up to the front. He didn't look back and see what he'd left behind. Hester just sat there. She couldn't move, couldn't breathe. The blood had frozen in her veins. Her lungs stopped. She could hear her pulse, her heartbeat growing impossibly loud until it was the only sound she could hear.

"It's just a car accident on Mountain Road..."

Like it happened all the time. Like it was no big deal.

A tear escaped and ran down her cheek. She could feel more tears building, a guttural cry rising in her throat that would need to be released soon. Time was growing short. Hester found her legs. She managed to stand and stumble toward the bathroom. When she was inside, she closed the door, locked it, and muffled her scream with her hand.

Hester couldn't say how long she stayed there. No one knocked on the door or any of that, so she imagined only a minute or two passed. No more. She got herself together. She looked in the mirror, splashed water on her face, and saw David's ghost in the reflection.

"It's just a car accident on Mountain Road..."

She wondered where Oren had been that night when he got the call. Was he at work, in a squad car, at Tony's like tonight—or was he at home with Cheryl? Did he get woken up in bed and Cheryl turned to him and asked if something was wrong and then maybe Oren shook his head and kissed her gently and told her to go back to sleep, murmuring...

"It's just a car accident on Mountain Road..."

This all made sense now. Hester considered herself neither pessimist nor optimist, but she knew somehow that this couldn't work, that the happy bubble she'd been in with Oren last night had to be too fragile not to burst. Now she understood. Oren had been there that tragic night. Like it or not, he was entangled in the worst moment of her life—and there was no way to change that. She would see Oren, maybe kiss him, maybe hold him, and she would always be transported back to that horrible night.

How could any relationship survive that?

She dried her face with a paper towel, took out her phone, and clicked for an Uber. Eight minutes away. Hester took a few more deep breaths and another look in the mirror. She looked old—like an old woman—which she was. It sucked to look in the mirror and see it sometimes. The harsh light of this stupid pizzeria bathroom amplified every wrinkle.

Her phone buzzed. She checked the number and saw it was Allison Grant, her producer. Hester said, "What's up?"

"You near a television?"

"I can get to one. Why?"

"Someone leaked a tape of Rusty Eggers."

Hester felt her back straighten. "Bad?"

"Very. There is no way Rusty Eggers survives this."

CHAPTER THIRTY-ONE

Rusty Eggers watched on the TV in his penthouse.

Gavin stood behind him. Rusty's two top aides—Jan Schnall, onetime chief of staff to South Carolina's Republican governor, and Lia Capasso, a campaign manager for two Democratic senators—sat on the couch taking notes. The crawl on the bottom of the screen unimaginatively screamed in red caps:

BREAKING NEWS: SHOCKING RUSTY EGGERS VIDEO

Anchorman Scott Gallett: *"The video is believed to be ten years old, from season one of* The Rusty Show*..."*

"They got that part right, at least," Rusty said.

"The young woman is Kandi Pate, the young star of the hit kid comedy Amazing Darcy, *who did three guest appearances on* The Rusty Show *that season. At the time of this taping, she would have been sixteen or seventeen years old while Rusty Eggers would have*

been in his midforties. Again we caution: This story is breaking. While the video appears to be authentic, we have not yet independently authenticated—"

"Not that that will slow the jackals down," Rusty said.

Gavin noticed that Rusty seemed remarkably calm. His two aides did not.

On the video, Rusty Eggers has his arm around Kandi Pate on a couch. Kandi seems to cringe at his touch.

Rusty Eggers: *Most guys your age don't know what they're doing. Sexually, I mean. You know what I'm saying?*

Kandi Pate: *Uh-huh, my agent is waiting downstairs.*

Rusty: *I don't think your agent is doing right by you.*

Kandi: (nervous laugh) *She's gotten me this far.*

Rusty: *Kiddie roles. You're a full-grown woman now. And so talented.*

Kandi: *Thank you.*

Rusty: *Why don't you come by my hotel room tonight and we can talk more about it?*

Kandi: *Tonight? I'm not sure—*

And then Rusty Eggers kisses her hard on the mouth.

"Look!" Rusty gestured to the screen. "She's not exactly fighting back, is she?"

But she wasn't exactly pulling him closer either.

Rusty's two female aides blanched.

Gavin asked, "Do you know where this was taped?"

"Looks like Maynard's New York studio," Rusty said.

The kiss ends. Kandi Pate quickly stands, smooths her skirt, wipes her mouth with the back of her hand. She forces a smile.

Kandi: *I have to go now.*

Rusty: *Tonight then? Nine o'clock. We'll just talk.*
Kandi rushes out of the room.

Rusty turned away from the television and looked at his two aides. "To answer your first question, yes, she showed up that night."

Anchorman Scott Gallett: *Kandi Pate ended up being fired from* The Rusty Show *for what was rumored to be drug use and insubordination, but we have our expert panel with us who now wonder about the veracity of those rumors and if she was a victim of—*

Rusty flipped off the television. "Expert panel," he repeated. "Give me a break." He rubbed his hands together. "Lia?"

Lia Capasso looked up in a daze.

"You have the bots ready?"

"They're on standby," Lia said.

"Good." Rusty began to pace. "So get the first group of them to claim that this tape was a teaching demonstration."

"A teaching demonstration?"

"Yes. That's why we filmed it. Kandi and I were acting out inappropriate workplace behavior, so that anyone employed by *The Rusty Show* would know that we would have zero tolerance for this kind of thing."

Jan Schnall said, "You think that will fly?"

"That's just bot group one, Jan. For bot group two, we say that Kandi was working on a 'Me Too' screenplay. Way ahead of her time. She asked me to act out a scene with her. Lia, get our graphic design people to create a screenplay with this exact dialogue. Use one of the big screenwriting programs from ten years ago. Final Draft or Movie Magic maybe. Tell them to add a page of dialogue before, a page of dialogue after, that kind of thing. Make it look legit. Then we leak it as the 'unproduced manuscript' Kandi Pate hoped to develop before her career hit the rails."

Lia jotted that down. "Got it."

"We say that as a mentor figure to many young people who appeared on my show, I was trying to be supportive in reading these lines with her, but I was clearly uncomfortable in what she wanted me to do. Jan, get a few body language experts to insist that I'm clearly acting and I look hesitant during the pretend kiss."

"Right."

"Next, we go right and left. Jan, get some right-wing bots to say stuff like 'How come the left is always into sexual freedom and women making their own choices and now they are saying that Kandi Pate is too weak to decide who to date?'—that kind of thing. Then Lia, get the left-wing bots to say, 'We don't belong in people's bedrooms and this mature woman should be able to make her own choices.' You know the drill. Do you guys know the age of consent in New York?"

Lia tapped something into her iPad. "Seventeen."

"California?"

"Eighteen."

He thought about it. "We also have an office in Toronto. How about there?"

Lia typed some more. "It was fourteen. Now it's sixteen."

"Okay, cool. Let's spread another rumor that this happened in our Toronto office. We also get another group of fake profiles to raise the 'macho man' excuse."

Jan frowned. "Macho man?"

"You know, like 'What red-blooded all-American male wouldn't make a move on a hot piece of ass like Kandi Pate?' and 'All the whiny babies online are just jealous of a real man,' that kind of thing. They should all keep repeating that Kandi was of legal age."

Lia and Jan both nodded, warming slightly to the task. Gavin just watched in silence.

"Finally, let's get the 'fake news' groups to say the tape had obviously been doctored. Again we have those social media accounts with various levels of"—Rusty made quote marks with his fingers—"'expertise,' right? Let's get them to work up the conspiracy nuts. Have them notice, I don't know, some kind of irregular shadows in the film and claim that it's a clear Photoshop job or that the sound is off. Have them make up those YouTube videos where they circle stuff and say, 'Whoa, this shadow or whatever can't be, someone had to have tampered with it, yada yada.' Oh, then get a few voice 'experts' to say that it's not my voice, that it is someone doing a bad impression. Have some of the bots say it sounds like it was spliced from old footage or something. With me?"

"With you," Lia said.

Jan added, "That's perfect."

Neither woman was blanching anymore. They were both, in fact, smiling.

"Then I want our own bots fighting with each other. 'Who cares if it's a Photoshop? It's totally legal anyway!' Or 'Stop worrying about the ethics—the tape is fake news, it never happened.'"

Lia asked, "You want to go with all these?"

"All these and let's come up with a few more. Like, why don't the networks show what happened *before* this—like when Kandi Pate was hitting on Rusty? Oh, that's good. Let's get a group posting 'Here's a link to the WHOLE tape where you can see Kandi is aggressively making moves on Rusty and he's trying to back off, why don't they show that?' But then—oh, I'm loving this—the link will lead to an error message and then the bots will claim the mainstream media or the government took it down. It's a cover-up, they'll scream. Full bot attack—get the right- and left-wing ones on that. I want people fighting over how we *can't* blame me for any of this."

"Love that," Lia said.

"And then let's do the standard attack-the-process. You know. The real crime isn't on the tape—the real crime is, who illegally taped us? What awful partisan with a clear axe to grind broke into my office and unlawfully spied on me? Those are the real criminals. Why are powerful people willing to break laws to stop my message from reaching the people?"

"Oh, that's good," Jan said.

"Right? Also, Lia, have one of our lawyers reach out to Kandi. Remind her of the nondisclosure agreement she signed. She's not allowed to say anything. If she does, we will destroy her a hundred different ways. If she backs us, let her know that we are financing a new film which we think will be a great comeback role for her."

"Got it," Lia said.

"One question," Jan said.

"Shoot."

"The media is going nuts right now looking for a comment. What do we put in our official press statement?"

"Nothing yet. Let's wait and see what social media looks like in a few hours. We should know better then. My guess is, our statement will be pretty vague. Something like 'We will not comment because we do not want to harm the reputation of Ms. Pate, who is a fine person and vulnerable mentee, and we find it disgusting that the media would drag her through the mud like this just to get some additional clicks and we won't participate in that kind of gossipy trash over what is clearly not what it is being made out to be.' That sort of thing. But not yet. I want to see which story takes root. Let's get the talking points to our people, so they can get on the air asap. We need to keep seeding confusion here, people."

"On it," Lia said.

The two women took to their phones and tablets.

Rusty pulled Gavin to the side. "You know where the tape came from, right?"

"I assume the Maynards."

"You were supposed to stop this."

"I told you. They fired me." Then, lowering his voice, Gavin added, "You also told me the tapes had nothing harmful."

"If this is the worst of it, we will be fine."

"If?"

"What?"

"You said 'if.' What else is there?"

"Get the car," Rusty Eggers said. "I want to go to the Maynards'."

Wilde was in the library with Delia and Dash Maynard when the newscasts began. They watched the "breaking news" in silence.

During the first commercial break, Wilde said, "I assume that was the 'very damaging' upload."

"We didn't want to release it," Delia said.

She stood and headed for the door. Dash looked surprised. "Don't you want to watch—?"

"I've seen enough. I need some air."

Delia left. Wilde looked up at the stained glass in the library's turret. It was dark outside, yet the windows somehow still glowed as though the sun were shining through them. The room, as before, felt off to Wilde. A grand library like this should smell of age—leather from the books, pine from the wood, must from usage.

"That should do it, don't you think?"

No one else was in the room, so Dash was talking to either Wilde or himself.

"Do what?" Wilde asked.

"Satisfy the kidnappers. End Rusty's campaign."

Wilde didn't know. He also didn't know whether Dash said this with regret or glee. There was fear in the man's voice. That much was obvious.

"So what do you think is going on here?" Wilde asked.

"Pardon?"

"With your son. Do you think he was kidnapped?"

Dash folded his hands and leaned back. "In the end, Delia and I figured that it was better to be safe than sorry."

"That doesn't really answer my question."

"It's the best I can do."

"There was more to your decision to release this video though, wasn't there?"

"I'm not following."

"The pressure is off now," Wilde said.

Dash sounded annoyed now. "What are you talking about?"

"The media demanding you release the Rusty Eggers tapes, everyone constantly screaming at you to do the right thing, to be a patriot—you would have been hounded forever. No privacy. No real freedom. Relentless pressure on you, your businesses, your family. But now that this tape is finally out, that's all over. There has to be some relief in that."

Dash turned back to the television. "I don't mean to be rude, but do you mind moving to another room for a while? I'd really like to be alone for a bit."

Wilde rose and started for the door. He was just in the corridor when his cell phone rang.

The caller ID read NAOMI PINE.

He put the phone to his ear. "Hello?"

"Hey, Wilde."

His pulse picked up a step. "Naomi?"

"Stop looking for us, okay?"

"Naomi, where are you?"

"We're fine. We're safe."

"Crash is with you?"

"I have to go."

"Wait—"

"Please. You'll ruin everything. We don't want to be found."

"You already tried this, Naomi."

"What?"

"When you did the Challenge," Wilde said. "Do you remember what you said to me?"

"In the basement, you mean?"

"Yes."

"I said I wanted to make a change."

"You said more than that."

"I said I wanted to make a total change. I wanted to do something so big it would erase my past and I could start again."

"Is that what you're doing now?"

"You're going to say I failed then, so I'll fail now."

"No, Naomi, I'm not. I believe in you."

"Wilde?"

"I'm here."

"Please. If you want to help me, you'll let me be."

Rusty Eggers sat in the back of the car with Gavin. He kept straightening and bending his bad leg. Gavin watched him reach into his pocket, pull out a small tin box, and open it. Rusty plucked out two pills, threw them back in his mouth, swallowed. His glassy eyes turned to Gavin.

"Tylenol," Rusty said.

Gavin didn't reply.

Rusty picked up his phone, dialed a number, and said, "Hi, it's me. Don't explain. I'm coming up to your place. I hear there's security. Just meet me out... yes, exactly. Thanks."

Gavin Chambers asked, "Are you going to tell me what that's about?"

"Do you remember when we discussed the horseshoe theory of politics?"

"Yes, of course."

"We talked about how most Americans used to be in the middle, relatively speaking. That's how America kept its balance all those years. The left and the right were close enough to have disagreements but not hate."

"Okay."

"That world is gone, Gavin, and so it will now be easy to destroy the social order. The middle has become complacent. They are smart, but they are lazy. They see the grays. They get the other side. Extremists, on the other hand, see only black and white. They are not only certain that their vision is absolutely correct, but they are incapable of even understanding the other side. Those who don't believe as they do are lesser in every way, and so they will kill for that vision. I get those people, Gavin. And I want to create more of them by forcing those in the middle to choose a side. I want to make them extremists too."

"Why?"

"Extremists are relentless. They don't see right or wrong—they see us and them. You're a baseball fan, aren't you, Gavin?"

"I am."

"A Yankee fan, right?"

"So?"

"So if you found out the Yankee manager cheated or that all your favorite Yankees took steroids, would you then become a Red Sox fan?"

Gavin said nothing.

"Well?"

"Probably not."

"Exactly. The Yankees could never do anything that would make you a Red Sox fan. That's the power I want to harness. I read a quote recently from Werner Herzog. You know who he is?"

"The German film director."

"Right. He said that America was waking up, as Germany once did, to the awareness that one-third of our people will kill one-third of our people while one-third of our people watches." Rusty put his hand on Gavin's shoulder. "You and I are going to change the world, my friend." He leaned forward. "Drop me off up ahead on the next corner."

"I thought we were going to the Maynards'."

"Change of plans."

"I'm not following."

They pulled to the corner. There was a woman by a bus stop. She had her head down.

"There's a diner three miles down the road on Route 17."

"I know it."

"Wait for me there. I shouldn't be too long."

They drove off. As they did, Gavin tried to make out the identity of the woman. He couldn't be sure—would never swear to it—but he thought that it looked very much like Delia Maynard.

CHAPTER THIRTY-TWO

When Hester woke up the next morning, it took her a minute or two to realize where she was. Her head pounded. Her throat was dry. The sliver of morning light sneaking into the bedroom hurt her eyes. In the distance, coming from downstairs, she heard voices.

She tried to piece it together. It didn't take long. After leaving Tony's Pizza and Sub, she'd come to her old home. No one was here yet. Matthew was out with some friends. Laila, well, from what she surmised, Laila was out on a date, which explained Wilde's remark earlier about him not sleeping over. Left alone, in the house that once held her own family—Ira, Jeff, Eric, David, all her boys, that was what she always called them, her boys, her beautiful, wonderful boys—Hester knew that the only way to quiet the roused ghosts was through some sort of chemical intercession. She found a bottle of Writers' Tears whiskey in the liquor cabinet and poured some over ice. That was a start, a good start, mellowing the ghosts, letting them sit beside her and hold her hand, but not ridding her of them, so she fumbled into her purse and found the pills. Hester rarely took them, only when she felt a strong need, and if tonight wasn't the dictionary definition of "strong need," then she wasn't sure anything would ever be. Even as she dropped them into her mouth, Hester realized that this wasn't a smart play on her part, that you never mix booze and medication, that she should be conscious and sharp in case either her family or Wilde needed her.

Most nights that would stop her, but again tonight was not most nights.

She squinted and reached for her phone. How, she wondered, had she made it into the bedroom? She didn't remember. Had Laila come home and found her former mother-in-law passed out on the couch? Had Matthew? She didn't think so. She conjured up a vague recollection of being cognizant of her state and preparing for bed before the inevitable overcame her. But she couldn't be sure.

Hester could still hear voices floating up from downstairs. For a moment she worried that perhaps Laila forgot that she was staying over, that Hester was actually listening to Laila make breakfast for whatever male may have stayed the night. She held her breath and strained to hear.

Two voices. Both female. One was Laila's, the other...?

Hester's phone was down to four percent charge. The clock on the screen read 6:11 a.m. She could see the notifications from Oren. He'd called several times. There was one voicemail. It was from Oren too. She hit play.

> "Hey, it's me. I'm... I'm so sorry. I can't believe how insensitive I was. I got the call, and I just rushed out, not thinking, but that's no excuse. I'm really sorry. Just so you know, the accident was nothing major, no serious injuries. I don't know if that matters or not. Call me, okay? Let me know you're all right?"

But she wasn't all right.

Hester could hear the worry in his voice. Oren was such a good man, but it was like in one of those movies where a witch cast a curse on you. Oren had been there the night David had died. He'd been called to an accident scene that night too, and there was no way she could shake that and be normal about it. Not now. Not ever. The curse doomed any chance, remote as it probably had been anyway, for them to be happy.

She didn't want Oren upset. This wasn't his fault, and he wasn't a young man anymore. No need to give him additional agita. She typed out a text to Oren:

All good. Super busy. I'll call you later.

But she wouldn't call him. Or reply if he called back. Then he'd get the message, and everyone would be better off.

The voices downstairs were getting louder now, on the move. Funny what you remember. This room, which Laila and David had turned into a guest room, had been Hester's home office way back when. She still could tell from the echoes and volume that the two women had originally been talking in the kitchen and that now they had moved to the foyer near the front door. Probably saying goodbye. Hester looked out the window as, yep, a young woman walked down the cobblestone path to a dark blue car parked in front of the house.

Hester threw on a robe Laila kept for guests and made her way into the hallway. Laila was at the bottom of the steps.

"Good morning," Laila said.

"Good morning."

"You were in bed when I got back last night. Everything okay?"

"Yes," Hester said through the hammering in her head. "Fine."

"I'm sorry if I woke you. A client who lives nearby needed to talk."

"Oh, I get it."

"There's brewed coffee in the kitchen, if you want some."

"You are a goddess," Hester said.

Laila smiled and picked up her bag. "I have to run before the traffic builds. You need anything?"

"Nothing, Laila, thank you."

"Matthew should be up soon. If you're still in town tonight, do you want to do dinner?"

"Let's play it by ear."

"Sure."

With that, Laila smiled, opened the door, and exited. Hester dropped her own smile and put both her hands on her pounding head, pushing at the sides to keep her skull from falling open. She started down the stairs because, no question about it, the coffee would help.

From the window by the door, she could see the young woman in the blue car hadn't taken off yet. Laila walked over to her. Hester watched them talk for a second or two. Laila put a comforting hand on the woman's shoulder. The woman seemed to gain strength from that. She nodded and hit the remote on her car.

"Hey, Nana."

It was Matthew at the top of the stairs.

"Hey." Still looking out the window, Hester asked, "Do you know that woman with your mom?"

"Who?"

"The one getting into that blue car."

Matthew bounded down the steps as only a teenager can. He squinted out the window as the young woman slipped into the car and pulled away. "Oh," Matthew said. "That's Ms. O'Brien. I think Mom is helping her with a case."

Why, Hester wondered, did that name ring a bell?

"Ms. O'Brien?"

"Yeah," Matthew said. "She teaches art at my school."

The Uber driver who, according to the app, was named Mike with a 4.78 rating, didn't like the looks of the crowd in front of the Maynard Manor security gate.

"What the hell is this?" he asked Hester.

A handful of protestors, no more than ten, stood outside with signs reading FAKE NEWS! and SPIES BELONG IN JAIL FOR TREASON and chanting. An equal number of local police were on the scene, keeping them back from the opening, and as 4.78 Mike of the gray Honda Accord pulled up, a uniformed Oren, of all people, strolled over, leaned his head in the front passenger side of the car, and asked 4.78 Mike, "Are they expecting you?"

From the backseat, Hester said, "Yes."

Oren turned toward her. "Oh. Hi."

And with just those two words, David's ghost materialized and sat next to her.

"Hi."

For a moment neither of them moved or said anything. Then 4.78 Mike broke the silence. "Can we go in or what?"

"The guard will let you drop Ms. Crimstein off inside the gate," Oren said. "Have a nice day."

David's ghost faded away as Oren pulled back and 4.78 Mike drove through the gate. Wilde was waiting for Hester with the golf cart. After Hester climbed in, Wilde said, "Naomi called my phone."

"What? When?"

"Last night."

"Why didn't you call me?"

"You were out on a date."

"What about later?"

Wilde tried not to smile. "I didn't know how well the date went."

"Don't be fresh."

"Sorry."

"So what did Naomi say?"

"To stop looking for them."

"Them? As in she wasn't alone?"

"Correct."

"Did she sound distressed?"

"Not like she was being-held-for-ransom distressed. Actually, she sounded pretty excited."

"Like the most popular boy in the school just ran away with you?"

"Could be."

They started up the drive.

"I got something too," Hester said.

"Okay."

"Ava O'Brien was at Laila's this morning."

That threw him. "Why?"

"Laila said she was a client."

"In what way?"

Hester made a face. "We can't ask—and she can't tell. Attorney-client privilege, remember?"

Wilde checked the time. "Ava will be getting to school soon. If I hurry, I might be able to catch her on the way in."

"And ask her what? I've been thinking about it. How would a legal matter with Laila have anything to do with this?"

Wilde had no idea, but with the deadline still five hours away, he felt antsy.

"I'll be back soon," he said.

"Where are the Maynards?"

"In their library. I'll drop you off before I head out."

The night had been long. Wilde hadn't slept, going instead for a late run through the woods. He liked running through the trees at night, seeing how fast his eyes adjusted to the darkness, the five senses—yes, you used all five—all blending together, making the whole somehow greater than the sum of the parts. He'd checked in on his Ecocapsule. He hadn't been back since Gavin Chambers's men surrounded it. He wanted to make sure none of them had come back and tinkered with it. They hadn't. He also hadn't showered and changed in a while, so he took care of that too.

When he was back at his capsule, Wilde thought about the decoy idea—the Ghost Army, the tactical deception. The military purpose behind all that had been simple: Create chaos and confusion. Judging by what he'd seen on the news, that was what Rusty Eggers and his people were doing too.

It was working. In a way, when you think about history, it always worked.

He took the Maynards' Lexus to the high school, hoping to catch Ava. Hester was right. There was probably nothing to learn here. But Wilde liked Ava. Part of him didn't quite want to accept it, but something made him want to see her again. Ava had been on the back of his mind since yesterday at the 7-Eleven, when he'd surprised himself by suggesting they get back together again. Nothing serious. He knew that. Part of the reason he rarely went back was that while he wouldn't form an attachment, the short-term partner might. That didn't seem right or fair. So no encores.

Except, if he could be honest with himself, he wanted one with Ava.

So was showing up at school just an excuse to see her?

Wilde parked across from the teachers' lot, got out of the car, leaned against it. A few minutes later, he saw Ava's car pull in and park. When she got out, he watched her for a moment. Ava O'Brien was beautiful, he thought. Strong. Passionate. Independent. Sensitive.

He took a step toward her when a car pulled in front of him, blocking his path.

The driver leaned his head out the window. "Get in."

It was Saul Strauss.

"Why the hell is everyone suddenly looking for me, Wilde?"

"You tell me."

"I had nothing to do with that tape going public."

"I know," Wilde said.

"So why the hell is Gavin searching for me? Why did you call me?"

"Long story."

"Get in the car," Strauss said, his eyes glancing left and right. "I need to show you something."

Wilde looked toward Ava. She was going through the entrance.

"It's important," Strauss said, "but I'm not going to stay out in the open with Gavin Chambers gunning for me. Get in now or I take off."

Wilde hesitated long enough for Ava to disappear. No better option now. He got into Strauss's car on the passenger side. Strauss hit the accelerator.

"Where are we going?" Wilde asked.

"Would it be too melodramatic if I answered 'to find the truth'?"

"Definitely."

"Then the answer is prison," Strauss said. "We're going to prison."

CHAPTER THIRTY-THREE

"What do you mean, prison?"

Saul Strauss kept both hands on the wheel. "Why is everyone so anxious to find me?"

"The better question might be, Where have you been?"

"I have enemies, Wilde. I'm sure that doesn't surprise you. So when a calculating fascist like Gavin Chambers, who is working for a pill-popping nihilist like Rusty Eggers, comes a-knocking, I don't make myself too available, you know what I'm saying?"

"I know you're not saying where you've been."

"Why do you care? Why does Gavin care?"

Wilde didn't see a reason not to tell him. "Crash Maynard is missing."

"What do you mean, missing? Wait, is that why that tape was released?"

Wilde said nothing.

"And, what, you guys think I have something to do with this?"

"Do you?"

"Yeah, right, I'm hiding Crash Maynard. How many armed men does Gavin have guarding that family anyway?"

It was, Wilde thought, a good point. "How did you find me?"

"Just now? I have a guy watching the Maynards' place. By the way, who the hell calls their house 'Maynard Manor'? Is that not the most ostentatious, over-the-top, obscene... I mean, if you wanted evidence the rich are too rich, I would make that place Exhibit A. Anyway, my guy tailed you here."

"And you were in the area?"

"I needed to see you."

"To take me to prison?"

"Yes."

"I have to be back at the Maynards' by eleven thirty."

"This won't take long. I hear Hester interviewed Arnie Poplin."

"You hear a lot of things, Saul."

"That I do. I assume Hester believes him now."

Wilde changed subjects. "The other night at the hotel bar, why were you so interested in Naomi Pine?"

"I wasn't. I was interested in Crash Maynard."

"Who is now missing."

"You didn't believe me, but I told you. The Maynards have damaging tapes."

"And they've been released," Wilde said.

"Yeah, I watched the news," Strauss said, "and the reaction. No one cares that Eggers kissed a teenage girl, except those who'd never vote for him anyway."

They crossed the Tappan Zee Bridge and headed north alongside the Hudson River. If Strauss was being straight about going to "prison," Wilde had a pretty good idea where they were going.

"Sing Sing?" Wilde asked.

"Yes."

"Why?"

"I need you to see for yourself, Wilde. I need you to understand."

Less than an hour from Manhattan, the Sing Sing Correctional Facility was one of the most famous prisons in the world. Built in the early 1800s, Sing Sing hid in plain sight. If you were one of the many commuters on the Metro-North train to Grand Central station, your daily journey actually bisected Sing Sing. If you took a boat up the Hudson, you'd see Sing Sing perched atop an otherwise enviable plot of land overlooking the river. The notorious electric chair "Old Sparky" had executed over six hundred people inside Sing Sing's walls, including the alleged Soviet spies Julius and Ethel Rosenberg in 1953. Supposedly, Julius was strapped to Old Sparky first and died quickly. Then Ethel was led to the same chair where her husband had so recently perished—what must that have been like?—but her execution had complications. Witnesses said it took several attempts to kill her, that her heart kept beating despite repeated electric shocks, that smoke started rising from the top of her head.

Wilde had no idea why Saul Strauss was taking him here.

Strauss parked the car in Sing Sing's visitor lot and turned off the ignition. "Come on. This won't take long."

Strauss had clearly called in a few favors, so they got to move ahead of the line. They emptied their pockets and walked through the metal detector. The visiting room looked like a school cafeteria on steroids. There were tables and chairs—none of that behind-glass stuff you saw on television. Prisoners were being openly embraced by loved ones. You expected adult spouses, partners, parents, siblings, but mostly the visitors were families with young children. Lots of children. Some spent time in the multicolored "family center," which looked like a daycare or preschool classroom. There were board games and picture books, crafts and toys. Others went outside and hung on the playground.

The guards assigned them a table in clearly marked Row Four right by the prisoner entrance. They were told to sit and remain seated until their inmate joined them. Wilde wanted to ask for details, but he'd gone this far and figured that he'd let Strauss play it out. There was a buzzing noise, and the door to the actual prison slid open. The inmates poured in and hurried toward their families. Wilde looked at Strauss.

"Our guy will be last," Strauss said.

Wilde didn't know what that meant, but he would learn soon enough. After the line of men (Sing Sing Correctional was an all-male facility) receded, one final man entered—via a wheelchair. Wilde understood why they were seated near the front.

It was handicap accessible.

The man in the wheelchair was black. His hair was cut short and gray, his skin leathery, his eyes jaundiced. Wilde guessed his age to be fifties, maybe sixties. It would be a cliché to say prison ages a man, but sometimes the cliché is apropos.

Saul Strauss stood and then he bent his tall frame down to hug the man. "Hey, Raymond."

"Hey, Saul."

"I want you to meet Wilde. Wilde, this is Raymond Stark."

Wilde shook the man's hand. Raymond Stark's grip was firm. "So nice to meet you, Wilde."

"You too," Wilde said, because he had no idea what else to say.

Raymond Stark smiled up at him. The smile lit up his face. "They found you in the woods when I was being held at Red Onion," Raymond said. "That's a maximum-security facility in Virginia. I'd just gone in, and I still had hope, you know? Like they'd realize they got it wrong and I'd be free any second."

This man, Wilde realized, had been in prison for more than three decades.

"I read every story about you back then. The whole idea…I mean, you had no connections, no family. No past, right?"

"Right."

"I don't know if that's a blessing or a curse."

Saul sat down and signaled for Wilde to do the same.

"Thanks for coming," Raymond said to Wilde.

Wilde looked at Raymond, then at Strauss. "Do you want to tell me why I'm here?"

"In 1986, Raymond was arrested for the murder of a young man named Christopher Anson. Anson was stabbed to death in the

Deanwood section of Washington, DC. The claim was that Anson had gone into the wrong neighborhood to buy drugs, though that part was mostly kept out of the press to protect the victim's rep. Anyway, he was stabbed once, in the heart, and robbed. You would have been too young to remember it, but it was a big case. Anson was a rich, white college student. There were calls for the death penalty."

Raymond put a hand on Wilde's arm. Wilde turned and looked into the jaundiced eyes.

"I didn't do it."

"You can imagine what it was like—the media, the mayor, the pressure to solve the case. The cops supposedly got an anonymous tip that Anson had been buying drugs from a black kid in Deanwood, so they dragged in every black kid they could find, stonewalled, kept them awake, started up with the enhanced interrogations—again you know the deal."

"I do," Wilde said. "What I don't know is why I'm here."

Strauss pressed on. "Eventually, one kid said that Raymond sold drugs to rich white guys."

"Marijuana," Raymond said. "That part is true. I mostly just delivered."

"A judge issued a search warrant, and a DC Metro detective named Shawn Kindler found a knife under Raymond's mattress. Tests showed it was the murder weapon. You can imagine how fast it went downhill from there."

"The knife wasn't mine," Raymond said. Again he met Wilde's eye. "I didn't do it."

Wilde said, "Mr. Stark?"

"Call me Raymond."

"Raymond, I've seen the biggest sociopaths look me in the eye like that and lie to my face."

"Yeah, I know," Raymond Stark said. "Me too. Every day of my life. I'm surrounded by them. But I don't know what else to say, Wilde. I've spent thirty-four years in here for something I didn't do. I've tried my best. I studied hard, got my high school equivalency, college degrees, even a JD. I wrote letters and briefs for other inmates and myself. But nothing happened. Nothing *ever* happens."

Raymond folded his hands on the table and looked off. "Imagine being in a place like this every day, screaming out the truth every way you know how, but no one ever hears you. You want to hear something weird?"

Wilde waited.

"I have this recurring dream that I'm getting out," Raymond said with a hint of a smile. "I dream someone finally believes me—and I get set free. And then I wake up in the same cell. Imagine that for a second. Imagine that moment when I first realize that it's just a dream and I try to hold on, but it's like grabbing smoke. My mother used to visit me twice a week. She did that for more than twenty years. Then they found a mass in her liver. Cancer. Ate her up. And I wonder every day, every hour, if the stress of seeing her son locked up for something he didn't do weakened her immune system and killed her."

"Raymond," Strauss said, "tell Wilde how you ended up in that chair."

Raymond slowly shook his head. "If it's all the same, Saul, I'll pass on that. A sad story like that won't make you believe me, am I right?"

Wilde said nothing.

"So I'm not asking you for pity or to believe my face or my eyes," Raymond said. "Instead I'm just going to ask you for a few more minutes. That's all. No pleading about how innocent I am. No emotion. Just let Saul finish what he wants to say."

Wilde was going to say that he didn't have the time right now, that he was in the middle of an industrial-strength problem of his own, that even if he was convinced that Raymond Stark had been railroaded, it would make no difference. Wilde couldn't do anything that Saul Strauss and his organization couldn't do better.

What stopped him from saying that was that Wilde realized there had to be a reason, a good reason, why Strauss had driven him up. Strauss had some idea what was going on with Crash Maynard and Naomi Pine, and yet he had still insisted on making this journey. So rather than lose time protesting his presence, Wilde saw little harm in showing some respect and giving them another few minutes. It wouldn't change anything back at Maynard Manor, which was more than ever feeling like worlds away from Sing Sing.

Raymond Stark nodded at Strauss to go ahead.

"Two years ago," Strauss said, "we at the Truth Program discovered that Detective Kindler planted evidence in at least three cases to reach his arrest quota and up his profile as a crime fighter. The DC attorney general's office is now being forced to reexamine a number of Kindler's arrests. They've vacated one conviction already. But they're moving slowly, and no one wants to touch the Christopher Anson murder."

"Why not?" Wilde asked.

"Because the case was so high profile. Everyone thought Raymond was guilty—fellow officers, prosecutors, the media, Anson's family and friends. It would be more than an embarrassment now if it came out that the knife was planted. And even if we could prove that, plenty of people would still say Raymond was the killer. It's like OJ. Tons of people think Mark Fuhrman planted the bloody glove—but they also think OJ did it."

Strauss handed him a grainy photograph of a young white man with a big smile and wavy hair. He wore a blue blazer and red tie. "This is Christopher Anson, the murder victim. The photograph was taken two weeks before his murder. He was twenty when he was killed, a junior at Swarthmore College. Christopher was the quintessential all-American boy—basketball captain, debate team, three-point-eight GPA. The Ansons are a big blue-blood family in Massachusetts. They summered in a huge estate in Newport. You get the idea."

Wilde said nothing.

"I tried to approach the Anson family with what we learned about Detective Kindler. They didn't want to hear it. In their minds, the killer is caught and got what he deserved. It's not an unusual reaction. You've been believing one thing for over thirty years. You become vested and blind."

"Saul?"

It was Raymond.

"Wilde has been very patient with us," Raymond said. "Show him the other photo now."

Strauss hesitated. "I'd rather put it in more context first."

"He'll get the context," Raymond said. "Show him."

Strauss reached into the manila folder and pulled out another photograph.

"At first, this didn't mean much to us. But then Arnie Poplin made that comment."

He handed Wilde a group shot of about thirty or forty young people, all well dressed, healthy looking, and vibrant. The photograph had been taken outdoors on white concrete steps. Some of the young people sat, some stood. The first face Wilde recognized was Christopher Anson standing second from the left on the top. Wilde quickly realized that the other portrait of Christopher Anson that Strauss had showed him had been this same photo, just cropped and enlarged.

In the background, above the smiling faces, Wilde could see the familiar white dome of the Capitol building in Washington, DC.

A chill began to creep down his neck.

"Christopher Anson spent that summer interning for a Massachusetts senator."

Wilde's eyes traveled along the picture. He got it now—saw it all—but he waited for Strauss to point it out. Strauss pointed to a face two away from Christopher Anson.

"That's Dash Maynard."

His finger moved down to the young woman who hadn't changed much over the years. "That's Delia Maynard, née Reese"—and then the finger slid to the face next to her—"and that, my friend, is the current senator for the great state of New Jersey, Rusty Eggers."

CHAPTER THIRTY-FOUR

Back in the Sing Sing parking lot, Wilde called the Maynards to see whether there had been any news. There hadn't been. Two hours remained until the kidnappers promised to release Crash.

When they got back in Saul Strauss's car, Wilde said, "So let me see if I have your theory right."

"Go ahead."

"Arnie Poplin claims to have overheard Rusty admit to killing someone and Dash having some kind of confession to it on tape. You figure they're talking about Christopher Anson."

"In short, yes. But there's more to it."

"Such as?"

"They were out that night."

"Who?"

"Christopher Anson and Rusty Eggers. That took a while to track down. These interns—they were all kids from pretty wealthy families, so their names weren't in the released report."

"In a case this high profile?"

"Even more reason. 'We will only cooperate if we're assured

our precious child's name will not be sullied.' They struck confidentiality deals before they'd testify. It turns out that the prosecutor didn't need them for court. The knife discovery was enough. But anyway, a bartender at a local hangout called the Lockwood saw a whole group of the male interns that night. Look, it took a while. We had our best people on this. Most of the interns wouldn't talk—heck, it's been over thirty years—but from what we understand, Rusty Eggers and Christopher Anson didn't get along. Both of them saw themselves as alphas in this group of interns. They were constantly competing. According to the bartender, they had words that night. One of their buddies had to separate them."

"Rusty and the murder victim?"

"Yes."

"Do you know who separated them?"

"Oh, you'll like this. We showed the bartender that intern photo from the steps of the Capitol. Guess who he picked out?"

Wilde saw it now. "Dash Maynard."

"Interesting, right?"

"So after Dash separates the two of them, what happened?"

"From what we can piece together, Christopher Anson storms out. He's first to leave. Then later—no one can say if it's half an hour, an hour—but the next person to leave was Rusty Eggers."

"The police knew about this?"

Strauss nodded. "Their theory was, Anson left early to buy drugs. He'd done it before. Anson was something of the group's... 'dealer' is too strong a word. Supplier maybe. So the police think Anson was drunk. He stumbled out to buy drugs in a bad neighborhood. He was well dressed—they were still in suits and ties from interning—and an easy target. Raymond Stark spots him or maybe Anson goes up to him to buy drugs. Either way, the white kid is an easy target. Raymond pulls the knife to rob him. Maybe Anson resists, maybe not."

"Raymond Stark stabs him."

"Right. But there are a lot of flaws in that theory."

"For example?"

"Anson's body was found in an alleyway. Our expert at the Truth Program examined the crime scene photos. He's convinced the body was dumped there."

"So Christopher Anson was killed somewhere else?"

"Our expert says yes."

"Did Raymond's lawyer bring it up at trial?"

Strauss shook his head. "He was pro bono. He couldn't afford an expert."

"And I assume the prosecution didn't let anyone know?"

"There's a chance their expert didn't come to the same conclusion, but it's probably classic 'don't ask, don't tell' prosecutorial misconduct. I don't think it would have made a difference to the jury anyway. If it had come up, the prosecution would just say Raymond stabbed Anson somewhere else and dragged him into an alley, so no one would see."

Wilde sat back. They took the new Tappan Zee Bridge across the Hudson back to New Jersey. A text came in from Hester:

> Rola may have a lead on Naomi's mother.

Wilde typed a reply:

> Be back in half an hour.

Wilde said, "So you think Rusty Eggers killed Christopher Anson?"

"He was there that night," Strauss began. "They exchanged angry words."

"Meaningless."

"On its own? Sure. But years later, Arnie Poplin hears Rusty admit killing someone to Dash Maynard and worrying about a tape." Strauss took one hand off the wheel and held it toward Wilde.

"And yeah, I know Arnie Poplin doesn't pour all his cornflakes into one bowl, but think about Rusty Eggers's behavior. He forces the Maynards to hire Gavin Chambers, maybe the best security man in the country, to guard them. Why?"

"Because there are indeed tapes," Wilde said. "Like the one just released."

"You think Eggers hired Chambers over that tape of him and Kandi Pate?"

"It could be."

"It could be," Strauss repeated, "but it's not. Because there is one other thing we are leaving out."

"What's that?"

"Rusty Eggers is a stone-cold sociopath. I don't know if he was born that way or that truck accident that killed his parents sent him off the rails, but it couldn't be more obvious. He's charming and ridiculously smart—but he's seriously damaged. If you look through his past, there are too many people who got in his way who ended up dead."

Wilde made a face. Strauss saw it out of the corner of his eye.

"What?"

"I'm not a huge fan of conspiracy theories," Wilde said.

"It doesn't matter," Strauss said. "What matters is, if Rusty Eggers gets elected, millions of people may die. That is how it is with charismatic leaders like him. You're a student of history. Don't pretend you don't see the danger."

They drove some more.

"You sound like a guy with a lot of motive," Wilde said.

"To do what?" Strauss smiled. "Kidnap two teenagers?"

Wilde turned to him.

"I told you I have sources," Strauss said.

"So it seems."

"And you're missing my point, man. Someone *really* wants that tape. They'll do pretty much anything, it seems, to get it. Including kidnapping kids. And their motives may not be altruistic. That's what I'm trying to explain to you. If they get it before we do, they may destroy it. Or cover it up. And if that happens, Raymond Stark stays in jail for a crime he didn't commit. That's the micro level. On a macro level, maybe Rusty Eggers gets elected. You aren't blind or as blasé as you pretend. You know what kind of destruction Rusty Eggers is capable of unleashing."

Wilde thought about the tape. He thought about Rusty Eggers. But mostly he thought about Raymond Stark's dream of being free. How soul-crushing it must be, on the cusp before you wake up, when you realize your release was just a dream, when you know the wisps of hope will soon be gone and you'll be back in that cell.

"How did Raymond end up in that wheelchair?" Wilde asked.

Strauss was a big man with big gnarly hands. His grip on the wheel tightened. "In a sense, it's part of the reason why Anson's family will never accept that Raymond didn't do it, even if we prove the knife was planted."

Wilde waited.

"The Ansons wanted the death penalty. There was a quote in the news after the verdict from his father. A reporter asked Anson Senior if he felt that justice had been served. He said no. He said that Raymond Stark will get free housing and free clothes and three meals a day while his beautiful son's dead body will be eaten by worms."

Strauss took a shaking hand off the wheel and rubbed his chin. His eyes started blinking. "Raymond was in four months when some guys grabbed him in the shower. They laid him on his stomach on the tile. Two guys grabbed his arms and pulled. Two guys grabbed his legs and pulled. Like he was on a medieval rack. Another guy held Raymond's face down, so that his nose was pressed against the ceramic. They held him and they pulled his limbs. Hard. And then another guy, a big guy, Raymond said, weighed over three hundred pounds, came over and said, 'This is from the Anson family.'"

Strauss's breathing was hitching now. Wilde sat next to him, almost afraid to move.

"The big guy is still standing. He straddles Raymond's stretched-out body. Then he jumps up in the air, like he's coming from the top rope at a wrestling match. That's how Raymond described it. The other men pull his legs and arms even harder, totally taut, painful, and this big guy's full weight slams into Raymond's lower back like a sledgehammer. Raymond hears his spine snap, he said, like a strong wind whipping a dry branch off an old oak."

Silence. A silence so deep, so pure, that it pushed against the windows of the car. A silence that smothered you, that didn't let you take a breath. A silence that felt like a scream.

"Saul?"

"Yes?"

"Two hundred yards on your right. There's a spot to pull over. I'll get out there."

Wilde needed the time in the forest.

It wouldn't be long. He had to get back to the Maynards. But that rain-gray visit to Sing Sing and the night-black story of how Raymond's spine snapped made Wilde feel that walls both literal and figurative were starting to close in on him. He didn't know whether he suffered from some form of claustrophobia—he doubted it was severe enough to be labeled a disorder—but Wilde knew that he needed the woods. When he was away from these trees for too long, he felt as though he was suffocating, as though his lungs were ready to completely shut down.

"Imagine being in a place like this every day, screaming out the truth every way you know how, but no one ever hears you..."

Wilde closed his eyes and gulped down deep breaths.

By the time he reached Maynard Manor, he felt stronger, more himself. Hester's Escalade was parked by the gate. Tim, her driver, opened the rear door, and Hester got out.

She pointed to him. "What the hell happened to you?"

"What?"

"You look like a kitten someone left in a dryer."

So much for stronger, more himself.

"I'm fine."

"You sure?"

"I'm sure."

"Rola found Naomi's mother. She's agreed to see me."

"When?"

"If I want to talk to her today, I have to leave now. She's back in New York."

"Go," Wilde said, "I can handle here."

"Tell me where you were first. So I know why you look like hell."

He gave her the heavily abridged version of his trip with Saul Strauss to Sing Sing. Turned out the abridged was more than enough. Hester's face darkened to a deep scarlet. Her fists tightened. With all the distraction of Crash and Naomi, Wilde had almost forgotten that Hester Crimstein was one of the most famed and dogged criminal defense attorneys in the country. Nothing upset her more than prosecutorial overreach.

"Those bastards," Hester said.

"Who?"

"Cops, prosecutors, judges—take your pick. Railroading an innocent man like that. And now they know this Kindler guy was crooked and they still have this man locked up? Disgraceful. Do you have Saul's number?"

"I do."

"Tell him I'll take Raymond's case pro bono."

"You don't even know all the details."

"See this?" Hester tapped with her finger.

"Your nose?"

"Exactly. The nose knows. This case stinks like the thirty-year-old garbage it is. Tell Strauss I'll make some calls and kick some ass. Tell him."

"One more thing," Wilde said. "Do you know anyone at Sing Sing?"

"Like?"

"Like someone who can let me see the visitors log."

She started back toward the car. "Text me the details, doll face. I'll get on it."

Tim already had the door open. Hester climbed back in. Tim gave Wilde a small nod, got in the car, and drove away.

Wilde trekked up the hill. Rola had the whole team here now—all women with hard eyes.

"The Maynards know I'm back?" he asked.

Rola nodded.

There was still a half hour until noon. No reason to go inside yet. If the Maynards needed him, they'd know where to look. He headed back toward the path in the woods, the one that led to where Matthew had first sneaked away with Naomi. He couldn't say why he came here. Mostly, he supposed, because he craved peace and quiet and the outdoors. The outdoors more than anything else. He didn't want to be inside that damned library any longer than he had to.

He checked his phone and was surprised to see a message from the genealogy website. The message came from "PB," the person who'd been listed as his "closest" relative. He debated just deleting it or at least leaving it unopened for now. It was probably nothing. Genealogy was a big hobby for many, connecting in a "fun and social way," as the website put it, maybe asking questions so that you can fill in empty branches on your family tree.

Wilde had no interest in doing that. Then again, rudeness and willful ignorance weren't his style either. Neither was procrastination.

He hit the message link and read PB's message:

> Hi. Sorry about not giving my name, but there are reasons I don't feel comfortable letting people know my real identity. My background has too many holes in it and a lot of turmoil. You are the closest relative I've found on this site, and I wonder whether you have holes and turmoil too. If you do, I may have some answers.

Wilde read the message twice, then a third time.

Holes and turmoil. He didn't need that right now either.

Wilde put away the phone. Then he looked up, past the branches stretching to the deep blue of the sky. His thoughts turned to Raymond Stark. When, he wondered, had Raymond last been outside like this? When had he last been surrounded by green and blue instead of institutional gray? Wilde reached into his back pocket. He unfolded the photograph of the Capitol Hill interns Saul Strauss had given him. He searched the faces again, finding Rusty Eggers, then Dash, then Delia.

The hell with it.

He hurried back into the Maynards' side yard. He took the steps two at a time and burst into the library. Dash Maynard was staring at the computer screen, as though it were some crystal ball that might tell him the future. Delia paced.

"We're glad you're back," she said.

He crossed the room. "Do you recognize this photograph?"

Wilde held it up so both could see it. He wanted to see if they'd react. They did—recoiling like vampires near a cross.

Dash snapped, "Why do you have that?"

Wilde pointed to Christopher Anson. "Do you recognize him?"

"What the hell is this?"

"His name was Christopher Anson."

"We know," Delia said. "But what the hell, Wilde. We're waiting for a word from our son's kidnapper. Don't you get that?"

Wilde saw no reason to reply.

"Why are you raising this now?"

"Because whoever has your son clearly wants a very damaging tape."

"Which we gave them," Dash said.

"Arnie Poplin said he overheard you and Rusty Eggers talking about a murder."

"Arnie Poplin is a lunatic," Dash said with a dismissive wave.

Delia added, "You can't possibly think we had something to do with what happened to Christopher."

"Maybe not you two," Wilde said.

"Rusty?" Delia shook her head. "No."

"You don't get how unreliable Arnie Poplin is," Dash said. "When we fired him from the show, he grew resentful. You mix his crazy with the drugs and the bitterness—"

"I don't understand," Delia interrupted. "Who gave you that photograph?"

"Raymond Stark."

Silence.

Wilde waited. He wanted to see whether either of them would go so far as to pretend that they didn't recognize the name. They didn't.

After a while, Dash said, "Oh my God."

"What?"

"Is that what Raymond Stark is saying? Is that what he's trying to pull now to get out of jail?"

Delia looked at her husband. "Could he be behind all this?"

"What?"

"Raymond Stark," Dash said, turning back to Wilde. "Maybe some convict he met in prison is doing him a favor. They kidnap our son and claim it's related to the killing of Christopher. They demand some tape that will prove his innocence."

"Maybe," Delia joined in, "Raymond Stark told someone the story and they are acting on their own."

"Wilde," Dash said, turning to him, "how did Raymond Stark reach out to you?"

That was when they heard the ding on the computer.

It was noon.

Delia refreshed the page and a message came up.

You can find Crash at 41°07'17.5"N 74°12'35.0"W.

Wilde felt his mouth go dry.

Delia pointed at the screen. "Are those—?"

"Coordinates," Wilde said with a nod.

But not just any coordinates.

Someone was seriously fucking with him.

"I don't understand," Delia said. "Where is that?"

Wilde didn't even have to bring up the map app on his phone. He knew where the coordinates would lead. "It's in the woods, about three miles from here, up near the Ramapoughs. It'll be fastest if I hike it. Give the coordinates to Rola. Tell her to get a car and meet me there."

He didn't explain more. He just took off, down the steps, out the door, into the sticky air. Sweat broke out on his face first. Would Crash really be there? In many ways, it was a great drop-off spot—remote, away from any roads or cameras, deep enough in the forest.

But why those particular coordinates?

Because someone wanted to seriously mess with Wilde's head.

Without breaking stride, he stuck an AirPod into his ear and called Hester. When she answered, he said, "The kidnappers sent coordinates forty-one degrees, oh-seven—"

"Speak English, Wilde."

"It's a remote spot in the Ramapough Mountains. By the old burial site."

"Wait. Are you saying—?"

"It's the exact location where the police found me when I was a kid."

"Holy moly," Hester said. "Who would know about that?"

"The specific coordinates? The cops, maybe the press, I don't know. It's not a secret."

"But it's not a coincidence either."

"No, it's not a coincidence."

"Where are you?" Hester asked. "You sound winded."

"I'm running there now. I'll call you back."

Wilde knew the route, of course. He knew it would take Rola and whoever she brought longer to drive because there was no immediate road access. You had to hike more than a mile off the road to find the spot.

So why there?

Wilde was starting to get it now, starting to maybe piece together what the hell was going on. They'd hope to seed confusion and chaos. But maybe for the first time, Wilde was seeing things clearly.

He dodged to the left, ducked under branches, tried not to break stride. Decades ago, when the park rangers and local police surrounded him, he'd been using a Coleman dome tent and an Eddie Bauer sleeping bag he'd stolen from a house in Ringwood. He didn't remember how long that particular camping site, far away from any hiking trails, had been his home, but when he saw them coming for him, young Wilde—what had he called himself back then? He didn't even know his own damned name—had been tempted to run for it. He had done that before, of course, whenever anyone spotted him or got close.

Why?

Why had he always fled? Was it some kind of primitive survival instinct? Was man's basic nature to fear rather than engage with other humans? He often wondered. Why, as a young child, had his instinct been to run? Was that genetic, human nature—or had something happened that made him that way?

But on that brisk early morning, with young Wilde in his tent and four officers and rangers surrounding him, he chose not to run. Perhaps because he realized that it would be futile. Perhaps because one of them was Oren Carmichael and even back then, Oren had a calming, trustworthy, safe aura.

Three, maybe four minutes until Wilde reached the coordinates.

He was north of the forest area called the Bowl, a mile or so from the New Jersey–New York state border. On the surface, this rendezvous had all the earmarks of an ambush. Wilde debated slowing down, taking some extra precautions now that he was getting nearby. Unless they were very good, he'd spot them with a fairly quick reconnaissance. If they were pros or snipers in trees, then his advanced scouting wouldn't do any good. They could simply take him out whenever they wanted.

There would be no reason for these dramatics.

So no, this wasn't an ambush. This was a distraction.

The woods grew thicker now, making it harder to see. Even as a child, Wilde had known not to make camp in clearings because he'd be too easy to spot. Most nights he'd surround his tent with twigs or even old newspapers. If someone (or more likely, some animal) came close, the sounds emanating from those twigs and papers would warn him. Wilde was a light sleeper, probably because he spent most nights as a child half listening for predators. Even now, while most people plunged deep into slumber, Wilde barely did more than skim the surface.

A hundred yards now.

He spotted something red.

Not a person. A few seconds later, as he hurried closer, he could see that the red thing was fairly small—maybe a foot high by a foot long.

It was, he saw now, a carry cooler, the kind that holds a six-pack and a couple of sandwiches.

Wilde felt the hairs on the back of his neck rise.

He couldn't say why. It was just a cooler. But instinct is a funny thing.

He ran over and flipped down the handle. Then he opened the top of the cooler and looked inside.

Wilde had braced himself. But not enough. Still, he didn't scream. He didn't call out.

He just stared down at the severed finger with the smile-skull ring.

CHAPTER THIRTY-FIVE

Naomi's mother, Pia, lived in an ornate four-story Renaissance Revival town house off Park Avenue in Manhattan. A woman in a black French maid's uniform opened the door and led Hester over the herringbone parquet floor, past the oak-paneled walls and the intricately sculptured staircase, and out back into a lush courtyard garden.

Pia sat in a chaise. She wore sunglasses, a beige beach hat, and an aqua blouse open at the top. She didn't rise when Hester came out. She didn't even turn and look at her.

"I don't understand why you keep hounding me."

Her voice was high-pitched and shaky. Hester didn't wait to be asked. She pulled a free chair next to Pia and sat as close as she could. She wanted to get in the woman's space a little.

"Nice place," Hester said.

"Thank you. What do you want, Ms. Crimstein?"

"I'm trying to locate your daughter."

"Your assistant mentioned that."

"And you refused to talk to her about it."

"This is the second time you called," Pia said.

"Correct. The first time you cooperated. You told me that you didn't know anything. So why the change?"

"I felt enough was enough."

"Yeah, Pia, I'm not buying that."

With the dark sunglasses it was impossible to know where the woman was looking, but she wasn't facing Hester. The former Mrs. Pine was, no doubt about it, a stunning woman. Hester knew that Pia had been some kind of bathing suit model back in her day, but that day was really not that long ago.

"She's not my daughter, you know."

"Uh-huh."

"I terminated all my parental rights. You're an attorney. You know what that means."

"Why?"

"Why what?"

"Why did you terminate all parental rights?"

"You know that she's adopted."

"Naomi," Hester said.

"What?"

"You keep calling her 'she.' Your daughter has a name. It's Naomi. And who cares if she was adopted or not? What does that have to do with it?"

"I really can't help you, Ms. Crimstein."

"Has Naomi been in contact with you?"

"I'd rather not say."

"Did you voluntarily terminate your parental rights—or were they taken away from you?"

Pia still looked off, but a small smile came to her face. "It was voluntary."

"Because you would have been brought up on charges?"

"Ah," Pia said, with a small nod, "you spoke to Bernard."

"You should be in jail."

From behind them: "Mrs. Goldman?"

It was a young woman with a stroller.

"It's time to take Nathan for his walk in the park."

Pia turned toward the woman. Her face broke into a wide smile. "You start, Angie. I'll catch up to you by the Conservatory Water."

The young woman pulled the stroller away and left.

Hester tried to keep the horror out of her voice. "You have a son?"

"Nathan. He's ten months old. And yes, he's biologically mine and my husband's."

"I thought you couldn't have children."

"That's what I thought. But of course, that's what Bernard told me. Turns out the problems were with him." She tilted her head. "Ms. Crimstein?"

Hester waited.

"I never abused her."

"Naomi," Hester said. "Her name is Naomi."

"Bernard made that all up. He's a liar and worse. I should have known what he was right away. Isn't that what they say? But I didn't. Or maybe I'm weak. Bernard abused me—verbally, emotionally, physically."

"Did you tell anyone?"

"You sound skeptical."

"Don't worry about how I sound," Hester said, a little more sharply than she intended. "Did you tell anyone?"

"No."

"Why not?"

"Do you really need to hear another abused-woman tale, Ms. Crimstein?" Pia smiled and tilted her head, and Hester wondered how many men had been smitten by that simple move. "Bernard can be very charming, very convincing. He's also extremely manipulative. Did he tell you the hot-water story? That's his favorite. Of course, if it had been true, she"—this time, Pia stopped herself—"I mean, Naomi would have gone to the hospital, wouldn't she?"

Fair point, Hester thought.

"I don't want to give you my whole life story. I came from a small town. I was... I guess the word is 'blessed' with a figure that drew too much attention. Everyone told me I should be a model. So I tried it. In truth, I was too short to make it big. I also wasn't anorexic enough. But I got some jobs, mostly in lingerie ads. And then I fell for the wrong man. Bernard was good to me at first, but then his insecurities ate him alive. He was sure I had to be cheating on him. I'd come from a shoot and he'd ask a million questions—did any men talk to you, did anyone flirt with you, come on, someone had to have flirted with you, did you smile at them first, did you lead them on, why were you late?"

Pia stopped, took her sunglasses off, wiped her eyes.

"So you left?" Hester asked.

"Yes, I left. I had no choice. I got help. A lot of it. When I was back on my feet a little, I met Harry, my husband. You know the rest of the story."

Hester made her voice as gentle as possible. "Has Naomi been in touch with you?"

"Why do you care?"

"It's a long story, but I will never betray Naomi. Do you hear me? Whatever you tell me, you can trust me to do whatever I can to help."

"But if I tell you," Pia said, "I'd be betraying Naomi's trust too."

"You can trust me."

"Do you work for Bernard?"

"No."

"Swear?"

"I care about your daughter, not your ex-husband. Yes, I swear."

Pia slipped the sunglasses back onto her face. "Naomi called me."

"When?"

"A few days ago."

"What did she say?"

"She said someone working for Bernard might call me again asking for her. Like you did last time. She said not to say anything."

"Why would she say that?"

"I think... I think she planned on running away from her father. She thought that maybe if people thought she was with me, it would throw him off the scent."

"And you were okay with that? With her running away?"

"I was happy about it. She needed to escape from him."

"I don't understand," Hester said. "You say he's abusive. Your ex, I mean."

"You have no idea."

"And yet," Hester said, trying to keep her voice even, "you left your daughter with him?"

She took off the sunglasses again. "I've gone through a lot of therapy. You have no idea how much, how weak I was, how troubled. There was nothing I could have done. And there was a hard truth I had to face, Ms. Crimstein—in order for me to recover and heal and move on."

"What hard truth is that?"

"Bernard was right about one thing. I didn't want to adopt her in the first place. The hard truth is—and it took me a long time to forgive myself for this—I couldn't connect to Naomi. Maybe it was because she wasn't my blood. Maybe at the time, I just wasn't cut out to be a mother. Maybe it was my chemistry physically reacting to hers or the bad situation with her father. I don't know. But I could never really connect with the girl."

The bile rose in Hester's throat. She swallowed it back down. "So you just left Naomi with him."

"I had no choice. You have to see that."

Hester pulled back her chair and stood. "If you hear from Naomi, have her call me immediately."

"Ms. Crimstein?"

Hester looked down at her.

"Who do you believe?"

"You mean you or Bernard?"

"Yes."

"Does it make a difference?"

"I think it does, yes."

"I don't," Hester said. "You either abused your daughter or you selfishly left her behind. Either way, you abandoned a little girl to a man you just described as a monster. Even when you 'recovered' and 'healed,' even when you got married and moved into this ritzy town house, you just left that poor girl alone with a damaged man. You didn't protect her. You didn't think about her. You just ran away, Pia—and you left Naomi behind."

Pia kept her head down, her eyes on the table.

"So in the end, I don't care if he's lying or you are. You are scum either way, and I hope you never have a moment's peace."

When Dash and Delia Maynard saw their son's severed finger, they reacted in two very different ways.

Dash dropped to the ground, totally collapsed, like a marionette with all its strings cut at the same time. His fall was so sudden that Wilde jumped back a step, careful not to jar the finger from its perch atop the ice pack. Not that the jarring would have any effect. If that was the case, the fact that Wilde had just rushed back from that spot in the woods, more sprinting than jogging, would surely have been the culprit.

Delia froze. For a few moments, she didn't move, didn't even react to her husband's fall. She just stared down at the finger. Slowly, almost imperceptibly, her face began to cave. Her head fell to one side. Her lips quivered, her eyes blinked. She reached out toward the finger, a mother wanting to offer some kind of comfort. Wilde pulled the cooler back, not wanting her to touch or contaminate it.

"The EMTs will be arriving soon," Wilde told her as gently as he could. He glanced at the gate behind him. "They'll do their best to preserve it."

When he closed the cooler, Delia let out a moan. Wilde handed the cooler to Rola and nodded. She took it outside the gate for the ambulance. There was, Rola had already learned, a decent chance that the finger could be reattached if they ran the proper medical protocols.

On the grass, Dash pushed up with his arms and made his way to his knees.

Delia finally spoke. "What do they want? What do they want?" Her voice started off in pure monotone, but slowly grew louder, more frenzied. "We gave them the tapes. What do they want from us? What do they want?"

There was a ping.

It took them all a second to react to it, but then Dash, his eyes doing the thousand-yard stare, reached into his pocket and pulled out his phone. His hand shook.

"What is it?" Delia asked.

Dash read it, got to his feet, and handed his wife the phone. Wilde moved close to read over her shoulder.

> Send the tape we want in the next thirty minutes or we will send the coordinates for your son's entire arm. If you contact the police, he will die in terrible pain.

"What tape?" Delia shouted. "There is no tape. We don't have..."

Dash started hurrying up the drive toward the house.

"Dash?" she called to him.

He didn't reply.

"Dash?"

She ran behind him.

"Oh God, what did you do?"

Dash still wouldn't speak, but tears streamed down his face.

"Dash?"

"I'm sorry," he said.

"What did you do, Dash?"

"I didn't think he was really in danger. I didn't..."

He broke into a full sprint. Delia called out to him, but he didn't respond. She continued to give chase. Wilde, his shirt already coated with sweat, followed them as they entered through the side door and up the turret into the library. Dash hurried up the stairs. He moved behind his desk and started typing on the laptop.

"Talk to me," Delia said.

Dash glanced up. He spotted Wilde and said, "Get out of here."

"No."

"I said—"

"I heard you," Wilde said. "But that's not going to happen."

"You're fired."

"Cool."

Wilde didn't move.

"You have no right to be here."

"Then throw me out," Wilde said.

"Dash," Delia said, "tell me. Please?"

"Not in front of him."

"Yeah, Dash," Wilde said, "in front of me. Stop wasting time."

Delia moved closer to her husband and put her hands on his face. "Baby, look at me," she said, turning his face to hers. The gesture was surprisingly tender. "Tell me, Dash. Please? Tell me now."

Dash swallowed, the tears back now. "He did it. He killed him."

"What are you talking—?"

"Rusty killed Christopher."

Her hands slid down off his face as she shook her head. "I don't understand."

"That night," Dash said. "We'd all been drinking at the Lockwood. Rusty and Christopher, you know how they were. The two of them almost came to blows. I broke it up. Christopher stormed out. Then I got a call at, I don't know, one in the morning. It was Rusty in a panic. He begged me to come over. I could tell from his voice that it was bad. So I went and, well, you know me."

Delia's voice was far away. "You taped it."

"It's what I do. You know that."

"Which camera?"

"Why do you—?"

"Which camera, Dash?"

"The hidden pocket one."

Delia closed her eyes.

Wilde took out his phone and checked the app. It was all coming together now.

"You were in Philadelphia that night," Dash said to her, "researching some project for that congressional subcommittee. When I got there..."

He stopped.

"What?" Delia said.

Dash seemed unable to speak now. He flipped the computer screen around so it was facing Delia and Wilde. He pressed the play button and collapsed back.

For a few seconds, the screen remained a grainy black. Then a door flew open, and a young Rusty Eggers was there. Judging by the height, the camera must have been placed somewhere near Dash's breast pocket. The view was grainy and somewhat distorted, like a fish-eye, like watching the whole thing through a peephole.

Several things struck Wilde all at once. First, the obvious: Rusty looked so damn young. He was probably around twenty years old here, and for some reason, even though he hadn't aged poorly or anything, the effect of seeing Rusty Eggers at this age was strange, like some kind of "before it all went wrong" picture.

The second thing was, Rusty seemed remarkably calm and controlled. For a moment, his gaze turned directly to the lens, almost as though he knew it was there.

Third: His smile was broad. Too broad.

"Thanks for coming," Rusty said.

"You said it was urgent?"

The voice of young Dash.

"Yeah, come in."

Rusty moved to the side, out of sight. The camera took two steps forward as Dash entered. There was the sound of a bolt slide. Wilde figured that Rusty had just locked the door behind them.

"What's going on?" Dash asked.

Rusty stepped back into view. "I really appreciate you coming."

"What the . . . ?" Dash suddenly sounded terrified. "Is that blood on your hand?"

With the broad smile still plastered to his face, Rusty reached toward the lens with an open hand covered with blood.

"Rusty?"

The hand moved north of the camera lens, grabbed what must have been Dash's shoulder, and jerked him forward.

"What the hell, Rusty! Let go of me."

He didn't. Rusty dragged Dash forward. The picture on the screen lurched. The breast-pocket viewpoint combined with the fish-eye quality of the lens made it difficult to keep track of what was happening when there was movement. Lots of things were a blur for the next few seconds. Wilde spotted a bookshelf maybe. A rug. Some wall hangings.

The movement slowed down a bit. A tile floor. A stove, fridge.

The kitchen.

Wilde risked a glance at Delia. She stared at the screen transfixed.

Then on the screen, Wilde heard Dash let out a sharp gasp.

Rusty moved close to him, blocking the camera for a moment. He whispered, probably in Dash's ear, "Don't scream."

Then Rusty let Dash go and took a step back. The camera panned down to the tile floor, swung a little to the right, and stopped cold.

There, lying on his back in a pool of blood, eyes open and unblinking, was Christopher Anson. For a few seconds, the camera didn't move, didn't jerk, didn't shake. It was almost as though Dash couldn't even breathe.

Then Dash said in a hushed, horrified tone, "Oh my God."

"It was self-defense, Dash."

"Oh my God."

"Christopher broke in," Rusty said. His tone was low and serene in a way that chilled the room more than the scariest of screams. "I had no choice, Dash. Dash? Do you hear me?"

The camera veered away from the dead body and back to Rusty, the fish-eye lens making his face look huge. There was still a hint of a smile, but Rusty's distorted eyes were black and cold.

"Christopher broke in," Rusty said again, as though he were explaining the situation to a small child. There was no mania in his tone. No emotion, no panic, no crazy. "I think he was high on drugs, Dash. That's my guess. He probably bought them after he left the bar. You saw how angry Christopher was, right?"

Dash didn't or maybe couldn't answer. Rusty moved closer. When Rusty spoke again, his voice—still calm, still in total control—had just a bit more bite:

"You saw that, right?"

"Uh, yeah, I guess."

"You guess?"

"I mean, yeah, I did, of course." Then: "We need to call the police, Rusty."

"Oh no, that's not going to happen."

"What?"

"I killed him."

"You . . . you said it was—"

"Self-defense, yes. But who's going to believe me, Dash—me against the Anson family and their connections?" Rusty's face grew larger as he moved closer to Dash's chest. His voice was again a whisper. "No one."

"But... I mean, we have to call the police."

"No, we don't."

"I don't understand."

Rusty stepped back. "Dash, listen to me."

The camera moved a little to the left. Casually, almost too nonchalantly, Rusty started to raise his right hand. Dash cried out. He startled back, so that everything was a blur. A few seconds later, the lens regained focus.

Now Wilde could see what was in Rusty's hand.

A knife still wet with blood.

Dash: "Rusty..."

"I need your help, my friend."

"I... I think I should leave."

"No, Dash, you can't do that."

"Please..."

"You're my friend." Rusty smiled again. "You're the only one I can trust. But if you don't want to help me"—Rusty turned his gaze to the knife in his hand, not overtly threatening, not even pointing it at Dash—"I don't know what to do."

Silence.

Rusty dropped the knife hand to his side. "Dash?"

"Yes."

"You'll help me?"

"Yeah," Dash said. "I'll help."

That was where the tape cut out.

For a few moments, Delia and Wilde just stood there and stared at the blank screen. No one moved. In the distance, Wilde heard a clock chime. He looked around at the opulence of the great library, but opulence is a false facade. It doesn't really protect or even enhance. It just fools you into feeling safe.

Dash had his head in his hands. He rubbed his face.

"So you tell me," Dash said. "Suppose I said no to him?"

Delia put a shaking hand to her mouth, as though muffling her own scream.

"Delia?"

She shook her head.

"Listen to me, please. You know Rusty. You know what he would have done to me if I had tried to walk away."

Delia closed her eyes, wishing it all away.

"So what did you do?" Wilde asked.

Dash turned his gaze toward Wilde. "I had a car. Rusty didn't. That's why he chose me, I guess. We moved Christopher's body into my trunk and dumped him in that alley. Then Rusty wiped his fingerprints off the knife and threw it in the dumpster. We figured the police would think it was a drug deal or robbery gone wrong. I hoped maybe later, I don't know, I would feel safe and then maybe I could send the tape in to the police. But of course, my voice is also on it. And when you watch it, Rusty didn't really threaten me, did he?"

Delia finally found her voice. "Rusty chose you," she said, "because you're weak."

Dash blinked, his eyes wet.

Delia looked down at him. "So you just kept the tape?"

"Yes."

"And at some point, you told Rusty you had it?"

Dash nodded. "As an insurance policy. I was the only one who knew what he'd done. But I made it clear if something happened to me—"

"The tape would come out."

"Yes. It bonded us in an odd way."

"And you never told me," Delia said. "All these years together. All that we shared, and you never told me."

"It was part of the understanding."

"We broke up right after that," Delia said. "Rusty and me."

Dash said nothing.

"Was that part of the deal, Dash?"

"He is a terrible man. I just wanted you to be safe."

She glared at him.

"Delia?"

Her voice was pure ice. "Send them the tape, Dash. My son's life is in jeopardy. Send the goddamn tape right now."

Wilde waited until Dash clicked the button. After it was done, Dash sat back in his chair, spent. Delia stood next to him. She didn't move. She didn't put her hand on his shoulder. She didn't look at him. Someone had just detonated a bomb in this room, leaving these two people in rubble and ruins that would be impossible to rebuild.

They were shattered and would never be made whole.

No reason to watch it.

Wilde turned and left. They didn't ask where he was going, or maybe they couldn't speak. It didn't matter. He wouldn't reply. Not yet anyway. He'd heard all he needed to hear from them.

He thought that maybe he had the answers now.

CHAPTER THIRTY-SIX

Rola drove him in the Honda Odyssey. There were three car seats in the back. Five pink sippy cups with screwed-on lids and side handles were on the floor by his feet. Cheerios and Goldfish crackers were scattered everywhere. The cloth seats felt as though they'd been coated in pancake syrup.

Rola smiled. "The mess is freaking you out, right?"

"I'm fine," Wilde managed.

"Sure you are. Want to tell me where we're headed?"

"Just keep heading north on 87."

Wilde had debated driving himself, but he might need someone for a variety of reasons, not the least of which was that Wilde wasn't a very good driver. He could do the local roads, but big interstates loaded with various trucks and cars and merging vehicles were not his forte. He also had the phone in his hand, tracking the two GPS locators, and he didn't want to do that and handle a busy highway at the same time.

He needed time to sort through his next move.

"Take exit sixteen," Wilde said.

"The one for Harriman?"

"Yes."

Rola asked, "Are we going to Woodbury Commons?"

"What?"

"It's a ginormous mall of outlet stores, right past the toll plaza. Nike, Ralph Lauren, Tory Burch, OshKosh B'gosh, a zillion others. Factory stores. The kids love the Children's Place. Ever been? Supposed to be huge discounts, but my friend Jane, who knows more about retail shopping than anyone, says, when you add in the travel and the lower quality—"

"No, we're not going shopping."

"I know, Wilde. I'm just babbling here. You know when you play the silent mountain man I get chatty."

"And even when I don't," he replied.

"Funny."

"Make the right. Route 32 North."

"How long has it been since you called Mom and Dad?"

She meant the Brewers. "I don't call them that."

"Do you call me your sister?"

He said nothing.

"The Brewers were good to us, Wilde."

"Very," he said.

"They miss you, you know. And I miss you. Of course, sitting here with you now I don't remember *why* I miss you. It's not like I miss this sparkling repartee."

"You have your gun?"

"I told you before we left. Yes. Where are we going?"

"I think I have a lead on where the boy is being held."

"You serious?"

"No, I'm kidding, Rola. I always was a terrific kidder."

She grinned. "That's more like it, my brother. And I call you that, by the way. My brother."

"There's a rest stop a couple of miles up the road. I want you to pull in and park where we can see everything, but no one can see us."

"Got it."

Wilde planned out their next moves. They'd park. They'd wait. It wouldn't be long. Twenty minutes tops. And then...

"Look," Rola said.

Damn, Wilde thought.

The blue sign read:

REST AREA—1 MILE

...in familiar white lettering. But there, slashing across those words, was a neon-orange sign with black letters:

CLOSED.

Closed? Wilde hadn't anticipated that.

"Now what?" Rola asked.

"Keep driving. Try to slow down a little, but nothing obvious."

The rest stop had clearly been shut down for a while. It had temporary fencing with a padlocked gate on the entrance ramp. Weeds sprang through the cracked pavement. The glass windows of the small convenience store were covered in plywood. A flat canopy led from the gas station's office to three nonworking pumps. There was a two-car mechanic's garage. A hut-like building on the right had a faded Dunkin' Donuts sign half falling off the facade.

Wilde looked for vehicles. None were visible.

That made no sense.

"Now what?"

Wilde brought up a standard navigation app and used his fingers to spread it out and see the map. "Take the next exit."

"Got it."

When they reached the end of the ramp, Wilde told her to veer right and then take the first right turn. He looked out the window and told her to slow down.

"See that Dairy Queen on the right?"

"Are we stopping for an Oreo Blizzard?" Rola asked.

"Your comic timing," he said. "It often sucks."

"Good thing I'm cute then."

"Uh-huh. Head to the rear. The lot should back up directly behind that rest stop."

Rola made the turn. No cars were parked behind the Dairy Queen. Wilde hit the button to lower the window. He looked up the hill and bingo—he spotted the back of the closed gas station.

"Stay here," Wilde said, reaching for the door handle.

"No way."

"Fine. Get an Oreo Blizzard."

Rola frowned. "*My* comic timing sucks?"

"If I don't check in every ten minutes, call the police."

"I'm going."

"I need you to—"

"—call the police if you don't check in every ten minutes," Rola said. "I heard you. I'll have Zelda do that via her phone. I don't know what's going on, but I don't want you going in unarmed."

"Fine, give me your gun."

"No offense, Wilde, but you're trash with a gun," she said. Which was true.

"This could be dangerous."

"I love danger."

"You have k—"

"Stop," Rola said, holding up her hand for emphasis. "If you're going to say I have kids or a family or any other sexist bullshit, I'll shoot you myself."

He said nothing.

"I'm going, Wilde. This is nonnegotiable, so let's stop wasting time."

Rola got out of the car. Wilde quickly followed and put a hand on her shoulder. She got it. Driving might not be his forte, but approaching quietly was. He should lead. She should follow.

They started up the hill, staying low. Rola took out the gun and kept it in her right hand, just in case. When they reached the top of the hill, they were maybe thirty, forty yards from the closed gas station. The back wall was cinder block and covered in graffiti, most of it a big bubble-letter tag spelling out the words SPOON and ABEONA.

Wilde crept closer, his gaze constantly on the move. No signs of life. No signs of a car. He risked a glance at the GPS locator on his phone's screen. No question about it. The car was right near here.

He moved toward the back of the gas station. When they were in the clearing, he picked up speed, hoping no one would spot them. Rola kept pace. They reached the cinder block and pressed their backs against it.

Rola gave him a look that said, *Now what?*

He mouthed, *Wait here*. He slid toward the side. The grass was overgrown enough to lose a third grader. He could see tires strewn about it, a few crowbars, a variety of rusted engine parts. On the side of the concrete wall, someone had long ago painted the words TIRE SERVICE in red and blue. The letters were faded now, beaten and stripped by years of sun.

Wilde stayed low and moved to the front. The garage bays were closed. Wilde looked at the bottom of the doors. Wind had covered one up, sealing the bottom. The other garage door though had a solid crack opening.

Someone had not shut it all the way.

There were tire tracks in the dirt leading up to it.

Wilde had been confused when he'd first seen that the rest stop was closed. He'd figured that this had been a meeting place, a spot they could come and hash out their kidnapping plan without drawing attention. He figured that maybe he and Rola would park and wait and follow—and that the car would lead him to Crash.

This, of course, was better.

Wilde lay on his stomach and moved closer to the opening in the garage door. He peered in. Yep. Just as he expected.

The car.

He was here.

Wilde moved back to the side of the garage. He peeked around the corner, taking it all in, before he saw something that made him pull up. The old Dunkin' Donuts hut. At first glance there was nothing remarkable about it. The windows were covered by plywood. A sign was hanging by one nail. It was run down and beat up and one day a wrecking ball would end its existence mercifully and effortlessly. There was only one odd thing.

The air-conditioning unit in the window toward the back.

It looked new.

Wilde's heart started pounding. He headed back to Rola. She greeted him with a *What gives?* shrug. He signaled for her to follow him. They slid along the back wall. When the Dunkin' Donuts came into view, Wilde pointed to the air conditioner. It took Rola a second to get it, but then she gave him a thumbs-up.

Wilde checked the locator app again. They still had ten minutes. As he put the phone back in his pocket, Rola again gave him a look as if to ask, *What was that?* He shook it off. No time.

They'd be out in the open. There was no way to avoid that. Rola had the gun out. Wilde gestured that he'd go first. If someone took a shot at him, Rola should be at the ready. She reluctantly agreed. Wilde made the sprint, and as he did, he heard a sound that made the blood in his veins hum. Over the sounds of the cars speeding by on the nearby highway, Wilde could make out the air conditioner.

It was on.

Someone was in that Dunkin' Donuts back room.

When he was up against the wall of the hut, he looked over his shoulder toward Rola. He was tempted to signal for her to wait there, but suppose whoever was inside the Dunkin' Donuts back room—assuming someone was inside and no one had just left the air-conditioning unit on—might be armed.

She had the gun.

He waved her forward. Rola kept the weapon at her side, pointed down. She was agile and quick, ever the athlete. When she reached him, they both ducked down. Neither moved for a moment, waiting to see whether they were heard or seen.

Nothing.

Wilde crawled toward the air conditioner. He gestured with his hand for her to stay down. She nodded. He lifted himself up. He could feel the exhaust air blowing out the back of the unit.

The window shade was drawn.

He couldn't see in.

Now what?

Time was a-ticking. He came back down to her.

"Someone is in that back room," he whispered, "but someone may also be in the gas station office. I need you to draw the gun and be ready. I'm going to open the window a crack and pull out the air conditioner. Quietly if I can. You be ready?"

Rola nodded. "Got it."

He stood and inspected the window. The unit didn't look screwed in or anything like that. All he had to do was slide the window up an inch and pull the air conditioner out, all in one swift move. Wilde rehearsed the action in his mind as he put his hands on the bottom of the window frame.

Rola stood with her back against the wall. The gun was ready.

Then Wilde mouthed the countdown to her.

One, two...

On three, Wilde pushed the window open and grabbed the air conditioner out. At the same time, Rola swung into action. She spun toward the opening, the gun up and ready.

When Rola saw who was inside, she pulled the gun to her side. Wilde dropped the air conditioner and looked too.

Crash Maynard was chained to a bed.

His hand was wrapped in heavy white gauze. Crash looked back toward them, stunned. Wilde moved fast. He put his index finger to his lips while slipping through the window. He hurried over to the teen and whispered, "Stay quiet, Crash. We're here to help."

Tears started rolling down Crash's face. "I want to go home."

He sounded like a little boy.

"You're going home," Wilde whispered. "I promise you. How many of them are there?"

Crash held up the gauze-encased hand. "Look what they did to me."

"I know. We're going to get you to a doctor. Focus, Crash. How many of them?"

"I don't know. They don't talk. They wear ski masks. Please. Please. I just want to get home. Please."

He started sobbing. Wilde checked the shackle holding the boy in place. The chain traveled from his ankle to a plate in the wall. He looked back at the window for Rola. He was surprised not to see her.

Two seconds later, Rola popped back into view, this time carrying one of the discarded crowbars. She handed it to him.

Crash cried, "Please..."

"It's okay, Crash. Hold on."

Wilde used the crowbar against the plate in the wall. It didn't take long. Two tugs and the plate popped out.

At sixteen years old, Crash was pretty close to fully grown. Wilde would be able to carry him if need be, but the teen rolled quickly off the bed and stood.

"Do you know where they stay?" Wilde asked.

Crash shook his head. "I want to go home. Please?"

"How about Naomi?"

He was pretty sure he knew the answer—but Crash's baffled expression confirmed it. "Naomi Pine?"

"Never mind."

They moved to the window. Crash climbed through first. Rola helped him. Wilde followed. When they were back outside, they ducked down and stayed as low as possible.

"Take him back to the car," Wilde told her.

"You come with us," Rola said.

"No. I have more work to do."

"You think Naomi might—?"

"Just go. Take him."

Rola's eyes bore into his. "We can just call the police, Wilde. They can have a hundred cops surrounding this place in ten minutes."

"No," Wilde said again.

"I don't understand—"

"No time to explain. Take him. I'll be fine."

Rola studied his face. Wilde didn't like that, but he gave her nothing. She frowned and handed him the gun. "In case you need it."

"Thanks."

"I'm giving you fifteen minutes. If I don't hear from you by then, I'm calling the police."

"Don't wait for me. When you get back to the car, take him immediately to the Valley Hospital. The finger is there. Every second counts."

"I don't like this, Wilde."

"Trust me, my sister."

Rola's eyes welled up when he called her that. She looked toward Crash. "Think you can make a run for it?"

Crash had stopped crying now. "I'm ready."

Rola took off first. Crash followed her, cradling his injured hand with his good one. Wilde watched until they were out of sight. He checked the locator app again.

There wasn't much time.

CHAPTER THIRTY-SEVEN

Wilde moved to the back of the gas station again, then to the wall with the faded TIRE SERVICE on the side. A few seconds later, he crawled in front of the mechanic bay door that had been opened a crack. He got on his stomach, making himself as flat as possible.

He needed to hurry.

Still on his stomach, he looked through the opening. Wilde could see that the door slid up and down on a track with wheels. Manual. Not electric. That was good. He got up on his knees now, cupped his hands to the bottom of the door, and using a bicep curl movement, he moved it up one inch.

The door squeaked.

Loud enough for someone to hear? That he didn't know. He assumed that no one was in the actual garage. The more likely place for the kidnapper to be—the only place left really—was in the adjacent gas station office.

Wilde stayed still, listening for anyone coming. No one. All he heard was the now-familiar cacophony of cars speeding by. He hoped that no one from the road would see him. He didn't want someone calling the police to report a strange intruder.

Not yet anyway.

He pulled up on the door another inch. Then another.

Squeak, squeak.

Enough. He forced it up another six inches. That was all he'd need. He got back on his belly and shimmied into the garage. It was dark. Dust came up and into his nose, but that wouldn't bother him. The garage reeked of spilled petrol and mildew. Wilde got up, stayed low, moved to the side of the car farthest away from the adjacent office.

He heard the clack of someone typing on a keyboard.

Wilde hadn't lied to Rola, but he hadn't told her the entire truth either. He hadn't told her that he'd figured out about this rest stop in the simplest way possible—from the GPS locators Rola herself had given him. He hadn't told her that the car he'd spotted in this garage bay—the car he was now hiding behind—was the same Chevrolet Cruze that Gavin Chambers had used to meet him at that 7-Eleven.

That had been a mistake on Gavin's part.

Wilde's suspicions, which had already taken root, blossomed the moment Gavin pulled into that 7-Eleven without his usual driver or SUV vehicle. Why suddenly come alone? Why would a guy with his money, a guy who normally got chauffeured around in a Cadillac Escalade, now be driving a Chevrolet Cruze, a car model used extensively by rental-car companies?

On its own, that meant nothing. But it was enough.

Still ducking behind the Chevy—still hearing the clacking of someone typing—Wilde checked the locator app on his phone.

Two minutes until the other car arrived.

He had to get ready.

Wilde crawled from the back tire to the front one, and then to the front bumper. He looked to his left, toward the door to the office.

It was open.

He could see a man's back, but he'd need to get closer to make sure. He moved a little farther out, toward the shelving. He stayed low. When he was about two feet from the back wall, he could make out the profile of the man who was typing.

Gavin Chambers.

Without warning, Gavin turned his head toward Wilde.

Wilde dropped flat on his stomach again. The gun was tucked into his waistband in the back. He reached now and took it out. Gavin Chambers, no doubt, would be armed. If Gavin had spotted him, if he was right now on his way...

But no.

The other car had arrived. On its way past the locked gate, it had tripped a sensor. That was what had alerted Gavin. That was why he'd turned his head.

Wilde crawled back so that he was hidden between the Chevrolet Cruze and the far wall. A minute later, he heard the fumbling of the other bay door. Gavin Chambers rose from his chair. From under the carriage of the Chevy, Wilde could see Gavin's feet go past. Gavin pulled the bay door all the way open. A car pulled in. Gavin immediately shut the door behind it.

The driver opened the door and stepped out.

"Did Maynard send the tape? Did you watch it yet?"

It was Saul Strauss.

Gavin said, "I'm just watching it now."

"And?"

"And it's solid gold," Gavin said. "Rusty admits he killed Anson, though he claims it was in self-defense."

"My God."

"Yes."

"We need to send it out now. Take no chances."

"Agree," Gavin said.

The two men headed into the office. Wilde stayed where he was.

"I knew it," Strauss said, a lilt in his voice. "I knew that tape existed. I didn't want it to go this far, but..."

"I could see why Dash was reticent about giving it up," Chambers said. "It ruins Rusty, sure, but it hurts him too. I don't know if Maynard can be charged for helping move the body. That statute of limitations has probably passed. But anyone who hears it will know what he did."

"And he let Raymond Stark take the fall."

"I know."

"It's one thing to help a buddy out, I guess. But to sit back while another man goes to prison for life."

"Scum," Gavin agreed. "Let's get the tape ready."

Wilde didn't move. He could, of course, stop them now. He could rise up and point the gun and not let them get back to the computer.

But he didn't.

Wilde waited.

"I got it keyed up," Gavin said.

"All the major networks?" Strauss asked.

"Plus some bloggers and Twitter accounts."

"This is it, my friend. Hit send."

One last chance for Wilde to act.

He heard the click of the key.

"Done," Gavin said.

The relief in his tone was palpable.

"We need to free the kid," Strauss said. "You have the coordinates to send to the Maynards?"

"Do you think we should wait?" Gavin asked.

"Why?"

"I don't know. They may have more."

"More?"

"More tapes," Gavin Chambers said. "They could be holding out on us."

"We can't," Strauss said. "This . . . it's gone far enough, Gavin. That boy . . ."

"Yeah." Wilde could hear the devastation now in Gavin's voice. "Yeah, you're right."

"Hand me the ski mask. Let's go finish this."

Wilde came out from his hiding spot and pointed the gun at them. "No need."

Gavin Chambers and Saul Strauss spun toward him. Wilde raised the gun.

"If you breathe wrong," Wilde said, "I'll shoot you both. Gavin, I assume you're armed?"

"I am."

"Holster under the left armpit?"

"Yes."

"You know the drill. Thumb and index finger. Throw it over here. Do it slowly. Saul?"

"I'm unarmed." Saul held up his hands and twirled slowly.

"Keep your hands on the desk where I can see them. Gavin, toss the gun."

Gavin Chambers took the gun out of his holster and tossed it on the floor toward Wilde. Wilde picked it up and stuck it in his waistband.

"How did you figure it out?" Gavin asked.

"Lots of things. But the main one was the most basic. I kept wondering how Crash could be kidnapped so close to his own home with someone as good as you guarding him. The simplest answer? He can't. So you had to be involved." Wilde looked at Gavin, then at Saul. "I assume you guys hatched this idea after Naomi Pine ran away?"

"We did," Gavin said.

"Made sense. Naomi goes missing. She has a tentative connection to Crash. So you know that if Crash goes missing now, everyone will tie them together. It gave you time. It gave you the ultimate diversion. You even said it to me, Gavin."

"Said what?"

"At my Ecocapsule. The Ghost Army. Everything you did was about tactical deception."

"And yet here we are."

"Here we are."

Gavin smiled. "We overdid it, didn't we?"

"You did."

"I didn't expect the Maynards to bring you and Hester in."

"Right, that threw you. It's why you kept insisting I concentrate on Naomi. You knew that even if I was successful in finding her, I'd be no closer to the truth about Crash. The problem is, you both gilded that lily. Saul, you show up at the hotel bar to ask me about Naomi the night Crash disappears. Why? I didn't realize it at the time, but even if you thought Crash and Naomi were close, why would you ask me to help you? You were just planting the seed so I'd go in the wrong direction. Then you"—Wilde looked back at Gavin—"you show up at the 7-Eleven with some suddenly unearthed secret message that again was supposed to make me think that Naomi was connected to whatever happened to Crash."

Gavin nodded, seeing it now. "You asked me for a ride to the Maynards'."

"Right."

"That's when you planted the GPS tracker in the car."

"You're a wealthy, successful man. You always have a driver or at least an expensive car. Suddenly you're in a Chevy Cruze? I figured it was a rental."

"But you didn't know for sure?"

"I was just covering my bases. Then today Saul conveniently shows up by the school. He claims to have men following me, that he has an inside source at the Maynards'. But who would that be? Hester wouldn't talk. Neither would my people. The Maynards? Not a chance. So it had to be the kidnapper. You, Gavin."

"Eliminate the possible and whatever remains," Saul said, quoting Arthur Conan Doyle, "no matter how improbable, is the truth."

"Exactly. So when Saul drove me up to Sing Sing, I planted another GPS locator in his car. After you dropped me back near the Maynards', you drove up to this rest stop. You didn't stay long. Just to feed the kid, I guess. Look in on him. But the day before, according to the locator in Gavin's Cruze, he had stopped here too. Why would both of you be in this fairly remote rest stop? You two had to be in on this together. Oh, and the finger coordinates being where I was found as a kid. Again, overkill. The only reason someone would do that would be to mess with my head. Of course, I got stuff wrong too. Like I figured you just rendezvoused at this rest stop. Met up, discussed things, whatever. But when I arrived just now, I was surprised to see it was closed."

"How did you sneak in here anyway? We have sensors by all the entrances."

"But not in the back. There's a Dairy Queen."

"So you found Crash in the Dunkin' Donuts hut."

"Yes."

"Where is he now?"

"Probably at the hospital. Rola took him."

"So Rola knows about this?"

Wilde chose not to reply.

"You get why we did this," Saul said. "You see the danger, right?"

"It took me a while to remove the blinders of self-interest," Gavin said. "You become so enmeshed in a charismatic leader, seduced by all that he can give you, that you can't see past his bullshit. Then Saul started pleading his case to me."

"You didn't need much persuasion," Saul said. "You were already starting to see."

"Maybe I was—the pill popping, the erratic behavior, the ease with which he could manipulate. I liked his idea of tearing down the social order to rebuild, but as I spent more time with him, it became clear that Rusty doesn't want to rebuild. Rusty wants to destroy this country. He wants to pull us apart by the seams."

"We two old men don't agree on much," Saul said. "I'm on one side of the political aisle. Gavin is on the other. But we are both Americans."

"Our views, opposite as they might seem, are in the realm of normalcy."

"That's not what Rusty wants. Rusty wants to make everyone choose a side, turn everyone into an extremist."

"Seems it worked," Wilde said, still holding the gun on them.

"What do you mean?"

"You two kidnapped a child. You cut off his finger. If that's not being an extremist..."

Their faces fell. Both of them.

Gavin said, "You think we wanted to do that?"

"Doesn't matter what you wanted."

"You tell me," Saul Strauss said. "Would Dash Maynard have given up the tape any other way?"

"Again: Doesn't matter. You made the choice." Wilde said it slowly and with emphasis: "You. Cut. Off. A. Boy's. Finger."

Gavin Chambers lowered his head. Saul Strauss tried to hold his high, but his mouth was quaking.

"Crash was drugged up when we did that, unconscious," Saul said. "We kept the pain and trauma to a minimum."

"You disfigured him. Then you threatened to cut off his arm. Suppose the Maynards didn't send the tape. Would you have gone through with that? Would you have sent them his arm?"

Gavin Chambers finally looked up. "How far would you go to save millions of lives, Wilde?"

"This isn't about me."

"We're all soldiers here, so it damn well is," Gavin said. "This battlefield might not be as obvious, but lives are at stake. Millions. So if disfiguring or killing one person, even an innocent kid, could save millions of lives, would you do it?"

"That's a pretty slippery slope you're standing on, Colonel."

"The frontline troops are always standing on a slippery slope. You know that. Would we have rather cut off our own fingers to save those lives? Of course. But that wasn't the choice. Life isn't lived in the black and white, Wilde. People like to think so nowadays. All the online outrage, things are either all good or all bad. But life is lived in the gray. Life is lived in the nuances."

"Even now," Saul added, "you standing there holding a gun on us. Gavin and I are willing to pay the price for what we did. We felt we had no choice. But we've now saved Raymond—"

"Righting a tremendous wrong," Gavin added. "Nothing hypothetical about that."

"—and on a much larger scale, we maybe saved this country. That tape we just sent out could change the course of history."

The two men waited now for Wilde to say something.

After a few moments passed, Gavin put his hand on Saul Strauss's arm. "Oh man."

"What?" Saul said.

"Wilde gets it."

Strauss frowned. "What do you mean?"

Gavin met Wilde's eye. "I mean Wilde has been hiding in this garage since before you arrived."

"So?"

"So he *waited*, Saul. He waited for you to get here. He waited until we sent out the tape."

Silence.

Strauss saw it now. He turned to face Wilde too. "You could have stopped us. You could have popped out with that gun two minutes earlier."

"And the tape would never have seen the light of day," Gavin added.

"But you didn't do that, Wilde." Both men were nodding along now. "You came out with us on that slippery slope."

Wilde said nothing.

"In the end," Gavin said, "we're just three soldiers."

"One last mission. You let us complete it."

"In my case," Gavin said, taking a step in front of Saul, "a suicide mission."

Wilde finally spoke. "Wait, what?"

"I'll be okay in prison," Saul said. "I'll still be able to speak out. I can still be a voice."

"But I'm an old man and I don't want to face that," Gavin said. He stood and reached out his hand. "Let me have my gun back, Wilde. Warrior to warrior. Let me end this on my terms."

Suicide.

"No," Wilde said.

"Then I'll run at you. I'll force you to shoot me."

"That's not what's going to happen either," Wilde said. "Listen closely. You had your mission, I had mine. Mine was to find two missing kids. I rescued one. I then stayed behind to search these premises for the other. That's what I'll tell Rola. Naomi isn't here, is she?"

"No," Saul said, confused. "We don't know anything about that."

"Then my mission here is complete."

"I don't understand," Saul said.

"Yeah," Wilde said, "I think you do."

Wilde didn't say another word. He just lowered the gun and walked away.

PART THREE

CHAPTER THIRTY-EIGHT

Three Weeks Later

Hester was finishing up a meeting with Simon Greene, the rich financial advisor who was captured on a viral video punching what looked like a vagrant in Central Park. She liked Greene, felt that he was getting a bad rap, but more important, the call from the Manhattan DA indicated that they wouldn't be pressing charges, in part because no one could locate the supposed victim.

Hester walked Greene to her office door.

Simon Greene thanked her. Hester gave him a buss on the cheek. That was when she saw her seated in the waiting room. Hester stormed over to her executive assistant Sarah McLynn and said, "Why is Delia Maynard here?"

"She asked for fifteen minutes. She said it was important."

"You should tell me these things."

"I did."

"When?"

"Did you check your texts?"

"A text isn't telling me."

"How many times have we gone over this? You told me not to interrupt you and to inform you of schedule changes via text."

"I did?"

"You did. Now you have fifteen minutes before your next client gets here. It's a billable fifteen minutes, and Delia Maynard is a client. Should I tell her to go home or—"

"Stop already. You're a bigger nag than I am. Send her in."

Hester had not seen Delia Maynard since that awful day at the manor three weeks ago—right before the finger was found. Sarah showed Delia into the office and closed the door behind her. The two women stood and stared at one another for a long moment.

"How is your son?" Hester asked.

"Better," Delia said. "They were able to attach the finger."

"Oh, good."

"Physically, he's doing fine."

"And mentally?"

"There are nightmares. It seems the kidnappers, whoever they were, treated him well, but..."

"I understand. And you've decided not to involve the police?"

"That's right."

"No one asked you how his finger got severed?"

"The doctor did, of course. We said it was a fishing incident. I don't think she bought it, especially since it was hours between the time the finger arrived at the hospital and the time Crash got there, but there's nothing that can be proved."

"So no one else knows about the kidnapping."

"No one."

Delia had no idea Gavin Chambers and Saul Strauss had kidnapped her son. Hester knew, of course. Three weeks ago, Wilde had confided in her and her only. She didn't like what Wilde had done in the end. You don't work outside of the system. The system may be flawed, but you don't cut off children's fingers, even to save a wrongly convicted man or even to save—ugh, such dramatics—the world.

She hadn't seen Wilde in three weeks either.

"So why are you here, Delia?"

"To say goodbye."

"Oh?"

"We are taking the family and moving overseas for a while."

"I see."

"Since that tape became public, you can't imagine what it's been like."

"I think I can."

"There are constant death threats coming from Rusty supporters. They think Dash made it up or doctored it to destroy their hero."

"Fake news," Hester said.

"Yes. As our attorney, you know that Dash can't comment or authenticate it."

Hester swallowed hard. "Right. It would be self-incrimination."

Dash Maynard had committed felonies that night by moving the dead body. Hester had wanted to work Raymond Stark's case pro bono, but unfortunately, she couldn't because of the conflict of interest in her representing the Maynards. Her hands were also tied. She wanted Dash more than anything to come forward, but as his attorney, she had to advise him against it.

The system was flawed, but it was still the system.

She didn't think Dash would come forward anyway. She also didn't think it would help. That was the worst part of it all. At first, the release of the tape seemed to destroy Rusty Eggers once and for all.

At first.

But mythical beasts don't die, do they? When you try to kill them, they come back stronger. So: The tape was a fake. If it wasn't an outright fake, it was doctored. If it wasn't doctored, it all happened thirty years ago, so it didn't matter. If it mattered, Rusty Eggers said on the tape that he killed the man in self-defense and that's not a crime. If it's a crime, it was thirty years ago, when Rusty Eggers was just a young student, and well, someone tried to kill him so he had no choice but to defend himself.

And if the death was later blamed on an innocent black man, that was the police's fault, not Rusty Eggers's. Blame that crooked cop Kindler. Blame the racist system. And if it's not racism, Raymond Stark had a criminal record, even as a seventeen-year-old, so he probably would have ended up in prison on another charge. Maybe Stark did other crimes that night, who knows? Maybe Raymond Stark was involved in Christopher Anson's killing anyway. If it was self-defense, maybe Raymond Stark joined forces with Christopher Anson to attack Rusty Eggers. Maybe Raymond Stark and Christopher Anson together tried to rob Rusty Eggers and Raymond Stark ran off with the knife. Maybe that was why the knife was on him.

Like that.

Most of the media scoffed at these theories, which just made the Eggers supporters, coming from both the far right and the far left, dig in their heels and back their man even more.

"You said that you would never tell," Delia said.

"Sorry?"

"No matter what. Even if it was to stop Hitler. If something was told to you under attorney-client privilege, you'd never tell."

"That's right." Hester didn't like the way this was headed. "You also told me that there was nothing on those tapes."

"I didn't know about that tape," Delia said. "I had no idea that tape existed. I had no idea Dash helped Rusty dump the body in an alley."

"Okay."

"Because I was gone by then."

Hester felt an icy hand touch down on her spine. "Sorry?"

"The two of them fought a lot. Rusty and Christopher. A lot of it was over me. Thirty years ago. You know how it was. Girls were things. Shiny objects. So I guess they had a big fight in the bar that night. I was dating Rusty then. We were getting serious. Rusty had gotten a plum assignment from the senator. Christopher had been overlooked. I don't know. Who cares anymore? So Christopher knocked on the door. I let him in. He was drunk. He tried to kiss me. I told him no. He didn't stop. No girl was going to say no to Christopher Anson, especially not his rival's girlfriend. You can guess what happened next. I hate the term 'date rape' or 'acquaintance rape.' Thirty years ago, it was pathetically considered 'boys being boys.' When I shouted for him to stop, he punched me in the mouth. I ran into the kitchen. He raped me right there on the floor. He was about to rape me again. Tell you the truth? I don't even remember reaching into the drawer or picking up the knife."

Hester just stood there. "You killed him?"

Delia moved over to the window. "I sat on the kitchen floor next to him. The knife was still in his chest. I don't think he was dead yet. But I couldn't move. He made gurgling noises for a while. Then those stopped. But I just sat there. I don't know how much time passed. That's how Rusty found me. On the kitchen floor. Next to the body. Rusty took over. He cleaned me up. He dressed me. He drove me to Union Station. There was a late Amtrak from Washington to Philadelphia. He got me on it and told me not to come back until he called. I stayed in a Marriott hotel room for three days. Ate room service. Rusty told me he moved the body, so nobody would know. When I came back to Washington, nothing was the same between us. You can imagine, right?"

Hester could feel her heart pound against her rib cage.

"We broke up. And I started dating Dash."

Had that been, Hester wondered, an arrangement between the two men? Was Delia still just a thing, a shiny object, being bartered for a favor? Or had Rusty really loved her? Had Rusty loved her so much that the politician so many believed would destroy the country sacrificed his own happiness to protect her?

Or does it go deeper than that?

Did Rusty's actions that night—getting rid of a bloody corpse, living with the awful lies and aftermath, losing the love of his life and then his parents—are those what warped Rusty Eggers? Had all of that nudged the young college student off the straight and narrow and veered him into becoming the irredeemably damaged man he was now?

Delia put up her hands. Her smile was sad. "The rest is history."

"After all that, you're staying with him?"

"Dash? We have a life together. A family, kids—especially a boy who suffered a great trauma and is going to need stability. We both kept secrets from each other. I at least know his now."

"And you won't tell him yours?"

"That I was the one who killed Christopher?" Delia shook her head. "No, never."

"Hell of a thing to live with," Hester said.

"Been living with it for over thirty years," Delia said. She made a production out of checking her watch. "I better go."

"People wouldn't blame you," Hester said, trying to keep the desperation out of her voice. "You were being raped. You can still come out of this doing the right thing."

"I am doing the right thing. For me. For my family."

She turned to leave.

"There was one secret you and Dash both kept," Hester said.

"What's that?"

"What did you think when you heard that Raymond Stark had been arrested for Christopher's murder?"

Delia didn't reply.

"You both knew the truth, right? You and Dash. You didn't talk about it with each other, but you both knew that an innocent man had been arrested. Yet you never came forward."

"And say what?" Delia asked.

"That you did it in self-defense."

"You think anyone would believe me?"

"So you just let Raymond Stark take the fall."

"I hoped he'd get off."

"And when he didn't?" Hester crossed the room and got into her face. "When he got sentenced to life in prison for something he didn't do? When he got beaten and abused?"

"I didn't sentence him. I didn't beat him or abuse him. Won't the tape free him now?"

"No, Delia. The tape won't be enough. Raymond Stark will stay in prison." Hester took a breath, tried to sound reasonable. "But please, listen to me—"

"No. I'm leaving now."

"You helped lock him up. You can't just—"

"Goodbye, Hester."

"I could tell."

Delia smiled and shook her head. "No, you couldn't, Hester."

Hester stood there, her fists at her side, her body shaking.

"First off," Delia said, "there is no evidence. I'll just deny it. But more than that, you won't violate attorney-client privilege. Even if it meant saving the world from Hitler. Even if it means an innocent man stays in jail."

The system was flawed, but it was still the system.

Delia Maynard left the office then. For a few minutes, Hester didn't move. Sarah McLynn came in and said, "Your next appointment—"

"Cancel."

"I can't just cancel. He's—"

"Cancel."

The tone left no room for argument. Hester circled back to her desk. With a shaking hand, she picked up the phone and dialed the number.

The voice that answered sounded tentative. "Hello?"

"Oren?"

She hadn't spoken to him in three weeks, not since the pizza date. She hadn't returned his calls or answered his texts.

"Are you okay, Hester?"

"I need you to take me someplace. I need you to take me now."

CHAPTER THIRTY-NINE

Two hours later, Oren pulled the squad car onto the shoulder of Mountain Road. He turned off the ignition. For a few moments the two of them just sat in silence.

"Are you sure you want to do this?"

When Hester nodded, Oren got out of the passenger side and opened her door. Up ahead, Hester saw the weathered makeshift cross. It was odd for her to see it here—her son had been raised somewhere between agnostic and Jewish—but for some reason, Hester didn't mind it. Someone had cared. Someone had tried.

Hester walked over to the edge of the highway and looked down the steep embankment.

"So this is where…?"

"Yes."

Hester had never had the courage—if courage was the right word—to come here. Ira had. Many times. He wouldn't tell her. He would say he was going out for a ride or to pick up milk at the 7-Eleven, but she knew that he would pull his car over on the shoulder, maybe in this exact same spot, and get out and look at the makeshift cross and sob.

Ira hadn't told her. She wished that he had.

"Where did the car end up?"

"Down there," Oren said, pointing to a spot far down the hill.

"You were one of the first officers on the scene."

Oren couldn't tell whether that was a question or a statement. "Yes."

"The car was on fire."

"Yes."

"Wilde had already pulled David out."

Oren just nodded this time.

"Wilde told me he was the one driving," Hester said.

"He told us that too," Oren said. "We didn't charge him though. No alcohol in his system. The roads were wet."

"Was Wilde driving?"

"That's what our report said."

Hester turned to him. "I'm not asking you what your report said."

Oren's eyes stayed on the ravine. "When the only survivor of a car accident tells you he was the driver, it's hard to prove otherwise."

"Wilde lied, didn't he?"

Oren didn't reply.

Hester stood so that they were shoulder to shoulder. "Wilde and David were best friends. You know that, right?"

Oren nodded. "I do."

"That night, they went to Miller's Tavern. In David's car. My David didn't drink much or go for bars much—that was more Wilde's scene, I think—but he was having problems with Laila. Nothing serious. Nothing they wouldn't get past. So the two best friends went out to blow off some steam or whatever men do. David drank too much. The hospital ran a toxicology report when he was rushed in—when they still thought my boy would survive. Wilde didn't want to get David in trouble. So he said it was him. That he was driving."

Oren still said nothing.

"Is that what happened, Oren?"

"Did you ask Wilde?"

"He insists he was driving."

"But you don't believe him."

"I don't, no. Am I right?"

Oren looked down. She watched his eyes. They were so clear, so honest, so beautiful. "Oren?"

Then he said something that surprised her: "I don't think you have it exactly right."

For a moment she couldn't find her voice. When she did: "What do you mean?"

"Wilde would never have let David drive drunk."

"So..." Hester didn't know what to say. "I'm not following."

"We checked Miller's Tavern. Wilde was a regular, as you said. David wasn't, but that night, yeah, he got pretty drunk. Anyway, nothing we could prove, but one patron said Wilde left at least half an hour before David. On his own."

"Why?"

"I don't know. Wilde would only tell us he was the driver."

"David was there alone?"

"Alone and drinking, yes. This is all just a theory, Hester. But at that time, Wilde was living in a tent not far from here." He pointed to the left. "Maybe three hundred yards in that direction. Again I don't have any proof. Wilde insisted that he drove, but yeah, I never believed it. I think Wilde was nearby. I think he heard the crash or saw the flames. I think he wanted to protect his friend. And I think he felt—feels—guilty about not staying at the bar that night."

Hester felt a thud deep in her chest. "So you think David was alone in the car?"

When Oren nodded, Hester dropped to her knees. She dropped to her knees and cried.

Oren let her. He stood there, close enough that if she needed him, he was there. But he didn't reach out to her. Thank God.

Thank God this man, this good and decent man, knew to not hug her or offer words of false comfort.

He just let her cry.

It took some time. She couldn't say how much. Five minutes, ten, maybe half an hour. Oren Carmichael just stood there, guarding her like a silent sentinel. At some point, she got back into his squad car. He started down Mountain Road. They drove in silence.

Finally: "Oren?"

"I'm here."

"I'm sorry I didn't call you back."

Oren didn't reply.

"When you rushed out of the pizzeria to go to that car accident, I realized that we had no chance—because no matter what, whenever I see you, I will imagine you at the scene of that accident. Whenever I see you, I will see my dead son. You'll always remind me of David, so we can't be."

He kept his eyes on the road.

"But then I started missing you so damn much. It was like there was a giant hole in my heart. I know how that sounds. I started thinking that even with that pain, I didn't want to be without you—and I didn't want to stop thinking about my David, not ever, because that would be the worst outrage. I'll never stop thinking about him. Do you understand?"

Oren nodded. "I do."

She reached out and put her hand on his.

"Are you willing to give us another chance, Oren?"

"Yeah," he said. "Yeah, I'd really like that."

CHAPTER FORTY

Wilde bought a round-trip ticket for the Delta shuttle flight from New York's LaGuardia Airport to Boston's Logan. He had no luggage. He didn't plan on staying in Boston long—a few hours tops. Then he'd fly back home.

In fact, he planned to never leave the airport.

When the plane landed, Wilde walked over from Terminal A to E. He positioned himself near Gate E7, where he would eventually watch passengers board American Airlines Flight 374 to Costa Rica.

Two hours to go.

To pass the time, Wilde opened the DNA genealogy website and found the message from "PB." He read it again, thought about it, then decided to write:

> I'd like to know more, PB. Can we meet?

He was about to put away his phone when it rang. Wilde checked the caller ID and saw that it was Matthew. He picked up immediately.

"Everything okay?" Wilde said.

"You don't have to answer the phone like that," Matthew said. "You can just say, 'Hello.'"

"Hello. Everything okay?"

"Yeah, Wilde. Except I haven't seen you in weeks."

"Sorry. How are things at school?"

"Calming down. Crash is back already. He keeps showing off this scar on his finger and saying some bad guys cut it off. Mom says it was a fishing accident. Wilde?"

"Yeah?"

"Everyone thinks Naomi ran away. They think she's somewhere on an island or doing something cool or exotic—which is ironic since they always thought she was such a loser."

"I know."

"Are you still looking for her?"

Wilde didn't know how to answer that, so he kept it simple. "Yes."

"Cool." Then: "Where are you? I hear a lot of noise."

"In Boston."

"Why?"

"Visiting a friend."

Matthew must have heard something in his tone. "Okay."

"How's Mom?" Wilde asked.

"Still with Darryl."

Darryl. Designer Threads had a name now. Darryl.

"They're getting serious, I think," Matthew said.

Wilde closed his eyes for a moment. "You like him?"

"He's okay," Matthew said, which in Matthew-speak was a rave.

"Good. Be nice to him."

"Ugh."

"Your mom deserves this."

"Fine, whatever."

The flight to Costa Rica was ready to board now. The gate agent called for passengers needing special assistance, passengers traveling with children under the age of two, active-duty US military members.

"Anything else?" Wilde asked him.

"Nope, all good."

"Call me if you need anything."

"Anything?"

"Yes."

"There's a new *Grand Theft Auto*, but Mom won't buy it for me because it's too violent."

"Funny."

"Bye, Wilde."

"Talk soon."

He hung up as the gate agent called for Group 1 to board. Wilde watched the passengers start to mingle near the boarding line.

Nothing.

The gate agent called for Groups 2, 3, and 4.

Still nothing.

For a moment Wilde wondered whether he had gotten it wrong or perhaps someone was again trying tactical deception with him. Perhaps they had booked more than one flight to throw him. Perhaps they'd never intended to fly today.

But when the gate agent called the final group, Wilde spotted a young girl getting into line wearing, yep, a baseball cap and sunglasses.

Naomi Pine.

Standing in front of her, holding both their tickets, was Ava O'Brien.

For a few seconds, Wilde didn't move. He didn't have to do anything. He didn't have to approach them. He could, like with Gavin Chambers and Saul Strauss, simply melt away.

But he didn't.

Enough stalling. Wilde walked over and tapped Naomi on the shoulder.

Naomi jumped, startled. When she turned and saw his face, her hand flew to her mouth. "Oh my God. Wilde?"

Ava spun now too.

For a few seconds, they all just stood there.

Ava said, "How did you . . . ?"

"Do you remember when you were leaving 7-Eleven and I told you to roll down your window?"

"What?" Ava looked baffled. "What about it?"

"I leaned in and put a GPS tracker in your car."

It was the same deal as with Gavin and Strauss—Ava, too, had overdone it with the tactical diversions. When he'd told her about Crash disappearing, all of a sudden Ava had remembered that Naomi had mentioned a possible romance with Crash, strongly hinting that the two teens had run off together.

Ava had been trying to throw him off the scent too.

The question was, why?

She clearly had nothing to do with Crash Maynard.

"You're from Maine," Wilde said.

"Yes, I told you that."

"Why would you move to New Jersey to take a job you were overqualified for?"

Ava shrugged. "I wanted a change."

"No," Wilde said. "You've also been back to Maine four times in the past three weeks."

"I have family up there."

"Again: No. You stayed at the Howard Johnson's in South Portland, where you had Naomi hiding. But more than that, you visited the Hope Faith Adoption Agency in Windham twice."

Ava closed her eyes.

"You didn't take the assistant teaching job because you wanted to live in New Jersey," Wilde said. "You did it to be closer to the daughter you had to give up for adoption."

For a moment, it looked as though Ava might deny it. But only for a moment.

"You have to understand," Ava said. "I never wanted to give Naomi up."

So there it was.

"I was only seventeen. I didn't know any better. But I just had… I don't know, it was a feeling or a want or a premonition or… So I went back to the agency. I begged them to tell me what happened to my daughter. They wouldn't. Not at first. So I paid someone off. They gave me Naomi's new name and address, but they explained that I had no rights. That was okay. I just wanted to see her, you know. So I just figured…"

"You'd take the teaching job to be close to her."

"Right. What harm would it do?"

"Wilde?"

It was Naomi.

"Don't make me go back."

"I just wanted to see how she was," Ava said. "That's all. I didn't want to mess up her life. But then I saw the hell she was living through. Day after day, I had to sit back and watch my child being bullied with no support from home."

"So you became her friend," Wilde said. "Her confidante."

"Is that so wrong?"

Wilde turned to Naomi. "When did Ava tell you the truth?"

"That she was my real mother?"

"Yes."

"After I came back from the Challenge," Naomi said. "At first, I thought she was making it up or like it was a dream come true, you know? Do you remember our talk in my basement? How I wanted to change everything?"

Wilde nodded.

"It wasn't just at school. It was everything. My father…"

Her voice just faded out. Bernard Pine would not come out of this unscathed either. Rola was working up a way to make him pay for what he'd done.

"So you two decided to run away," Wilde said.

"I didn't want that," Ava said. "I wanted to do it legally."

"Which is why you went to Laila."

"Yes. I told her how awful Naomi's adoptive parents were, but I still had no rights. Laila said it would take months or years to prove neglect or abuse, and even then, winning was unlikely."

"So that's when you hatched this plan," Wilde said. "You'd run away and hide. You"—he looked at Ava—"you'd get Naomi a fake ID while finishing out the school year. If you left your teaching post right away, that would draw suspicion. So you two waited. And now it's time to flee the country together."

Ava just looked at him with her big brown eyes.

The boarding line was clear. The gate agent made another announcement.

Naomi stepped forward and put her hand on his arm. "Please, Wilde, if we're caught, I'll have to go back to him. Ava might go to jail."

"She's my daughter," Ava said, her tone never steadier. "I love her with all my heart."

They both stood together and faced him.

"I know," Wilde said.

"So...?"

"I just came to make sure you were all right," Wilde said. "And to say goodbye."

Naomi threw her arms around him so hard she almost knocked him over. Wilde usually recoiled from this sort of embrace. But he didn't. Not this time. He let the girl hold him, and it felt right.

"Thank you," Naomi whispered.

Wilde nodded. "If you ever need anything..."

The boarding agent was back on the loudspeaker. "Final call for Flight 374 with service to Liberia, Costa Rica."

"You guys better get on board," Wilde said.

Naomi looked at Ava. Ava looked back. Then Ava turned and took Wilde's hand and said something that caught him totally off guard: "Come with us, Wilde."

"What?"

Naomi put her hands together. "Please?"

Wilde shook his head. "I can't."

Ava held on to his hand and said it again: "Come with us, Wilde."

"No," he said.

"Why not?" Ava asked.

"It's crazy," Wilde said.

"So?" Ava gave him a smile that dazzled and stunned. "Everything about this is crazy."

Wilde shook his head again, even as he felt something in his chest crack open. "You guys need to get on board."

"Come with us, Wilde," Ava said again. "Naomi needs you. Maybe I need you too, I don't know. If it doesn't work out, you just come back."

"I can't," Wilde said.

The gate agent came over, cleared her throat, and said, "I'm closing the door in thirty seconds."

"They're boarding now," Wilde said in a tone that left no room for debate.

Naomi's eyes were wet with tears when she threw her arms around him one more time. Then Ava handed the gate agent their tickets to scan. Wilde watched them start down the jet bridge. Naomi turned and waved. Wilde waved back.

Ava's eyes lingered on his a little longer. When she broke eye contact and turned away, Wilde felt his chest crack open a little more.

He watched them disappear from view.

The gate agent reached for the door. As she was about to close it, Wilde asked, "Is there any room on this flight?"

"What, you want to buy a ticket?"

"Yes."

The gate agent squinted at her computer screen.

"Well, what do you know?" she said. "There's one more ticket available."

ABOUT THE AUTHOR

With more than seventy million books in print worldwide, Harlan Coben is the #1 *New York Times* bestselling author of numerous suspense novels, including *Run Away*, *Don't Let Go*, *Home*, and *Fool Me Once*, as well as the multiaward-winning Myron Bolitar series. His books are published in forty-three languages around the globe and have been number one bestsellers in more than a dozen countries. His Netflix series include *Safe*, starring Michael C. Hall, and his adaptation of his novel *The Stranger*, headlined by Richard Armitage. He lives in New Jersey.

For more information you can visit:

HarlanCoben.com
Netflix.com/HarlanCoben
Twitter: @HarlanCoben
Facebook.com/HarlanCobenBooks